P9-BXW-989

# COVENANT OF GRACE

Books by Jane Gilmore Rushing

WALNUT GROVE
AGAINST THE MOON
TAMZEN
MARY DOVE
THE RAINCROW
COVENANT OF GRACE

Jane Gilmore Rushing

# COVENANT OF GRACE

DOUBLEDAY & COMPANY, INC.
GARDEN CITY, NEW YORK
1982

Library of Congress Cataloging in Publication Data
Rushing, Jane Gilmore.
Covenant of grace.

1. Hutchinson, Anne Marbury, 1591–1643—Fiction.
I. Title.
PS3568.U73C5 813'.54
AACR2
ISBN: 0-385-17702-X
Library of Congress Catalog Card Number 81-43307


Printed in the United States of America
First Edition

To Sally Arteseros, with love and gratitude

# COVENANT OF GRACE

# PROLOGUE

There was a time when religion was the overpowering concern of all the world, or at least the world as it appeared to the people who first settled on America's northeast coast. In England, in northern Europe, religion raged. Families, even nations, were split asunder by differences in their understanding of the lessons Jesus Christ had come to teach on earth. "Not peace but a sword" often seemed the aptest words He spoke.

In those days no one doubted that a state church was a natural consequence of true belief. There being only one way to salvation, a godly nation would inevitably find and follow that way: every priest would preach that way, and both ruler and subjects would adhere to it. Sometimes wrong thinking prevailed in a country. Then some of the righteous became martyrs. Or if the true believers were numerous and desperate enough, a civil war might ensue. In the seventeenth century, in the time before their High Church king was beheaded, Englishmen often chose another course—removal to a new world, where Christians might do well in worldly endeavors and at the same time build a pure Church of Christ, such as the old world had not known since the days of Paul the Apostle. In this wide, waiting wilderness, God was the only landlord; and by virtue of the grand charter given to Adam and his posterity in Paradise, the elect could dwell there like freeholders in a place of their own, with assurance of security and prosperity forever, so long as they did not defraud God of His rent by failure to serve Him well and teach their children likewise how to serve Him.

Men and women of the Massachusetts Bay Company heard

the great minister John Cotton explain this covenant with God when he preached his farewell sermon to them as they awaited a fair wind at Southampton. In their hearts they earnestly accepted the terms of this bargain, and few ever forgot them. Cotton himself, driven out of England three years later by the policies of Archbishop Laud, entered into this same covenant and came to preach at New Boston, the chief town in the colony of Massachusetts Bay.

Others followed, and not all who came were godly men and women. But most of them were, and most of them strove diligently to keep their bargain with God.

# I

On a bright September day in 1634, a ship called the *Griffin* sailed into Boston harbor, bringing among its passengers a large family named Hutchinson, from a village near old Boston in Lincolnshire, England. There was one among them, and one only, responsible for their coming to the New World. She was the wife and mother, the mistress of the household, and her Christian name was Anne.

By the time the ship dropped anchor, passengers crowded the main deck, pressing against the bulwarks. Anne Hutchinson stood among the foremost, a tall figure wrapped in a gray woolen cloak that was somewhat too warm in the afternoon sunshine. The way she gathered it around herself, holding it close, suggested some need of it though, as if she were insulating herself against the consciousness of her surroundings—the pushing and shoving of her fellow passengers, or the crude cries of sailors in the rigging overhead. But her attention was upon the drab peninsula she had chosen for her family's home. Beyond the flat wet sands at the seaside, past bleak, encroaching marshes, her gaze traveled. A straggling village spread like some wasteland weed along the shore and up the slopes that rose from the harbor toward a tripartite hill. She could see no trees anywhere, and though she might guess at gardens behind the stake fences, she could as well believe she faced a land where nothing fresh and fruitful ever grew. She drew her cloak yet closer, shivering, and let escape a small sigh.

"What is it, sweetheart?" anxiously inquired the man at her

side. He was of about her height or slightly less, sturdily built and well dressed, in everyday russet-colored breeches and doublet.

She turned to him, letting her hood fall back to reveal a pale, strong-featured face, with large dark eyes. "Oh, William," she said, "I cannot believe that any place marked out by God for His own people could look so desolate and forlorn. If I had not a sure word that England would be destroyed, my heart would shake."

He put an arm around her and drew her close to him. "Hast thou not often scolded me for judging by outward appearances?" he asked gently.

Neither of them noticed the thin little man who stood within hearing while she spoke and then moved silently away. But Anne well knew the narrow frown, the puckered mouth no wider than the base of his oddly flaring nostrils, and the glitter of his light blue eyes. Had she seen his expression now, she might simply have said that one cannot judge by outward appearances. On the other hand, she had reason to know that the Reverend Zachariah Symmes found some of her opinions distasteful.

Neither she nor William noticed Symmes slipping away; for it was just then they recognized, in a boat rowing out from the shore, the figure of their eldest son.

"There's Edward!" cried Anne, and forgetting her momentary sense of desolation, she happily waved her hand.

Much of the population of Boston had come to the harbor. Some were there to meet friends or relations, but many came simply because the arrival of a ship from England was an exciting event in the life of the town. Those who had no one to welcome watched others meet, as the passengers were rowed ashore.

Almost everyone in Boston had some acquaintance with everyone else, for it was still a new settlement and by necessity a close-knit community. The two Edward Hutchinsons were well known and respected—the young man whose parents were due on this ship and the somewhat older man, his uncle, who with his wife and children was also on hand to greet the new arrivals.

And so there were many to look on in sympathy and curiosity as the Hutchinson family came together, with tears, embraces, and prayers of thanksgiving.

There came upon the group a little old woman—a hunchback she appeared to be, or perhaps she was only bent through a perpetual seeking for things on the ground. She had been foraging somewhere northward along the shore and came now to watch the unloading with her basket full of herbs and roots and God or the devil knew what. A good many people thought it was the devil that knew the most about Goody Hawkins' undertakings. No doubt it was this suspicion that kept them always a little away from her. Even at Sabbath Day meeting, which the old woman regularly attended although refused communion by the church, the women seemed reluctant to approach her, while she was always edging a little nearer to whoever sat beside her on the bench.

Just so, now when everyone else kept a proper distance from the Hutchinsons out of respect for their evident joy in coming together again, this little old stooping woman went directly up to them. She had heard all the talk, too (overheard it, more likely), and knew who was coming, even to the names of the ten children and the identity of the four grown women—Anne, her sister, and two cousins of Master Hutchinson. Goody Hawkins' round brown peering eyes moved from one to another, like hungry hovering birds, and settled at last on the handsome, dignified woman who stood, smiling with calm happiness, a little apart from the rest. The two women, so unlike in manner and appearance, looked at each other then and for about the space of an eye blink let their gazes hold together. They felt, it might be (but without naming any such feeling to themselves), some fleeting sense of sisterhood.

In any case, it was then that Goody Hawkins stepped up close and cried in her high creaky voice: "Welcome to Boston, Mistress Hutchinson!"

"Come on, Mother, come on!" then called out Samuel, the ten-year-old. "Brother Edward is taking us to our house." So that the mother turned away abruptly and the old woman never even knew if she heard the greeting. But others heard, and there would be someone later on to remember that Goody Hawkins was the first of all the women in Boston to speak a word to Mistress Hutchinson.

2

Young Edward was indeed impatient to lead his family to the house he had found to hire for them, where they would live until such time as their own house could be built on land to be allotted by the town. The family had not known till now where they might live, expecting to crowd with Brother Edward's family into their one-room cottage or perhaps to dig a cellar on their own land and stay in it through the winter months. But the young man had happened to hear of a merchant returning to England on business matters that would keep him abroad a year and had hastened to secure the use of the man's good-sized dwelling for his father's family. William was exceedingly well pleased with his son's astute action; for to find a house to rent on any terms was rare in Boston, as he had already ascertained, and Edward had driven a good bargain.

Anne was pleased, too, as ever she was with son Edward; but she hoped the family would not forget one very important thing. It was not by accident, she reminded them, that the house had fallen vacant just as Edward began to seek a place for them. If anyone had entertained any doubt that it was the hand of God guiding them to New England, this latest sign should make His will clear to them all.

The gaunt gray house Edward brought them to might earlier have deepened Mistress Hutchinson's gloom at the sight of her chosen homeland; but that shock had passed, as she reminded herself that the glory of God shone on this town more brightly than any spot in poor, benighted England. Also, having walked through several Boston streets, she felt satisfied that this was as fair a dwelling place as any they were likely to find here. It stood behind a paling fence in a narrow, crooked lane, and rosemary grew by the door. Anne's oldest daughter, the grave-eyed Faith, broke off a sprig of it that day they first came there, and the scent made her weep for the garden at home.

"This is home," said Anne, and pushed open the door.

The mother and daughter were the first to step into the dimly lit, barn-like room that covered the entire ground floor. They paused and looked at each other, unwittingly keeping the others outside.

"Something strange will happen here," Faith said.

Anne nodded. "Some beginning," she confirmed. The sense of it touched her at first like a glimpse of golden sunrise, but in passing left upon her soul some trace of troubled dark. "Pray that it be something of God."

The little children, including those belonging to the elder Edward, pushed past them then, filling the room with the noise of their excitement, dispelling whatever spiritual shadow had come over the two women. Yet Anne did not dismiss the incident from her mind. It was some true sign from God, she thought, which He would clarify in His good time. The uncharacteristic doubt that briefly touched her sprang from some temporary weakness in herself. A physical weakness, more than likely, resulting from the long, wearisome sea voyage now over at last. She knew a strong temptation to sink down upon a crude bench that stood before the fireplace and close her eyes while the children streamed past her, to play as they pleased through the bare, dusty house.

But Anne Hutchinson never sank down when her duty was clear. Many accusations would in time be hurled against her, but no one ever said she neglected her duties. She did not sit down but stood tall and straight-shouldered—having moved unconsciously toward the tempting bench, into a patch of light a-swim with golden dust motes—and in a high, clear, commanding voice called the family and servants around her. Quickly they all came, the children readily leaving their play, and stood while she prayed, thanking God for their safe arrival in the place He had picked out for them, asking His continued blessing on their lives as they began now to go about His service in this new land where freedom to worship according to His true dictates would never be denied them.

When she had finished praying, they all stood in silence, waiting for her to dismiss them, watching her face, which was tender and bright, and her dark eyes lit by love that flowed through her and shone on them all—on all the world, it might be, for surely there was no limit to this love that was the love of God. They waited—all those gathered there waited—until the light faded, and the mistress of the household set in motion the business of moving into the new house.

## 3

Meanwhile, Zachariah Symmes had made up his mind to his duty. He was on his way to Charlestown, where he had been called to preach, and he wanted to be there by nightfall. But the woman called Anne Hutchinson disturbed his thoughts. That strange prophecy she seemed to be making, about the destruction of England, had reminded him of certain opinions she had vented on the way over from England. Undoubtedly, she would apply for membership in the Boston church as soon as she could, for he knew the Hutchinsons intended to settle in Boston, where Master Hutchinson would establish a mercer's trade, the same he had plied in Old England. It would be remiss and even un-Christian of the minister to let his own convenience prevent his warning the appropriate authorities about this woman's dangerous beliefs.

He was not quite sure whom he ought to approach, whether ministers or magistrates. This was properly a church matter, and yet he knew that, in this colony of Massachusetts Bay, church and state kept close watch upon each other. It seemed clear that the effect Mistress Hutchinson's opinions might have upon the colony was grave enough to warrant going to the governor, who to the best of his knowledge was John Winthrop, a man he had met once or twice in Old England.

As soon as he was set ashore, he looked about for some responsible citizen of the town, and having settled upon one, put his question at once.

"I pray you, sir," he said, "could you be so kind as to direct me to the governor's house?"

"The governor dwells in Newtown, across the River Charles," the answer came.

"But I understood John Winthrop lived in Boston," Symmes protested.

"Aye, that he does," said the citizen. "But you see, in this colony the governor is elected by the freemen, and this year some thought it was time for a change. Master Winthrop might be thinking he was king, some people said, after four years in the same office."

"And who is the new leader?" Symmes asked.

"Thomas Dudley," the man said proudly. There was no doubt which one he'd voted for. "Master Winthrop is a good man, but if the truth be told, a mite lenient. Dudley is a fair one, but he won't tolerate any free thinking or bad acting. Winthrop admitted he thought some allowances might be made in a new colony like this, but Dudley says once you start countenancing toleration in any form, you've opened the door to licentiousness."

"And you agree," said Symmes.

"That I most certainly do," said the citizen. "I brought my family here to worship in a pure church and walk in a pure way."

"So I should hope," said Symmes. "And I thank you very much, sir, for telling me about Thomas Dudley. I believe you have directed me to the man I want to see."

Unbeknownst to the townsman, as to the newly come minister, Thomas Dudley was in Boston as they talked. Having heard that the *Griffin* had been sighted, he was anxious to learn whether an expected messenger had come from England. He had indeed come, bringing secret word that confirmed what Dudley had suspected: King Charles would soon send for the colony charter again, with threats to take it by force should the leaders once more refuse him. If he ever took the charter out of the hands of the Massachusetts Bay Company, he would appoint a royal governor—someone totally out of sympathy with the pure church. And if the people felt themselves oppressed or misgoverned, there would be no way then to go and vote for a new governor.

This matter of the charter was a continuing concern, one Dudley as deputy governor had often been consulted about by John Winthrop. Out of courtesy now, as well as a true respect for Winthrop's knowledge and judgment, Dudley went with this latest news to Winthrop's house, where the two men conferred for several hours about the threatened danger.

Two things they agreed upon. Since news had also been brought of problems in England between the King and Parliament, it was possible that the royal attention might be kept away from Massachusetts, as long as no upsetting incidents occurred in the colony. In the past, just punishment of wicked unbelievers (imprisonment or even so little a thing as cropping off a man's ears) had at times created controversy in New England and provoked the King's ire. There must be nothing now to suggest that the colony contained dissension within itself or disloyalty to King Charles.

Their second consideration was that this time the King might really carry out his threats. The charter was too precious to be relinquished without a fight, and the two agreed that the militia was scarcely prepared to meet royal troops. They were still discussing that problem when Dudley saw that he must go or else miss the last ferry.

When at last he reached home, he learned that a stranger had called to see him and left not an hour earlier. Mistress Dudley could not tell him exactly who it was, though she believed the man had come to be pastor at Charlestown and had gone back there for the night. He had arrived this very day on the ship from England and had wasted no time seeking out the governor. He had something to impart—something about a fellow passenger, Mistress Dudley thought—but his manner had been rather queer and he had refused to say much. He promised to return early the next morning.

And he proved a man of his word, for the governor, an early riser, was still seated over his breakfast beer and porridge when the visitor was announced.

Although Dudley's house provided no separate room for gubernatorial business, there was a corner furnished with a sturdy oak table and two armchairs, where he customarily retired with anyone upon whom he wished to impress the high dignity of his office. He placed Master Zachariah Symmes there, and sat facing him across the table. "Now, sir," he said gruffly, "what can we do for you?"

"I came to speak to you about a woman," said Symmes. "A Mistress Anne Hutchinson, who was a passenger on the ship with me from England."

"The *Griffin,*" said Dudley.

"Yes, sir," said Symmes. "And it may be you will say, why come to the governor about such a matter?"

"You must tell me what the matter is," said Dudley, "before I can say anything."

"It is the woman's opinions," said Symmes. He spoke indignantly about her interpretation of a certain passage of Scripture he had preached on. He said it might seem to the governor a matter for the ministers and magistrates of Boston, since Mistress Hutchinson would no doubt join the Boston church, but that there was something about her—a fierceness of manner, coupled with the narrowness and corruptness of her mind—that seemed to threaten the foundations of the colony as a whole.

Dudley sat frowning, looking down at his paper-strewn table top. He could not make out exactly what manner of threat it was that Symmes feared. What he said did not seem altogether to explain the anger so evident in his countenance and the trembling of his voice, which he tried not quite successfully to control. Observing him closely from under his bushy gray eyebrows, the governor suspected some personal affront suffered by the minister at Mistress Hutchinson's hands. Yet he was certainly a minister of the Lord, and there was no reason to doubt his veracity. The woman might well have expressed opinions that could prove dangerous, though what effect a single female could have upon an entire colony Dudley could no way imagine.

Mistress Anne Hutchinson. He almost believed he had heard some report of her, but perhaps it was only the family name that was familiar. Some persons of that name had arrived in Boston in the last year, he knew. They were moderately well-to-do and, as he seemed to remember, known to John Cotton from the time he lived in Lincolnshire. The woman was not likely to be a troublemaker, surely, if she belonged to that family; but one had to suppose that Symmes possessed a certain amount of perception. And this was no time to tolerate dissension anywhere.

"Come with me to Boston," he said to Symmes at last, but the minister said church duties would keep him busy all day in Charlestown.

Dudley would go alone then, for he wished to waste no time about the matter, and consult with John Cotton and John Wilson, teacher and pastor respectively of the Boston church. The governor and the minister walked together to Charlestown, Symmes carefully going over one more time the doubtful expressions he had heard from Mistress Hutchinson. He said he would come to Boston later if the ministers wanted him: his presence might be useful when they came to question the woman.

4

In Boston, John Winthrop strode along the dusty high street toward John Wilson's house by the market place. The former governor seldom set out to stroll or amble anywhere; he had no time to waste. He had looked for some leisure when Brother Dudley gained the highest place—some compensation for the hurt he couldn't help confessing to himself at this evidence that the people were turning a little away from him. But there had not been much change, after all. Boston remained the center of the colony, and with Dudley in Newtown it fell to Winthrop to transact much of the commonwealth business. He had agreed that he would go today and confer with Captain Underhill about an intensification of militia training, and so he would; but first he wanted to see Pastor Wilson about some matters of private concern.

So his days ever went, no time to spare, and yet as often happened he felt his pace slowing in spite of himself as he walked the streets of Boston. He could not help marveling at what with God's help men had wrought on this bare peninsula in the four years of settlement. There across the market place stood the center of everything, the meetinghouse, mud-daubed and ugly he could not deny; but its thatched roof could shelter the population of the town when it came together for holy worship, and God had never asked for towers or stained glass. Even apart from the spiritual unity it betokened, the meetinghouse might stand as an emblem of the entire town, which was growing too fast to allow anyone time for thoughts of town planning or architectural style. Paths crisscrossed the market place as persons took the nearest way to their destination. Hogs rooted there; chickens scratched in the dust and raised their contented voices to blend with the sound of saws biting into logs, shaping planks for the new houses rising everywhere. Scattered along the high street and up and down the narrow lanes running every which way, the houses stood, of new pine glowing yellow in the sunshine or older wood already weathered gray. Winthrop might be forgiven if he saw his own hand in all this growth and progress, for he never forgot Whose hand guided his. Indeed, he felt called upon to pause for a moment and thank Him for the prosperity of this town and the commonwealth that Winthrop hoped would prove a model for the entire Christian world.

There was also the necessity—a pleasurable duty—of pausing to greet the numerous men and women who would always want to stop and have a word with him. All Boston knew his figure at any distance—somewhat slight but well proportioned and well clad, with an aristocratic bearing that stopped sufficiently short of being haughty. "Your servant, sir," one would say to him, tipping his scarlet cap; and Winthrop, looking down his fine long English nose, would produce a grave smile from above his thick Van Dyck beard and answer him, "Good morrow, Goodman Brown, how fares thy ailing child today?" He would be governor again, and yet again. God had him marked out for that.

John Wilson, like many others in Boston, still often unthinkingly used the old title. He flung open his door when he saw Winthrop coming. "Good morrow, Governor!" he cried heartily.

Master Wilson, whose long creased face had the expression of one constantly striving to nose out the work of the devil, was packing a chest in preparation for a journey to England. Though his departure was still some weeks away, Winthrop knew the pastor was already sealing up chests and boxes; and therefore he had brought some books and papers that he hoped to have safely delivered in Suffolk.

Wilson planned to visit Suffolk and would take the articles himself, he said. He knew that part of England well. So did Winthrop, for it was his native place. The two men allowed themselves to be led into nostalgia, and spoke of spacious stone manor houses, of hedge-bordered fields free of stumps and stones, and well-kept roads that led to busy market towns. It was seldom that either of them, or any other right-thinking man of Massachusetts Bay, allowed himself such thoughts: they might almost feel themselves upon the verge of sin, should they regret those worldly things left behind for the sake of God and His pure church.

There came a knock at the street door as they talked, hard quick raps such as an officer of church or state might produce at the door of some wrongdoer. The two men looked half guiltily at one another, but before they could either comment or get up to answer the knock, Mistress Wilson entered, ushering in the governor.

"I trust I do not intrude upon private affairs," said Thomas Dudley, not as though he cared very much what their affairs might be.

They assured him he was no intruder, and he said well, then, there was business, something to be approached in a church way, and perhaps Brother Winthrop would do well to hear it himself, since it closely concerned the town of Boston.

## 5

John Cotton liked his snug house and the location of it. Set back against the easternmost of the three low hills Bostonians called the Trimontaine, it was sufficiently removed from the hustle and bustle of the booming port town that he could withdraw into his study as from the world. He could have stayed shut up there from early morning and never looked up till candlelight time, had not Mistress Cotton always come insisting that he had to eat his dinner. Since Cambridge days, he had taken his greatest pleasure in books, especially all that derived from the thought of the great theologian to whom he devoted himself. "I have read the fathers, and the schoolmen, and Calvin, too," he was fond of saying, "but I find that he who has Calvin has them all." Deprived of every book except the Bible and the *Institutes,* he could have happily spent each day behind his study door.

He was glad Pastor Wilson had chosen to live by the market place: people wanting to discourse of church matters would naturally come to him first. Occasionally some church member would make his way to Cotton Hill, in need perhaps of the teacher's gentle understanding; but Mistress Cotton had been trained to screen all comers carefully. Not everyone who sought admittance there was allowed to come between Calvin and John Cotton.

One midmorning, when—could Cotton but have known, or cared to know—the hillside was washed gold by the rich light of the September sun and the sky cupped a blue like the surface of calm seas, Mistress Sarah Cotton tapped at his study door and called him timidly. Sarah knew the day was dazzling blue and gold, but it would not have occurred to her to call her husband forth to see that sight.

"Yes, dear heart?" he called at last, remotely, from within.

She opened the door. He was sitting by the window at the plain pine table that had replaced the handsome oak desk he used in former times. He lifted his hand to tuck a wisp of straw-colored hair up under his black skullcap. The way that soft hair framed his face against the sunlight made her think of the name they used to call him in Old England: the angel of Botolph's.

"What is it, Sarah?" he asked her, with a conscious air of patience.

"John, Thomas Dudley is here," she said.

"What does he want?" he asked, with somewhat less patience.

"John, I did not ask," she said. "Brother Wilson and Brother Winthrop are with him."

He regretted at once the slight irritability. "Of course, dear," he said. "I was thinking of old Dr. Sibbes"—he glanced at the portrait of the black-gowned clergyman hanging on the wall in front of him—"and what he used to preach about negative righteousness. The covenant of works was what he meant, you know."

"John, the governor—" she said.

He rose quickly, spoke apologetically. "Yes, dear, of course." Of course one did not keep the governor waiting; nor would he wish to appear wanting in respect toward the other high-placed men. It struck him for the first time that those three calling together could mean a matter of some gravity.

He hurried down to the parlor. Although he appeared somewhat heavy in the loose gown he wore to work in, his footsteps on the stairs seemed surprisingly light.

Sunshine streamed in through the open front door, but the visitors sat on benches placed against the wall, their faces in deep shadow. He peered at them, trying to read their expressions, as he offered his apologies for making them wait.

Dudley hastily denied any cause for apology. "Nay, we have interrupted you, brother, as well I know," he said. He stood up: with an old-fashioned padded doublet adding to his naturally bulky trunk and his legs encased in Florentine hose, he might have made a comic, gamecock sort of figure, but the absolute certainty that he was in command of every situation glinted in his gray eyes and kept anyone from ever saying so. "Yet it is true that we all have our work to do, so let me say at once that we are here about a former parishioner of yours in England, a Mistress Hutchinson, who it seems has vented strange opinions."

Cotton shook his head doubtfully; he could recall no such person from among his flock in old Boston. "Mistress Hutchinson?" he repeated.

"Anne Hutchinson," said Dudley, "so I believe."

Then Cotton remembered a woman who used to come to hear him preach at St. Botolph's and sometimes take part in discussion meetings at his house. She could ask questions that showed an uncommonly good understanding of theology.

"She was not in my parish," he said, "but I remember a Mistress Hutchinson who used to come in from Alford sometimes. She said she gained no benefit from hearing the vicar there."

"Now that I think of it," said Dudley, "I believe Master Symmes did mention Alford." He went on to explain who Symmes was. "He was alarmed at some of her expressions on the ship," he concluded.

"I never knew her well," Cotton said, "but I find it difficult to believe she holds unorthodox views."

"You had better hear what Brother Symmes had to say, John," said Pastor Wilson. "You may then believe it."

Cotton realized this was not, as perhaps he had halfway still hoped, a thing to be settled in a word or two down here in his sunlit parlor.

"Come then," he said. There would have to be a conference—in private, where neither Sarah nor the servants would have a chance to overhear. He led the way. In his study he regretfully closed the book of Dr. Sibbes's sermons that lay waiting on his table. He gestured toward the bench and two extra chairs that he kept for such unavoidable occasions. "Well, brothers?" he said.

# II

On the third day after arriving in Boston, Anne Hutchinson awoke with a feeling of joyful excitement. As was her custom, she lay a few minutes gaining full awareness of the day, recollecting its expected duties and events. Ah, but this would be a glorious day. It was Saturday—or rather seventh day, as Christians here called it, preferring not to name the pagan gods. It was seventh day, and it contained within it the beginning of the Sabbath.

At three o'clock in the afternoon, as Anne had learned, all work in Boston ceased. Laborers went home. Shops closed. Children were called in from their play. Observation of the Sabbath began at that hour, with family prayers and religious instruction for children and servants, and continued until sunset of the next day. Anne allowed herself a few minutes to lie silently thanking the Lord for bringing her to this place where His pure way was the way of all the people. For so at that time she believed it was.

She turned then to her husband. He lay still beside her, but she knew he was awake, waiting for the signal that her time of secret thought and prayer was ended.

Daylight had grayed the narrow windows but scarcely lit the interior of the room and penetrated not at all the darkness within the high, curtained bed that stood in one corner. But Anne unerringly reached out and touched her husband's face.

"Dear William," she said.

He turned to her and embraced her, and almost in the same

moment baby Susannah began to whimper in her cradle by their bed.

Anne kissed William and pulled herself from his arms. "I must suckle the babe," she said.

So her days ever began, and so her life was ordered: first God, then William, and after him the children.

They rose and dressed. Then she sat on a stool and gave Susannah suck, while he brought the fire to life in the great chimney place. At the same time, the members of the household began stirring in the rooms above. The house, like most of the better houses of Boston, had three levels: the ground floor, comprising one large room called the hall, where Anne and William slept and the daily activities of the family centered; the second-floor room, of the same size as the hall, where the three kinswomen and eight of the children slept; and the garret, where up under the steep wood-shingled roof slept the two eldest sons and the two menservants.

While Anne still sat with the baby at her breast, the two servants came downstairs, took milk pails, and hurried to the barn. Son Edward had bought cows before the family came and had been milking them; with the help of Brother Edward's wife Sarah, he had a supply of milk and butter and cheese already on hand.

The next to appear downstairs were Anne and Frances Freestone, cousins of William, unmarried sisters who long had dwelled beneath his roof. They came excusing themselves for being late, though they were as early as there was need of them, and began to make preparations for breakfast. Gradually, through the years, they had taken the kitchen work as their province; Anne had the care of a large house and many children, so the arrangement suited her well. Here there was no kitchen, only the space around the fireplace at one end of the hall, where already the sisters had set out on shelves or hung up on the chimney breast the cooking utensils and tableware brought with the Hutchinsons from their old home.

Very shortly, for no one dawdled, the rest of the family descended: the two grown young men, Edward and Richard; Francis, a boy of fourteen, characteristically apart from the rest; the oldest daughters, Faith and Bridget; Anne's sister Katherine Marbury, with three-year-old William in her arms; and following her the other young children, Samuel, Anne, Mary, and Katherine.

There were affectionate greetings among them, but no conversation until after the men had come in with the milk, prayers were said, and the family sat eating warmed-up pease porridge. As they were finishing, scraping their bowls, the deep, sad sound of the herd's horn reached them. Towards the North End somewhere, coming their way, was the boy who daily drove the cattle to the common, and whose horn blast meant the work of the day ought to be well begun.

So at least said Anne Hutchinson, as she talked to the household gathered around her, reminding them of the imminent beginning of the Sabbath. There was much to be done, and on this day all tasks must be finished early, so that by three o'clock their minds and hearts should be cleared of all except the consciousness of God. To that end she prayed with them, and then sent them all to their separate kinds of work.

Sister Katherine, with the help of the younger girls, set about to complete the cleaning of the house, which had stood unoccupied since the owner's departure some two months earlier. They still had not dusted all the shelves and ledges or swept down the cobwebs that clung along the exposed beams and joists. Faith and Bridget were charged with unpacking and airing all the children's clothes, and making ready the garments chosen for wear on the Sabbath. Kitchen work well sufficed to fill the sisters' time, since they had to prepare enough food for the four meals that would be eaten during the time when no work could be done.

Anne, as she went about a variety of duties that she felt no one else could be trusted with, had her thoughts directed always toward the climactic events of the Sabbath, the services conducted for the worship of the Lord. She could not suppress completely, though, a lurking sense of disappointment. Before coming here, she had not realized that John Cotton was not pastor of the Boston church. At his arrival—she now had been told—the congregation already had a pastor, John Wilson, with whom they were well pleased, and they had not wished to turn him out, even for the greatest nonconformist preacher in England. As soon as the elders learned that Cotton had been silenced in England and must leave that country if he would escape imprisonment, they began to plan how they could entice him to Boston and keep him there. So when he came they were prepared to offer him the position of teacher in their church; and understanding that Boston was the leading town of Massachusetts, the minister accepted their terms. He may have thought (what Anne herself believed) that it was the only appropriate dwelling place for a preacher destined to become the spiritual leader of the entire colony.

Anne could not but resent his being given second place, though assured by some Boston members she had met that Master Cotton's position was in effect as exalted as the pastor's. His duties were as numerous and important, and within the year that he had been in Boston many people had learned to trust him more than John Wilson in questions of doctrine and faith. And although it was the pastor who preached at the morning service, so that Anne would have to wait until the afternoon to hear the soft voice and sweet words she had so long been starved for, she kept one consolation in her heart. It was as her teacher that he had (if unknowingly) drawn her after him, and so the place he held here might be considered the fulfillment of a prophecy.

While the women and girls stayed busy inside the house, the men and boys were at work building a lean-to where the mercer's goods could be stored and his trade carried on. At first, William had meant to keep his goods in the hall until such time as he could erect his own house, but when all the family's belongings had been fetched from the ship, he could see no space to stretch out a length of cloth and hardly room for a customer to stand while he examined it. He had soon ascertained that it would be feasible and permissible to build a lean-to onto this house and then remove it when he built his own dwelling.

So like many other men of Boston, the Hutchinsons were at work with hammer and saw. But about midmorning Brother Edward came along from the harbor to say that a ship was in with a cargo of fine silk, and William determined to go find out about the prospects of acquiring some of it.

Stopping in the house to tell Anne where he was going, he found her engaged in lifting out clothing from a long, deep chest of unornamented oak. He put an arm around her and said, as a question, "Thou art happy?"

"I am here," she said simply, "where he is."

It had become almost a condition of her very life that she follow John Cotton to New England. Because his own life was of no value to William if this woman were not content, he had agreed to give up comfort and security in Old England, leaving behind his aged mother and most of his brothers and sisters, in a radical change totally incompatible with his own nature. Yet because he could not understand her restless seeking, her desperate need for something he could never give her, he was happiest when he knew she was satisfied, as now, with womanly, domestic tasks.

"What dress hast thou found for tomorrow?" he asked.

She lifted a pair of slashed silk sleeves trimmed in lace and gathered into puffs with velvet ribbons. "Will these be suitable to wear on Sabbath Day in Boston?" she wondered.

William smiled. He liked those sleeves. "Very suitable, I would say," he answered. "They have passed sumptuary laws here lately, but they say that such garments as a person has on hand should continue to be worn, for thrift's sake."

"Nevertheless," said Anne, frowning slightly, "I should not wish to wear anything not deemed sufficiently modest for a Christian gentlewoman."

"The law allows one slash in each sleeve, as long as it be not immodestly large and puffed. I think thou hast never worn anything as extreme as the clothes this law refers to."

"Very well," said Anne, "for I have not got the wear out of this pair of sleeves."

"The sea-green gown goes with these sleeves very well," William said. He thought it went with Anne herself very well: the silvery green was an excellent color against her pale skin, and the stuff it was made of fell in soft folds that revealed without clinging her full and well-shaped figure. He would not say these words to Anne, not about a dress she might think of wearing to church, but she must know very well that he thought them.

"I have given it to Bridget already," she said. "It no longer suits me at my time of life, and she has grown almost as tall as I and can wear it."

He was sorry for that, but did not say so. "It will look well on her, too," he said. "The children too must look well dressed according to our station in life, for that is what is expected in Boston."

Anne smiled. "When in Rome, do as the Romans," she said, "as long as no sin be involved."

"So I believe," he said. He kissed her lightly on the cheek. "I must go to the harbor," he told her. "My brother has brought word of a ship that is in with some silk that I may want to bid for."

"Watch the sun and be home for dinner," she said. "Cousin Frances found a good piece of beef at the market and is roasting it."

He assured her he would be on time, and as he turned away was pleased to see her draw out of the trunk another gown of a stuff he had chosen, a tawny satin that looked sumptuously rich yet was made up in no showy style.

Thinking how "brave" she looked in that dress, he walked jauntily along to the harbor, heartened by his wife's brisk interest in clothes for the Sabbath Day. But it pleased him too to think that soon she would hear John Cotton preach again, for she had grieved a long time over his loss.

It was an easy, simple doctrine Cotton taught, or so Anne loved to tell people. Not by good works does a man reach salvation, nor by any thought he can take, but by union with Christ, which comes only through the grace of God. The assurance constantly sought by every Christian could be found through his awareness of this union, the sense of the Holy Ghost within. William had often heard John Cotton preach these words; yet the more he would think of them, the more their full meaning would elude him. With Anne it seemed to be the other way: she grasped them at once and could make them clearer, it seemed to him, than even the preacher himself could ever do. William was not by any means as well read as Anne or as anxious to question what was taught. Left to himself, he would probably have been happy with the Church of England as he had always known it; and yet he could see the clear logic of what she would explain as she went over the fruits of her long meditations in the evening after family prayers.

Like Anne, he thought of the Sabbath Day worship service

and looked forward to it for several reasons. He had met a few merchants and tradesmen, but he wanted to see who the leaders of the community were. He was curious about the service itself, which would be plain and simple compared with anything he had known up to now. He thought he would like that: he was a plain man, and he had a simple belief in God. He had always left church matters to Anne and would still. He would attend to his worldly affairs, in which he had always been successful, and he would support his family and give generously to whatever church Anne believed in. He had heard Cotton himself preach on this subject of worldly affairs, and it seemed to him that the preacher made good sense when he talked about business. A man must work in his calling, Cotton taught, to the best of his abilities, for the good of himself and his family, as well as for the public good. "Diligence in worldly business," Cotton said, "and yet deadness to the world. Such a mystery as none can read but they that know it." William thought he understood that. There was a time to think upon the quality of silk and upon the demand and ability to pay for it that might exist in this new colony. He had already made some inquiries about that. He thought he might invest in this unexpected shipment Edward had learned of. On the other hand, he might not, for he had brought a considerable stock with him and had established credit in London sufficient to order what he needed when he needed it. Still, this might prove a good bargain. He deliberately turned his thoughts to business, to the calling God had fitted him for. Thoughts of Sabbath Day meeting could wait upon the time.

2

The Lord's Day dawned bright and fair. Except for milking the cows (for necessary care of animals was allowed on the Sabbath), there was no work to be done. They ate cold porridge for breakfast and would eat it again, with cold meat, when they came home for a short stay at noon. The task of dressing for the service was all that remained now to be done. Anne had assigned to Faith and Bridget the washing and dressing of the younger children, except for Susannah, whom she must nurse and then would clean and dress.

They were ready in time for a short prayer service at home before the sharp rattling summons reached them from the drummer who walked along the high street.

"Mother, it's time to go!" shouted little Anne, jumping up from her low stool with a rustle of her taffeta petticoat.

"Hush," said Anne sternly, and the single syllable was enough to quiet the child and stop her in her tracks, for she knew at once what she had done. "Thou hast desecrated the Sabbath, and thy father will have to whip thee after sunset."

She had wounded God and thereby her beloved mother. For these reasons and also because her father would himself be hurt because he had to whip her, and not least at the thought of the rod upon her bare skin, she began to cry. Then there had to be more stern talk and a face washing, and because she had delayed their departure, the prospect of additional licks when the Sabbath ended at sunset. Poor little Anne. More than any other of the children, so she thought in her heart, she wanted to please God and her mother and father. But somehow the joys of life always seemed to overpower her sense of duty.

The incident of Anne's excited outburst served one good purpose. All of the children were suitably grave and silent as they walked behind their elders on the dusty way to church. Faith, as the oldest daughter, was given the privilege of carrying Susannah in her arms. Bridget held William's leading strings, and Mary (taking the place of little Anne, who now must be deprived) held little sister Katherine by the hand. The older boys brought up the rear.

All over Boston, family groups were emerging from their front doors in much this same fashion. Bright-colored clothing, gold belts and hatbands, trimming of gold and silver lace, all shone bravely in the bright sunlight. A stranger might have thought the town was turning out for some gay celebration, some fair or festival, until he observed the sober, measured gait and the grave, unsmiling faces.

The Hutchinsons had not far to go before they reached the market place—the open square seemed strangely lifeless today, compared with the bustling noisy state of it the day John Winthrop passed through on his way to see the pastor. A few hens sang as they scratched in the dust: one would have liked to silence them some way, for the glory of God. Now crossing toward the west side of the market place, the family had facing them the house of God, to which all feet were directed.

"What is that big, ugly house there, sister?" whispered Katherine to Mary, who hurriedly said "Sh!" and pinched the little one's hand. The parents did not look back; gratefully, the girls could hope they had not heard. In any case, it was becoming clear to them that this could only be the church—the meetinghouse, as it was called in Boston.

"We are not to call the building a church any more," their mother had instructed them. "The church means the people who join together for the worship of God."

Church or meetinghouse, it was unbelievably ugly: a square, mud-plastered building with a steep thatched roof rising to a point at the center. William led them to the doorway, where they were met by a tall man who nodded and called William by name. He directed them to sit at the front of the hall, on the second row—the women and girls on the right side, the men and grown boys on the left. The younger boys had to sit on the floor beneath the pulpit, and there was a little cage, or wooden frame, where children too young to sit alone and yet no longer babes in arms were kept. Edward had already told them that although noncommunicants ordinarily were required to sit at the back of the building, they would be received and seated according to the position it was expected they would take in Boston and the church. Their acquaintance with John Cotton and William's unquestioned position as one of the "richer sort" assured them a place near the front even at their first coming.

Damp and dim was the interior of that strange meetinghouse. The golden morning sunlight reached in at the front door but could penetrate only a few feet in the direction of the tall pulpit built against the opposite wall. The pulpit was still empty as the family made their way down the aisle, but most of the seats were filled already. On either side of the pulpit were raised seats where, on one side, the officers of the church were seated, and on the other, those members of the General Court of the commonwealth who resided in Boston. Beneath their stern gaze,

Anne and her daughters found seats along a row of hard, backless benches, where they must learn to sit for hours with rigid backs and unswerving eyes upon the pulpit.

Soon after they were seated, the ministers came in. The congregation stood as the two men in skullcaps and black Geneva gowns made their way down the aisle to the pulpit. One climbed the narrow, ladder-like stairs and took his place behind the lectern where the Bible lay open at the text chosen for that morning's sermon.

Anne waited with apprehension to see what sort of man this was who as pastor came first before the congregation and would preach the sermon at this morning's service. In the dimness it was hard to discern the separate features of his face; it was long and lean and appeared dark in expression as well as complexion, though had the sunlight been able to reach this distance from the entrance door, it is possible his visage might have appeared more fair. He raised his voice in prayer; and to one eager for the sweet angelic tones that used to fill St. Botolph's, the pastor's speech—harsh, unclear, unmodulated—did truly seem to grate upon the ear. Yet one must not judge too soon: the sermon was yet to come. One of the ruling elders rose and announced a psalm, which was sung without benefit of any instrument by voices mostly unmusical and untrained. Anne joined in wholeheartedly and uncritically. Music was never her favorite part of the service, but she would not wish to slight any portion of the worship of the Lord.

As soon as Pastor Wilson rose again, it became clear that his preaching voice was no better than his praying one. Yet as for that, he had to make do with what God gave him. It was the matter, not the manner, of his preaching that concerned Anne Hutchinson. She listened, bent forward a little, the frown lines on her forehead drawn just perceptively closer together than ordinarily they were. If there were a text or a doctrine, it would seem to be "He who falls into sin hates the Lord," and if there were a logical plan of developing that text Anne could not discern it. There was a great quoting of Scripture, and a great exhortation to listen and take heed. The monotones employed in the prayer were punctuated in the sermon with angry shouting as the pastor bethought him of the great sins committed against God. When at last, after some two hours, he sat down, Anne's inward condition was indicated by the fact that, very faintly and unobserved by anyone who cared, she involuntarily wagged her head. Who could quarrel with a preacher who opposed sin? But who could possibly find enlightenment in such murky matter as John Wilson placed before them?

Anne thanked God it was sweet-voiced John Cotton who gave the closing prayer and dismissed the congregation from the morning service. The worshipers went home for an hour, to eat cold porridge and otherwise refresh themselves, before coming back for the afternoon service to hear John Cotton preach. In keeping with the day, they said very little to each other. Tonight after sunset, when little Anne had been whipped and all the children put to bed, and Anne was lying beside William, she would have her say about John Wilson. It was clear already what comparisons would be made.

When at last she heard John Cotton preach again, Anne could not keep back the tears. All the glory of God's promises came flooding over her; bathed with the sound of this voice, lifted upon the hope of these words, she felt baptized anew in the sea of God's loving grace. Here in Boston, as she had long believed, she would find food for her spirit, to keep her strong in the worship of the Lord. That Pastor Wilson provided nothing, less than nothing, was regrettable; but placed against the benefits of Master Cotton's preaching, his great negative seemed of no account. Anne moved slowly toward the door of the meetinghouse. Without noticing, she lagged behind the women of her family, among whom she had been sitting. Neither was she aware of others edging past her.

"Mistress Hutchinson! Mistress Hutchinson!" a soft but commanding voice behind her called. Indeed, her name was spoken several times before she heard it; the women going ahead of her were turning back to stare.

She paused still hardly convinced she had heard anything. She knew there was no idle talk in the meetinghouse on the Lord's Day, or even in the yard outside or the streets and lanes that people followed homeward. She half suspected she had dreamed the calling of her name.

"Mistress Hutchinson." The words came again, and she knew that voice, as well as William's or any of the children's, as well as the very voice of God.

She stood stock-still. She scarcely dared turn and look behind her, for fear she was mistaken about whose voice she had heard. She knew she was not, and yet she could not believe she was being singled out by John Cotton. Although as her teacher he was immeasurably dear to her, and although she had gone to him in old Boston as often as she could, she had doubted he would recognize her face.

While she stood doubting, the congregation was moving on outside, until at last she knew she was alone in God's house with the man who she believed came closer than anyone else in the world to thinking His thoughts and speaking His words. She trembled in hope and fear. Could he be about to tell her of his pleasure in learning she had followed after him? Nay, for such a presumption lay close to blasphemy.

At last she turned to him, stood face to face with him, tried to look him in the eye as if he were some ordinary man.

"I hoped for a word with you, if you will pardon me," he said gently.

"Sir, I have come thousands of miles to hear a word from you," she said, and marveled at her boldness.

"First," he said, "I may tell you that it seems to me a sign of your honest conviction that you have come so far, and brought your family to this harsh new land, for the sake of the true faith."

"I came because I believed I could hear true preaching here."

"And therefore I suppose you do intend to join with the Church of Christ in Boston."

"I do," she said. She knew then he had not singled her out to praise or welcome her. His words came like a blow from some unsuspected hand, for they clearly presaged some objection to her as a member of a Christian congregation.

"You may know," he said, "that as we strive here for a pure church, we must make sure of the fitness of every communicant. Not as in England do we have churches made up of true believers mingled with hypocrites and even the openly ungodly."

"Of course I knew I would be questioned before the congregation," said Anne—and then added something she had never once thought of till that moment: "If so be I do decide to seek membership when I have learned more of the church."

Cotton smiled. "It is but right that you should wish to be assured," he said, "as we must be of you."

Anne suddenly became impatient. If something more than the ordinary questions put to every new member awaited her, then she wanted to know what it was. "Hath anyone reported aught of me to make you doubt me?" she asked outright.

"Somewhat," said Cotton, "and yet I daresay there may be some misunderstanding." He paused, peered into her face as if searching out something hard to discern in that dim light. "I believe you are acquainted with my brother minister, Zachariah Symmes."

So he was the one. His pursed lips and suspicious little pig eyes rose before her and she flushed with ill-controlled ire. "Aye," she said, not risking more, for her voice was unsteady.

"He has come to us casting doubt upon the soundness of your opinions," said Cotton, "and although I have sufficient knowledge of you to think he must be mistaken, you will see that we are bound to pay attention to the honest questions of a brother minister."

With this assurance that John Cotton did truly remember her, Anne began to feel less threatened. She knew well that all her opinions derived from his teachings, and she thought she knew exactly which one had set Zachariah Symmes against her.

"Sir," she said, "once and once only did I dispute something Master Symmes said at a worship meeting on the ship. He spoke some words about the evidencing of a good estate, which made me wonder if he preached a covenant of works, and gave as proof that place in John you will remember."

"We know that we are translated from death to life because we love the brethren," murmured Cotton.

"And I remembered how I had asked you once to clear that text, and you explained it perfectly. I tried to explain it then to Master Symmes, but he could no way take my meaning, so I told him when we came to Boston he might have new food to feed his soul."

Cotton shifted his feet slightly, turned more directly upon Anne. "You did not mention my name?" he said.

"No, sir, I did not," she said. "And yet I think you can be sure I did not alter your meaning."

"Nay, I meant not that," he said. He said nothing of what he did mean; she thought it was some doubt of her.

"And so you mean to question me," she said.

"We have thought it well," he said, "for your sake as well as our own, since Brother Symmes is minister of another church, to hold a conference with you in private before you seek admission to the Boston church."

"Should I so decide," said Anne.

"I think you will," said Cotton, "and I think we shall be very glad to have you. But we should like to hear you express your thoughts upon such matters as this place in John."

"I should like that, too," said Anne, "for I want you to be assured that I have understood your teaching."

"Then it is agreed," he said.

"When do we meet?" she said.

"Since Brother Symmes must find a time when he can leave his duties and come here from Charlestown, we have agreed to wait upon his convenience."

"You will send me word?" she said.

"Aye, you will hear," he said.

They walked out of the meetinghouse together, blinking in the bright sunshine, and she saw William waiting for her at the edge of the grassy yard. She longed to run to him, throw herself against his broad chest, and give herself up to weeping. But she walked to him quietly and slowly, with the great minister at her side, and when the two men had greeted each other, in solemn Sabbath restraint, John Cotton turned one way and they the other. And she said not a word to William, nor did he question her, until they had reached home and shut the door against the curious eyes Anne seemed to feel upon her.

# III

At the family gathering that Sabbath evening, Anne explained what had delayed her at the meetinghouse. She said she held no opinions differing from John Cotton's, and she had no fear of being rejected by any church where he was teacher. No, no, they all cried, at least the adults and the children who were old enough to know what questionable opinions meant. "Thou art a dear saint and child of God," said William to her openly, "and no man of good faith could find a word to say against thee."

There must have been, however, some disturbance in their thoughts, for no one remembered the punishment that was due to little Anne. The child herself did not forget, of course, but neither did she feel called upon to remind her parents. She simply thanked God for directing their minds elsewhere.

Only after Anne and William lay in bed together, with the household sunk in dark and silence, did Anne remember the promised whipping. She spoke of it to William, who said, "Methinks we have been more troubled in our minds than we wish to believe."

"Truly," said Anne. "And must she still be punished?"

"She has suffered enough in expectation, I think," said William.

"So think I," said Anne. "I shall talk with her on the morrow, but we shall forego the whipping this time."

William turned to Anne and embraced her. "I love thy gentle and merciful heart," he said softly.

She returned his embrace, and in so doing learned his mind was no longer on any of their troubles. She might have denied him, and he would have understood why; but she had from weariness put him off since their arrival, and she knew he had hoped this night at the Sabbath's end would bring him comfort.

Her mind was in such turmoil that she scarcely knew what he had done when he finished; and this troubled her, for she believed God created man and wife to find joy in the carnal knowledge of each other. She realized she had never been as deeply affected as William by the act of conjugal love: the first night they lay together he wept as they were truly joined and made one flesh. Although she had known William all her life and never wanted any other man for her husband, it was many months after that first time before she knew such pleasure in his bed as she had thought a wife's part; and even then she surmised her pleasures were less frequent than his and less complete.

And yet in truth she loved him and was glad tonight as always to satisfy his need. Even so, the while he wooed and won her (for always the act seemed a brief recapitulation of their long-drawn-out courtship), her mind would keep going back to the encounter of the afternoon. She was reminded of those six years she lived in London. Though she thought often of William then, as a dear childhood friend, and wrote to him whenever she had a chance to send a letter, her mind strayed easily to other concerns. At that time she used to spend many hours in studies directed by her father, reading Scripture and books of theology, for in his view the only worthwhile purpose of study was to know God. In order to teach her to reason upon what she had read, he engaged her in long arguments which she must with all her powers try to win while evincing the full respect due a parent from a child. Then as now, seeking always to grasp every aspect of God's plan for His children, she would often find her mind wandering down some new track she hoped might lead to greater understanding. And always, since understanding God involved convincing her father, the image of Francis Marbury would be rising before her (even coming between her and the paper on which she tried to put down words that would speak to William far away in Lincolnshire), demanding her attention, just as tonight the face of John Cotton appeared somehow between them, smiling approval or frowning in doubt.

Throughout the night, her moiling mind would torment her.

Yet she knew she slept a little because she awoke several times as though aroused by an urgent need to set aright some terrible but forgotten displacement. Then all the same questions would return to her, recalling once more the whole distressing interview in the meetinghouse. When at last the time came that she awoke and saw the diamond-shaped windowpanes grayed with dawn, she thanked God that the night was over. In the light of day, she told herself, reason must prevail and she would clearly see that because she was right she need fear no man's questions.

But as the day wore on, she had to confess to herself that her mind was far from settled, and she recalled with deep longing how in Alford she used to retire to her chamber daily for a period of restoring solitude. At one troublesome time in her life (not long before the immigration to New England), she had even spent whole days in Scripture reading and meditation. It seemed that in Boston there was no hour in her busy day and no corner in her crowded house for this kind of luxury.

Late in the afternoon, weary from a day spent washing soiled clothes worn by the family on their long journey, she paused by the open east window while the breeze from the sea cooled her face. A tall oak armchair stood there, the only chair in the house, and except for some simple wooden chests the only furniture brought from England. It had been set at an angle to the window, facing the bed she slept in, which was nothing more than a crude framework left there by the owners of the house. Anne rested a hand on an arm of the chair, and seemed to see how that small space between it and the bed could even become a retreat in her dire need.

Just then came little William, running from the open back door, calling, "Marmie, Marmie! Come see!"

She turned to him and held out her arms; but Francis, who had just come in at the front door, strode across the room, picked up his young brother, and tossed him in the air. Setting him down again, he said, "I shall come and see in a moment. Marmie is busy and tired." Then looking to Anne, he said, somewhat anxiously, "Are you all right, Mother?"

"Aye," she said, smiling at his tender concern. She brushed back a sweat-damp lock of hair that had escaped her coif, then sat in the chair and took William on her lap. "I had just stopped a moment to let the breeze blow in my face," she said.

"Mother," said Francis then, looking at her keenly, "can you not take time now to sit alone awhile, as you used to do in your bedchamber in Alford?"

"Not now, I think," she said, "though I confess I have been wishing that I could find an hour."

"You shall find it today," he said. "I shall see that you do." He picked up William out of her lap and set him on the floor. "Run outdoors," he said, "and in a minute I will come and look at whatever it is."

"Wilt thou go with brother and show him?" Anne asked her small son, and he said solemnly, "Yes, I will, because Marmie tired."

William ran back outdoors, and Francis said to his mother, "Shall I not bring you the large Bible before I go back to help Father?"

"I should like it above all things," she said, "but I have not unpacked it." It was an old book, much like the one her father had used, and in Alford she had been accustomed to sit with it open on her lap in her times of quiet solitude. But on shipboard, and since landing, she had kept with her only a smaller Bible, the one she always used for family services.

"I know where it is," said the boy. "It's in a stack of books that I took from a crate two days ago, and yet have not had time to make a shelf for."

Anne smiled. "Then I should like it." He was the one of all the children who had been eager to unpack the books, and perhaps the only one who would know where the great Bible was.

He fetched the cumbersome book and laid it on her lap.

"I thank thee, Francis," said Anne. "And one more thing I would ask: do please see if little Anne is remembering to watch the younger children while she knits."

"That I will, Mother," he said, and she knew he would.

Left alone, she sighed. There would be little time left to her today, but she was grateful to Francis for seeing her need and trying to help her. She seemed to know that henceforth she would have a time and place for meditation. And this proved true; her daily withdrawal to this spot became a custom respected by the household. The little children called it Marmie's hour with God.

## 2

The chair she sat in, called a wainscot chair, had a high panel back incised with scrolls and diamonds and crowned with a carving of something resembling the face of the sun. At first, before they knew her better, Boston women believed she had brought the chair with her out of vanity, as a sign of her husband's prosperity in England. Certainly it looked out of place in that household, but it was not for any love of show or wealth that Anne clung to that chair. She kept it because it was the last thing she had of her father's, and because it had stood all the days she could remember of his life in his study among high walls of books, where she sat often at his feet and listened to him reading from the Scriptures or other books that he accounted useful for the hearing of a child. It was the only thing she had asked for when, soon after his death, she left her home to marry William Hutchinson. She would take it with her to the ends of the earth, if ever she were called to travel that far.

This first day in Boston that she sat in the chair to read and meditate—after Francis had scolded William and brought the Bible, and then sister Katherine had come to her and then seeing the Bible apologized for interrupting her—when Anne finally sat alone, she tried to direct her thoughts to the accusation Zachariah Symmes had brought against her. It was a vague and shadowy accusation and would amount to nothing, so she truly believed. Even so she could not help a fear, a vague and shadowy fear, of the outcome. It was hard to fix her mind upon the exact nature of the questions that might be put to her. She opened the Bible to that place in John, but still her thoughts lacked discipline. The memory of her father came to her—he too had once stood falsely accused. He had gone to prison rather than deny the truth, and so would she. She sharply shook her head to rebuke herself. So weary she was, she must have fallen half asleep. There was no question of her going to prison; her mind had been led astray by drowsiness.

Still in that state, not really asleep, for she noticed movement at the other end of the room and a seagull mewing somewhere toward the harbor, she became aware that her father stood by the chair just a little behind her. She could never see him clearly —she felt him more than she saw him; yet so clear to her was his presence that she could readily have described him. The loose study gown he had worn when they lived at Alford and the thick unsilvered hair made him seem the man he was in those years when he was deprived of a living in the Church of England, before he was recalled to be a pastor in London. Also his deep-set dark eyes (not brown, but gray to blackness, like her own) burned with a fierceness that often flamed in those Alford days. The fierceness now seemed directed at her, as seldom it had been in real life, and she thought she said, "What is it, Father? What have I done?"

She might have spoken aloud. The sound of her own voice perhaps awakened her. He was gone, or the sense of him—whatever had stood there—and she was left with a feeling of uncertainty. What had this strange dream been sent for? It almost seemed as though her father had been demanding that she give him back his chair. Could he deem she somehow was not worthy of it? Could he have brought some warning about the ordeal she soon must pass through? It was not conceivable that he disapproved of her because she dared to disagree with a minister; he had taught her to speak the truth in the face of any threat.

There seemed no way she could straighten out the muddle produced by the dream or vision. She had no doubt there was meaning in it for her, but she was not to know now, that was sure, and so for comfort and clarity of mind she turned once again to the Scriptures. As the passage in John did not at this moment seem fruitful, she closed the book and opened it again at random. The thirtieth chapter of Isaiah lay before her, and she took it as a sign. It was not that God had miraculously inserted His finger there, however; the reason was not far to seek. She had read a certain passage so many times in the last twelvemonth that the book opened there of its own accord.

> And though the Lord give you the bread of adversity, and the water of affliction, yet shall not thy teachers be removed into a corner any more, but thine eyes shall see thy teachers.

Now as she had often done before, she thanked God for that promise, which came to her again and again, ever refreshing her spirit, no matter how troubled and doubtful she might still sometimes become. What agonizing months—nay, years—had she spent before the voice of God led her to an understanding of this Scripture. John Cotton, the teacher who had first made clear to her the truth of Christ, having been threatened with imprisonment in England for his nonconformist ways, had fled to New England, and the meaning for her was that she should follow him.

"Thine eyes shall see thy teachers," God said to her, and she had explained to William then what they must do. It was not hard to convince William, for many with nonconformist tendencies had gone already with the Winthrop fleet to Massachusetts Bay. Word came back that men prospered there, while they worshiped God freely and truly, as their consciences directed.

The two Edwards, with nothing to prevent them, were eager to leave immediately, so as to reach New Boston before the winter set in and have a year to prepare for the arrival of William's family. The year was none too long, either, for the financial arrangements William had to make and the many kinds of work that must be done in the household. At last the time came, the ship sailed, and now after the long tedious voyage they had reached the place of promise.

Going over once more the long anguished time before God told her what she must do, and remembering the assuring faith with which she planned and completed the journey, Anne felt convinced afresh that she had done right in speaking to the preacher on the ship. Nor would any wrong be found in it. God had led her and her family here, and would not have her cast out from among His people. What would happen she could not predict. It might even be that God had not truly blessed the church of Boston and would have her keep apart from it awhile. But she believed now that she could stand up to the ministers' questions without anxiety. While she still sat letting strength and certainty well up in her, she heard the lowing of cows coming home from the common. The evening work of the household must now commence.

"I am ready to go back, then," she said to herself.

Later that evening, Francis said to her, "Is it well, Mother?"

"Very well, I thank thee, son," she said.

# IV

Anne had rested her burden on God. This she said and believed, and even so knew very well that the conference with the ministers was always on her mind. It lay before her like the Last Judgment. It would come, but she knew not the day or the hour.

"They must surely send for me before another Lord's Day, dost thou not think?" she said to William one day about the middle of the week. "For they must expect that I should wish to present myself for membership at the earliest possible time."

"Is this indeed thy wish?" he asked her.

"Nay, I know not," she said.

And this was true. Whenever she had time to look back over the Sabbath services, as in the daily period when she sat to read and meditate, she remembered how light came with her teacher's sweet voice into the duskiness of the meeting hall; yet in retrospect the pastor's exhortations produced a cloud that in her mind bore heavier and heavier until it threatened to put out that light. No, after much consideration of the matter, she was still not sure the preaching in Boston church placed sufficient emphasis upon the grace of God. Which man exerted the greater force was perhaps the question, unanswerable now. But certainly John Cotton was an honored member as well as teacher of the church; that much was clear from the faintly sighing breath that rose from the congregation as he mounted the pulpit. Were it not for Master Wilson, she would feel herself deeply drawn to that communion. And one thing was sure: whether she joined or kept outside, she wanted the decision to be hers.

In her heart and with all her rational being, she understood the way to salvation and she knew what it was to be ravished by Christ Jesus. Taking notes as she had sat in St. Botolph's Church in England, she had written down these words of John Cotton's: "We live, and yet not we but Christ lives within us." Nothing could be clearer than those words, it seemed to her, but she remembered the astonishment that widened the eyes and pursed the lips of Zachariah Symmes when she spoke them in his presence on the ship. John Wilson's face, she suspected, would darken with anger: his sermon savored too much of the covenant of works, of earning by deeds what could only be freely given of God. Well then, she thought, if she were to be judged by men she knew how to be prepared. They would understand nothing but the letter of the Scriptures, which though nothing in itself (nothing but dead words, like the body from which the spirit has departed) might be the only means by which such men could be brought to know the spirit. And so she sat every afternoon searching the Scriptures for those places already known to her, refreshing her knowledge and her own sense of the spirit.

Never at those times would the children or kinswomen disturb her or allow her to be disturbed. Nor was it easy to distract her. If a visitor came to the door, she quite likely would not hear a sound. But one day—sixth day it was, the week almost gone—there came a knock at the door and the soft voice of someone who did not enter the house. And that voice reached her. She closed the heavy Bible and laid it on a stool by her chair, then hurried to the door where Faith stood holding a paper in her hand.

It was a message from Master Cotton; he had delivered it himself.

"I knew you would want him to come in, Mother," Faith said, "but he bade me tell you that he could not stay."

Anne walked out to the gate and looked after him, a black-clad figure that dropped out of sight down the hill toward the harbor while she watched.

Then turning back to Faith she sighed. "Yes, I should have liked him to come in," she said, "but that cannot be until this time of doubt has ended." Standing in the doorway, she looked at the paper with her name inscribed upon it, folded and sealed with red wax. "That may be soon," she said.

She did not open the paper until she was sitting in her chair again. There were only a few lines, scarcely more than a summons. She was bidden to Master Cotton's own house—"It is a clapboarded house, facing east, set up against the easternmost of the three hills known as Trimontaine"—at ten o'clock in the morning of the seventh day.

She reread the terse message and dwelled upon its closing: "Your brother in Christ, J.C." There was, at least, that.

## 2

Mild sunny days had prevailed since the Hutchinsons came to Boston, but on the day Anne went to be questioned by the ministers the weather changed. Before dawn a strong wind blew in from the sea, waking her with the sound of heavy blows against the house walls, and when she set out for Master Cotton's, walking at first in a northerly direction along the high street, a cold mist wet her face. When she turned into Prison Lane, with the wind at her back, she felt warmer; but the force of the wind was such that at times she could hardly keep her footing. The lanes of Boston were nowhere smooth, and roots of long vanished trees bulged out of the ground here and there along the way, so that one had always to take care in walking. Anne, with her mind taken up by the coming ordeal, stumbled over a root and fell to her knees.

She was not hurt, but her cloak was muddied somewhat. She took the incident as a sign, as though God said to her, "Be careful, child, lest thou stumble, in answering the ministers." It was a warning not to be too confident. Though she would certainly speak nothing but the truth, she would have to be very careful to choose words that left no room for misunderstanding.

All three ministers were waiting when she arrived in John Cotton's parlor. There was no sign of Mistress Cotton or any servant. John Cotton himself opened the door, which he had difficulty closing against the wind, and bade her be seated on one side of the long table that stood at an angle to his great fireplace. The three men in black sat opposite her, so that she could not help remarking the great outward differences among them and relating them to the differences she suspected lay within.

John Cotton, his face open and clear, his pale, fine hair flying out from his black skullcap, seemed almost to reflect some ray of light even in the dimness of the narrow-windowed hall. John Wilson, his eyes hard under heavy dark brows, his dark face unsmiling, his lank hair lying close against his cheeks, would add no light of his own anywhere. Zachariah Symmes sat well back in the shadows, and it was just as well, Anne thought. Too much light on that subject, she surmised, would show its emptiness, both of the intellect and of the spirit.

She exchanged polite greetings with the men. Then Pastor Wilson spoke at some length, appraising her of what she already knew, that certain expressions of hers on the ship had given rise to doubts about her opinions. They had some questions they would like to ask her, with her consent.

She readily gave it.

Master Symmes prefaced the questions with his account of Mistress Hutchinson's expressions. "I must explain at the outset," he said, "that I have never been acquainted with Mistress Hutchinson, only I saw her once or twice in London, whilst we waited for the ship to sail. Even then I noticed she would sometimes slight some of the ministers that we talked of. Then on the ship I would preach to the passengers, and after the sermons would allow a time for discussion. When I preached about the evidencing of a good estate, and cited that place in John concerning the love of the brethren, she took strong exception to that, and said it showed I was under a covenant of works. When I asked her to explain, she would only say that when we came to Boston I should hear something to a good effect. 'I have many things to say to you but you cannot bear them now,' said she in the words of our Saviour, and went on in such a vein until I could only stand amazed at the corruptness of her opinions, and my thought was that she should not be admitted to the church until I had made these matters clear to someone in authority. And so I went to Governor Dudley, and he properly brought the matter to the attention of these my brethren."

"And what, Mistress Hutchinson, have you to say to that?" asked Pastor Wilson.

"Only that in truth I made such statements and asked such questions as Master Symmes has told you of."

And Pastor Wilson said, "Will you please explain your objection to the passage in John?"

And she recalled it and repeated it. "By this we know that we are translated from death to life because we love the brethren," and then said, "It did seem to me that Master Symmes preached as if to say that by taking thought in ourselves to love the brethren, we could assure ourselves of everlasting life."

And Pastor Wilson said, "You think not so?"

And she answered, "Nay, not so. I have heard Master Cotton preach upon the same text, and he doth not think so either."

And Pastor Wilson said, "Can you cast light upon this question, Brother Cotton?"

And Teacher Cotton said, "Yea, for we may borrow light from Calvin here. A man may preposterously conclude, said he, that life may be acquired by love, whereas our spiritual life can come only from one foundation: the grace of Christ Jesus."

And Anne said, "That is what I said that day. We are saved by grace alone."

Then they must say all the same things again, and Master Symmes must take the occasion to doubt that this was really what the gentlewoman said. But at last they did reach agreement upon the passage about the love of the brethren.

And then Pastor Wilson said, "So it is not as Brother Symmes hath understood it, that you say our works can be no evidence of a good estate."

And Master Symmes said, "I dare affirm she did say so, and can bring witnesses who did hear her on the ship."

And Anne said, "What I said is that anyone who rests his hope on such evidence is walking in a covenant of works, the same as Adam did before God's covenant with Abraham."

And Master Symmes said, "I do not perceive the difference."

And Anne said, "Ah, but my teacher does. I have heard him speak it lovingly and clear."

And Pastor Wilson said, "What have you to say to that, brother?"

And Teacher Cotton said that it was true, and he explained the difference. But he must explain it over and over, in different words, before the other ministers accepted this: that anyone who thinks that because he obeys the Commandments he has evidence of Christ within him may be sadly deceived—he has got the wrong end of the stick, and is no better than a hypocrite. A

Christian obeys the Commandments, but so may any Jew or infidel.

Words, words, words they spoke until Anne began to feel the breath pressed out of her beneath the deadly weight of them.

Then Master Symmes said, "As to justification and sanctification, I am satisfied. Brother Cotton says that justifying faith must come first, but that it may be evidenced by our sanctifications. Mistress Hutchinson professes to agree with that, and so I find no scruple. But what is this of Christ within? I would have the gentlewoman explain that."

Would have her explain it? Would have words, dead words, to show forth the living Christ? He stirred within her. And she longed to say to the purse-mouthed man, "If thou knowest not, none can tell thee." But her training in disputation was strong and she remembered her father. Something she had heard John Cotton say came to her mind, and she spoke it, not expecting that merchant of dead words to understand. "We live, yet not we, but Christ liveth in us."

The two dark ministers frowned and set their jaws.

And Pastor Wilson said, "You will have to explain your explanation, Mistress Hutchinson. Do you wish to say the Christian hath no will of his own?"

Struggling to keep her voice even, Anne answered, "The words I spake came from my teacher's tongue. Yet I daresay he will tell you the Christian's will is Christ's will."

Then Pastor Wilson questioned, "Brother, did you speak those words?"

And it was strange that when she looked at him Anne half believed she saw her own teacher's face darken. Or she fancied that he closed his eyes against the light.

But then he said, "I spake them."

And she knew what she had seen was fancy, and that what she had been about to fear would not happen.

But he went on and said, "I spake them. Yet I would have it understood that we are not the same person with Christ. There may still be actions that come from the old unregenerated man; yet the spiritual life within is from Christ."

And Pastor Wilson said, "Is this what you meant, Mistress Hutchinson?"

And the dark men and the light mingled before her eyes; she put her hand to her head to stop a moment's dizziness. Was it? Was it indeed what she meant? But then of course it must be. The words belonged to her teacher. He knew their meaning if any man did. There *was* union with Christ, but maybe not a complete union. She would have to pray about that. But yes, it must be. Whatever John Cotton said must surely be. "Yes, the spiritual life is of Christ," she said.

And the men went on talking, yet the last spark of life had gone out of the words they said. They no longer reached her. She sat with her eyes turned modestly down toward the table, and those men could never any way have guessed the things she saw.

She became aware that Pastor Wilson was addressing her. "Mistress Hutchinson," he said sharply, and she looked up. "I said do you agree that Brother Cotton rightly expresses your opinion on this matter?"

"I agree," she said.

"There is one more thing, then," said Zachariah Symmes, and it is that as we stood in Boston harbor Mistress Hutchinson spake some words that seemed to mean that she had had some revelation."

"A revelation!" exclaimed John Wilson. "Then it could not be of God, for we know He has given all His word already in the Scriptures."

"I know not what speech of mine you refer to, sir," said Anne to Master Symmes, "for I am sure I had no revelation."

"You looked out upon Boston and it was a sad and sorry sight, I will agree. And you said something to the effect that you would be tempted to go back home if you had not a sure word England would be destroyed."

"I was speaking to my husband," Anne said, "and knew not anyone else was listening. He knew I referred to a prophecy made by Master Hooker in a sermon that he preached before he left for Holland."

"I do not believe Brother Hooker said any such thing," snapped Symmes.

"I confess I heard it not with mine own ears," said Anne, "but I had it on good authority that he did speak so."

"Then this about the destruction of England was not revealed to you," said Cotton.

"No, sir, it was not," said Anne.

"Then I have no more to say," said Symmes, "for it seems the gentlewoman can explain everything away, at least to Brother Cotton's satisfaction."

Then Cotton stood and said, "Let us ministers retire to my study for a few minutes, and discover what agreement there may be among us."

And Anne had done what she could; the ordeal was over.

## 3

The ministers told her they would recommend to the ruling elders that they accept her profession of faith. She would have to meet with church officials and then stand before the congregation, but she understood that all the rest was but form. She could have membership in the church now.

"If I choose to ask for it," she said to herself as she struggled against the east wind, toward William coming to meet her.

"Is it well?" he said.

"It is well," she said, but she did not talk to him about the conference and when they reached home, she said, "I shall have to be alone awhile, and think of all that was said to me, before I speak of it."

She took her Bible and sat down in the great chair, and the family ate their dinner and went quietly about their necessary tasks.

Opening the Bible, not really at random for she knew it as though every page were engraved upon her heart, she came to this Scripture, that he who denies Christ to be come in the flesh is Antichrist. Thus she had come upon it once before, when it seemed as irrelevant as it did now; and now as then she waited to see what the Lord would open unto her. She remembered how that other time she had been brought to see that whoever did not teach the new covenant had the spirit of Antichrist. And having pondered this, and read again the two passages, she began to know what she must do, and it was as though the Lord had spoken—not through the Scripture, not even with words, for even the use of words would have interposed between her and what was spoken. "Listen to the voice of my beloved." Not those words but the sense of them, and she saw what it meant to her now.

She must join the church at Boston, but not until John Wilson had departed for England, as everyone knew he would do within a few weeks. He would be gone a long time, perhaps he would never come back. And in his absence she would listen to her teacher, the true minister, in such a way that if there still remained obscurities in her understanding they would be cleared away. By the time the other returned, if ever he did, she would have been free to hear the true teacher for so long that her spirit would be merged with his (with Christ's) and she would know without a question what to do. "Something more will be asked of you," the wordless voice spoke clearly. "You will know when it is time."

# V

Until Anne Hutchinson was welcomed into the Church of Christ at Boston, she often felt unsteady and unsure, as though still tossed about in a fragile ship on the waves of the stormy Atlantic without knowing whether she should ever reach the shore. True, she might have joined the congregation sooner than she did. Yet it seemed to her better to be tossed at sea than to sail deliberately into a dark and doubtful harbor. She had come to this country to hear truth preached, the clear, blissful doctrine of grace, the easy covenant by which God saves His chosen ones without demanding of them any reckoning. Having experienced such agony of mind and spirit before she understood what she must do, she thought it would be false and ungrateful of her to join a church where the pastor preached the same dismal doctrine she had fled from through God's guidance.

And so she waited for John Cotton. Even when William decided to go ahead and petition for membership, she chose to wait outside until the day she deemed God meant her to come in.

Once part of the church, to which John Cotton now preached three times a week, she knew not what more she could wish for in this world. Apart from the spiritual satisfaction now afforded her, life went on much the same as it had done in Old England. She had lost nothing, so it seemed, while gaining much. With so many women and girls in her family, she had less work to do than many wives in Boston, so that she might scarcely have had enough to fill her day, once her household had been set in good order, had not word soon gone around town that she was skilled in sickness and childbirth. Then she was often sent for, and would go, either by day or by night, just as she had always done in Alford. And as in her old home, she still enjoyed each day a period of meditation.

Even so, with every hour filled, God found some lack in her. Now and then, as she entered her front door, especially if the house seemed uncommonly quiet, and if no fire burned brightly, she was carried back to the first time she stepped into that dimness and the sense that something out of the ordinary would happen to her there—would be demanded of her. One day in her hour of silent thought, still seized by this strange certainty, she began deliberately to seek the meaning of it, but many days passed and still she got no farther than that dim perception. One thing did begin to seem clear though: she had not uprooted her family and come all this way only for the satisfaction of hearing the sweet words of John Cotton. Terrible as her longing for him seemed in those days when he had been taken from her, still she knew he was not the embodiment of God's grace. The living Christ was within her no matter where in the world John Cotton was. Surely God had not guided her here simply for her own gratification. She began to feel convinced that He had some special need of her in Boston. Yet if that were so, she had but to wait until such time as He revealed the nature of it. She could rest content till then, for unlike such ministers as John Wilson, who preached that salvation depended upon a person's earthly actions, she knew (as her teacher had long since made clear to her) that her salvation was sealed and sure, no matter what she did or failed to do.

And so when William asked her (as he still sometimes would do), "Art thou happy?" she would answer in all truthfulness, "Yea." But at the same time she was waiting and watching, certain that there was some space in her life that remained to be filled when God saw fit to let her know what more He wanted of her. Whenever a new experience was opened up to her, or a favor asked, or a task that she could do made evident, she thought, This may be what God has held in store.

So it was that some slight expectancy tightened her throat one morning in November (or ninth month, as they called it then) when her door opened to three women come to call. They were Mistress Hibbens, Mistress Coddington, and Mistress Dyer—

Anne knew them all already, though only by sight. It was a cold day, with remnants of a recent snow scattered over the streets and gardens of the town, so she brought them quickly to the fireside and set stools for them there.

Anne's feeling that their coming might hold something portentous in it was perhaps increased by the fact that they were a rather unlikely threesome, both as to their appearance and their positions in the community. Mistress Hibbens was the wife of a wealthy merchant, but better known as the sister of Master Bellingham, a rich man himself but more important in Boston, a powerful man politically. An older woman than Anne, she had perhaps been comely once, but a perpetual expression of ill humor had etched itself deep into her face. The black velvet hood tied under her chin increased the effect of a dark and bitter nature. Yet she smiled and bowed, and spoke words that were gracious, so that Anne said to herself that the darkness might be only seeming.

Mistress Coddington was the wife of a man whom William Hutchinson had known in a business way in Lincolnshire—a rich man, too, the richest man in New Boston. He had built the only brick house in town. Yet his wife, though sumptuously dressed, had not the haughty bearing of Mistress Hibbens. She was plump and somewhat untidy, amiable, and even perhaps inclined to be merry, had merriment been the fashion in Boston.

Mistress Dyer (so Anne had noticed on Sabbath days) sat farther toward the back of the church than either of the other gentlewomen, yet she was the wife of a merchant too, a milliner in the New Exchange. No doubt for this reason she wore a hat while the other women were satisfied with hoods. It was a high-crowned beaver hat, of a style much worn then by both men and women, and she had a silver band around the crown. On account of the Dyers' small means, the decoration might have been considered ostentatious, had not the court concluded that the hat with a modest silver band might appropriately call attention to her husband's trade.

Though the lowliest and youngest of the three, it was Mary Dyer who spoke first to Anne about what they had come for. With a shy glance at the other two, as though asking their pardon for her boldness, she turned on Anne her large, soft, blue-gray eyes. "Dear Mistress Hutchinson," she said, "we three are all accustomed to meet with a small group of women for a little spiritual refreshment in the middle of the week. All of us live within a few streets of each other, and as you now dwell right in our midst, we have come to say, pray join us in our devotions."

The purpose of their visit was something of a disappointment to Anne, as she knew already about these neighborhood prayer meetings. Her sister-in-law Sarah, who lived some distance away, toward the North End, sometimes attended one of them. The women met more for the pleasure of each other's company than anything else, Anne suspected, and she had already decided she did not have time for such gatherings. Now, though, because of the quiver of expectation the first sight of her visitors had stirred in her—and partly because of some spiritual yearning she glimpsed in Mistress Dyer's soft eyes—she did not refuse as hastily as she might have done. She said to herself that in fairness she should find out more about the meetings before closing her mind against them.

"I do thank you," she said, "but I will not come yet awhile. At the present I find my days so full that it is hard to find time for my own meditations."

"Hmph," said Mistress Hibbens.

"Do come when you can," said Mistress Coddington.

Mistress Dyer said nothing at all, but looked at Anne with widened eyes and slightly parted lips, as though there were some question that she feared to ask.

The women stayed not much longer, though the two younger ones talked a little about housewifely things. As they were leaving, Mistress Dyer asked permission—which Anne readily granted—to take the baby Susannah from her cradle and hold her for a moment in her arms.

Then Mistress Hibbens, declaring that her time was as precious as anybody's, went on out the door and did not wait for the others.

"You must try to forgive her," said Mary Dyer, "for it is only her way to have a hasty temper."

Anne smiled. "I am sure it is not your way," she said. She prayed them both come back another time, and thanked them again for their invitation.

During the visit, the cousins and Katherine Marbury had gone on with their work, but as the callers departed, came and bade them courteous good-bys. Then Mistress Coddington said, evidently as an afterthought, that they would all be welcome at the meetings along with Mistress Hutchinson. But as the door was already open, letting in the cold air, she did not stay for an answer.

Now it was time to set up the table board for dinner, bring out the wooden trenchers, and put the porridge off the fire to cool. The little girls were sent to call their father and brothers from the shop, and the women found time for little more than a phrase or two about the visitors.

"They did not come to invite us," said Frances Freestone to her sister Anne, "and yet we might go. It would be a change from housework."

"Yes, go," said Anne. "You need a change." She herself felt no such need, nor did—she thought—her sister Katherine.

At table, after grace was said, William asked about the visitors. He had seen them come up to the door, he explained, and thought he recognized one of them as William Coddington's wife.

Yes, one was Mistress Coddington, Anne said, and told the names of the others, what their purpose was, and what her answer had been.

"Very well," said William, "if that be your considered view. And yet I conceive such gatherings could do no harm. And a merchant's wife could do him good by making herself agreeable among other women."

"If you wish it, William, I will go," said Anne. "But my true feeling is that meetings of this kind may be a form of self-deception, if they be held in the name of devotion to Christ."

The cousins exchanged a glance with each other, but Anne had forgotten already that those two wished to go.

"Nay," said William, "it is not so necessary to me as that, to have you go."

"Yet methinks it be true, sister," said Katherine, "that you created no good will by the answer you gave them. Especially with that Mistress Hibbens, who I believe is the highest placed of them all."

"Then what answer would you have given, sister?" asked Anne.

Katherine smiled. "The same, yet not so soft," said she. "I

might be sorry of the consequences, but Boston will have to learn that we Marburys can brook no hypocrisy where our faith is in question."

William laughed gently. "So I learned long ago," he said, "and never would I urge a word against such faith."

"Think you, Father," then spoke up Francis, "that true faith be at odds with trade?"

"Not at odds, but I agree with your mother that religion should not be made to do the work of trade."

"Yet a man knows that his brothers in Christ will come and buy from him because he is a brother."

"A man cannot help what he knows," said William.

"And consider too your work for the town and the colony. I have heard they want you for a deputy to the General Court."

"Aye, I may stand for election."

"Will such a service also improve your trade?"

"That it may do. And is that any reason to forego it?"

"No, sir, I did not mean that. It is but a new thought to me, that is all, that all these parts of a man's life may serve one another. Even friends, I suppose—"

"Certainly. We do not choose our friends that they may buy our goods, but if we possess some wealthy friends and they wish to deal with us—well, I don't mind saying I hope to have Will Coddington as a friend. He is a man I admire, and did in Old Boston. I have met him twice and again here in this place, and I find him still to be admired: one of the richer sort, helpful in government and church. A man I should like for my friend, no matter what my calling might be. Therefore, you see, I hoped your mother might make a friend of his wife."

"So I may very well do, William," said Anne, "for I saw not that she took offense at my words, any more than the other young woman. And I thought she had a pleasant way about her."

Thus Anne began to form some friendships—sometimes, as in the case of Mary Coddington, from a desire to please her husband. More often, acquaintances began as she watched by sickbeds or attended some woman in childbirth.

By the time winter set in—and winter came early and hard in New England—the Hutchinson family was well absorbed into the pattern of Boston life. It was not a gay life; there was a sameness about it, a gray with only shades of difference, as in the weathered wood of the houses and fences. Yet it was not a life devoid of incident. The Sabbath services were an ever-recurring joy, and fifth day, likewise, added interest to each week. This was both lecture day and market day, the time when people came from all over the colony, in order to buy needed goods and, not secondarily, to hear John Cotton preach a weekday sermon.

Lecture day was a favorite time for inviting friends to dinner. One day Anne and William went to the Coddingtons' brick house and met there such dignitaries as Governor Dudley and John Winthrop, with their quiet, modest wives.

But such events were rare. Especially in wintertime, the days held not much variety. Women and children, with their small tasks, kept mostly to the chimney corner, and even so would feel their backs freezing while their faces burned. Anne would set Susannah's cradle right inside the huge chimney.

At such times, while the workers sat silent, as if frozen within their own thoughts, Anne often wondered when the summons to her special task would come. She did not know that events leading up to it had already begun to transpire, nor did she recognize any part of God's plan in the strange little visitor who came in out of the snow one day. It was on a morning towards noon, when the pot was boiling briskly and dinner was on their minds, that they heard the fateful knocking at the door. William and the older boys had already come in from the lean-to shop, because it was much too cold in there to stay for regular business hours, and so William went to admit this unexpected visitor.

She was thin and small and inclined to be hunchbacked. She hopped in like a sparrow, peered out of her huge enveloping hood with round bird-like eyes, and when she spoke she chirped. (Much later, there would be someone to claim she had seen this old woman in the form of a sparrow perched on a paling of her garden fence, and that afterwards her peas shriveled in the pod to the size of a wheat grain.) The Hutchinsons had seen her first at the harbor when they landed from the ship, and since then everywhere about the town. If Anne chanced upon her in the market place, or at the town spring, the old woman always bobbed her head and cried in an excited voice: "A very good day to you, Mistress Hutchinson!"

Anne knew that for some reason the little hunchback longed to speak with her and know her; yet she never lingered, but hurried away, as though saying, "You have better things to do than talk to one like me."

Now inside the house, and invited to come by the fire, the old woman responded quickly, holding out her skinny hands to the blaze. "My name is Jane Hawkins," she said. "You may not know me, but I have known you since the first moment I saw you, before ever anyone told me your name."

"Yes, Goodwife Hawkins," Anne said, "I know your name too."

"Will you come with me and help someone?" the goodwife asked. "Someone in childbirth, who I fear may die."

There was no need for Jane Hawkins to say more than that. Anne drew on her cloak, took up the basket she kept ready for such cases, and said, "Let us go."

The two women walked in silence over the frozen snow, their faces wrapped against the cold. Out of the narrow lane where the Hutchinsons lived, along the high street, and across the fields towards Boston Neck, they made their way, through a broad expanse of lightless white, with here and there a spot of gray where stood some poor man's house or a clump of stunted trees, the only sort that grew on the peninsula. They came at last, through low-lying ground where marsh grass reached up through the snow, to a thatched hovel set near the seashore, far removed from any other habitation. No smoke rose from its mud-daubed wood chimney.

The door opened before them, as of its own accord, but a gray-faced young man stood inside it. He must have heard their footsteps on the frozen snow. Anne had seen him somewhere, she fleetingly observed, but she took no time to wonder where.

He did not greet them. "She has fainted," he said. "Or she may be dead."

Anne knelt at once to the figure that lay bundled in ragged, sweat-drenched clothes before the hearth, which was growing cold as the last coals faded. The girl turned a swollen, tear-stained face to Anne and opened wide, frightened eyes.

"She is alive," Anne said, "though worn out from travail. Why do you not build a fire?"

"There was fire," said Goody Hawkins, "when I left."

"The wood is gone," the young man said.

"Go at once," Anne said to him, sharply as she might have spoken to a lagging child, "to my house. Do you know where it is? Master Hutchinson's house?"

"Yes, mistress," he said.

She rose and faced him. "Go there and tell them to help you bring wood. And tell the women to send sheets and blankets."

He stood dumbly.

"Can you not understand?" she demanded.

"Go, Jacob," said Goody Hawkins.

While he stood there an anguished shriek came from the girl on the floor. He half turned, then went out the door.

"Will he remember what he is going for?" Anne asked Goody Hawkins.

"He is no fool," she said. "But he is afraid. I could not make him leave her, or I would have sent him to you and stayed by her side."

"Yes, I see," said Anne, kneeling to the girl again, placing her hands on the swollen belly.

Jane stood a moment watching, then quickly said, "Have you a daughter eight years old? For I fear the child be dead, and the girl is but sixteen."

Anne did not need to ask her what she meant. "My little Anne is eight," she said, "but surely you know better ways of bringing away a dead child."

"I will run after him," said Jane, "and have him bring a lock of her hair. Have you ants' eggs in that chest?"

"This is a spell you speak of," Anne said. "I do not deal in spells."

"No, mistress," said Jane, "but I am no learned gentlewoman. Whatever I hear of that has effect, I use it."

"I have brought dittany," said Anne. "It will serve much better than any spell, if we can have hot water to steep it." She looked around the room. "Break up that stool," she said.

Jane Hawkins did not protest, or say it was the only stick of furniture in the room, except for a rough board laid across two trestles, where wooden bowls with dried-up porridge sat abandoned. They might presently burn the board and trestles, too, and the dirty bowls as well, and she would say never a word. She had known from the first glimpse she had of Anne Hutchinson, stepping off the ship, that she would follow that woman anywhere, and obey her every command.

The girl began to scream again, and Anne held her, while Goody Hawkins built the fire and made the drink. It might help; they could but wait and see.

Meanwhile the husband made his visit and returned, accompanied by young Richard Hutchinson, drawing a sled piled with wood, bedclothes, a straw mattress, and food from the dinner pot. And while they came over the snow, the child was born. The women had washed it and wrapped it in a tattered cloth, and they placed it in the young man's arms.

"It is a woman child," said Goody Hawkins.

"She is dead?" he said.

"Aye," said the old woman.

He thrust the baby at her and ran out into the snow.

"Go after him, Richard!" cried Anne. "He thinks it be his wife that's dead."

Richard caught him and struggled with him until they were both well-nigh frozen, before he was able to make the young man understand that it was his baby and not his wife who had died. When they came in, Anne, fearing frostbite, had them wrap themselves in blankets and stay by the fire, though she had great difficulty keeping the young husband away from his wife until the women could wash (with melted snow) the blood and filth from her, and put on Faith's nightgown that the girl herself had sent. She lay (the young wife, looking like an underfed child), wrapped in blankets, upon the straw mattress placed on the earth floor. Anne gave her a drink made from a packet she had brought from her chest, and she slept a deep and motionless sleep.

The husband came and stood over her. Tears ran down his cheeks. "You are sure she's not dead?" he said.

"She is alive," Anne said, "and will be well." She turned and looked at him searchingly, saying, "But you will have to bury the baby."

He looked toward the little bundle that lay on a mat in the corner.

"Tomorrow," said Anne. "I will send someone to help you tomorrow."

He went and sank down by the fire again, looking as if all that happened was too much for him to understand.

"When has he slept?" Anne asked Jane.

Jane pointed to the porridge bowls. "It was dinnertime yesterday," she said, "when it started."

Suddenly Anne realized how long it had been since either the young husband or the midwife had slept or eaten. They had taken a few bites of the food Richard brought, but they had not slept at all.

"Where do you live?" Anne asked Goodwife Hawkins.

"Not far from here," she said vaguely.

"Have you a man at home?"

"Aye."

"And plenty to eat?"

There was a pause. Then, "Oh yes, mistress."

"Will your husband be expecting you tonight?"

"Oh no, he knows I may need to stay here."

"Then here is what we shall do. I will stay here. You will go home with my son Richard, and eat with them there, and stay the night. Tomorrow some of the men will come and bury the child. You come back with them, and stay here as long as you wish to or are needed."

The old woman looked at the younger for a long moment, her round eyes unblinking, and at last said only, "Yes, mistress."

When Richard and Goodwife Hawkins were gone, Anne made the young man eat his supper (the remains of what Richard had brought, for there was nothing else in the house) and then lie down by his wife on the mattress of straw. Though he protested, he fell asleep almost at once, and as he slept put his arms about the girl. So they lay till morning, while Anne kept a fire going and watched over them. She looked for a Bible, but found none —probably, they could not read. But she herself could read the Scriptures in the flames of the fire.

2

Jacob Hickson was a fisherman. He had not always followed that trade; he had come to New England as a bond servant, but his master having fallen on hard times was forced to release him.

Finding no man to hire him, he was like to starve, but one day along the shore of Boston Neck he found a battered boat. Without stopping either to thank God or look for the owner, he set about repairing it, as best he could, with scraps he came upon and tools he carried in his pocket. He had no experience fishing, and could get no work on any of the shallops that regularly went out to sea. But with this boat he could fish close to shore, and working all day could catch enough to keep himself from starving and sell whatever surplus he enjoyed at the back doors of goodwives who lacked the means to buy the more desirable fish offered in the market place.

You would not expect a man in such circumstances to take a wife, nor did he himself expect it. But in much the same way that he stumbled on the boat on the beach, he found a girl one day. She was weeping in the sand because she had found no clams for supper. As soon as he picked her up and wiped the dirt off her face, he kissed her; and as soon as he kissed her, he determined to marry her. From the looks of her ragged gown and the bony frame beneath it, she could not be much worse off with him. She agreed that this was so: she was a stepchild whose mother had died and left her stepfather with a house full of children. She had taken her mother's place in every way, and the burden had become well-nigh unbearable.

Because no single man could be allowed to live alone in Boston, the town fathers had put Jacob in the house with a poor shoemaker; but now that he had found the girl, he looked about for a place to live with her, and down along the shore, not far from the spot where he found the boat, he came across the abandoned cottage. It was no cottage really: a hovel was more nearly the right name for it. The shoemaker, who had nothing against Jacob Hickson but did not prosper from having the young man in his house, went with him to the town officials and inquired about the cottage. If he was married he could live there, they said, and pay no rent if he would keep it in repair.

So the couple put up the banns, but by the time the requisite three weeks had passed and they had found out where to go to get married, the girl was already pregnant. Her name was Elizabeth Joan. One day the tithing man found them together in the cottage, and though it was no business of his (or so they thought, for neither of them belonged to Boston church or would ever be accepted there), he reported them to the court, who convicted them of fornication and sentenced them to wear the label of their sin for six months.

In the weeks that followed the birth of their dead baby, Anne came every day to bring food or medicine and help with the care of Elizabeth Joan. It was during that time that she learned their story, and she remembered then, of course, where she had seen them: on the scaffold, on lecture day, with paper F's pinned to their backs.

Jacob was an orphan. He had never had anyone to love before. Elizabeth Joan had loved her mother but could not remember whether her mother had ever loved her. Neither seemed ever to have heard of the love of God. And so they loved each other, desperately.

"I must get up and cook for him," Elizabeth Joan said often, until at last Anne and Jane gave up and said she might try. She grew stronger then day by day.

"Don't bring no more victuals or wood," said Jacob, "for I can take care of my wife."

How he could, they could no way imagine, for the waters were frozen still. But the two older women agreed to leave the young couple alone as much as they could. More than on food or fire, their lives seemed to depend upon each other.

Every few days, the little midwife stopped at the Hutchinson house. The first time, she pretended to have come to ask Anne's advice about the condition of a woman who, though clearly pregnant, was bleeding at her monthly time.

"I think you know what to do, Goodwife Hawkins," Anne said to her.

Jane ducked her head and said, "Aye, but I long to see you."

Then Anne began to understand the other woman's need. "Make no excuse to come to me, dear Jane," she said, using the goodwife's Christian name for the first time.

"Truly?" cried Jane. "May I come to you when I need you, and will you talk to me the way you talked to Elizabeth Joan?"

Anne was not altogether sure what Jane meant. She had asked the young wife questions about her childhood—her life in London before she was brought to New Boston, whether she had ever been taught about Christ. The girl had not, and seemingly did not wish to know. The time might come though: the girl had a capacity for grace and Christian love, so Anne believed. Goodwife Hawkins, it seemed, did wish to know, and perhaps the time was now.

She had already learned that Jane and her husband, Richard, had applied for membership in Boston church and been rejected. Even so, Jane usually went to church, as the whole population was expected to do—though so many did not that there was talk of passing a law that would compel them to. Before Jane came to her, Anne had been aware of the little old dried-up creature, crowded with the poorest sort, the outcasts, at the back of the meetinghouse.

"Do you want to tell me why you have not been accepted in the church?" she asked now.

"They say I am a familist," Jane said.

"Are you?" asked Anne.

"Nay, I know not what a familist may be," Jane said.

"Yet they must have some reason," said Anne.

"When I lived in St. Ives, on the River Ouse," said Jane, "I visited, twice or thrice, the Isle of Ely."

"I have heard very much of the Isle of Ely," said Anne, "and of some who took refuge there because of their beliefs."

"When I was there, I heard a woman preach," said Jane.

"Ah," said Anne, "word came to us in Alford of the woman of Ely, that she might do no more than stand up in the market place, and hundreds gather round her, as a flock that is waiting to be fed."

"Aye, so it was," said Jane, and sighed. "Never was there preaching in any church that fed my soul as hers did."

"But was she a familist then?"

"I know not. But when the elders questioned me, it happened that I mentioned her. 'Aha, the Family of Love,' they said, 'and is your husband likewise infected?' I told them we knew nothing of the Family of Love, but I said something that made them think I lied."

"What was it you said to them?" Anne asked.

"I spake of a Scripture the woman told us of. They asked me if I read my Bible, and I remembered this: that the Scriptures are a light to us, shining in a dark place, till the day star rise in our hearts. And that day star was, I always thought, the love of Christ, and when we had that we needed no Scriptures. So I told the elders when they asked me if I read my Bible, because the truth is that I have no Bible and I never learned to read."

Anne did not answer for a while, but pondered what Jane said. It was not, in one way, so far from the truth as she had learned to know it through the preaching of John Cotton. It might be the woman of Ely preached very well, and poor ignorant Jane had but somewhat misunderstood her. Anne had once planned to make the journey to Ely in hopes of hearing this woman; but circumstances interfered (another pregnancy) and somehow the time never did come again when she and William both could get away.

"I have heard of this preacher," she said to Jane at last, "and I never heard she was a familist. All I know of the Family of Love is that its members say they hold together through the love of Christ, without regard to dogma. But this is what that place in Second Peter means, that place you heard her preach about: that the Scriptures give us comfort, as from a light that cheers us in the dark; but the day star rises in our hearts according as God grants us grace. We cannot any way, by reading Scripture or taking any other action, bring to ourselves this saving grace. We read Scriptures because they help us understand God and His way, but when we are saved, we are saved, whether or no we ever read a word." She paused and looked into the old woman's face. Could she possibly, Anne wondered, understand what she was saying? "Is that quite clear?" she asked.

Jane looked solemnly into her eyes. "Yes, mistress, very clear," she said. "But have I Christ within me?"

"By His voice you may know," said Anne, "and have you not heard it?"

Jane's face clouded. "Nay, I know not," she said.

"It may be you have become confused by legalistic preachers. But listen, and wait, for He will come to you as readily as to any man who has learned to read and dispute of Scripture. And He will come to the greatest sinner more readily than to one who thinks to seize upon Him by following the letter of the law."

Before Jane went away, and after they had talked of other things, she said, "Yes, you are very like the preacher on the isle. You might even be her sister, for your face is like hers, and your dark eyes that burn when you speak of the living Christ."

## 3

Had the leaders of the colony known what new acquaintances Anne was making—had they been able to overhear some of the words she spoke—could they have guessed at her thoughts as she sat every day in her great oak chair—they might have paid further attention to this woman who even as she first set foot on Massachusetts soil had caused alarm. But as far as they were concerned, that slight disturbance was over and done with.

Other troubles that concerned them at the time of the Hutchinsons' arrival had not so readily vanished. Either the hostility of the King or the savagery of Pequod Indians marauding in the Connecticut Valley seemed far more likely to overwhelm the colony than any strange opinions expressed by a middle-aged housewife. In any case, the ministers appeared to find nothing very strange in her opinions and certainly no danger therein. Thomas Dudley and John Winthrop were wasting no thought on Anne Hutchinson in that winter of 1634. They were making certain that in every town the militia were given strict and regular training.

A militia had been maintained from the beginning of the colony, but now there was a greater sense of urgency than had been felt for some time. Whereas men had been careless about doing their duty, now on train days every able-bodied man in Boston appeared on the common, armed and dressed in as nearly military a manner as he was capable of achieving. And thereby they provided a spectacle that drew out wives, sweethearts, and children in the greatest crowds seen anywhere except the meetinghouse on the Lord's Day.

Anne Hutchinson herself never went to watch the train band, though her husband and three oldest sons were all part of it. No one asked her for the reasons she preferred to stay at home; perhaps she did not wonder herself what they were. She simply had no inclination for the pageantry of war. Most people did—her children did; and on a bright white Saturday in January (called eleventh month), they had permission to go to the common.

Bridget Hutchinson had a secret reason for wanting to go and watch the train band—powerful enough to make her volunteer to be responsible for Samuel, Anne, Mary, and little Katherine.

Faith lacked Bridget's enthusiasm but would accompany the group. The cousins were going with friends of their own, and Katherine Marbury had no more interest in the show than her sister Anne; hence the older girls would have to look out for the younger children.

"There ought to be a married woman with them," said Cousin Frances.

So Boston women would decree, Anne knew, though she was not concerned for her children's safety. Anyway, there was no one—so Anne said at first—and then she thought of Elizabeth Joan. The girl was no older than Bridget, and no better versed than little Katherine in deportment becoming to a Christian matron; but she was known to be a married woman. In the past few weeks, mostly because of Jacob's proud attempts to reject charity, Anne had been having Elizabeth Joan come every day or so to help with the work of the kitchen. She would stay through the morning and eat dinner, then take something home to Jacob. She had recovered very well from her ordeal and in fact was plumper now, so she said, than she had ever been in her life. She looked very comely wearing some of Bridget's old clothes. She was grateful to Mistress Hutchinson for this chance to go with the children, for she had only once or twice before been able to see Jacob march with the band.

All over town little groups like this were setting out for the common, and Captain John Underhill thought everyone was coming to see him. Well, naturally, all eyes would be upon him, for he was Boston's professional military leader. He had a pretty raggle-taggle company to try to mold into some sort of military fashion and order, but if he dressed and bore himself like a soldier the rest might learn to follow him in this as in other matters. So he explained to his wife, Helena, while she helped him on with the armor she had just finished polishing. When she watched him stride off down the lane, shining in the sun like the sparkling snow, his helmet adding several inches to his unimpressive height, she smiled to herself. Yes, of course a military leader would have to look the part; but it wasn't the eyes of the men on the field John Underhill would feel upon him.

John Cotton came now, starkly black against the white landscape, in a fur-lined wool cloak and steeple-crowned hat worn over his customary skullcap. And when he had taken his place beside Captain Underhill, for by then the whole company was ranged in proper order, with halberdiers and flagbearers standing stiff and the drummer ready to drum, the opening prayer began. One might think Master Cotton would pray a short prayer, in consideration of the people standing still on frozen ground, but in truth it was not much colder there than in the meetinghouse, and in neither place would it ever occur to John Cotton to stint the Lord.

When the prayer was over, and the black crow flapped away, it was—though hardly anyone in Boston would have dared say so—like the lifting of a paralyzing spell. The spell-breaker was Lieutenant Sanford, as polished and handsomely clad as Captain Underhill, who called out (in deep tones that vibrated in someone's heart) the names of all the men who stood there armed and waiting. Or the drummer, Arthur Perry, might have been the one who stirred them all to life. No one forgot that they were building military strength for the perpetuating of the New England Zion—or at least not for very long—but there were more immediate concerns: for the participants, to load and fire, and wheel and file and face about; for the spectators, to stamp their feet in rhythm to the beating of the drum, and to move back and forth as the marchers moved, hoping to catch the eyes of the one for whom each braved the bitter cold.

The catching of eyes that day was a wonderful thing. Bridget exchanged a glance that calmed her turbulent heart with the certainty that now she knew the man that she would marry, and Faith realized that someone looked upon her with a feeling she had never guessed at. Captain Underhill caught an eye that quickly turned away and in so doing tantalized him and led him to abandon one of his basic rules for dealing with the other sex. Until this time he had known when to be satisfied with a glance, though it was true what he explained to the elders on the occasion when they asked why he did not look upon Mistress Newel or Mistress Upham instead of the young woman who wore wanton open-worked gloves slit at the thumb and fingers for the taking of snuff. He never had cared to look upon dames who were not desirable women as to temporal graces.

Others likewise looked briefly into each other's faces. William saw his young son Samuel gaze with pride upon his martial image. Richard surprised a look that gratified his vanity though it failed to touch his heart. He never even learned the name of that girl, but someone said she came from Marblehead.

Anne Hutchinson, at home in her father's chair with her Bible on her knees, had no thought of such wordless fleeting moments. If she had let her mind wander to the people on the common, she might have felt the force of their glances, for some of them would have a bearing on her life. But she was now gone in too deep toward God for any sense of earthly loves to reach her.

# VI

For some days after the marshaling of the train band, the sun still shone bright, and people began to talk about the chances of a thaw. There was indeed sufficient warmth during the days for ice to begin breaking up in the harbor, but those who had been longest in New England predicted river waters would not be freed until the tenth day of February, or twelfth month. Newcomers thought there was reason to hope that the worst of the winter was over already.

Jacob Hickson came in one morning from a walk along the shore and said to Elizabeth Joan that he could not set himself up as a prophet, but this day was sunny and the sea clear enough of ice that he could take his boat out and try to catch some fish. He might be able to land someplace where he could pick up some wood as well. He said he was tired of being an excuse for that Puritan sister to do her good works.

"Well, you are wrong about that, Jacob," said Elizabeth Joan. "Mistress Hutchinson does not even believe in good works. When she does something for somebody it's because she likes to do it."

"That may be," Jacob said, "but she's a pious, prating, prying—"

Elizabeth Joan interrupted. "She does not pry. I tell her about our troubles because she comforts me, as you might imagine a mother comforting her child."

"Well, neither you nor I ever had such a mother," said Jacob, "but now we have each other, and that's enough for me."

Elizabeth Joan said nothing to that. She saw he was jealous and felt pleased, in a way. She loved him more than anything in the world and was always looking for evidence that he felt the same way about her. There was no use, anyhow, in going on with talk about Mistress Hutchinson in the hope of persuading him to keep at home. "Just wait a few days," she begged, "before you take out the boat. The weather is not settled yet. I heard Goody Hawkins say yesterday she could feel in her bones that a new storm is brewing."

"It seems to me you must always be listening to either a witch or a female god-damn-me," he said.

She guessed he wanted to provoke a quarrel, to make it easier for him to go and leave her. She threw her arms around him, and kissed him long and hard. "Don't go, Jacob," she pleaded. "I fear for thee."

Without another word he grabbed her and shoved her to the floor, to the pallet where they slept, in the same moment pulling his breeches down and pushing up her skirt with rough hands raking her thighs. Then he had her, quick and hard, and as quickly left her there, making little high moans of grief and love.

He might come back. She lay a little while waiting, needing to have him touch her one more time. Though he hurt her sometimes, this was better than anything else that had ever happened to her. She hardly ever thought about her stepfather any more, but he came to her mind now, and she thought with wondering amazement (as early in her marriage she had often done) about how much better it was to lie with a man when you loved him.

Finally she dressed and went to Mistress Hutchinson's. She wasn't expected, but there would be work to do and dinner when it was over. And love. She was not altogether sure about the nature of the love that filled the rooms of that tall house on the high street, but it was not the same as what she had here in this damp and always slightly stinking hovel.

Jacob went along the shore to the harbor, where now in the winter weather he liked to keep his boat. In summer he might launch it almost anywhere, for it was a small boat, and usually he would beach it near his house, but in this season he preferred the convenience of the wharf. There wasn't much activity around the harbor. No ship had been able to come in for many months, nor were the fishing shallops working at this time of year; and so he could make use of facilities ordinarily denied him. As he was getting ready to push off, he heard someone call out, "Young man! What do you think you're doing?" Whoever it was, it was none of his business, and Jacob turned to tell the man so. He knew who it was then: King Winthrop, with his holier-than-anybody look and his long thick pointed beard.

"You would be wiser not to take that boat out today," John Winthrop said. He recognized the young man now. He had been hesitant about encouraging the lad to marry by letting him have the abandoned cottage to live in last summer. He was not on the board that had to approve him, but he could easily have put a stop to the whole thing by saying a word or two. This Jacob Hickson would be no asset to Boston, he was sure of that.

"Me and my wife has got to eat," Jacob said. "I aim to catch some fish."

"There's too much ice in the sea," Winthrop said, "and the wind is already changing."

"We have got to eat," said Jacob stubbornly.

"But your wife is working for Mistress Hutchinson now, I believe," said Winthrop. "Surely you can find nets to mend or repairs to make on the cottage while you wait for the weather to improve."

"How is it that every god-damn-me in Boston knows what every honest man is doing every minute of the day?" Jacob demanded. "Have you wrote down every time we piss and every time we shit?"

Winthrop's jaw stiffened and his eyes flashed. "That is blasphemy," he said, "and God will punish you."

"God be damned," said Jacob, and he turned back to his boat.

"I'll have you before the court for that," Winthrop shouted.

Jacob gave his boat a push, leaped into it, and rowed it out into the harbor. "I'll send you word when I have time to be there," he called back.

Winthrop sadly shook his head. His anger had already cooled; he was not a choleric man. Such men as Jacob were hopeless, he supposed, but he had come as a servant to a respected church member. It was impossible to examine everyone who landed in Boston, desirable though it would have been to do so. His first vision of this settlement had been that of a colony of God's elect, one that could serve as a model to all the Christian world, a city upon a hill. Already he could see that vision fading, feel himself losing the hold on his dream. He sometimes feared there might be more people in Boston now outside the church than in it. And one could not even depend upon church members to walk without swerving in the way of the model citizen. Forgotten doubts about Mistress Hutchinson returned as he considered this young couple she had taken under her wing.

He sighed as he watched the man raise his tattered sail and move out to sea. God might take care of this problem, he thought. Otherwise, he himself certainly would. He had been accused sometimes of being too lenient, for he had thought that in the beginning of a colony people might need a little time to adjust to this new idea of a whole community living in complete accord with God's will. He might be wrong, though. His brother Dudley might have banished this boy long ago, when he was first found lying with the drunken cooper's daughter. At least he himself had found a way to send the cooper and his brood back to England. He was thankful for that. He supposed the girl was, too. He did not know what had gone on there, but he could make a pretty good guess.

Jacob might have been more nearly right than he suspected when he taunted this man. Sooner or later, John Winthrop knew everything that happened in Boston. And when it was evil, either God or Winthrop meted out the proper punishment.

By mid-afternoon, when Elizabeth Joan went home along the seashore, the wind had already filled the sky with thick clouds and the cold hung in heavy invisible curtains hard to walk through. She took the long way in order to look for Jacob's boat sail, but there was nothing save hunks of ice in that gray, churning sea. She knew he wouldn't be foolish enough to stay out in such weather, though the Hutchinsons assured her he could not have returned. He would be at home when she got there, with a fire burning and a pot boiling. Something else would be hot and ready, too, she made no doubt. That thing inside her that he called her little coney reached for it eagerly. She quickened her steps.

No smoke rose above the huddled roof when she came in sight of it. Nor could she see a boat anywhere, though he might —she decided to believe—have left it out of sight in the little cove he had sometimes sailed into in the summertime. He might have come home in the last few minutes and be making a fire right now, while she hurried as fast as she could toward the door where he would meet her and grab her in his arms.

It was cold and dark inside the cottage. No one was there. The door had not been opened since she closed it, that was certain. She sank down on the bench by the table. (Jacob had built it in the past few weeks, with scraps of wood that William Hutchinson gave him.) She looked at the door, but she did not expect it to open. How long must I wait? she thought.

She sat there until she knew by the cold in her bones that she must not stay still any longer. She never went through the stages of anxiety, anger, and terror known well by wives who wait in vain. She felt very little, as if even her emotions were numbed by the cold. Presently she thought, If I do not build a fire, I shall freeze to death. Still she sat with no real thoughts of moving, until at last there came a knock at the door. Her heart beat wildly, but she said to herself, "Don't be a fool, he never has knocked on the door."

She flung it open and William Hutchinson stood there amidst thickly falling snow. "I came to see if Jacob is here," he said. "Mistress Hutchinson began to fear that you would be alone tonight, and wants you to come home with me."

"I need to make a fire," she said. "I have to wait for him."

William came in and closed the door. His task would be to make her see that Jacob wasn't coming home. There was no way he could sail that fragile boat of his through the sea that was tossing out there now.

"He must have found somewhere to take shelter for the night," William said. "Or else he would be here by now."

She seized upon that. For the first time, her mind seemed to come to life enough to picture situations that might account for Jacob's absence. He might easily, when he saw how the weather was changing, have made for the nearest shore—for one of the islands, most likely. He could make some sort of shelter there, to keep from freezing.

"But what if he should come home?" she said.

"You could leave word."

"How could I?" she asked simply. "I cannot write, and he cannot read."

"Come, girl," said William then, with authority she could not deny. "There is no way he could reach home until the storm is over, and if we do not set out soon we may become stranded ourselves."

She let him wrap her in an extra cloak he had brought and lead her out into the storm. Dark came on as they made their way across the open fields and into lanes now filling up with snow. Dark and cold, dark and cold, the words filled the consciousness of Elizabeth Joan; she used them to stamp out crazy images of Jacob on some bare rock shore, with the boat and the sail for shelter.

In Mistress Hutchinson's house, candles glowed from tables and shelves, and flames leaped in the fireplace. "Oh the glorious light!" cried Elizabeth Joan, and collapsed, senseless, as she stepped into the room.

2

Two days later some men found his body, naked and torn, flung up on an icy shore. They never found a scrap of his boat, so they never knew where he had got to, or whether he drowned or froze to death or was battered to death by the sea. Some said it might have been all three, but most people favored one over the others and took pleasure in explaining their reasons at great and logical length. Jacob's death was an exhilarating experience for Boston, because it provided something right out of the ordinary to talk about, yet posed no sort of threat to their well-being, as did the Pequod Indian threat, or letters from the archbishop and King. On the contrary, it was for most people (at least for the godly folk of Boston church) a comfort and a cause for self-congratulation. His last words to John Winthrop were quickly known throughout the town, and all who heard of them marveled at the swift justice with which God had meted out this fitting punishment.

John Winthrop went to John Cotton about the matter. Not for the first time, he regretted the absence of the pastor of the church. Master Cotton was undoubtedly a brilliant preacher and theologian, with a reputation among English nonconformists that Pastor Wilson could never aspire to; but in dealing with a happening like this John Wilson would do the expected thing and make it the subject of a sermon leaving no doubt in the minds of the congregation about the terrible wrath of the Lord. Who knew what John Cotton would do?

"Of course the boy was not a Christian," Cotton said, as the two men sat facing each other across the table in his study, "so his behavior is not subject to the action of the church."

"It was, however, subject to the action of God," said Winthrop, "and His quick retribution must have been intended as a lesson to Boston. Otherwise, the punishment might as well have taken place in some less public way and the manner of the death have been less horrible to look upon. Or the young man might not have spoken to me as he did. Although it may be true that he had many times used such language in speaking of God and His ministers and magistrates, privately, among his own friends—whoever they be—it seems to me providential that I came upon the scene precisely in time to warn him against his rash endeavor and so to hear him curse God and his fellow man. Jacob Hickson thus became the perfect type of the unregenerate man who mocks God and refuses his own chance of salvation."

John Cotton gravely shook his head. "Undoubtedly, some mention should be made of it," he said.

John Winthrop persevered. "A sermon should be preached upon it," he said flatly. "Believe me, the people of Boston expect it."

When he thought about the matter, Cotton knew Winthrop was right. He examined his own reluctance to grant the request and could not determine the source of it. If it was only pride, reluctance to let his pulpit be influenced by a lay person, then no doubt he had better consent. He might want to protect the feelings of the young man's wife—but it was doubtful she would even hear the sermon, and he had to admit that, if she did, painful as it would be to her, it might be the means of her awakening. There were others who had concerned themselves with Jacob Hickson's welfare, but not, presumably, with any great degree of personal affection, so as to make them suffer at his use as a public example.

"If you are thinking of the Hutchinsons," Winthrop said bluntly, "it seems to me that through taking to herself this couple known for filthy living and the rejection of God's ordinances, she gives some credit to the word we first had of her, that she is inclined toward strange opinions, and even it may be toward the Family of Love."

"Nay," said Cotton, "not so. For one thing, the teachings of that sect, though in error, are not what you apparently believe. Still, if there be such doubts and whisperings among us, then I suppose I needs must preach the sermon you demand."

3

Elizabeth Joan had soon awakened from her swoon. Then, bathed in the light of Anne Hutchinson's hall, and warmed with the fire and a cup of wine and Mistress Hutchinson's loving words, she began to believe that Jacob was well and would soon return to her. Through the two days before the messenger came to them (nearly night it was when he came, nearly suppertime), she went almost cheerfully about the tasks Anne found for her, talking from time to time about where she thought Jacob might have taken refuge and when he might be expected to come back. Just before the messenger came, she had been asking William whether he did not think a search party might be arranged (now that the snowfall had ended and the winds calmed), in case Jacob's boat had been damaged so much that he was stranded somewhere, perhaps on some island, with no means of getting away.

Then the knock came, and the messenger entered. It was the tithing man, feared figure in the cooper's family, when Elizabeth Joan had lived with them—the black man, one of her little sisters had called him, because he dressed in black and wore a black beard. And when she saw that black man in the Hutchinsons' doorway, she knew what he had come to say. Almost, she could have predicted his exact words: the unstinting, detailed description of the noseless flayed body flung upon the hard shore. She could have predicted it, but she never heard it. She could not bear to listen, and so she did not hear. She never heard even who had found him: servants of John Winthrop they had been, and they had gone to him, and he had guessed immediately whose body it might be. Anne, seeing the girl had ceased to respond, ceased to move, thought at first she had fainted, for she seemed subject to such fits; but she appeared fully conscious, her breathing and her heartbeat both regular and strong. She simply did not seem to hear the words anyone said, if they were anything to do with Jacob, and she never gave any sign of understanding the news that had been brought to them about his death.

Presently she got up and went to bed, and the next morning she arose and went about such tasks as she had become accustomed to doing each day.

"The men will go and bury the body," Anne said to her.

"I will go and get some snow," said Elizabeth Joan, "for we are in need of water to boil the meat."

Anne wondered if the girl could be thinking, as she herself was, of the job the men would have shoveling off the snow and digging a grave in the frozen ground.

"Would you like to go with the men?" Anne asked.

Elizabeth Joan had already turned away.

Anne had sometimes been displeased by the practice in Boston of burying the dead without religious rites, without even a minister present. The Church of England service had been a comfort to her more than once. Yet the belief here was that only the elect were entitled to such a service, and since logically it was not possible to determine with finality anyone's election, it was better for the church to forego the old ceremonies (which in any case smacked of popery). She had not quite determined what to think about this custom—she meant sometime to talk to Master Cotton about it—but today she was glad not to be faced with making Elizabeth Joan go to a funeral. The few men who cared about Jacob Hickson would go and stand by the grave while her own sons shoveled in the frozen clods. The end would come thus simply.

That night when she and William were in bed Anne asked what he thought of keeping Elizabeth Joan as a maidservant. They could use another pair of hands about the place, inexperienced as Elizabeth Joan's hands undeniably were at most kinds of work in a gentleman's house. Then by the time the oldest girls were married, Anne might have a servant trained and ready to be depended on.

"Married?" he asked in astonishment.

"Of course married," she said. "When hast thou ever looked at them?"

"They are very comely maidens," he said thoughtfully.

Anne laughed. "I can tell thee something else," she said. "Thou art not the only man that thinks so."

"Why?" he said, aroused. "Hath any man said so?"

"Nay," she said. "Be not alarmed. 'Tis only that a mother's eye may see. But Bridget and Faith will both be married before another year is done—they are ready and it will happen, that is all. But what dost thou think of Elizabeth Joan?"

"I am inclined to think she is demented," William said.

"Nay, William," Anne said, "it is only her way of protecting herself against hard truth. She will be all right, and I verily believe will come to know Christ Jesus, in His good time."

"Whatever thou sayest, Anne," he said. "And what would the girl do, anyway, if we turned her out of the house now?"

"Dear William," Anne said, and turned and embraced him.

Elizabeth Joan showed no surprise at being told she could stay with the Hutchinsons as their only maidservant. Since the menservants and oldest boys slept in the garret, she would continue to sleep in the room with the women, girls, and younger children. But she would understand that it was necessary to keep up the forms of propriety and so she would not eat at the table with the family now.

"Yes, mistress," said Elizabeth Joan, as though she had been a servant all her life.

On Saturday, Anne took out an old black dress of her own and showed Elizabeth Joan how to shorten it. "You can wear it to meeting tomorrow," she added, and Elizabeth Joan dutifully obeyed her and on the Sabbath dressed and walked with the household to church, with never a word as to whether any of it pleased her or no.

In the meetinghouse she unhesitatingly went to the back row of seats, where as an unregenerate and a member of the poorest class she had been accustomed to sit whenever she happened to attend the church service. Anne nodded at her approvingly, as she with the other women of her family moved to their regular seats near the front. The meetinghouse was crowded today; but so it had been, increasingly so, every Lord's Day, since John Cotton had been acting as pastor. A good-sized portion of the increase was due to new members in whom Master Cotton's preaching had awakened the spirit of Christ. Anne often thanked God for that increase and did now, as she stood while the pastor came down the aisle and mounted the stairs to his pulpit. Filled with anticipation of the sermon, she paid little attention to the crowd this day, or she would have noticed that it included many not usually seen there, and that everyone, whether saint or stranger, was vibrating with a kind of expectancy vastly different from hers. Half the congregation knew or guessed what the sermon would be about that day, but Anne's concept of the ways of God toward mankind differed so completely from theirs that the prospect had never occurred to her.

Hence it was a shock when Master Cotton announced his text —from First John, Chapter Two—and she realized what the application of it would be. "He that hateth his brother is in darkness, and walketh in darkness, and knoweth not whither he goeth, because that darkness hath blinded his eyes." John Wilson would have chosen a different text. Many people, aware of this fact, wondered whether Cotton would disappoint them and fail to preach on Jacob Hickson after all. Anne knew immediately what darkness he would speak of, and what he would preach: that hatred of both man and God had thrust Jacob into such abysmal darkness that he stumbled as though blinded into his eternal destruction. She wished she had defied proper order by keeping Elizabeth Joan at her side this day. Cotton did not mention Jacob's name at first. The congregation was hushed, puzzled, inclined to feel duped. Then he came to the pronouncement they were waiting for. "Jacob Hickson, a man known to this multitude, was offered a candle and dashed it to the ground out of hatred for the Giver of all light, and so by his own act is doomed to darkness."

Cotton paused. The house was absolutely quiet and motionless now, waiting for the full recounting of the story they already knew, hoping to hear the pastor repeat the words spoken by Jacob to John Winthrop, certain of having a detailed description of Jacob in hell.

Then suddenly from the back of the house came a terrifying, inhuman shriek, rising and falling, then rising again to a dreadful crescendo. Most had never heard anything like it in their lives. Some of the men who had been in the wilderness likened it to the savage yell of Indians on the warpath. Elizabeth Joan ran down the aisle toward the pulpit, tearing the borrowed black hood from her hair, ripping open her borrowed black dress of mourning, until only her streaming yellow hair concealed her bare breasts from the eyes of the craning, pushing mob that a moment ago had been a circumspect congregation.

Elizabeth Joan knew what she was protesting: that this man who seemed to speak in God's name would force her to accept a reality she could no longer deny, strip her in public of the only man who ever in her life had loved her, strip him of all dignity as his very skin had been stripped by the hands of the cruel God. But she was not a very articulate girl, nor was she now, her protective shell rudely broken, able to think out any acceptable means of expressing her grievance against this man. At the foot of the pulpit, she stood, and tearing her bodice open to the waist, kept screaming "I hate God" until four tithing men came to her and pinned her arms and stopped her mouth.

Then Anne Hutchinson stepped forward before them all, draped her own cloak over the girl, and put her arms around her.

4

When they had taken the girl to prison, Anne Hutchinson resumed her seat and John Cotton finished his sermon. Under the eyes of the tithing men, no one dared leave the meetinghouse or turn and whisper to his neighbor. Nothing could be done, by the Sabbath Day laws, until after sunset. Then Anne set out with a bundle of clothes, left it at the prison house, where the jailer refused to let her speak to Elizabeth Joan, and continued along Prison Lane to John Cotton's house at the foot of the Trimontaine.

She had not been there since the conference in October. She was doubtful of her reception in October. She was doubtful of her reception now, but she boldly knocked on the door. "They are at supper," the servant said when Anne asked for Master Cotton. But he heard her, and left the table, and came to her himself. Cotton's first floor was divided into two large rooms, with the huge central chimney opened to each one. Now with his family still in the kitchen at the supper table, Cotton led

Anne to the settle facing the fireplace in the parlor and sat down with her and took her hand.

"You are worried, sister, about the girl," he said, thus inviting her to speak.

"Do you think I was wrong to cover her nakedness in church today?" Anne asked him.

"Nay, you showed compassion," he said. "And I understand that you feel responsible for her."

"You are a compassionate man yourself, sir," Anne said to him.

"I think I may be," he said. "I could almost regret having preached that sermon today, if I were not convinced it opened some hearts to the workings of Christ."

"I pray it may have done so," Anne said. "But I could wish Elizabeth Joan had been better prepared to hear it." She tried to explain to the minister what the girl's condition had been. "If there had been any sort of service at the grave, it might have helped her," Anne said, "but since there was no service and since she refused to pay any heed to what I said to her about the burial, I did not force her to go."

Cotton frowned. "Yes, I see," he said. "I see there might sometimes be that need. But in the case of Jacob Hickson—"

"Even in his case," said Anne. "And sometime I think we may speak of this need. But what I need to know now, what I need to go and tell Elizabeth Joan as soon as they will let me see her, is whether you did indeed mean to say today that Jacob Hickson stepped through the darkness straight to hell."

"Let no man judge," said the minister.

"But I must know," said Anne. "I have always understood you to mean that through God's covenant of grace, man is neither saved nor damned by any act of his. Is there not a possibility, in spite of all the evidence, that Jacob Hickson was one of the elect?"

"Of course there is a possibility," Cotton said. "It seemed to me that his experience made an instructive example and served as a warning to those who may be rejecting Christ. Yet I would not say the young man did not come to a glorious awareness of Christ alone in his boat in the last hours before he died. Though we must doubt he had been vouchsafed any experience of grace at the time he spoke to Master Winthrop at the harbor, no man can tell what happened in his heart in those last days or hours."

"I am sure," Anne said, "that Elizabeth Joan, being scarcely in possession of her senses, half believed she was hearing the voice of God declare he had gone straight to hell."

"That would be a great pity," the minister said.

"Oh, sir, could you not come to her," Anne said, "and speak to her about the covenant of grace? It would be such a comfort to her in her bereavement and might, I hope, in time lead her to open her own heart to Christ."

Cotton smiled—the same smile he often shed on his congregation as he preached of God's wonderful plan. "I will come, sister," he said. "And yet it might be God will make better use of you in this instance."

The following day, William went to William Coddington, as the one of the magistrates he hoped to find most understanding, and explained to him Elizabeth Joan's condition and his wife's desire to care for her—how by employing her as a household servant, she hoped to provide for both her physical and her spiritual needs.

"She will certainly have to be punished," Coddington said. "Winthrop will demand that. And yet I will do what I can. With a Christian woman like Mistress Hutchinson ready to offer pity and aid—and I assume to take responsibility for her actions—I feel sure the punishment can be lessened."

He had a certain degree of success. The prisoner was released that day in the custody of William Hutchinson, and when the court met it sentenced Elizabeth Joan Hickson to sit an hour on the scaffold every lecture day for six months, wearing a letter B, three inches high and of a proportionate bigness, pinned to the back and front of her bodice.

Afterward, safe at home with Mistress Hutchinson, Elizabeth Joan smiled and observed that she had been there before.

Anne sighed and did not answer. The girl had truly very much to learn. Anne prayed she might learn it on the scaffold in the market place.

# VII

One thing about living in Boston, as poor Jacob Hickson had observed, was that a person had very little privacy; there undoubtedly must have been secret sins, but there were so many public ones, at least among what people called the poorer sort, that sitting in the stocks or standing on the scaffold was not really much regarded as a mark of shame. There were various ways in which the richer sort could keep their sins more to themselves, but the fines they frequently had to pay were no more of a secret in Boston than the badges worn in the market place to proclaim abroad the nature of a sinner's transgression.

For some the badges might even be a mark of distinction. Anne noticed this when she heard young Samuel pointing out to his friends on lecture day, "That's our maid up there."

"What's the B for?" one little boy asked.

"Blasphemy!" announced Samuel proudly, as though this were a hard sin to outdo.

Anne said nothing to the boy then, but she scolded herself for having been so careless about his education. When next she gathered the children together (with Elizabeth Joan) for catechism and general instruction, this incident would provide a fitting subject. Even so, she was not very sorry to observe that no one appeared scandalized by the various public punishments taking place. Anything cruel or unusual might have driven Elizabeth Joan back behind the wall she had erected after Jacob's death.

With Elizabeth Joan's mental and spiritual condition Anne felt, for the moment, content. She had adopted the proper manner of a maidservant, yet seemed as friendly and open as in the days when she first used to come to Anne's house. Anne had taken the girl to see John Cotton, who—though rebuking her for her behavior in church—had talked with her in the way he had promised; and although it was not clear how much the girl understood, she had not again declared she hated God, but had gone sedately to meeting with the household on the Lord's Day, behaving herself very much as any young widow would be expected to do. Anne herself never talked with her about the renting of her clothes, believing she had not been conscious of what she was doing. When the time came, Anne would have some private talk with her about her salvation. Meanwhile, she drew her into family prayers and sessions of instruction with the children, waiting patiently for signs of Christ within her.

In general, Anne was pleased with her servant, and well believed that God had sent her; for as Elizabeth Joan was learning the manners and duties of her position, Anne grew steadily in greater need of her. It seemed that with the approach of spring God was opening a new way of life for her, one that took her more and more often away from her family and house.

Goody Hawkins was to some extent responsible for this change, but it would have come about sooner or later, with or without her. God needed an instrument, that was all, and so He used Jane Hawkins. Some might have thought it strange that He would use this humpbacked old woman, unchurched and suspect, but Anne did not. She was inclined to take almost everything as an instrument of God, and hardly ever suspected the devil's hand in anything.

From the time when word first went around that she had saved the life of Elizabeth Joan (Jane Hawkins spread that word, there was no way of knowing the truth of it), more women had been calling on Anne for help in sickness and childbirth. Jane, as the more or less official midwife of Boston, would often suggest she be called, even when there was no indication of a crisis.

"You have such a good way with you, mistress," Jane said, peering into Anne's face, moving in close, as though seeking help for herself from this good way. "It makes women feel better, just to know you're in the room."

It was hard to know exactly what comprised this way of Anne

Hutchinson's. Partly it was knowledge and experience. She had borne fourteen children, all of whom lived past infancy, and in Alford she would often help in neighbors' sicknesses. She had a good stock of medicines and instruments brought from her former home, as well as apparatus for distilling more preparations as she had need of them. But the good way was more than having a physician's stock and knowing what to do with it. It was an emanation of love and concern—something invisible that reached out to the person lying in pain and doubt and drew her close as within a mother's arms. All without any word or a gesture more intimate than a hand on a weak, fretful arm.

Goody Hawkins tried to imitate it—whatever it was, some sort of faith, some force derived from faith, she seemed to feel—but could only bend close to her patient, blinking her glittering eyes, and murmur, "If you believe, I can help you. If you *believe*."

Later, a close inquiry would be made into what she was asking people to believe. The truth was, she didn't know herself, but how she did love to hear Anne talk about her own beliefs—her certainties—about the grace of God. Anyone at all—anyone in the world, Anne seemed to be saying—can hope to go to heaven. You don't have to do anything, Christ just comes to you, out of His great love, and joins Himself to you. He's really part of you, and when the right time comes He draws this part of Himself, and you with it, up to heaven—a fisherman pulling in a fish, was the picture that came to Jane's mind. Jane had the greatest difficulty imagining any portion of Christ anywhere inside her own bony chest—but where else could He be? She never asked Anne Hutchinson about that, never asked anything much; she had a feeling of delicacy about Anne's beliefs, as if too much probing would expose something hard and rocky that a person like Jane would have to stumble over, or a pit for her to fall into. So, when Anne would ask if all she said to her was clear, Jane always answered eagerly, "Yes, very clear." And in fact, at the time, it always did seem so, as if nothing in the world could ever be easier and clearer than the love of God. It was only afterward, walking some lonely path by the seashore, that she would see there must be something else she didn't understand—some trick to it.

Her old man thought so too. "That sounds too good to be true to me, my duck," he would say. But he didn't argue much. If

Jane wanted to follow after this woman like a little puppy dog, he couldn't say he cared—certainly not while she brought home victuals from the Hutchinson house two or three days out of the week.

Goody Hawkins couldn't keep quiet about Anne Hutchinson's wonderful covenant of grace. At times Anne suspected, from the questions some woman would ask, that Jane's talk about this subject was the real reason she had been called in. Well, no better reason, she would say to herself and go on to explain, perhaps through an explication of one of John Cotton's sermons.

Her talk with the women of Boston revealed to her a strange discrepancy. In spite of the fact that John Cotton's sermons were so popular and had brought so many new members into the church, there was still a surprising number of people indoctrinated with grim John Wilson's sterile covenant of works.

Mary Cogshall, for example. She had had an easy time of it with her last baby, and as Anne talked about the meaning of the covenants with the women gathered at her bedside, she had listened as avidly as anyone. Then in visits afterward, Anne found her uncommonly intelligent and inquisitive.

"Are you saying," Mary asked earnestly, deepening the lines drawn across her broad, fair brow, "that we cannot find assurance of our salvation in any deeds we do?"

"That is true," said Anne.

"Not helping our neighbors, or caring for the sick?" Mary said slyly.

"Not even that," said Anne.

"Then why are you here?" asked Mary.

Anne laughed gently. "Because I want to be," she said. "It may be that I want it because of the portion of Christ that lives within me. As to that, I cannot say and need not know."

"And you do not think this doctrine of yours would make a person so arrogant in his certainty of salvation without works that he or she might smugly live a selfish, sinful life that would fly in the face of the teachings of Jesus."

"I know it would not," said Anne, seeing no reason to argue any more.

"I believe you," said Mary.

The next time Anne saw her, Mary said, "My husband would like to hear what you have to say. He has long been restless in this doctrine Pastor Wilson preaches, without quite seeing a clear difference between him and Master Cotton."

"When you are better, you must bring him to my house, and we shall talk," said Anne.

So it often went. Anne would see light dawning in the eyes of a woman who had long been lost in darkness, thinking to build her spiritual estate upon her worldly actions, and then the wife would awaken her husband to the presence of grace. (The old Eve artfully at work on the heart of man, as Winthrop later would interpret such changes in religious allegiance.)

Anne could still find time every day to sit in the wainscot chair by the window with her Bible on her lap. Humbly she would try to discover whether this new way of life, offering aid for the bodies and souls of their neighbors, was the thing God had told her to wait for. She was not sure.

2

Faith and Bridget, like other marriageable maids, were concerned with matters vastly different from those that occupied their mother's thoughts. They came to her one morning as she sat spinning by the fire, and asked if she would listen to a request they had to make.

Ever since the January training day, Anne had known there were two young men singled out by her daughters. Faith preferred Thomas Savage, who looked so brave on the marching field and made so much money as a tailor that he was one of her father's best customers. John Sanford, her sister's choice, was richer, and at the age of thirty already a selectman of the town and cannoneer of the militia, but Thomas had deep, far-seeing eyes that both excited Faith and made her certain that in his care a wife would ever be secure. Bridget was very sure that John would like to know her better. Faith was not quite so sure about Thomas but was eager to give him a chance. What they wanted was a large dinner party, to which the young men might be invited without appearing to be singled out.

Anne said she would discuss the matter with William. She felt rather sure that he would like the idea himself, and so he did. Now that he was serving on several committees and commissions, and certain of election to the General Court, he could be considered one of the leading men in Boston. It would look very well if he were to give a dinner for his friends, particularly since the Hutchinsons had attended several dinners and suppers during the fall and winter. Anne told him the girls' secret, and he was not displeased. He knew both the men and found them trustworthy in their dealings and successful in the building of their worldly estates.

The girls were already planning the party, and Anne decided that she could allow them to have it very much as they pleased. They wanted it at night: the bare walls and crude, scanty furnishings looked better by fire and candlelight. They needed another table: couldn't Father and the boys bring in boards and trestles from the shop? They needed more room!

Anne laughed at that. Nothing could be done about it now, although William was drawing plans for a new house to be started as soon as the weather allowed. There would be a great hall in it —with room for several tables. But they would have to wait for it, perhaps till the end of summer, and the girls assured her they would rather be crowded.

As indeed they were. By the time they had set up boards enough to accommodate themselves and all the guests they wanted to invite, there was scarcely space to walk around the room. But so it was in most houses in Boston when a great feast was spread. The only thing that really mattered was that the tables be equally crowded with platters of meat and fish and fowl. William readily procured them, and the girls, with the help of Cousins Anne and Frances, cooked at the fireplace for two days before the dinner. During those same two days, Elizabeth Joan and the two Hutchinson menservants were being drilled to wait at the table. These young men no longer lived in the Hutchinson house, having both married and found places of their own, but they still worked for William and could be pressed into service for the household when they were needed.

Elizabeth Joan was trying hard to be a good servant. There was very little in the world she wanted now more than to please Anne Hutchinson, who was the first person ever to be kind to her. Jacob had loved her, but Mistress Hutchinson both loved her and was kind. The whole family were kind to her most of the time—Bridget sometimes grew impatient, and the little children sometimes teased, but all of them were kind and the kindness derived from Anne Hutchinson. She would have done anything she could for any of them, but there did not seem to be anything she could do except follow her mistress' instructions day by day. If she could have seized upon Jesus Christ and violently thrust Him into her bosom, for the sake of Mistress Hutchinson she would have done so. She knew that would please her beloved mistress more than anything else, but she could see no way to reach Him. Secretly, she thought she knew why, but the reason was something she could never tell. Yet it was a very simple reason, and one that Mistress Hutchinson, having had fourteen children, would quite possibly have understood. Sometimes this possibility occurred to Elizabeth Joan, but she could never bring herself to imagine Mistress Hutchinson in bed and enjoying a man. She might almost as easily have believed the children came into being through some miracle like the birth of Christ.

Anyway, she couldn't go to her mistress and say, "I can scarcely remember when I didn't have a man coming to me in the night, and you don't know how it is to do without it." If she had Jesus Christ, she wouldn't miss that. That was what Elizabeth Joan believed. Mistress Hutchinson always seemed to be saying that when you had Christ nothing else mattered. You would not sin, you could not sin, something like that, and yet you could never take the fact that you weren't sinning as the sign that you had found Christ and were saved. When Elizabeth Joan tried to think about it all, she became very confused and sometimes would go away into a corner and cry. And they would think that she was crying about Jacob.

The great stir about the dinner party almost made her forget the ache in her heart and even the one between her thighs. The girls brought out satin gowns she had never seen before, and she helped them to air and smooth them, and later helped them dress. She knew what they were hoping for, and she guessed they would get it. But they would never understand all they were bargaining for until they were properly wed and had a husband in bed every night. She truly hoped their marriage beds would bring them joy.

"Plenty of meat and Madeira," was what William said when asked for his ideas on planning the party. He provided both wonderfully well, and the guests partook of them freely. Toast after toast was drunk: to the master and the mistress of the feast, to the town, to the colony—Elizabeth Joan stood back and watched in amazement, as they drank and drank and never slipped under the table. She was accustomed to seeing people drink themselves into insensibility, but these people kept cutting their meat and laughing and talking as though they were drinking clear water. The pewter cups were not filled as deep as she supposed, of course, but there were some very experienced drinkers at the table that night.

Only old King Winthrop passed on the cup without tasting when it came to him—not John Cotton or anyone else would do that—and muttered something about the joy of the Lord being enough. Anne noticed that, too, and remembered hearing he had done and said the same thing at the banquet before the company sailed to the New World from Southampton. But she had seen him drink wine on other occasions, and felt the action was an affront to her and William. She had been doubtful about inviting him—he was out of their class, wasn't he? But William said he wasn't, not in Boston, and she said nothing more because she felt her reluctance might be due to some other cause she could not quite define.

Some few might drink too much, of course. She began to keep an eye on Captain Underhill. She might suggest before long that William take him out for fresh air. The air in the house was certainly not fresh. It was filled with odors of smoke and wine and food and old sweat soaked into fine clothes that were aired and shaken and put away, but not washed sometimes for years, because they would never appear so grand any more once they had been through the rubs. But nobody minded the odors, everyone was used to them.

There was good talk to go with the food and drink—gossip about ordinary happenings of the colony and discourse upon the grace of God. These people made religion so much a part of their daily lives that they noticed no discrepancy, and almost everyone listened with pleasure as Cotton, at a question from Anne, explained the precise location of faith in the order of salvation.

At last it was time to bring forth the puddings, a job that for Elizabeth Joan required complete concentration. She was afraid she would dump one in the face of some magistrate or his lady, while squeezing between the tables where there seemed for some reason to be less space than there had been when dinner began. Something pressed against her buttock—she thought it must be the elbow of somebody cutting the last of his meat—and then she felt a sharp nip that caused her to start, suppressing a scream, and to dish the soft pudding right onto the head of a fine handsome gray-haired gentleman, who rose up cursing. "Damn the doxy!" he said, and then started a spell of coughing which he must have hoped would cover up what he had already said. The poorer sort were sometimes set in the stocks for saying damn in public, but this man was not going to be punished. Everyone pretended not to hear what he had said, while Mistress Hutchinson rushed after extra napkins, in order to give the gentleman her personal attention, and all the rest were busily talking to their neighbors, so as not to appear shocked at what had been said by Captain Keayne. Under cover of all this, as Elizabeth Joan bent to scoop up the portion of the pudding on the floor, someone whispered in her ear, "If you meet me at the spring gate when the horn blows, I will beg your pardon."

She looked up and met Captain Underhill's eyes. Gray-green, deep laughing eyes they were, in a square, spade-bearded face. His somewhat too thick lips parted in a polite smile that revealed his tobacco-stained teeth. She gave him no sign. No one could have guessed he had spoken.

The dinner moved on, and ended. By that time Captain Keayne was able to make a joke of the pudding dumping; he wanted to speak to the girl about it, he told Mistress Hutchinson. He patted Elizabeth Joan on the head and told her not to worry. There was a gleam in his eyes, too—he was certainly no fatherly old gentleman. Suddenly she remembered why the men looked at her so. She had almost forgotten what she did in church that day the preacher said that Jacob was in hell. She had never, in fact, been willing to think of it or try to imagine what she had really done and what she looked like. But in the bleary eyes of this tottering old man (tottering from drink, because she realized now he was not extremely old), she saw as though the scene were mirrored there how she stood before the congregation with her bosom bare. Her face flared redder than the old man's nose. She bowed, said, "Thank you, sir," and fled up the stairs to her garret room.

On the pallet there, she wept uncontrollably until her mistress came to her.

"They've all gone now, it's all right," Mistress Hutchinson said.

"Oh yes, mistress," Elizabeth Joan sobbed. "I will come." The work of the dinner party was not over; it might go on far into the night.

"It's all right, you may come when you are calmer, but no one blames you about the pudding. The room was too crowded. The best trained servant might have done the same thing."

"It's not that," sobbed Elizabeth Joan. "It's not that."

Then the mistress became, as she might do, the mother, and enfolded Elizabeth Joan in her arms. "I know what it is," she said to her. "I know that Captain Keayne, and I know what sort of look a man like that may offer a woman."

"But it was what I did in church, wasn't it?" cried Elizabeth Joan. "That's what made him look like that." They had never before discussed this precisely, what she had done to bring about her punishment.

"Don't worry, don't worry," said Anne. "It wasn't as bad as you think. Your hair well covered you."

"But that was it, anyway. Will men of that sort always look at me that way?"

"Perhaps some will," said Anne, "but you must not care. You will learn to walk in the ways of a virtuous, Christian woman, and no one then can wound you with a look."

"But I am not a Christian," said Elizabeth Joan.

"That will come, too," said Anne. "Do not worry."

She left Elizabeth Joan to finish composing herself. "But you must come soon and help with the cleaning."

"Yes, mistress," said Elizabeth Joan.

Comforted once more by this kindest of mistresses, she felt her distress gently fading. Nothing so very bad had happened tonight, after all. But she knew very well, all the time, that she had kept from mentioning the one unequivocal thing; she had evidently not wanted to ask her mistress' advice about that.

Back downstairs, Elizabeth Joan couldn't help feeling a little surprise that no one paid attention to her. Then she remembered that after all she was only a servant girl. It was not a thought that bothered her very much, either. She liked quite well being left alone to wonder when she would go to the spring for water tomorrow morning. When the herd's horn blows, very likely, she said to herself.

# VIII

One morning two or three days after the party, Mary Cogshall called on Mistress Hutchinson. Something about Mary's expression—her broad smooth brow a little wrinkled, her clear gray eyes a little clouded—made Anne guess she wanted to speak privately. Having invited her to sit down, Anne looked around to see where everyone was. The older boys and their father were away at work, of course, and the little children were all out of doors in the mild sunshine. Anne, with her knitting, was watching over them all, while Mary and Katherine had been put to plucking fowls to be roasted for dinner. Sister Katherine had gone to have some shoes repaired, and the cousins had gone to the market place. Bridget and Faith had just been telling their mother what they wanted to do this morning, if she could spare them from household chores. They wanted to go through all their clothing, sun it and air it and mend whatever needed mending. She could foresee that they would discover the need of new gowns to be made for them this summer. They would be finding reasons to look over their father's stock of silk, she suspected.

She knew where all the children were, but she seemed to have mislaid her maidservant. "Where is Elizabeth Joan?" she called to the girls, who came halfway down the stairs to answer her.

"Gone to her little old house to look for something," Bridget said. "She said she couldn't find you, and so she asked Father, and he said it would be all right."

"What could she have left there?" Anne wondered, thinking the action strange and remiss, unlike Elizabeth Joan.

But as long as she had spoken to William before going, Anne supposed it was all right. She excused the girls to go on with their task upstairs.

"They have become more interested in their clothing than they have ever been before," Anne said.

Mary smiled. "They are two very fine young men that your daughters save their smiles for."

"I suppose you noticed at the supper," Anne said. "I hope they were not bold."

"Very modest, I would say," said Mary. "Very courteous to everyone, comely young women and well behaved. You can only be congratulated upon your children."

Anne set a plate of cakes on a stool by Mistress Cogshall and took a seat near her. She smiled (a modest smile much like her daughter Faith's) and said, "I thank you."

"You are all so courteous and well disposed toward everyone. All Boston is pleased to know you and your family."

"So I should wish," said Anne, raising her eyebrows somewhat as she realized Mary must be coming to the purpose of her visit.

"Of course you know I have a reason for saying these things," said Mary, answering her unspoken question, "other than the pleasure in telling such a truth."

"Then do say what it is, Mistress Cogshall," said Anne.

"It's something women talk of, here and there," said Mary. "They wonder, as you seem so open and friendly with everyone, why you care not for our neighborhood meetings."

This was not the first time the meetings had been mentioned to Anne since the invitation she received soon after she joined the church, but she had never suspected Boston women took her absence amiss. Mistress Hibbens did, perhaps, but it seemed she took almost everything that way, had quarreled with most of her friends, and ceased attending meetings herself. Mary Dyer and Mary Coddington were always pleasant when Anne met them; she would not believe they ever spoke against her.

"I have thought I might go someday, with my husband's cousins," Anne said. This was true. She had never quite decided not to go, but there was always something else she needed or preferred to do.

"There is really no reason you should go," said Mary. "And yet I thought—well, I don't know whether opinions of other women make much difference to you. Very likely not, nor do they much, to me. Still, you have come to live in Boston—"

"And when in Boston do as the Bostonians do?"

Mary shook her head. "Nay, I would not say so."

"But some might," said Anne. "Do tell me, Mistress Cogshall. I shall be very glad to know."

There had been some talk, evidently at these meetings where the women gathered for their spiritual edification. Anne was too proud to come to them, some said. She thought she knew it all. Others, who felt they had been delivered from a spirit of bondage by her talks about the covenant of grace, tried to defend her, but they did not know what to say. It was conjectured that she held such meetings unlawful. Some wondered if she despised all ordinances, having heard her say that observing them was nothing in the building of a spiritual estate.

"Of course I do not despise the ordinances," said Anne. "Is there one they have seen me neglect?"

"So it was answered," Mary said. "They see you in the meetinghouse twice on every Lord's Day, and others said they know for sure you do hold family prayers."

Anne thoughtfully nibbled a seed cake, baked by Elizabeth Joan yesterday under Cousin Anne's supervision. With that reminder there slipped in among her concern for her own reputation in Boston the puzzle as to why the girl had wanted to go back to that hovel. Then it slipped away again.

As Anne did not speak, Mary went on. "I think I know why you don't go," she said. "I believe you hold them a waste of time, and I have to say I believe you are right. I would stop going myself, if I knew how to do it without hurting somebody's feelings."

"And yet," said Anne, "if women do have time and feel drawn together in this way, it is a pity if there be not something helpful and instructive they can gain there."

"So I think myself," said Mary, "and I might as well say that it is just for this reason I have come to you today."

Something pricked Anne's heart just then. Be alert, be alert, some signal warned her. She sat a little straighter, and laid down her cake.

Some of them had been talking together, Mary said. All of them had happened to hear Anne talk somewhere, during sickness at their own houses, or gathered together for the birth of some neighbor's child. All of them said they would give anything to be with her more, hear more of what she had to say about the covenant of grace. So often, they felt they understood Master Cotton's sermons better after they had the good fortune to be in a house with Mistress Hutchinson. So why—the question seemed to come to all of them at once, as if something outside them had slipped it into their minds—should she not hold regular meetings, to which all who needed the spiritual uplift of her words could come? Then no one could say Mistress Hutchinson was too proud to attend women's meetings, and no one would be kept from her helpful discourse.

Anne was silent, looking down. Mary wondered if she were praying, but she was not. This question was not in her view a reason for prayer, but it might have to be decided after some time in private meditation. Actually, there was no reason why she should not hold the kind of meeting Mary was suggesting. She would like to do it. Her heart beat a little faster at the thought of it—the opportunity every week to speak to women ready to feed upon the fruits of her long silent hours with the Scriptures and her own thoughts. But why did she want it so much—suddenly so very much, as if it was what she had long been waiting for? Could it in fact be the thing God was holding in reserve for her?

"I shall have to think about it," she said to Mary.

"Of course you would," Mary said. "But let me know, if you decide this pleases you. I will send the word around."

"How many would come?" Anne asked.

"There were four or five of us talking about it," Mary said. "Not many more than that. I know you would not want a great crowd."

"Oh no," said Anne. "I was thinking that if there were only a very few we could talk together more intimately. Otherwise it might as well be a sermon in a meetinghouse—and I never could presume to try to preach a sermon."

"You will really think about it then?" said Mary.

"I am already thinking about it," said Anne.

"Then I must go, and not disturb your thoughts, for I must tell you we are all in great hope of something wonderful from you."

2

Elizabeth Joan barely got home in time to help put dinner on the table, but no one asked her where she had been. Mistress Hutchinson seemed hardly to know she was there—or indeed, even to notice her own husband and children. This condition in her mistress was uncommon but not unheard of. Everyone recognized it, and no one—not even the smallest children—bothered her with questions or tugged at her skirt. The house became, as it always did at such times, unnaturally silent. As soon as the meal was over, the children rushed back outside, the men to their shop, and the girls upstairs to their wardrobes. Not to anyone's surprise, Mistress Hutchinson took her Bible and went to sit in the big chair and look out the window.

Elizabeth Joan breathed a sigh of relief as she went about the task of voiding the chargers left on the table after the meal. She walked on tiptoe, not really expecting Mistress Hutchinson to come out of her trance and ask why she had gone out this morning, but certain that the longer such questions could be put off, the more hopeful her situation would be.

She had been very much afraid her plan wouldn't work, but it was the only thing she could think of. With any luck, she had thought, her master and mistress would both be so busy with their own affairs, the question would never be asked. "What did Elizabeth Joan want to go to the cottage for?" she had imagined the mistress asking. "What?" the master would say. "Why I never knew she went anywhere."

Because Elizabeth Joan had lied. That was all. Had outright lied, and lying wasn't a common practice with her, either. She had been taught *something*, when she was a child at home, before her mother died. That was just all she could think of to do, and she wanted to go—oh, God, how she wanted to go. It seemed she would have to go to him, or die.

At the spring gate he was so courtly, such a fine figure of a man, really had more the appearance of a gentleman than she had noticed before. She had seen him in his uniform—had noticed him at the training day, as she had admitted to him this morning, and she had seen him at the supper. But on the first occasion she was truly thinking of no one but Jacob, with his pike in his hand and his armor shining, and at the supper there was such a crowd she had hardly known what he looked like except for the deep secret laughter in his lazy gray-green eyes. Those eyes gave him away. He was a fine soldier, she had no doubt, and knew how to look the part too. But he knew how to play another role, she instinctively knew that, and would choose it over any other, she would vow.

Oh, he did look so fine at the spring gate. Funny, too, with the water pail in his hand. On his head, a cap with a feather in it. Over his broad chest, a slashed leather doublet showing his soft tawny shirt. Full breeches in the Dutch style, and as he stood there swinging the pail, talking to her, she could see that something moved inside them. It was all she could do to keep from laughing, even while she felt her own thing swell somewhere inside her. There was no one else there, except a few servants. They too knew very well he hadn't come for water. He gallantly took the pail from her hand and stooped to fill it for her, and she heard one of the young men say something about the captain filling her pail right well, he would be bound. But she kept her manner as modest as Mistress Hutchinson's daughters might have done.

He talked fast, and under his breath, and with a pain in his voice that might convince any maiden he was wounded unto death and only she might save him. Elizabeth Joan knew better than that, so she told herself, but he did make his tale sound true: how he had glimpsed her at the training meet, and loved her from the first. How he had seen her in the meetinghouse, in her great grief. She felt herself begin to blush, and he said, "Nay, no one blamed thee. So tender a little wife, so cruelly deprived." Yet he could not help seeing those round little breasts peeking through her golden hair. He called it golden; she knew it was not.

They must meet somewhere, he said. He only wanted to talk, to comfort her, to touch her hand. He would never ask of her more than she was willing to give. He was lying in his rotten teeth, and she knew it, but she thought of a place—the old cottage, where she had lived as a wife. He said the town leaders had voted to have it repaired and offer it for sale, but he knew it would be a few days before anything was done there. So they had agreed on a time: the next day, at midmorning.

All the way to the cottage this morning, she had thought about Jacob, but after she got there she didn't, much. It seemed many years since she had lived there. She had forgotten the dampness and the stench. Someone had taken away the ragged old blankets they used, but the straw mat Mistress Hutchinson had brought was still there. It was full of fleas.

Still, they lay on it. He was the third man she had known, and different from either of the others. Her stepfather had used her. Jacob had loved her, but she saw now in what a rough and ignorant way. Captain Underhill wooed her, fondled her hair and kissed her breasts, until she was moaning and begging him to put it in. This he did several times, before she suddenly feared it must be dinnertime and she looked for at the Hutchinson house. He said they would meet again. He would find some way and let her know. He kissed her good-by lingeringly, and then she went, alone. He would remain awhile, in case someone with prying eyes had wandered down the beach.

Out of the dark hovel and into the wide bright open world of sea and sky, she became anxious. The sun seemed very high in the sky; undoubtedly, she would be looked for. She ran a good part of the way.

No one ever did ask her why she went to the cottage, and evidently Master Hutchinson was never questioned as to why he let her go. All during the afternoon the house was as quiet as the grave. It was strange to look at Mistress Hutchinson, sitting in her chair. She sat staring straight out the window with those great full-seeming eyes of hers, and yet it was doubtful that she looked at anything at all. Elizabeth Joan had seen her old grandam sit that way once in a chair, and grow still, and never wake up. She knew a temptation to bang a pot in her mistress' ear, or go to her and shake her and say, "Are you dead?"

Of course she was not. But the family were already gathering for supper before Mistress Hutchinson rose and turned to them, returned to them, as though she had been on a long journey.

It must have been a glorious journey. Wherever she went, she had seen something wonderful. Elizabeth Joan would have given much to know what it was. Her mistress' dark eyes glowed as though candles had been lit behind them. Her face, somewhat sallow as a rule, was rosy and gold like a sunrise. She came to them slowly, and holding herself tall.

"I have great news for you," she said, "but we shall wait until after prayers, when we are at table."

She never ate a bite, but talked to them throughout the meal of the new way God had opened before her. Mistress Cogshall was His instrument, she said, and she told how Mary had come to her with the request about the meeting.

"I shall consent to their request," she said, "and it will lead to something greater than I have yet experienced in my life. God hath not yet revealed to me the full extent of it, but it will be what He brought me here to do."

3

Early on the day of the meeting, Goodwife Hawkins came to the back door, asking for Mistress Hutchinson. She had a basket of herbs on her arm. She had been in the forest, she said, since before sunrise.

"Do you think," she asked Anne seriously, "that there be more virtue in plants when they are gathered at midnight?"

Anne smiled and shook her head. "Nay," she said. "I think there be no matter about the time of day or night, so long as they be fresh and full of juices."

Goody Hawkins shook her head doubtfully. "All but one, mayhap," she said. She moved on into the kitchen as Anne opened the door wider in invitation, and spoke excitedly. "Ah, mistress," she said, coming close to Anne and peering up into her face, as she was wont to do. "I know about the meeting, and that is why I have come, to see if you would let me be there with the gentlewomen."

"Why of course, dear Jane," said Anne. "Why should I not?"

"I am not of their sort," said the goodwife.

"But, Jane, no woman will be barred from this meeting," Anne said. "Anyone may come who wishes to hear us discuss the meaning of Master Cotton's sermon."

"To hear *you*, mistress," Jane said. "That is why I wish to come."

She was there, crouching on a stool in a dim corner, before

the rest arrived. Elizabeth Joan was present, as were the cousins, Katherine Marbury, Bridget, and Faith. From outside the household, four women came that day. Mary Cogshall, of course, she of the placid brow and friendly air. Mary Coddington, whose husband had become a good friend of William Hutchinson and more than once—on some occasion when he and Anne sat at the same table—had inquired into her opinions. He may have been more interested in them than his wife was; Anne guessed it was on account of him that Mary came, for she never seemed to care for anything much beyond her house and children. Elizabeth Aspinwall, another whose husband had seemed to express more interest than she. Mary Dyer, youngest of them all, and fairest, with patient, seeking eyes. Anne had had long talks with her during childbirth vigils, and deemed her most capable among the four of understanding all John Cotton taught.

Anne seated them all—urging Goody Hawkins from her stool —along either side of the long trestle table. Anne had asked Richard and Francis to set it up in the center of the room that morning. Something else she had them do, as well. It was a thing that had come to her in the night, in a vision of her father as he was when he explained to her so long ago—before she ever heard of John Cotton—the meaning of Calvin's statement about the covenant of grace. Francis Marbury said he was somewhat doubtful about Calvin and whether he understood aright the doctrine of the elect. (Secretly, Anne did not understand it herself, did not even believe it could be understood, and that might have been the basis of the difference—so long unrecognized by them both—between the minister and his avowed disciple.) Never mind, it was not precisely her father's teachings that came to Anne in her seeking, but rather the manner of them, the way he talked to her and questioned her, from a certain height and distance that all her life she had associated with the great carved wainscot chair. She had it placed at one end of the table, and she sat there, removed by half the length of the table from her listeners, and (that first day) repeated in her own words and her own way the gist of John Cotton's Sabbath morning sermon.

The women may have noticed from this first day some slight difference between the Mistress Hutchinson they sat with in the sickroom, talking together in low tones about assurances of salvation, and this one here in the big chair, tall and unbending, yet somehow warm and close to them, speaking words that went straight into their hearts. When at the last she asked them for their questions, she might have seemed more familiar, for they freely asked what they wanted to know, and she freely shared with them the light she had on some of Cotton's darker texts. When it was time to go, they could hardly tear themselves away from her; but what held them was no desire to linger gossiping with old friends.

They went out quiet and wondering, no more inclined to chatter among themselves than when they went out of the meetinghouse on the Lord's Day. But when they separated from each other at the corner of the lane, they all said they could hardly wait until the next week.

Afterwards, though, the next day when they no longer experienced so strongly the force of her feeling for God's promise (her passion, her flowing love for Him and them), they would talk of the event with their neighbors. "What did she say?" one would wish to know. Nothing very different from what Master Cotton said in the pulpit, the answer would be. Perhaps it was only the excitement in their way of describing the meeting that led so many more women to Anne's door the next week.

The room was crowded. Goody Hawkins kept this time to the low stool in the corner. Faith and Bridget sat on a bench near the door, with Elizabeth Joan, a little apart from them, on one end, at the edge. Nearest Anne's chair, on a joint stool, sat Katherine, frowning a little, leaning somewhat toward her sister, with her long hands opening and closing, as if determined to grasp the full import of every word. The cousins sat on a short bench side by side, with gray and noncommittal faces. Sarah Hutchinson had come this time—her children were playing outside with Anne's. Then there were the three Marys—Mary Cogshall, Mary Coddington, Mary Dyer—and Elizabeth Aspinwall. At least a dozen other woman were there, crowded together on stools bunched in the center of the room. Anne knew them all. With most she had watched by sickbeds or worked in borning rooms.

In her great chair she sat as though raised above them. She lifted her chin, looked out over them with an expression of benign concern, then began to speak. Words came rather slowly at first, familiar words about the sad delusion suffered by those who think to build their spiritual estate upon no more than earthly works and sinlessness. Though familiar, the words brought ever-renewing comfort to the women, who would sometimes look covertly at one another, as though to say, "Just see how we have been misled." They could certainly not blame this misunderstanding upon Master Cotton, for he talked about the same thing twice or thrice a week, but God's plan became so simple and clear, as the words dropped from Mistress Hutchinson's lips, that each time she spoke, it seemed more wonderful. She herself may have thought so: as she went on, she would begin to speak faster, and somewhat breathlessly. Her eyes would shine, her trembling lips would shine, and her hands (long-fingered, like her sister Katherine's) would squeeze the mellow oak chair arms worn smooth long ago by the similar delicate hands of her learned and passionate father.

For an hour perhaps, she would give and they would gratefully, greedily, take. Then, as if she were quite used up, she would droop in her chair, looking down, silently—only a moment, a long moment, and then she would look up, smiling, inviting, and say to them all, "Dear sisters, was that perfectly clear?"

"Yes, clear," said one—this was at the second meeting—"but Master Cotton sometimes talks of sanctification. And Master Wilson talks of little else."

"Ah," said Anne, "that is true. It is part of the doctrine. They must fit it in, you see. But some men are so narrow, that is all they can understand. The outward signs of faith, they call it, but anyone with any wit must know how men and women may dissemble. They may be deliberate hypocrites, or they may deceive themselves. Anyone may go to church, or hand out a crust of bread to a beggar. But this is to no avail if Christ be not alive in our bosoms. Master Cotton knows this, and preaches this. And sweetly doth he preach it, yet sometimes may cloud it with talk of what can be a result but never a cause of salvation. But if you listen to him carefully, you will see: it is grace, and grace, and grace, that Master Cotton preaches. The covenant of grace, by which God freely offers Christ to man made helpless by the sin of father Adam."

"Is that perfectly clear?" Anne asked them.

"Yes, perfectly clear," the answer came.

"Oh perfectly clear," Goody Hawkins squeaked, all but clapping her hands from her corner.

Week by week, the meetings grew. Women began to bring their own stools, for there were not enough seats in the house for all who would sit at the feet of Mistress Hutchinson.

4

By this time William was building their house, on the half-acre lot granted him by the town at the corner of Sentry Lane and the high street. They were more and more pleased with the site. It was close to everything, and they had some of the best people in Boston for their neighbors. Next door lived John and Mary Cogshall, already good friends and sure to grow dearer. Catty-corner from them on the other side of the high street lived John and Margaret Winthrop, although that small fact was perhaps not one to cause much gratification. "There won't be much running back and forth between here and that house," said Katherine Marbury with a tight little smile.

Now they would be directly across the street from the town spring, a convenience to be glad of. Through the long winter of snow and ice, the location of the spring had seemed of little moment; but they had already learned how much time could be consumed carrying water. Also they would enjoy the convenient proximity of the meetinghouse and the market place. The whole Hutchinson household became impatient for the move.

Viewing the crowds that came to his house every Monday afternoon, William began to revise his building plans. He spoke to Anne of this change. "Dost thou think," he asked her, "that these meetings will continue to grow larger? Must we have a hall the size of the meetinghouse yonder?"

They stood together, with the wind from the harbor cooling their faces, looking at the new site.

Anne turned quickly to look at him.

"Dost thou wish me to put an end to the meetings, William?" she asked.

He shook his head, returning her gaze with mild, untroubled eyes. "Thou knowest," he said, "what God asks of us. We shall build a bigger hall."

He showed her where small stones marked the dimensions of the house he planned. He moved them a couple of feet farther apart. This could all be one big room, he said, as they would need no partition on the ground floor. The second story would be divided, for it would be well if the boys and girls could sleep in separate rooms. There could be windows at the front and back in every room. There would be a garret, too, for storage and sleeping.

"When can it be ready, William?" Anne asked eagerly.

By the end of summer, he thought, if all went well.

Her eyes shone. He thought she was seeing the great hall filled with women come to drink the truth from the fountain of her lips. He prayed to God it was a true vision, and he vowed within himself to build her a meeting hall as big as he could possibly afford and as speedily as Boston workmen could be made to function.

# IX

In May, William was elected a deputy to the General Court. Dudley and Winthrop were both left out of the chief places, and Dudley moved to Ipswich shortly after the election. Winthrop, however, still strode about Boston casting dark looks down his long nose. "He bides his time," said Goody Hawkins. She was not the only one to make this observation, but was perhaps the only one to shiver when she said it. She was ever afraid of Governor Winthrop.

With the new house a-building and his new position in the court, William was busier than he had ever been. Edward and Richard from this time began to take over the management of the shop. Francis, at fifteen, acted sometimes like a man and sometimes not. He had been made a freeman at the March court, along with William and Richard, so that he was able to cast a vote for his father on election day. But he gave not much sign of wanting to settle down to business. He was expected to help in the shop, but they stopped leaving him alone there after he wandered away and left the place unattended for several hours. He explained he had remembered a line of Scripture that he felt compelled to go and search out in his mother's Bible.

At the supper table William often would talk about the affairs of the commonwealth and town. He was on a committee to allocate land outside the town to residents of Boston, so that every man should have some plot to cultivate. Bridget always liked to hear about that work, but her real interest was in young John Sanford, who was also a member of the committee.

Some of the liveliest discussions concerned the Salem minister,

Roger Williams, an avowed separatist who made a habit of causing dissension in the colony and had recently been teaching that no oaths should be tendered to the unregenerate, no matter how this rule might disturb the business of the state.

"He is right, though," said Katherine Marbury. "Roger Williams is right." She made the pronouncement as though she meant he was innately and unalterably right, about everything.

Anne looked at her keenly. "I agree with you about oaths," she said. "But in that matter of cutting the cross out of the flag, I do believe he is mistaken."

She referred to a strange happening in Salem. John Endicott, the leading magistrate there and captain of the militia, had one day taken his sword and slashed the cross out of the royal colors, influenced by Williams' preaching that the symbol of the papist cross was evil wherever it might be found.

"Just as you observed when the thing first happened, Mother," Francis said, "it is not likely that either man would refuse the King's coin because it bears a cross."

"Nobody dared say that to John Endicott," William said, "but the court has decided on a punishment. He will be disabled from office for a year, and that is all."

That would be no solution to the problem, William predicted. Too many freemen agreed with Endicott and Williams. The militia would be restive now, whatever the court might do.

There was one, not at table with the family, but sitting on a stool in the chimney corner with a wooden bowl of porridge in her lap, who pricked up her ears at mention of the militia. She did not know much about it. In Elizabeth Joan's few, snatched hours with Captain Underhill, there was little time or inclination for discussion of the relation of the military to the commonwealth and town. He did tell her a funny story once about a servant who wounded himself and three others trying to handle a fowling piece he had brought to the training field. He had also told her that the Indians were causing trouble again down toward Plymouth, and he might have to leave Boston with short notice, at any time, to lead this stupid untrained militia into battle and perhaps (through their stupidity) himself be wounded or killed. He wanted her to worry about that, to cry and clutch at him, and beg him not to leave her, and as best she could, she gave him what he wanted. She would indeed be sorry to see him go: never had any man aroused in her such raging need and then satisfied it so blissfully and fully. Yet when she sat listening to Mistress Hutchinson talk about being filled with the love of Christ she felt ashamed and at odds with herself. Sometimes when the two were alone, and sometimes in meetings, Mistress Hutchinson's large heavy-lidded eyes would rest on her searchingly, and she would say, resting her hand on her bosom, "Dost thou not feel something there, Elizabeth?" Elizabeth Joan would duck her head and, turning red, admit that she did feel something.

So few people had been kind to her in her lifetime that she longed to give anyone who treated her well what he or she asked for. So it was with Captain Underhill, and so it was with Mistress Hutchinson. She knew it wasn't Christ within her, but she wanted to please her mistress. Sometimes at the meetings, it seemed to her that Mistress Hutchinson was saying you could have Christ and still do bad things. She would say something like: "If one who has Christ within begins to fear eternal punishment for any sin he may commit, that is to go aside to a covenant of works. You can no more turn Christ out than you can by your own action obtain God's grace in the first place."

Then when she would look to Elizabeth Joan and say, "Is that quite clear, my dear?" the girl could only echo Goody Hawkins and declare, "Yes, mistress, very clear." That was a lie, though, just as Goody Hawkins' protestations may have been lies. Elizabeth Joan did not understand, and in any case knew very well indeed, whatever Mistress Hutchinson might say about not taking any action to receive the grace of God, that as long as she allowed Captain Underhill to come to her, there was no hope Christ ever would.

2

John Underhill, who had long since taken his place among the saints, having received the Witness as he was taking a pipe of tobacco, knew moments of doubt himself. He encouraged his wife to attend Mistress Hutchinson's meetings, and would have her repeat over and over such teachings as this about the impossibility of ever falling from grace. Helena would gravely repeat them, word for word, in her heavy Dutch accent, but she never quite understood some of the English expressions. If she wondered why her husband seemed so importunate about this point of doctrine, she never said so. She had accepted the vagaries of his religion long before, and liked her rest at night.

Underhill was not very well versed in the subtleties of the doctrines taught in the meetinghouse at Boston. It seemed logical to him that the God who made us would understand our weaknesses, and that when He sent Christ to save us, He would save us, weaknesses and all. Yet it seemed that when anyone's sin came to light, the doctrine was not just what John Underhill had understood it to be. They even had a law in Boston making adultery punishable by death, though up to this point it had not been put into effect.

What Underhill really believed, or hoped he believed, was that—though of course God was opposed to adultery, as witness the Commandment—the sins of the elect were endlessly forgiven. Probably there was no reason to fear hell. The punishment meted out by men was a different thing altogether. And though he might not fear hell (except sometimes, under the vigorous preaching of a man like John Wilson), he did not at all care to be executed, or even to stand in the pillory with an "A" on his back, or especially to be deprived of his position in the community.

Not quite clear on his reasoning, he had somehow arrived at a commandment of his own, which ought to save him from the fury of both God and man. He would never, never touch a virgin, he would have nothing to do with women of the street, and he had no intention of ever becoming involved with a woman who had no husband of her own to father any child she might conceive. God knew Elizabeth Joan was no virgin, and presumably she had never worked at any trade, but there was every other reason for him to keep as far away from her as if she were a pox-carrying London whore. First, Mistress Hutchinson. That girl still kept without the church, but she worshiped her mistress. Captain Underhill was not precisely sure what Mistress Hutchinson's position was, but as far as he could tell she was (within the bounds of all the laws) as close with Master Cotton as two halves of a clamshell. And Master Hutchinson was quickly rising in the commonwealth hierarchy; so that to run afoul of either one of them would be dangerous for Underhill's position in either church or state. He was as careful with Elizabeth Joan as he could be, and she was a sly one (so he deemed her) who knew how to pull the wool over anybody's eyes; but he sometimes had the feeling those big bulging eyes of Anne Hutchinson's could look through the thickest curtain. If she suspected Elizabeth Joan were deceiving her, she would probably go to both her husband and John Cotton. All Boston already knew William Hutchinson would do anything his wife had a fancy for, and Underhill suspected she would have influence with John Cotton, too. After all, the minister could hardly be anything but well pleased that in repeating his Sabbath and lecture day teachings, Mistress Hutchinson was drawing the biggest crowds ever gathered in a private house in Boston.

If only that girl had not undressed in the meetinghouse! It was true what he told her: he had seen her on training day, when her face still turned with every move her husband made, and he liked what he saw. Once, just once, he had caught her eye, and though he could tell she was besotted with that boy, he recognized a flicker of response when he saw it. At that time he was thinking of Goodwife Faber, the cooper's round, red-cheeked, black-eyed wife, who would be ideal for his needs: at home in her little house alone all day, where Underhill could easily find a way to get in and out unseen, safely married so that if any seed of his should sprout, that ground was lawfully cultivated and sown already so that no one could suspect him and even the woman in question could never know for sure. But he had not made up his mind about Goodwife Faber, and decided he might wait a little longer until this new little wife was ready for a change.

Then when he heard that Jacob Hickson was drowned, he said to himself he would continue to give his attention to the cooper's wife, and truly would have done, but for those rose-tipped rounds of milk-white flesh winking coyly through the mass of golden hair. He groaned aloud when he saw that, and knew he could never rest till they were his.

Often he cursed himself. The wench was willing, but never had he found such difficulty discovering a place to copulate. The best place, after Elizabeth Joan's old house was occupied, had been a barn near a burned-down house; but then one night they came so near being caught by the owner that he had not dared go there any more. Most recently, with Master Hutchinson's house a-building, he had solved the problem as well as he supposed it ever could be solved. As captain of the militia he could make sure the watch passed down that lane at an early hour, and then calculate what time he and the girl were most likely to be spied in coming to and fro, or interrupted if some noise haply escaped them as they lay together. There was still the question of Elizabeth Joan being missed from the house. She said she did not dare try to come more than twice a week. She had to wait till the family were abed, then slip down the stairs and out the back door. She meant to say if caught that she was going outside to relieve herself, but if she had to use that excuse one time, it would never be quite so safe again.

He tried not to think of the trick nature might play upon them —of the seed that might sprout in a field where no other man sowed.

When that cold fear crept in, he turned to God for comfort. To God and Mistress Hutchinson. To God's convenant of grace as Helena conveyed it to him from the mouth of her teacher. God made him as he was, and so through His grace would protect and forgive him.

# X

On the anniversary of their arrival in Boston, the Hutchinson family had been living in the new house about a month. There had been some small delays in the building of it. For one thing, William had to go before the court about the exorbitant wages asked by his workmen. His success in this effort (the men were required to forfeit part of what he had paid them) resulted in his appointment to the new wage and price committee, and thus his public work increased along with his private business. He was gone almost every day, either somewhere about the town (perhaps to the harbor, where he and some merchant friends were preparing to build a dock), or to the mainland looking over land to be allotted there or making plans for the good-sized parcel he expected to be given at Mt. Wollaston.

His wife's business had likewise increased, for she was as busy about the work of God as he was about his own trade and his public service undertakings. He scarcely realized how much it had increased until one day he happened to come home when one of the meetings was in session. Even the spacious, open room they had planned for this purpose scarcely seemed big enough. He counted over fifty women there that day, besides the members of his own household. He stood a few moments in the open front door, seeing how they all sat rapt before his wife in her tall armchair, while she spoke to them in her high, clear voice of things that made her face glow and her deep eyes bulge with the sympathy she seemed to create between them all and God.

Dear God, how he loved her. To stand here and see her face

lit up with joy was as great a reward as he would ever ask of God, on earth or in heaven. Perhaps he would have to accept the reward on earth, for he sometimes doubted he would ever get to heaven. Anne assured him he had Christ within, and he never wanted to worry her with doubts. But he did doubt, for the simple reason that as he stood watching her face he knew it was not her work for the Lord that thrilled him but the delight she found therein. He would give up any part of his own success, or all of it, would do anything in the world to keep his wife as happy as she was at that moment.

At supper, on the day of the anniversary, Anne wanted them all to count the blessings they had received from God in the first year in this new land where He had led them. She began by speaking of the many people who came to her to say how happy in the Lord they had become through her teaching. William mentioned his own successes, but said he believed that the work of the Lord must be what they had come for.

Edward and Richard, taking their turns, murmured only that they considered their father's business in part their own, as they had come to believe that his sort of work was also their own calling. Then Francis spoke, lifting his chin, opening and closing his long-fingered hands. "It is true," he said, "that Mother's meetings are the greatest blessing we have known this year. I think they be the greatest blessing known in Boston. And yet they are not enough. God asks for more."

"What canst thou mean, Francis?" Anne asked sharply.

"Have you not realized, Mother," he asked, "that the husbands of these wives who come to you are hungry for the same food? But the door must be shut in their faces."

William nodded. "This is true," he said. "William Coddington was saying to me only a day or two ago that he could almost find it in his heart to envy his wife Mary the spiritual pleasure she finds in this house."

Anne shook her head. She felt bewildered. "But I could not teach men," she said.

"You teach us all, Mother," Faith said then. "All of us in the family, men as well as women and girls. And sometimes when there are guests at table, you speak just the way you do at your meetings, and I see the men sit up and stare at the words you speak to them."

"Well, it is one thing at my own dinner table," Anne said. "But I conceive that I would cross a rule of Scripture in setting myself up as a teacher of men."

"If there could be another meeting sometimes, to which the men might come as well as women—" William said tentatively. "For I have observed from the doorway how our hall already is filled up with the women that come every week."

Anne felt a thrill of recognition. There was something else to come, she had known that. And since this new thought came from the men in her family, and was not of her own making—Yet she could never presume to set herself up before men, to lead them. She did not know how her eyes and cheeks were blazing. "I must keep a day of meditation," she said. "It may be we shall find a way."

As if with physical effort, she turned her table talk back to the course she had planned for it. No one else had anything unexpected to say. The cousins declared themselves well satisfied with Boston. Katherine said her meeting with the teaching of Roger Williams—the full freedom of God's laws from the interference of men—was the enlightenment she had hoped for.

"Well," said Anne, "he is not the greatest minister in New England, but I know of nothing in the man that stands outside the covenant of grace."

"No, you do not, sister," said Katherine. "He is a man of clear grace, without that cloudiness that sometimes drifts across the preaching of your favorite."

"It is not cloudiness," said Anne. "It appears so to you because you have not my teacher's great learning."

"That may be," said Katherine. Though the sisters never quarreled, each was too much a Marbury to give way to the other. "But I wonder if Master Cotton would enjoy such a following, were it not that a certain housewife comes just behind him, sweeping the clouds away."

Anne said nothing to that. The meal was over anyway. She asked Francis to say a prayer before they left the table.

2

Evening prayers and duties past, Anne lay with her husband surrounded by the hangings of the bed and the silence that prevailed in the household. The bed filled one corner of the main first-floor room, as in the first house, but the cradle no longer stood at their bedside. Susannah slept upstairs.

They lay side by side, each aware that the other was awake yet unwilling to push back the curtain of silence. The whole household seemed asleep, and the house itself was too new and well made to be host to creakings and whistles of wind in the night.

William imagined Anne was going over in her mind all the implications of Francis' startling declaration, but in fact she was making up her mind to speak to William about the empty cradle. She had earlier in the day determined to wait no longer about telling him her news. There could hardly be doubt of it now, and this anniversary of their arrival in the New World seemed a good time to tell him that God would give them a child to be born here. But at bedtime she had still been unsettled by her son's strange new notion, and she needed time to put away all thoughts of what that might mean.

"Art thou awake, William?" she finally asked.

"Yes, sweetheart," he answered.

"I have something to tell thee," she said.

"And what could that be?" he wondered.

"We shall have to bring the cradle down from the garret," she said.

"Thanks be to God," he said, and turned and took her in his arms.

3

In the garret Elizabeth Joan lay alone, afraid of the dark and the silence. For darkness and silence were death, and death was waiting for her now, not far ahead. If there had been anyone to turn to, speak to lovingly in the night about this expectation, death might have changed to life. Elizabeth Joan had guessed her mistress' secret and knew how it would be with her, with a man in bed beside her, to turn to and rejoice. Never mind if it would be the fifteenth child Anne Hutchinson would bring into the world. She was strong and happy and provided with a loving husband. Anyone would thank God for another such sign of His pleasure in His chosen children.

Elizabeth Joan knew whatever grew inside her did not come from God. It did not come from love. How it did come she half believed she did not know. When she used to lie with Captain Underhill (how strange to think it was beneath this very roof), she never once took thought that anything like this might happen. In a remote part of her mind she sometimes grew aware of something like a threat; but she pushed it away with the recollection of all the years in her stepfather's house, when nothing ever happened. There were women it wasn't easy for a man to get with child. It was comfortable to think that she was one of these.

A month ago she had still not been quite sure. Yet she thought she might tell him. It would have to be the last time they came together here, she knew that, but she supposed he would have found some other way, worked out some better plan. Maybe she would wait—she had about decided to wait. Then when he arrived, impatient as always to get his breeches off, she let him woo her and take her, as he had always done, thinking, Afterwards, I will. But he spoke before ever she had made up her mind, saying, "We shall have to be done with this. It has grown too dangerous."

Someone had seen them, he said. He did not think Elizabeth Joan had been recognized, but someone might make the connection with the Hutchinson house. He must tell her anyway—though he loved her dearly, there was someone else, a woman he had loved a long time without ever speaking of his feelings. A safer woman to love, she was. He explained that point to Elizabeth Joan: she could see this new arrangement would be better for everyone.

How for her? Elizabeth Joan never asked that. Perhaps she never even thought of it, at least for many days. His leaving her was a stunning blow because it had simply not occurred to her to wonder if he would. She had never looked any farther ahead than the next time he could find a way for them to be together. She let him go without even remembering to tell him that her terms had not come down. Later, when she remembered, she knew he would have left her there on the floor anyway, with her lips still lifted to the pressure of his and her ears still ringing with his last good-by.

## 4

A few days later, on a morning of September gold and blue that recalled the way the weather was a year ago, when the Hutchinsons first came to New England, Anne sat spinning where the sun streamed in upon her through the open doorway. A house cat slept on the floor nearby; she felt as warm and content, as comfortable with herself, as that cat. In such times of her life, when she felt well pleased that she bore within her another new being, and sure that through her own abounding health it would be brought to full fruition, flesh would for a time prevail over spirit. She would be more aware than ordinarily she ever was of the warmth of the sun, the hum of her wheel like the sound of summer insects, the sense of skill in her fingers as the wool spun out thin and strong. So far she had not felt quite ready to go to God with her doubts about the men's meetings that Francis hoped to instigate.

Elizabeth Joan would have been amazed to learn that her mistress was experiencing something resembling her own feeling that what she bore within her left little room for Christ. Anne Hutchinson never questioned what Person still dwelled within her; but just for some little while, her consciousness would be dominated by this tiny, growing person made of her flesh and William's. Christ was not displaced in her; but for a few weeks He might lie low. Before the birth, He would stir to renewed activity within her, in something of the same way the baby stirred in her womb. She had sometimes imagined this was because the baby's soul was beginning to be present in its body, and that while she had responsibility for two souls as well as two bodies her keen desire to act in complete accord with Christ was necessarily sharpened.

Now, though, was the time of drowsiness, of sweet fulfillment, of dreaming in the sun. She was alone in the house. She had sent Elizabeth Joan into the back garden, to pull up what root vegetables remained and prepare them for winter storage. The older girls had gone to the market place, having heard of some kitchen utensils just in on a ship from London. Anne could watch the younger children playing along the lane, but they had no thought of her as they tossed their large yarn ball to and fro.

Then Francis came around the house from the direction of the lean-to shop, shouting to her, "Mother!" in an excited voice. He had much the same air as little William when he came running to her with a green grasshopper he had caught in the garden. She felt as little inclined to hear whatever he had come to tell as she was to take the hard-shelled leggy insect from William's hot grubby hand. But she would never turn away from her children when they sought her, any more than Christ would ever turn away from one of His.

He came looking more than ever like her father. His hair, through the summer months just past, had bleached in the sun, and now, cropped short, above his ears, tumbled about his head in straw-gold curls. Her father's hair, though it fell about his shoulders, and was in the last years more silver than gold, had sprung away from his head in that same untamed fashion. She had always known Francis had a head shaped like his grandfather's: large, broad at the top, tapering down to a slender neck. His mouth—wide, with full, curving lips, parted now with excitement—and his deep, dark, brooding eyes lit now with some inner thrill and bulging with it slightly: she had seen her father look just like that, as for instance when he would recall the chain of events that had led him to Marshalsea prison. She had never seen her own eyes and lips when she sat in her father's chair and opened the whole glorious meaning of the covenant of grace to the women ranged before her.

"Mother," Francis cried, "I have had a revelation!"

Her heart beat harder. She surmised it might be so. Almost, she feared it might be so.

"We must be very careful, Francis," she said. "A person can be mistaken about that."

"Oh, Mother, no, I am not mistaken." His mouth drooped ever so little; she had withheld something he had come for.

Still, it was true, what she said. They must be very careful. "But have you not been keeping the shop?" she asked. "When did this revelation come to you?"

"No, Mother, I have not been in the shop. Richard came back. They did not need me, and I wanted to be alone." He sat down on the doorstep, just in front of where she sat with her wheel. "Mother, please, do stop spinning and listen to me. For you see, it concerns you."

She took her foot from the treadle. In the silence she almost deemed she could hear her heart pounding. She might expect anything of this son, with the golden hair and the Marbury eyes. She recalled now how even as he lay in her womb he had been different from any other of her children. There had never been a time, with him, when she was allowed this period of physical contentment that usually came in the early part of a pregnancy. From his very conception there had been a spirit active within her.

"Tell me, Francis," she said softly.

"I walked by the sea," he said, "and I watched the waves pounding. And beat the shore, and beat the shore, and beat the shore. Such power, such force, it seemed it well might bear me down, and yet I knew I need not fear, because they had no power against the power of God."

"Jeremiah, Chapter Five," murmured Anne.

"Yes. That came to me. And then I thought, I fear not, for that power is in me. And, Mother, though I have said and believed that I knew Christ within me, I truly did not till that moment know Him fully. I felt Him there, so clear, so strong. . . ."

"Thank God," said Anne.

"And then I knew I must use that power. Just as the power of God holds back the waves of the sea; and then in the same instant my thoughts went on, just as my mother uses her strength against that false teaching of the covenant of works. But what shall I do? I cried. Where shall I use the force of Christ in me? I do think I cried it aloud, Mother, and I know an answer came. At thy Mother's side. I know not how it came, not in words, and yet as clear as though the greatest voice had shouted."

"Yes," Anne said, "I have heard those voiceless words, that wordless voice."

"And do you know what it meant, Mother? What I must do?"

"Nay, son, I know not." She was not striving to know, but waiting for him to tell her what she knew would be the truth.

"I kept on walking, and thinking, and praying to God. I prayed aloud, but could not hear my own voice for the waves pounding. And finally I knew what we must do. It is I who must teach the men who want to come and sit at your feet. I am to stand before them, while you sit beside me in your chair. And if sometimes they ask questions I cannot answer—as of course they must—then I will turn to you, and you will speak, quietly, modestly, as ever you do. But you see, it will be only at my behest. And you see, Mother, I am a man."

She smiled at him gently. No more now than when he lay unformed in her womb would he let her rest. "Yes, Francis," she said. "Thou art a man."

## 5

Elizabeth Joan was not digging in the garden. With muddy clogs in hand, she had tiptoed through the house and, finding Mistress Hutchinson in earnest talk with Francis at the front door, she flitted out the back door and, pausing to slip on the heavy wooden shoes, set out through back lots, behind the meetinghouse, and down a narrow crooked lane to the little hut where Goody Hawkins lived, with no furniture except a bench, a table board, and a cabinet full of strange roots and herbs that the women of Boston whispered about to each other whenever the subject of women's ailments arose.

"By the time they miss me, I'll be there," said Elizabeth Joan to herself. "Perhaps it may even be over."

For she had made up her mind at last what to do. Or, as she said to herself with a bitter little laugh, it might be she had had a revelation. The word came out of the very corners of this house she lived in. She had heard it just now from that strange-looking son of the mistress who stood in the doorway. So why should she not have a revelation too? Such things might come from many different sources.

She hoped Goody Hawkins would be at home alone. Her old man was not always working, but Elizabeth Joan had heard the goodwife say he had got a job cutting wood at Muddy River. There was no babe a-borning anywhere in Boston that Elizabeth Joan knew of, and so she hoped the silly old woman was at home.

Elizabeth Joan did truly think her foolish, the way she came creeping around Mistress Hutchinson's door so many days about dinnertime. Did she think the mistress really believed it was the word of God the old woman hungered after? Lately Elizabeth Joan had even begun to wonder if her mistress were not a little foolish herself. There had been times when those words about the grace of God and Christ within had sounded good to her, too, so good she would find herself believing that for people like Mistress Hutchinson nothing bad ever happened because their lives were filled with nothing but love. She didn't know, she supposed it might be true. But you couldn't just decide to have Christ within you and there He would be. She knew that very well, for she had tried. And because Mistress Hutchinson cared so much, looking down at her with those eyes full of love for her —even for her, who never did much to give anyone cause to love her—ah, just because she cared so much, and prayed, and kept asking her questions, Elizabeth Joan had finally said, with an enormous effort to make her face reflect whatever it was that glowed in Mistress Hutchinson's, "Oh yes, mistress, I do. I do feel Christ within me."

And now, unless something could be done, the mistress would find out she had lied. She seemed to say Christ kept loving you anyway, no matter what you did, and that might be so. But Mistress Hutchinson wasn't Christ, and Elizabeth Joan knew well and truly what good Christian women thought of girls like her. Even in London she had known that; she had seen them come down the alley bringing baskets of food, but when they came to a girl great with child, still living at home with her parents, they used to preach and rant and appear half a mind to take their baskets home again.

She had known ever since she started going to Captain Underhill that the mistress could not love her if she ever learned the truth. But while the affair was going on, she had simply not been able to stop herself. She won't find out, nothing will happen. Elizabeth Joan said things like that to herself, over and over, till she even believed them. Now she said to herself, with her bitter little laugh, that she was indeed a one to think about any woman being silly or foolish.

She would die. She had almost died before; but for Mistress Hutchinson, she would have died. That was what Goody Hawkins always said. And she would not have Mistress Hutchinson this time. She knew she would not, because before she let herself go far enough for anyone to guess, she would be gone. Where, she had no idea. She would be gone, and she would die. There was only one way she had been able to think of that her life could go on. One way she could go on living in her mistress' house, being loved and cared for. She might die this way too. Indeed, she knew she was more likely to die this way. But at least she wouldn't know when they all began to hate her.

The Hawkinses lived in a cottage just about like the one Elizabeth Joan had lived in with Jacob, only at the other end of the peninsula. It had a thatched roof and a dirt floor. But it did not stink. Goody Hawkins stood in the door nodding and winking and drawing her in, into something that felt like a dark cave but smelt the way an apothecary's shop might if all the bottles were emptied and the contents stirred together.

"I need help," said Elizabeth Joan. Briefly she told why, and yet without naming the man who had brought her to this need.

"I see," said Goody Hawkins, and she screwed up her face and sat for a while with her eyes closed.

Elizabeth Joan knew she did see. She would understand why Elizabeth Joan would rather die than be a disappointment to her mistress, for both women had a deep abiding need of Mistress Hutchinson. Neither believed she would continue to support them with her love and concern if she understood what was really in their minds, or knew their secret sins. Nor was it clear to them why they cared so much. Those who said Jane Hawkins hung onto Mistress Hutchinson's skirts for the sake of a few bites to eat were unfair. Jane had been close enough to starving in her lifetime to be grateful for a seat at anybody's table, but she knew she would cling to that wonderful woman through any trouble that might ever come to her. She would have thanked God for the privilege of starving with this woman she had adopted as her mistress.

Then why, she might be asking herself, with her face still screwed up and her eyes tight shut, would she for even a moment give serious heed to Elizabeth Joan's cry for help? There was a chance the girl would suffer nothing more than a temporary indisposition, and Mistress Hutchinson need never know anything had happened. But there was also a chance that something might go wrong. It was unhappily true that with all Jane's skill and good intentions, the girl might die in her hands. Then Mistress Hutchinson, with her vast experience and her keen observation, would immediately know the whole story. And whatever her attitude toward Elizabeth Joan's behavior might be (and Jane was by no means certain she would utterly condemn the girl), she would certainly blame Jane if she died.

Yet Jane knew from the instant she first saw Elizabeth Joan in her doorway (for she guessed her mission at once, before any word was even spoken) what she would do. She might have spared Elizabeth Joan those moments of anxious doubt, spared herself the pretense of searching her soul. She knew what she would find there. It was her earnest conviction that she had bartered her soul long years ago for such knowledge as this that would enable her to give Elizabeth Joan what she wanted.

"All right," Jane said at last. "I can do it, and I will." And her heart beat faster with the sense of power that ever gave her so much pleasure, though from so detestable a source.

"Will it hurt?" asked Elizabeth Joan.

"Yes," said Goody Hawkins.

## 6

"Go to the shop, and ask your father to come and talk with us," Anne said to Francis, "if he be not busy with some customer."

"Will you tell him, Mother?" Francis asked.

"Aye," she said.

There was never complete understanding between William and this son. Francis was shy with his father, knowing himself inferior to his older brothers in his grasp of the family trade. He could never pay attention to what they told him about the quality of cloth in terms of pounds, shillings, and pence, because—so Anne believed—his thoughts were on a higher plane. She had once hoped this son might have a university education and carry on the tradition of his grandfather Marbury, who had gone to prison for being too outspoken about the need for an educated ministry. She had dreamed of sending him to Cambridge, although even before they left England she had realized that Francis could never take the conformist oath required for matriculation there. Now she had begun to hope again, for there was talk of establishing a school in Massachusetts Bay that would compare to the universities of England. Francis had spoken to her of this possible opportunity, but was doubtful of securing his father's approval. "Wait," was Anne's advice. She thought William would agree if ever Francis felt himself called to the ministry. And she expected that call.

William and Francis came and sat near her in the doorway. She told William of Francis' plan, and he found it reasonable. Without any consultation between them, mother and son both refrained from saying whence the idea had come. Talk of revelations (though he accepted those which had come to Anne) made William a little uneasy.

Bridget and Faith and the cousins came home from the market place and edged past the three who sat crowding the doorway.

Almost immediately Bridget called out, "Mother, is it not almost dinnertime? And where is Elizabeth Joan?"

"In the back garden," said Anne, but she realized as she said it that more time had passed than she had been aware of and the servant girl ought to have been in the kitchen preparing the meal.

Bridget looked out the back door and saw how the vegetables had been left wilting in the sun. There was no trace of Elizabeth Joan.

"She is simply gone," Bridget said.

Then they all went and looked, and then Anne sent Faith up to the garret, but nowhere was there any trace of Elizabeth Joan.

"Well, Bridget," Anne said, "help me to prepare our meal. She is a strange girl. Some fancy may have taken her away to the harbor or the market place. It has happened before, and may again, no matter how I scold and try to teach her better ways."

Bridget and Faith did not much like the girl, Anne knew. They might have thought she took advantage of their mother's kindness, but Anne felt no necessity to explain her actions to her children. She might not have been quite sure herself why she was willing to overlook so many small transgressions to keep Elizabeth Joan in the house. She did believe though, with Goodwife Hawkins, that she had saved the girl's life. God might therefore hold her responsible for her soul.

They were sitting at the table when a small boy came hollering and pounding on the door. It was hard to tell what he wanted because he was breathing hard from running and excitement, and besides spoke a dialect they had trouble understanding. "Missus 'Utchins," he cried. And then something about Goody 'Awkins, and that "'er wants 'er." Somebody was sick, that was clear. That girl, the boy said.

Without wasting any more time trying to find out what the situation was, Anne rose and took her cloak from a peg by the door. "Give him dinner," she said to Bridget. Faith she took with her. She might have to send back for medicines or other aids, and Faith she deemed the one most able to carry out such a mission.

They walked very fast, too fast for talking. Faith had at first wanted to conjecture about what they might find, but Anne had not answered her. She thought she knew. It was impossible that she should not have guessed Elizabeth Joan's condition, just as Elizabeth Joan had guessed hers. And it was entirely predictable that she would make a visit to Goodwife Hawkins, as other girls in like distress had done before her. Anne scolded herself for waiting in the hope Elizabeth Joan would come to her.

She lay on Jane Hawkins' bed, as still and white as on that other occasion when Anne had been called to save her. There was blood, too much blood. Anne feared at first that life had all flowed out in that red stream, but soon was satisfied that the heart was still beating.

"What have you done, Jane?" she asked.

"What you see, mistress," the old woman answered.

They said no more, then or ever, of what had happened here. Neither did Elizabeth Joan ever speak of it, when after many weeks of her mistress' nursing, she grew able to take up the life she had made up her mind to lay down.

Anne stayed with her in Jane Hawkins' house until she thought the girl fit to be moved, and then had her carried home, where she lay on a bed made up for her close to the chimney in the second-story room. Even through fever and delirium, she never spoke the name of the man who had brought her to this pass, and Anne never asked it.

During the time Elizabeth Joan lay ill, Goodwife Hawkins never came to the house, except to creep into meetings after they had begun, sit hunched in the corner until Anne had ceased speaking, and then creep away again while most of the women stayed, asking more questions, crowding as close to their teacher as they could come, as though it were necessary to touch her in order to take her answers into their very being.

Finally, when Elizabeth Joan was well enough to sit wrapped in a rug before the small autumn fire, Anne sent for Jane Hawkins. The old midwife came in at the back door, turning her head every which way like a bird who fears a cat lurks in the shrubbery.

"Come here, Jane, and sit by the fire," Anne said.

The three were alone. Anne had sent everyone else out of the house or upstairs, to work at some task she assigned them. Elizabeth Joan sat erect, wrapped in her rug, and stared into the fire. What she saw there she did not say, but always now it brought to her mind what preachers preached about the flames of hell.

Jane Hawkins looked everywhere rather than into the eyes of this woman who for reasons Jane never even tried to understand seemed to hold all hope of heaven in her hands.

"Art thou afraid, Jane?" Anne asked softly.

Then the old woman began to cry, sobbing and snuffling and hunching up her crooked shoulders, covering her face in her brown clawlike hands, digging her sharp chin into her bony chest.

"Why dost thou weep?" Another soft question came, and still Goody Hawkins, racked in sobs, made no answer.

"Do you not see, mistress," said Elizabeth Joan, and she began weeping too, so that she must make a great effort and try to speak again. "Do you not see," she repeated, tears streaming down her face, "that we are afraid because we belong to the devil?"

"No," said Anne, speaking now somewhat sharply, "for this is not the reason. If that be true, you did not learn it in these few minutes with me today. And how is it you have ever ceased weeping, once you learned that dreadful news?"

Both women hushed and turned their eyes on Anne's face, and this woman each one called her mistress rose and stood sternly before them.

"Now answer me, Jane," she said. "And take good thought of what I say. Why hast thou wept?"

"Oh, mistress," then said the little midwife, lifting her head to Anne like a beggar in supplication. "I fear it be true I am the devil's own, but I weep because I never wanted you to find it out."

"Ah," said Anne calmly, "and that's the truth of it."

And Elizabeth Joan said, "Yes, mistress, that is the truth."

"Then you do not see," said Anne, "you two silly women? You are not, you need not be, afraid of hell. God, who loves you and sent Christ to save you, would have you come to Him through love, not fear."

"But we have sinned," said Elizabeth Joan.

"Of course you have sinned," said Anne. "But you weep for your transgressions, because you love your Saviour."

"But it is like Goody Hawkins said, mistress," protested Elizabeth Joan. "We cried because we disappointed you."

"But it is out of love, you see. You may think you weep for love of me, because Christ is not yet clear to you. But it is love and not hate, and therefore you cannot belong to the devil." Anne paused now and they saw how she stood before them with lifted chin and blazing eyes, as though she herself had triumphed over Antichrist.

"Now is that clear?" she said, as she might have done at any meeting, for what she had just explained to them was the doctrine she ever taught, the covenant of grace, in terms of common understanding.

"Yes, mistress, very clear," said Goodwife Hawkins.

Elizabeth Joan nodded her head, but inside herself was saying, "Even now, when I have confessed to her, she does not see how wicked and unworthy I am."

## 7

On a brisk, sunny day at the end of September, about an hour past dinnertime, John Winthrop stood looking out the window of his upstairs bedchamber. He would have liked to be outdoors on such an afternoon, looking over new houses a-building in Boston or visiting his farm lands across the bay. But there was a committee meeting—there was always some duty of government to keep Winthrop from impromptu pleasures—and he was awaiting the appointed time for that.

Unavoidably, his eyes settled on the house recently completed across the high street. It was a well-built clapboarded house, not as large as his own but substantial, exactly the sort of structure he liked to see rising in Boston. William Hutchinson, indeed, was the sort of man he liked to see prospering in Boston. Yet he could never look across at that house without some small prick of misgiving. That woman—something about her had from his first sight of her stirred up some apprehension that she would in the long run do Boston no good. Many would disagree with him, he knew. It had even been necessary for him to forbid his own wife to go to Mistress Hutchinson's meetings, for although it was true he heard nothing but praise for them, he could not believe it was in accord with Scripture for so many women of all ages to leave their proper work to go and be taught by another woman. He told Margaret he could not allow her so to waste her time. If she thought she needed more light on Master Cotton's sermons—which was ostensibly what these women went for—he would give it himself or, if that did not satisfy her, arrange a conference with Master Cotton.

It was a shame, in Winthrop's view, that so many men seemed unable to control their wives. If they would only perform this one clear Christian duty, all these silly women would be at home where they belonged. Or if even one man—William Hutchinson—would keep his wife in her place, there might be no problem at all. This characteristic of Hutchinson's he had been aware of already; it was the only thing that ever made him doubt the man's ability as a leader in the colony or church.

His eyes returned from wandering over the more distant view. He became aware that a goodly number of persons, both men and women, were arriving at the Hutchinson house. And that was strange. He could conceive of no occasion at this hour on this day of the week that could draw so many to that door.

He went downstairs to find Margaret. "Has something happened across the street?" he asked her.

"No—where?" she asked.

"I mean there"—he pointed—"where that woman keeps her meetings."

"Oh," she said, "they are having a new meeting today—one for men as well as women, so I've heard."

It would seem to him later that this was the precise moment at which he ceased to have doubts and knew for sure she was a danger to the colony. "A meeting for men!" he exclaimed angrily. "And she teaching?"

"Oh no," said Margaret quickly, wanting to soothe him. "No, dear, do not fear that such a thing could happen in Boston. They say one of the sons will teach."

"Hmph!" said John Winthrop.

"I could wish," Margaret dared to say then, "that you had not such a strong dislike for Mistress Hutchinson."

"And I," he said sternly, "could wish you might never speak her name to me again."

"No, John," she murmured, but he never seemed to know she spoke. The woman was a troublemaker, he said. He had feared this since the first word he heard of her, when Brother Dudley came to bring the minister's complaint against her opinions expressed on the ship. There ought to be a way, and when he was governor again he would do everything in his power to provide a way, to keep people of such doubtful and dangerous opinions from settling in the colony. He held a vision in his heart of a glorious city of God on earth—a city in some great metaphorical sense, for he meant something much more than that, perhaps an entire nation. He considered that this colony was a city upon a hill, the eyes of all people upon it; and he wished men to say of all colonies yet to be founded: "The Lord make it like that of New England." This model colony would be a place where the order of God's laws prevailed forever—where even beyond the law God's love prevailed, and citizens so loved their fellow beings that no poor man would ever go in need, no sick man lie untended, no orphan remain unwanted and uncared for.

He did not say all those words to Margaret that day. She had heard them before, and she shared his heart-lifting vision. But in this perfect community of God and His children, this marvelous city upon a hill, was a woman never to be allowed to teach even in her own home the meaning of the word of God as she had been led to understand it?

That question came to her, and with unwonted thoughtlessness or daring, she asked it.

And once more he was compelled to speak to her in tones he misliked using. "Margaret, thou must never in my hearing even allude to that vile woman. Of course a woman may teach, for so it is written. But I tell thee this woman is a troublemaker. There is something fierce and terrible in her eyes—a blaze of dark fire capable of turning to ashes even the truth of God."

Watching her husband's face, Margaret Winthrop had the conviction, for one fleeting, incredible moment, that an unfamiliar flicker of the muscles around his mouth betokened fear.

# XI

On a morning in October, the women of Anne's household were gathered in the hall. Only Katherine was absent, having gone to the shoemaker's on some errand she did not explain. Anne was at her spinning wheel, and the women and girls of the family were all sewing or knitting or mending. William and Susannah were playing with a pumpkin shell, dropping into it small blocks of wood, smooth pebbles, and seashells brought home from the shore, then pouring them out again. Elizabeth Joan was picking the worms out of dried peas to be boiled for supper porridge.

The three Marys also were present, having separately and with different excuses, come in for short visits. The three were not close friends, and indeed Mary Dyer with her inward-looking eye seemed no close friend of anyone's; yet it often happened that the three appeared together at Mistress Hutchinson's house. William, if he chanced to come in and find them there, would hum the tune of an old ballad he knew about Queen Mary of Scotland's three waiting women, all like herself named Mary. Anne would frown slightly; though a profane song, of no religious significance and thus perhaps harmless as it might be hummed on a weekday at home, it suggested a sort of papist sympathy that repelled her. At one time in her desperate attempts to discover the pure way of God, she had not even been able to see why papists, who worshiped the same God as she, might not be as truly Christian. But she thanked God He had sent her light on that subject.

This day William did not come in while the company were gathered. He had goods from London due on a ship standing outside Boston harbor, and had gone to find out when they might be unloaded. The house was occupied entirely by womenfolk, with the one exception of little William on the floor with his pumpkin shell, and as often happened an unscheduled gathering had become a session of teacher and pupils concerning themselves with the questions that ever sprang from the teaching of Master Cotton and his self-declared disciple.

The children all knew better than to come bursting into the house on either of the regular meeting days. But this was not an announced meeting, and so young Samuel, thoughtless and boisterous as he was always inclined to be, did come bursting in, calling "Mother, Mother! I have just seen the passengers that have come on the *Abigail.*"

Some mild punishment would have to be devised for this disrespectful interruption. Meanwhile, it was clear the entire company wanted to hear what Samuel had to tell.

He stood among them talking excitedly. "The old pastor's back, for one," he said, "that one that left Boston a long time ago, right after we first came from England."

The women smiled. Pastor Wilson had been gone less than a year, and they felt they had scarcely had time to miss him. The news came unexpectedly to Anne, with a heavy dread that moved into her bosom at the thought of the change that must come in the Boston pulpit now.

"There's another preacher too," Samuel went on. "I didn't hear his name."

The women appeared disappointed at that, but he went on, hardly pausing for breath, "and he was with the finest gentleman that ever was before in Boston."

The expressions of his hearers livened greatly at that, and Anne said, "How can you say that, Samuel?"

"Well, because he's dressed fine. Not lace and big sleeves and all that. But big handsome boots and the best cloth you ever did see. Fine linen and silk and wool." That was the mercer's son speaking; unlike his brother Francis, he knew and cared about quality already.

"But who is he, Samuel?" That was one of the cousins (Frances); those two were ever interested in hearing of fine-looking men.

"I don't know his name, but they say his father is somebody with a title in the King's court. They say he knows the King and talks to him the same as any duke or earl might do. And I know he is handsome, for I heard a girl say so. And young—he looks no older than Brother Edward does, to me."

"But what is he doing in Boston?" Bridget asked.

"That I don't know," Samuel said. "But Father may, when he comes home, for I saw the two shake hands."

When William came in to dinner, he too was talking of the young man, who was Henry Vane, son of the comptroller of the King's household and personally acquainted with King Charles, who it was said had prevailed upon the father to let the son come to New England. He was a fine young man, William said, as friendly with all the men at the harbor as if he'd never even seen a king. He had come with a preacher named Hugh Peter. Those two and John Winthrop, Jr., had been commissioned to look after the interests of Lords Say and Brook in the settlement of the Connecticut Valley, but several of the men said, and William agreed, that it would be a great thing for Boston if they could keep young Vane here and give him some office in the government.

"I wonder, though," said Anne, "if he be bound up with all the ordinances of the Church of England."

"They say not," said William. "They say that is why he has come."

2

Throughout Boston, at least in the houses of the well-to-do, there was nothing worth talking of but Henry Vane. The poorer sort, it might be, had failed to hear of him, or cared not if they had. Henry Vane had not shaken their hands, or turned upon their faces that charming glance in which wisdom and youthful innocence seemed equally shown forth. Neither did they perceive (for of course it was not their business to perceive) what a connection at court might do for the prosperity and security of Boston and the Massachusetts Bay.

Young Henry (twenty-two years old when he came) had little notion of the impression he was making on Boston. He was very much more taken up with the impressions Boston made on him. When he first saw the place, from the ship, he was like many another sensitive person on his or her first view of that dismal gray port village. He had seen the greatest capitals of Europe and—though he had talked to people returned from New Boston, and formed some reasonable conception of its character and appearance—found the contrast something of a shock to his spirit. Like others, though, he quickly reconciled himself to the appearance; it was not the outward seeming of the place upon which his hopes rested. He had heard, here and there, among such nonconformists as it was his fortune to meet, about the true, half-secret purpose of the company known as Massachusetts Bay. It was no commercial venture, or so he had come to believe. The company must achieve financial success, must become self-sufficient, but only in order to work toward its real goal, the building of that city upon a hill which John Winthrop had preached of on board the *Arbella.* Vane had seen copies of that sermon in England. If the men of Massachusetts could make such a dream come true, there was no place he would ever want to live but here—here under God's law, where love of fellow men was everyone's deepest concern, so that no one need ever go hungry or lie untended on a bed of pain.

At the age of fifteen, after a period when sin and death had invaded his consciousness, a stream of grace had come washing all his fears and griefs away. Since that age he had read a great deal, and traveled, but whatever he undertook was always in the hope of coming closer to an understanding of the truest, simplest way of living by God's plan. In the Low Countries he had learned so much about New England ideals that he began to dream he might one day experience them for himself. To please his father, he tried to be a diplomat. He went to Vienna in the King's service, and many saw in him the promise of a great career at court. But all the time he was slipping farther and farther away from the forms of worship and the style of life to which he seemed destined, until one night when he refused to drink a toast at dinner, and his father roared out at him: "'Dost thou think because thou art virtuous, there shall be no more cakes and ale?'"

Henry knew where those words came from, even though he

never went to plays any more, and he felt the implied comparison unjust. Cakes and ale they might all have a-plenty, so long as he was allowed to go on seeking one place in the world where people lived by choice according to the laws of God. So he told his father. So he even dared say to Archbishop Laud. But they both opposed his coming, until King Charles put in a word on his behalf.

Then this project for a new settlement was discovered and it served as a good pretext for making the trip. Henry was granted a license to stay three years, but in his secret heart he thought a way might be found to extend those years indefinitely; and if Boston and Massachusetts Bay proved to be all he hoped for, he was not very sure he cared about helping settle a new place.

One thing had disturbed him, though, even on shipboard. That was the preaching of John Wilson, who they said was regular pastor in the church at Boston. Henry knew John Cotton's reputation and had looked forward to hearing him preach; but he had never heard of Wilson at all, until he found the man a fellow passenger and himself forced to listen to the dark priest's thundering threats of impending doom. Those depressing sermons, coupled with his first look at the town of Boston, were enough to stir up some doubts in his mind.

It was likewise true that, although generally so well received, young Vane on his part encountered among the passengers some criticism of himself—not of his behavior or opinions, as did happen with some others, but of his appearance. Although he considered his manner of dress quite modest, several had taken exception to a silver-embroidered doublet he sometimes wore and sundry articles of velvet and lace. And even more offensive than his apparel, it seemed, was the length of his hair. He had heard that nonconformists here were cutting their hair extremely short, but he kept his as he had always worn it, parted in the middle and falling to his shoulders in thick curls. When he arrived in Boston, he observed that most men were wearing their hair shorter than the fashion was at court, but not so short as he had been led to believe. Thinking that there might be some vanity in his preference for his long chestnut tresses, he made up his mind to visit a barber within the first few days of his arrival.

The barber's name was Dinely, and he liked to talk. As soon

as the desirable length for Henry's hair was established (not too short, they agreed, but not quite touching his shoulders), Dinely began to snip and chatter. Since the young gentleman, as he had heard, was religious, what did he think of the preachers of Boston, Dinely wanted to know.

Vane answered cautiously. By this time he had heard Cotton preach on lecture day, and he could hardly keep from making comparisons between the teacher and the pastor; yet he spoke moderately, as became a newcomer who had not even been in Boston long enough to attend a Lord's Day service.

"You come with me," said the barber, "and I'll bring you to a woman that preaches better Gospel than any of your blackcoats that have been at the Ninniversity."

"But is she of the church?" asked Henry.

"Sits on the front seat," said the barber. "She come here on account of Master Cotton, so they say, but she takes what he says and puts it in words a man like me can understand. And she'll take you farther than that sometimes when the spirit moves her. And for my part, I had rather hear such a one that speaks from the mere motion of the spirit, without any study at all, than any of your learned scholars, although they may be fuller of Scripture."

Although he respected theological learning, Henry Vane was something of the barber's mind. Through many hours of solitary meditation, he had come to believe that the truth of God could be conveyed directly to the meanest mind. He thought he might like to see this woman the barber admired so much, and he asked John Cotton if he knew of her. It had fallen out that Henry and the Reverend Peter had been invited to spend a few days in Cotton's house, and the three men sat together in Cotton's study, under the benignant pictured eye of Dr. Sibbes.

"I do know the gentlewoman," Cotton said. "And though I do not attend the meetings, nor would it be suitable for me to do so, I have talked with her often enough, and heard such good of her, that I daresay at least that it would do no harm to go."

"But what sort of person is she?" Vane pressed.

"Well, as to that—a woman. Not learned of course, though her father held learning in such high regard he went to prison in defense of it, and therefore I do think she may have gained some better understanding of logic and some further knowledge than most women have. For her sex she is keen of comprehension and doth express herself very well. And I think she hath brought a good many people to see that they cannot hope for any saving union with Christ merely by doing good works and refraining from evil. Many have come to me for confirmation of what she says, and I have found it ever true and helpful."

It seemed to Vane that for all Cotton said he had some reservation about this Mistress Hutchinson and her meetings. But he pressed no further. He would go with the barber and form his own opinion.

Hugh Peter, though he could know nothing of her, said that from what he had heard her meetings had grown so large and taken on such a character that Mistress Hutchinson might be little better than a woman preacher. "Even such," he said, "as the woman of Ely."

"Oh no, brother, you are mistaken about that," Cotton said.

And they talked no more of Mistress Hutchinson, but at the time of the next appointed meeting for both sexes, Henry went to William Dinely and said that he was ready to accept his offer.

3

A slender, dark-eyed boy with wheat-gold hair stood at one end of the large barn-like room that was crowded with men and women on backless stools and benches. Near him, facing the crowd, sat a woman in a heavy, high-backed armchair. Their smoldering, somewhat bulging eyes, high-bridged noses, and prominent cheekbones proclaimed them mother and son, as Henry knew already they were, from what the barber had told him.

"He will give us the gist of Master Cotton's sermon," Dinely said, "and then there will be questions from the congregation." Henry took note of how unconsciously the man compared this meeting in a private house to a gathering of the church. "He may answer some of the questions," Dinely went on, "but it is his mother people come to hear, and he will turn to her more and more. You will get a good idea of what her teaching is, even though the boy fills the place of teacher at these mixed meetings."

Since Henry had carefully listened to the sermon, he could recognize the effectiveness of Francis Hutchinson's summary. The son had been well taught by his mother, so the barber said. He had, besides, a sweet boyish voice with only a trace of manly huskiness, and an ingenuous manner of delivery, involving pauses in which he looked at his audience with widened eyes, as though to say, "Is this the way it seemed to you? Have I not got it right?"

At the end of Francis' talk, a man with one of the more desirable seats in the room—rather a large, florid, handsome man in a beaver hat—rose to ask a question. "It seems to me," he said, "that Pastor Wilson has told us we must first have faith and works." (Vane looked searchingly at the man, sure he had been introduced to him but unable to remember his name.) "Yet can you say our consciousness of Christ is our first and sufficient evidence of salvation?" It seemed to Vane that the man was not really asking for clarification, but that he rather wished to point up a difference between the two ministers.

The boy smiled sweetly. "So I understand our teacher, Master Coddington," he said, then hesitantly looked toward his mother.

The woman in the chair then leaned forward a little, lifted her chin, and looked out over the assembly. This question more visibly stirred her than any previous one had done, and it was clear she would speak, and at some length. When she had spoken before, her words came low and somewhat terse. But now her voice was high and clear, less musical than her son's, yet pleasing in its vigor of expression.

"I speak when I can in the words of our teacher," said Mistress Hutchinson, "for he brings so plain before us these matters that may sometimes seem confusing, even to some of the ministers of our churches."

Vane detected no undercurrent of accusation but noticed a number of people look at each other and nod knowingly.

"Faith comes to us not through our seeking but through God's grace, out of our union with Christ. Union comes first; then are we filled with faith, as a vessel is filled with oil. We need do nothing more, nay *can* do nothing more than the empty vessel can do. To say that we must have faith—even to say that merely by taking thought we *can* have faith—is to give us power beyond the power of God. We can do nothing till we have Christ within us, except to wait with loving patience till He come."

She sat silent and very still a few moments. She might have been waiting for more questions; but no one spoke—it was as if her silence commanded theirs. Then she began to speak again.

"I shall tell you how it seems to me. You have heard how Christ is likened to a bridegroom. We seem to me all like a poor virgin, and she with her whole heart desireth a great and handsome man who sometimes rides along the road before her hovel. Something inside her heart gives her hope that one day he will look down and see her at her window, will knock on her door, and when she answers will dismount and set her on his horse and ride away with her to a glittering palace. Yet there is nothing she can do but wait and hope, just as we, who know that all our hope is in the grace of God, may wait for Christ."

Vane saw how her eyes shone and the bright color came to her forehead and cheeks, as though she herself had long waited and now heard the knock on the door. He wanted very badly to ask a question, to have her notice him. He wanted to tell her that he understood what she meant by longing for the bridegroom. From his boyhood he had been longing thus, for something nameless, and he wanted her to know she had brought him closer than he had ever felt to an understanding of what it was he longed for. But he was seized by a wholly unaccustomed timidity. He opened his mouth, then closed it again, and let the occasion pass.

While he still wondered if he dared to speak, the meeting had begun to break up. Many of the people were pushing toward Mistress Hutchinson's chair. William Dinely asked Henry if he wanted to go and speak to her; and at first he thought that he would, if only he could say a few words, apart from the rest and unheard, and then he was afraid if he tried he would burst into tears. He shook his head.

A few days later, Henry met Mistress Hutchinson at a dinner party given by William Coddington. He was surprised to see she was with child, as her condition had not been apparent to him when she sat in her armchair at home. Neither was she as beautiful or perhaps as young as he had believed, but rather was modest-appearing and gravely smiling (like the best of the other gentlewomen), not strikingly different from them, though taller and of a more graceful carriage than most. She spoke to him, and her voice was low and deferential.

She said she had seen Henry at her house and was pleased to know him now. He said he would like to come again. Their eyes met, and he knew that what he had seen before was the true essence of this marvelous woman. It was her soul, and it matched his soul.

She saw that, too, and on the days of mixed meetings she looked for him, not anxiously, for she had no doubt at all that he would come. She had realized for some time that there was more involved in these meetings than she could have foretold when she agreed to let Mary Coddington bring some women to her house to talk about sermons—more than she had yet seen, and of a nature she had still to determine. And she knew now that whatever was to happen, that pink-cheeked boy would play some considerable part.

But it was several weeks before he came again, and when he did he hurried away without daring to go and speak to her. He had seen some part of himself in Anne Hutchinson's eyes, and was not yet ready to confront any fuller self than he knew already. Meanwhile, as he was waiting to be ready, the leading men of Boston drew him into their endeavors in a way that seemed to confirm what he had hoped concerning the opportunities in Boston for a young man of his abilities. Thus he was grateful, but not altogether surprised, when after only two months in the colony, he was informed of a decision requiring whoever wished to sue anyone else to first submit his case to Henry Vane and two of the elders.

As he learned more of the colony, he saw that it was by no means a community to which all nations might look as a model of Christian harmony. Trouble appeared on every hand, and as if in evidence one saw the militia exercising beneath a strange flag that bore no cross upon it. Vane was not displeased at the sight, until he learned what dissension it was causing and then was told of further unreasonable actions and demands by Roger Williams, that same minister who had first prevailed upon Endicott to slash the flag. Williams went to unbelievable extremes, he was told, even refusing communion with his own wife because she attended a church not separated from the Church of England. More threatening to the very foundation of the colony was his strange notion that the King, not having covenanted with the Indians, had no true title to the lands of New England. In the privy circle to which Vane now had access, the consensus was that for the sake of internal peace, the Salem minister would have to be banished. Such extreme opinions as Williams held were dangerous, Vane could see that, and yet no one seemed to doubt that he was a true Christian. Vane believed harmony among the people was the most essential requisite for a stable government—but must it be achieved by banishing Christian men of good will?

Many troubles were caused, and crimes committed, by both Christian and non-Christian. Vane had been led to think the colony was made up entirely of professing Christians, but in Boston more than half the population remained outside the church. It was not clear to Vane how many had asked admittance and been denied.

More than one of the magistrates confided to him that many of the troublemakers were to be found among those who kept outside, but they believed a pure church was more pleasing in the eyes of God than a more peaceful community that was built upon compromise and hypocrisy. Although it might not be possible in every case to identify the elect, they believed they had to come as close to purity as human frailty would allow.

Much unrest in Boston was due to a different kind of problem. Food was scarce, and prices were high. Winthrop told Vane privately he sometimes feared the colony would not support the population unless workmen and tradesmen could be persuaded to adopt a more Christian attitude. He related an incident that had occurred in the country somewhere nearby. A farmer, who like some others had failed to prosper, had paid his servant with a cow. At last he said he could pay him no more; his money was gone. "You can pay me another cow," said the servant. "But what shall I do," said the farmer, "when all my cattle are gone?" "Why then," said the servant, "you shall serve me, and thus may have your cattle back again." Vane smiled at that story, but

Winthrop did not. The implications were too serious for him to see any humor in it.

Another time, Henry talked about this problem of food and prices with William Hutchinson, who was on a committee to draft a new system of wage and price controls. Although he had met William before then, on social occasions, he had never sat and talked with him. He liked the man. There was nothing about him to suggest that exciting force one felt in the presence of his wife, but he was a thoughtful, friendly person. He was a merchant, earnestly trying to see a way to combine the interests of himself and his merchant friends with what he called the public weal. He discussed with Henry the famous sermon Winthrop had delivered on board the *Arbella.*

"He begins," William told Henry, "by saying that God hath so disposed the condition of mankind that some must be rich, some poor. And near the end he says we must abridge ourselves of our superfluities, for the supply of others' necessities. It seems to me that in this wise God's disposition will be thwarted and we shall all be poor."

Unlike Winthrop, he was able to smile, but clearly he was worried. He did not want anyone to go hungry, but he had been a prosperous merchant for many years and had not come to the New World to embrace some vow of poverty.

Vane saw how far from reality were those ideals he had so much admired. The colony was still new, and the leaders were hopeful and earnest. The trouble might lie partly with the leaders, though. Here and there, wherever he went throughout the colony, he heard this criticism, particularly of the two top men. Winthrop and Dudley, still the true rulers, were often at odds, especially on matters concerning the quality of justice. People said it was hard to know what to expect of government in the colony of Massachusetts Bay.

Vane was disappointed. All this dissension in both church and state was far from what he had been led to expect in New England. He felt depressed, uncertain. These men of government seemed to expect something of him; he knew not what.

And so it was in some distress of both mind and spirit that he went again to the house of Anne Hutchinson. Having been so much involved with affairs of state, he had once more remained away from her for some weeks. Then on a day of deep snow and bitter cold, having earlier decided he would spend the day reading by Cotton's fireside, he suddenly found himself throwing on his fur-lined cloak and departing without a word to anyone. Without even any clear word to himself in his thoughts, he knew where he was going.

Almost as many were present as on that sunny day in autumn when first he had shivered at the sound of her pure voice that rang like thin-beaten bells. Again the boy Francis stood before the group, and again, as questions from the floor began, the mother spoke and the boy said less and less until in the end he was standing silent by her side. As deeply moved as he had been before, Henry sat for a while uncertain as to whether he would go or stay. While others were still stirring about in talk with one another or in asking further questions of the woman in the chair, Francis came and spoke low in his ear: "My mother would be glad if you would stay for supper."

It was then he went to her; and the members of the household milled about them as they sat, the woman in her great chair, the young man on a stool at her feet. The movements and noises might have been those of wind-blown leaves in a forest or waves breaking on some rock shore. They sat as though alone among the winds and breakers.

"Why have you come to me?" she said.

"God sent me," he said.

4

After his talk with Anne Hutchinson, Henry knew what to do. It was hard to say why he should see his way so much clearer, because they had not even touched on politics.

"Dare to recognize what is in you," was what Anne had said. "Through Christ you have reached union with the Holy Spirit. If you listen to that spirit, if you heed that inner voice, you will know then what you have to do. Now you may understand your true calling, and go where it leads you. Now in trusting Christ you trust yourself."

So it happened that when the magistrates spoke to him again about Roger Williams, he answered them, "Yes, I should banish him."

Most likely they would have done so anyway. The move

seemed clearly necessary to the peace and unity of the colony, for it was threatened both at home and abroad by Williams' strange actions and pronouncements. But when they called the minister before the court, and Vane had the opportunity to meet and talk with him, he knew there was a power for good in that man. Still, he might use it elsewhere to greater advantage. The man himself would probably not be hurt by the banishment. Could it be possible it was the colony that would be hurt? The new thought just went through Vane's head that honest, well-founded dissent might be incorporated into the fabric of a colony without destroying unity and indeed perhaps to strengthen it. He was not sure he would so easily condone banishment again.

Yet perhaps the action was right for the times. Convinced Roger Williams had a place to go and would not suffer, Henry determined not to dwell upon this happening. Right or wrong, it did not solve the problems of Massachusetts Bay.

Devoting his attention to that undeniable if negative fact, Henry asked himself whether there might be any one action that could solve them all. He reckoned not, and yet (it suddenly came to him) there was one thing awry that almost certainly affected everything connected with the government of the colony. That was the dissension within the government itself, and at the highest level. He jumped in excitement from his seat by Cotton's fireplace. Winthrop and Dudley had to be publicly reconciled, and he had to begin at once doing something to achieve that reconciliation. It would have both practical and symbolic value. It might even change the whole course of the colony.

Hugh Peter, who like Henry had been persuaded to stay in the Bay Colony and leave the affairs of Connecticut to young Winthrop, was living with Cotton at this time, and the ministers as often happened were in the study. Henry always supposed they were deep in some theological discussion, and he rarely disturbed them. Now he could not restrain himself, but raced up the stairs and knocked on the closed door. Actually the two men were talking about Peter's new scheme to establish a fishing industry for New England, something to make the colony less dependent on the mother country.

Peter said something about the plan when Henry came in, but

the young man brushed it aside. He thought it a good idea, he had said so before, but it would be a long time coming to fruition. He himself had an idea that might bring almost immediate results.

The ministers might have smiled inwardly at the boyishness evident in Henry's flushed face and sparkling eyes, but they listened to his proposal and found it worth consideration.

Thus it happened that for two days in January, at the request of Hugh Peter and Henry Vane, Dudley and Winthrop came together in the meetinghouse at Boston. Protesting nothing but brotherly love for one another, they yet agreed to discuss their differences in the presence of the governor and deputy governor and three leading ministers—Cotton, Wilson, and Thomas Hooker of Newtown—with Henry Vane presiding.

The chief difference, as Vane had everywhere been told, was in the matter of leniency. Winthrop thought that people in a new country, facing unaccustomed hardships, and unfamiliar with the laws, might be forgiven some transgressions. Dudley felt that just because the colony was new and unsettled, every man should be held strictly accountable for every act.

Henry, inclined to agree with Winthrop, was surprised when the ministers decided in favor of Dudley's policy: "that strict discipline was more needful in plantations than in a settled state, as tending to the honor and safety of the Gospel." But he said nothing to indicate any private opinion of his own; for indeed that was one of the conclusions of the ministers—that once a matter was settled in the proper body, no one should privately or publicly complain.

The two magistrates expressed their thanks to Henry Vane, and it was strange to see these middle-aged men, weathered by long winters in New England and seasoned with success in many affairs of state as well as their private business, bow before this smooth-faced boy.

"I see where I have failed," said Winthrop solemnly to Vane, "and shall take care not to be so remiss in the future. Whenever I see any questionable act or hear of opinions that threaten the peace of the colony, I shall act with all the strictness my authority allows."

There was little reason to suppose that any threat lay veiled in that amiable expression of defeat. Certainly Henry Vane saw none, as in the ensuing days he heard from every side, from ministers and magistrates and common citizens, the words "well done."

# XII

On March 25, the first day of the year 1636, Anne Hutchinson offered prayers of thanks to God for the end of a difficult time in her life and the promise of new beginnings.

This had been another long, hard winter in New England; neither had her pregnancy been easy. For several weeks she had been forced to give up her meetings, and on some few cold and bitter Sabbath Days had not even felt able to walk the short way to the meetinghouse. In those bad times, hope itself sometimes seemed frozen in her bosom, and she wondered if spring would ever come again. Though sure of Christ within her and satisfied that she had turned many good people away from their misguided walks in the covenant of works, she had even feared she might return to a period like that years ago in Old England, when doubt and black depression seized her soul.

That was in the time when John Cotton was ill and like to die of a tertian ague, which had taken away his wife Elizabeth already. The Earl of Lincoln, that faithful Christian who helped support the Massachusetts Bay Company, took Cotton home with him, and it was nearly two years before he returned to old Boston. In those days Anne was still little more than a novice in the mystery of grace; she felt directionless and desolate without this man whom she had learned to look to as her guide.

And then, even while she mourned the absence of her teacher, two of her children died, a month apart. In spite of all her skill and love she lost them—her first-born daughter, her first Susannah, age fourteen and a comely young woman already, and then eight-year-old Elizabeth, her wise and gentle middle child.

When Susannah died, she knew a temptation to lay herself down and never arise, but Elizabeth was growing worse day by day and baby Katherine still depended on her mother's milk for nourishment. Anne lived on; she conceived again.

But doubt chilled her soul and darkened her life. She kept asking herself where she had failed, that God took away her children. Or perhaps the punishment was directed at the children themselves, for sins they never knew they committed. It seemed to her that if she could hear John Cotton preach the covenant of grace once more, she could be freed from these terrible doubts. But he was gone. Not far away in Bilsby, her brother-in-law John Wheelwright served as vicar. She had barely begun to discover there was comfort in his preaching, when suddenly he was silenced by the church. And then came word John Cotton was really gone—completely, finally gone, away to a different world.

She felt disconsolate. There was no hope anywhere, in pulpit or book, until after a long time of troubled seeking a light shone directly from God into her soul.

But in this winter ending in New England now, in the long uncertain days before Zuriel was born, that light had grown dim. The baby lay so still in her womb she began to fear he would never know life outside it. Her own death seemed a clear possibility (as indeed it must always, in childbirth), but of that she was not afraid.

Then help came from one whose knowledge and abilities she had never been quite sure of. Crooked little old Jane Hawkins came one day declaring she would not leave Anne's side until the baby was safely born, and she scarcely did. She made Anne rest for long hours, and she gave her soothing potions. When the time came, the little midwife was in full control. The birth was easy, and the baby strong and healthy after all.

But still Anne felt tired and depressed. For one thing, she was forty-five years old. This would almost certainly be her last baby: in the past few months she had lost more of life than she had gained. Faith and Bridget were both married; happily and well, to be sure, but they were gone from under her roof. Her son Edward had gone back to England to marry. When he returned, part of him would belong to another woman, one whom his mother was scarcely acquainted with. Anne's sister Katherine had suddenly married the shoemaker; and then, as unexpectedly, the couple announced they would follow Roger Williams to Rhode Island. Anne realized there had been clear signs of Katherine's deep respect for the minister, but she had not suspected the attachment was so strong.

"You followed John Cotton much farther than the distance I'll be going," Katherine reminded her.

But that was not the same, Anne could not see that it was any way the same. And now her last contact with the Marbury family was gone. It seemed to her quite likely that she would never see Katherine again.

From morning till night, people came calling to see the baby and find out when the meetings would resume.

"Not quite yet," Anne would say to them, but could not tell what she was waiting for.

Then one afternoon near the end of the year, as she sat by the fire with the baby at her breast, there came a knock at the door that for no clear reason stirred in her the hope for an answer. Elizabeth Joan went and opened the door, to a young man with long brown hair lit gold by the sunlight that came in with him. His back to the light, he had to come close before Anne could clearly see his face; but that slender, graceful form belonged to no one in the world but Henry Vane, and her heart reached out to meet him.

He came and knelt beside her, where she sat in her wainscot chair. (She had seldom used this chair except for meetings, but since she had the new baby it had seemed a great convenience.) A length of soft blue wool cloth lay across her shoulder, partly covering the breast where the baby sucked. The flickering fire cast a light on her face, which was framed by a white cross-cloth pinned over her coif.

"You are like a picture," Henry said. "A rich and glowing picture painted by some old papist, such as I have seen in Paris and Vienna."

He fancied she frowned. "Oh my dear sister," he said. "It was only a painting of a woman with a child, a comely woman with a fair and tender child. Such things are beautiful to look upon, though it be a terrible sin to worship them as papists do."

"I know thou art no papist, Henry," Anne said softly. In that moment it seemed as natural to say *thou* to him as though he were a son or (as in truth he was) a beloved brother. "I think I have seen such a picture myself, though not so fine a one, perhaps, as those you speak of."

He drew close a stool that stood at the opposite side of the chimney. "I have wanted to come," he said, "but I feared you were not well, since you did not resume your meetings."

"No, I am well," she said, "or very nearly so. I have thought of you, and I have heard some talk of you. They say you did something no one else in the colony had ever dared attempt, in reconciling John Winthrop and Thomas Dudley."

"I dared because of you," he told her. "I remembered what you said last time we met."

She looked down. The baby had fallen asleep; she laid him in her lap, fastened her bodice, and draped the blue wool across her bosom. Then she looked at him. "I thank God," she said.

He looked up at her face. "Shall I tell you?" he said, not as though he were asking a question; but musing, perhaps, within in his own mind. Without pausing for an answer, he went on: "They say they'll make me governor."

She reached out for his hand. "Of course they will," she said.

"But I am young," he said. "Some think too young, I know."

"Master Winthrop may think so. Master Coddington does not."

"You know about it."

"I have heard talk. There are many men who very much desire to see you in the governor's office. When they have asked me, I have told them you will do God's work there."

His soft lips seemed to tremble on the brink of something he could never say. Their eyes met—their dark eyes with the liquid depths of joy and pain—and as once before their souls seemed to mirror each other.

"As you will do here," he said. "In this house, in this chair."

"I have wanted some assurance," she said.

"All Boston is longing to hear you speak again. Is that not enough?"

She sighed. "Perhaps," she said. "And yet some talk has come to me—that some there be who think I do neglect my proper calling."

He smiled. "Have they not all heard Master Cotton preach

upon Christian calling? That when anyone has God-given talent for work that serves the public weal, this is a proper calling?"

She gently shook her head. "They think he speaks to men, not to my sex," she said.

"I cannot believe any think so," he said. "For God would not bestow His gifts to be wasted."

"There is one more thing about a calling though," she said. "God's hand must lead me to it."

"And has it not already done so?"

She looked down. The baby lay milky and rosy in her lap, and his urine had soaked through all the thicknesses of cloth wrapped around him. She could not sit much longer without calling one of the girls or rising herself to attend to him.

"Lately," she said, "I grow weak and I wonder. If God give a woman children, it may be that the care of them must be her only calling."

His eyes changed as he looked at her, their dreamy softness gone. "You have the healthiest children in Boston," he said, "and the best content. I have heard both men and women say that." His mouth tightened, and his eyes glinted to fierceness. "My sister, I say this from the depths of my own soul: thou must not deny God's true calling. He hath opened thine eyes to the truth, and speak it thou must."

How could he say that, how could he know? Anne Hutchinson did not even pose the questions in her mind, but knew, with certainty, God spoke to her through Henry Vane. The two of them were joined, their souls were one in Christ, the spirit strong within them. But God, to dissipate her doubts about the part a woman dared to play, had spoken in the voice of a man strong enough to be governor of this Christian commonwealth. She knew for sure. He would be governor: she was able to prophesy that, in the Lord. He would be governor, and she would sit here and help disseminate the light, combating the dark force newly prevailing in the Boston pulpit. Together they would work to create what God had meant the colony to be: a place of love and grace and Christian charity.

She looked at him softly, and once more his eyes matched hers. "Very well," she said. "There will be a meeting next week."

"My beloved sister," he said, close to tears.

She knew for an instant a desire to hold Henry Vane, as an infant to her breast; and then an unmistakable odor filled the air and Anne found she had to smile, both at herself and the tender young man leaning toward her.

"But you must go," she said, "for I am still a mother and you may guess I have work to do in that calling now."

Then once more the meetings held sway, and they were the talk of Boston. Mistress Hutchinson had never spoken so freely, with such power. Since the birth of her baby, she seemed to have regained all her accustomed vigor and more: a state of health that so much affected her that people who never thought her a comely woman now found themselves much attracted by her appearance. Her eyes and face glowed, and her carriage was queenly.

On a day in early May, with the doors thrown open to the sun and the damp cool air, men and women poured into the Hutchinson house for a meeting. Never had the big hall been so full. Goody Hawkins and Elizabeth Joan, squeezed together in the kitchen corner on one stool, had been whispering about almost every person that came in.

Anne, with Francis standing beside her, sat in the wainscot chair and looked out over the crowd. Soon she would give the signal to begin, but she was still waiting for someone. Busy as he had recently become, Henry Vane never let any duty keep him from a meeting. Anne had no doubt that when he was governor he would still come. Even if he had to walk out in the middle of a session of the General Court, he would be at Anne Hutchinson's meeting. (She had heard William Coddington make that observation one night, in a group of men who did not know she was listening. None of them seemed to feel such loyalty would prove in any way a disadvantage.)

Now a pair of male figures appeared in the doorway. One was slender and smooth-faced, and his thick curly hair fell almost to his rather narrow shoulders. The other, more stockily built, short-haired and bearded, stood with broad shoulders thrown back and a proud chest straining his doublet. No one would be surprised they came together, the delicate young aristocrat and the seasoned professional soldier, for Henry Vane had recently been appointed to the commission on military affairs. Though Henry's dislike of war had been one of the points of contention between him and his father, he had been persuaded that a well-supplied and well-organized militia would be a means of keeping peace; so that in those days he frequently consulted Captain Underhill.

"There's your man," whispered Goody Hawkins to her companion on the stool. Elizabeth Joan did not answer. The old witch knew everything, somehow, and so must know she had not been with Captain Underhill since late last summer; but she might know, too, he still pursued her.

Two rudely dressed young men who might have been fishermen or sailors got up from a bench near the entry and gave their seats to the new arrivals, then seated themselves on the floor against the wall. There was no formal order of seating here, as in the meetinghouse, but the abolition of social distinctions would not occur to anyone.

Anne nodded, as though in approval, then turned to Francis and smiled. At this small gesture from the woman in the chair, the congregation grew still and quiet. Francis, as was always the custom at the beginning of his mother's meetings, spoke to welcome them, and then with a small black notebook in hand undertook to recapitulate John Cotton's lecture of the day before. It was much concerned with the experience of the spirit, the necessity of knowing Christ within. But it turned from that to the question of whether, once sealed by the spirit, a Christian may doubt of God's love again, though he fall into scandalous sinning. That he may both sin and doubt was Cotton's answer, though the child of God surely falls much more rarely to gross sinning. That God may sometimes leave His children to a time of doubting, the better to raise their hearts to greater joy, the preacher well believed.

Many listeners scribbled earnestly in their notebooks. John Underhill wrote: "Sinne and Doute can be meens to more Joye in crist." He had tried several times to explain this to Goodwife Faber, who had not after all proved as ready for him as he had believed; but now (as he had noticed) she was here at the meeting and so perhaps would have more confidence in what he told her. She had some scruple yet to be overcome. Certainly it was nothing about his own person that made her keep on withholding her favors.

A woman rose to ask a question. It was Mary Cogshall, with her incipient and endearing little frown faintly creasing her wide brow. "Do you think, brother," she inquired of Francis, "that Master Cotton's lecture is quite in accord with Master Wilson's preaching on the Lord's Day, when he said that visible sin should be taken by the elders as evidence a man has not been saved?"

He did not need to look at his mother before answering. "No, sister, I do not," he said firmly. "The pastor of Boston church is preaching nothing but a covenant of works."

The audience gasped as with one breath. No one had thus publicly made such a statement before, though whispering a-plenty there had been about Pastor Wilson's dark sermons.

A man stood up. This was Atherton Hough, whose wife Elizabeth had attended Anne's meetings for women. "This seems to me a rather extreme statement," he said, "coming from so young a brother. I do not doubt the truth of it, but I think we all would like to hear what Sister Hutchinson has to say upon this subject."

Expressions of support arose throughout the room. "Aye, we have waited long enough," one clearly said.

Anne heard that and knew it was true. Since resuming her meetings, she had become keenly aware of the differences between John Cotton and John Wilson and had begun to suspect that most other preachers in the colony were, like Wilson, enmeshed in the old covenant of Adam. But it was a strong accusation she was asked to make now, and she was reluctant to make it. Unavoidably, comparisons had arisen as she talked and answered questions; people knew what she thought, and were in any case capable of drawing the evident conclusion. Yet they wanted to hear it from her.

She must speak now, but what she must say was not clear to her. She looked out over the gathering of her followers, all very quiet now and waiting. She looked at Henry Vane. His smoldering eyes were fixed upon her, his full red lips just parted as though to say, "Half the truth will not do, Sister Anne." He had said something like it before, in another context, but he was saying it to her now as clearly as if he shouted, though his lips never formed a word. She knew what she had to do, to be true to the Christ that was in her.

She lifted her chin and straightened her back. "My brethren and sisters," she said, in a voice that embraced them. She paused. "I have been disappointed," she finally said, "to notice when I have heard Pastor Wilson in the pulpit, that he seems to feel his purpose is only to rebuke sin, to pour out such hateful wrath upon his people as the God of Israel once heaped upon His enemies. I have not been able to help discerning the difference between his thundering voice and dark expression and the sweet smiling tones in which our teacher tells us about the promise of God's grace. You may remember, as I have heard tell, that in the days before I came here Master Cotton persuaded the elders to change the manner of deciding on new members of the church. In those days, under John Wilson, one had to make a statement of his doctrine and offer evidence of well-behaving. Then when Master Cotton came, he prevailed upon the other ministers to base admission upon the experience of conversion. John Wilson scarcely seems to have heard of Christ within us. John Cotton bases all on that one glorious experience.

"In the past few weeks, I have heard Pastor Wilson say that through faith we may lay hold of Christ Jesus. He does not seem to understand that by the wonderful covenant of grace we can do nothing, need try to do nothing, until Christ comes to dwell within. I have heard him say that he who walks not by the law of God will be smitten down by God. Brothers and sisters, this is legalistic preaching. I believe he thinks we are still under the covenant of old Adam, by which God promised death for breaking His one law. I have heard him say that the commission of sin will separate a man from God, as though God would deny His own covenant of grace. I have not heard an expression from Pastor Wilson to show he understands that promise—the spirit that transcends the word. Will you allow me to leave my expression of opinion at that for today? May I say only that a preacher who says no more of grace than I have heard John Wilson say preaches nothing but a covenant of works?"

She ceased, and dropped her eyes.

There was a stir of comment. "Aye, she speaks well." "It is true, she speaks fairly." And the question: "Has anyone ever heard him preach of grace?" And the answer: "No, no."

As the meeting ended, people were still excited by this first clear public statement of a division in the ministry of their church. They were a long time parting from each other. Many as always gathered around Mistress Hutchinson, and every two that faced one another must go over all they had heard these differing preachers say upon the crucial subject of the covenant.

Henry Vane went to Anne at once; people stood aside to let him pass, and stepped back from her chair when he approached it. "I thank God for your speaking," he said to her.

"You did not think I was afraid to face the truth?"

"You told the truth as you have seen it," he said. "It was a joy to hear. God could ask no more."

Meanwhile, John Underhill had sought out Goodwife Faber and said to her, "Now you have heard with your own ears, and will you not believe?"

"Perhaps I may," she said. "Come to me tomorrow and explain your doctrine again."

As he stepped out the front door, into the sunny yard where the scent of some bruised herb rose around him, he saw Elizabeth Joan standing away toward the fence, talking to another servant girl. She had thrown back her hood, and her pale hair fell around her face and onto her shoulders. It brought a certain picture so clearly before his eyes that he felt his member swelling.

"But I shall see her once again," he said, "whatever Goodwife Faber may decide." He walked briskly across the yard to her, as though he had some public business to speak of, and then he managed a private word or two.

2

John Cotton sat in his study at the table by the narrow window, which was thrown open to the gentle winds of May. He did not notice the gentle wind, or the salty, weedy smells wafted upon it. He was frowning at a letter brought to him an hour ago by a messenger from Newtown. In an hour more, the messenger would be leaving Boston, and the Reverend Thomas Shepard of the Newtown church had requested a reply with his return.

It was a letter asking urgently for clarification of some points made in his lecture the day before, all of which Cotton felt quite capable of writing about fully and clearly—and had in fact, from time to time, done so. It was the last several lines of the letter that puzzled him, a reference to something Cotton had said about familists which led into some veiled suggestion about some unnamed members of his church. "This I speake," wrote Master Shepard, "from the enforcement of my conscience, lest under this color of advancing word together with the spirit, you may meet in time with some such members (though I know none nor judge any) as may doe your people and ministry hurt, before you know it; and thus I have plainly writ my heart unto you, being persuaded that in the spirit of meekness, you will not think I have thus writ to begin a quarrel; but to still and quiet those which are secretly begun and I feare will flame out unless they be quenched in time."

What quarrel? What members? It was not in the least clear to Cotton just what Thomas Shepard was most objecting to. It seemed to him that such questions as he had raised about the word and spirit, about sanctification as evidence of redemption, about the doubts in a sealed Christian—all these were open and clear, and subject to clear answers. The real purpose of Shepard's letter lay in this last part. "I desire therefore that you would answer me in wrighting as soone as ever you can; and I do beleeve we shall not differ when things are hereby ripened for we are desirous and glad to learne; thus beseeching the god of all grace and peace to fill blesse and prosper you; with remembrance of my respect to that precious gentleman with you, and to your wife I rest. Yours in the Lord Jesus."

Cotton had always believed Thomas Shepard to be closer to him in his emphasis on the covenant of grace than most other pastors in the colony. What had stirred him up to write this letter he could no way conceive, and yet he was trying to answer it in as friendly and respectful a manner as he knew how. Nearing the end of his own letter, he could not refrain from a line or two that did not quite conceal his resentment. Restating his central doctrine of the promise, he then went on: ". . . though your expressions seem to feare some such danger in this manner of holding out of christ, which I have applyed my ministery unto these many years both in old Boston and in New; wherein if any error be discovered to me, God forbid I should shutt mine eyes against it, but I suppose wee differ not here in, nor any of my

Brethren if wee understand one another. Nor doe I discerne (though after diligent search) that any of our members, (brethren or sisters) doe hold forth christ in any other way. . . ." He wrote on, responding to the polite utterances with which Shepard had ended his own letter. "Your salutations to Mr. Vane I will god willing present to him anon, who hath bene a broad all this Day." Finally he signed the letter "Your affectionate though weake Brother, J.C." and sat rereading the last lines he had written.

Henry Vane, he said to himself. The whole colony seemed enamored of Henry Vane, and he believed with good reason. The young man was pious, well favored, of aristocratic bearing and useful worldly experience. They had had many good talks together about Henry's conversion experiences when a boy in England, and Cotton could not doubt the spirit lived in that aristocratic breast. But where was Henry now? Cotton knew very well where he was: at a meeting in the house of Mistress Hutchinson, where his own lecture of the day before would be—he understood—the subject of discussion. He had heard much from Henry, and from other brethren and sisters of the church, about these meetings. He approved of them, as far as he could know what went on there; and as he had always been told it was mainly a rephrasing and discussion of what he himself said, he could hardly be expected to feel a strong objection. Yet other ministers might feel it strange—might even in weak moments know a twinge of jealousy, that Cotton's preaching should be so widely followed and admired.

Still, he supposed he might by the same token be too complacent and self-pleased. He made up his mind to find out from Henry exactly what went on at the meetings such as he was this afternoon attending. If anything had ever been said to arouse such concern as Thomas Shepard expressed in his letter, then certainly Cotton ought to know about it.

3

John Wilson was in his study, too. About the time John Cotton was rereading his completed letter, Mistress Wilson appeared at the door and asked if he would like to come and take a cup of wine with some gentlewomen who had called upon them. He was in a foul humor, for some reason he did not quite understand; a little wine would be welcome.

When he saw who they were, he was almost sorry he had not told Elizabeth he was too busy to be interrupted. They were silly creatures, both of them, without enough at home to keep them busy. Now they were excited and flushed about something, and babbling over their wine, and he supposed they were bearing some tale he would have to investigate. Wickedness enough of all kinds went on in Boston, but he abhorred hearing about it this way. Still, he knew his duty.

They were Mistresses Newel and Upham, both of them overdressed in terms of the sumptuary laws, but being of the richer sort, not therefore ever admonished.

"Oh, dear Master Wilson," cried the first, Mistress Newel. "You cannot guess where we have been and what we've heard."

"No, Mistress Newel, I cannot," he began to say, sitting down at a small table and taking from his wife a cup of wine.

Before he had finished, the other woman spoke—Mistress Upham, who ever seemed just holding back the tears. "Oh, sir, if you only knew," she wailed.

"I should be very glad to know, my dear sisters," he said impatiently.

They looked at each other; they held out their open palms, each offering the other first chance.

"Do tell him, Mistress Newel," said Mistress Upham.

"No, pray do you, dear Mistress Upham," said Mistress Newel.

John Wilson looked at the two and wondered if either would ever succeed in conveying what they wished him to know.

"They have been to Mistress Hutchinson's, John," said Elizabeth at last.

Well, he might have guessed, after all. He did know this was the day for the meeting, and long had he wondered what sort of thing was said there.

He spoke sharply then. "Now, Mistress Newel, do calm yourself and say what you have come to say."

"She compared you to Master Cotton," said Mistress Newel.

"Aye, surely, a natural thing to do," said the pastor.

"She says you preach a covenant of works."

"And can you tell me what she meant by that?"

"Well, no, not exactly," said Mistress Newel. "But, sir, she says you never speak of grace."

"Of course I speak of grace, and often. I know not why she would have said that."

Mistress Upham could no longer keep quiet. "Oh, no, Mistress Newel, 'twas not that she said. But only that he knows it not, how Christ within us saves however much we sin."

"Without a word, she said, but only in the spirit," Mistress Newel cried, her voice breaking. "She says there never needs to be a word."

"Oh no, I think not that," said Mistress Upham. "But I know she said that Master Wilson is like Adam-before-the-fall."

Silently John Wilson begged the Lord to deliver him from babbling gentlewomen, especially those who thought a comparison to Adam in Paradise was an insult; then downed his cup of wine and tried to speak graciously. "I thank you for this news," he said. "For the time being, I hope you speak no more of these things, for it is possible you misunderstood what you heard. I shall know how to find out more about Mistress Hutchinson."

He excused himself then and went back to his study, where he sat grinding his teeth and gripping one hand in the other. He had tried to minimize those women's silly words, to deceive himself, and perhaps (in his fragmentary prayer) to keep the full truth from the Lord. He had suspected ever since his return from England that there would have to be a battle for the pulpit of the Boston church. But he would bide his time. Mistress Hutchinson might bring out the full truth of what John Cotton taught, and in her misguided zeal secure the victory for the man she most opposed.

# XIII

He was not a tall man, but Elizabeth Joan could look up into his eyes. At the meeting, when for an instant he stood near her, and his velvet doublet came briefly against her like the touch of a cat arching by, and he breathed upon her that old familiar odor of sour wine and stale tobacco, an ache she had not known for months came poignantly back to her. Then he spoke, in a voice husky with pain, and said, "God help me, I must have you one more time. Come out to the back lane tonight."

He was gone without waiting for a word, leaving her pale and a-tremble with anger. She thought it was anger. How dared he come near her and speak so, there in plain sight of such a crowd? Still, looking around her, she decided it was just the presence of the crowd, with every two or three talking earnestly together, that made it unlikely they had been noticed. If Goody Hawkins had been there, she would have seen everything, but she had been called in the midst of the questions at the end of the meeting to a childbed in some cottage toward the Neck. And Mistress Hutchinson, who in any case had not the midwife's prying eye, was still in the house with some of her closest followers. Bold and clever he was, a soldier experienced in war; he knew when and how to take chances.

On into the evening, through supper and prayers, her anger burned in her cheeks and eyes, till her mistress inquired if she suffered a fever. She said she thought it was excitement over something she heard at the meeting, an answer that well satisfied Mistress Hutchinson. And it was true—oh, God knew that it was true. How dared he speak so to her, she kept inwardly saying, as though he had only to set out the bait and she like a coney would come running to be caught.

It was a long time since she had lain with a man—so long she had begun to think all that desire was dead in her forever. Even when she had seen John Underhill in the meetinghouse, she had deliberately kept her eyes from meeting his, and had never felt anything stirring inside her. And was not the absence of such sinful desire, she could not help asking herself, a sign at last that she had Christ within her? It seemed so reasonable to hope it was, and yet Mistress Hutchinson always said that such things could not be. People who think they are saved, just because they keep from sinning, are the devil's dupes, Mistress Hutchinson said. On the other hand, you might have Christ and still go on in sin. You would be sorry, and Christ would be wounded again as with the nails on the Cross, but He would never go back on His promise.

This was not at all what Pastor Wilson said. "Depart from Me, ye cursed," God roared in Wilson's thundering voice to all who persisted in sin. Mistress Hutchinson said that was wrong; that was what God might have said to old Adam, but it was out of date since Abraham. Still, without seeing exactly why, Elizabeth Joan found it completely reasonable when she heard it in the meetinghouse. Then at Mistress Hutchinson's meetings, it was Christ, always Christ; if you had Christ you had everything, and you had it forevermore. And when Mistress Hutchinson spoke, what she said seemed so true it was like a candle lit in her breast, driving out old Pastor Wilson's fearsome dark.

But Elizabeth Joan did not know how to have Christ. Sometimes she thought it was easier not to sin than to have Christ. You need not do anything, to have Him, so Master Cotton and Mistress Hutchinson said. Worse than that, you couldn't do anything. "Wait and hope," said Mistress Hutchinson. But what if He never did come?

"How will it be when He comes?" she asked. "How will I know?"

"He will tell you."

"What will He say—I have come?"

"Yes, but not in words. His spirit will unite with yours; in the very person of the Holy Ghost He will unite, as He enters you, becomes verily another part of you, and you will be so full of

Him you will think you are bursting. You might even faint, from the pure joy of it, for it is almost beyond human strength."

There was only one experience Elizabeth Joan had known that was anything like what her mistress described. Because she thought only of that other joy as Mistress Anne talked of Christ, she still feared she belonged to the devil—though she never spoke her fear to her mistress, and indeed spoke less and less to anyone. And sometimes in her despair she thought, And if I'm the devil's, that is so for all eternity, just the same as if I was Christ's, and there is nothing I can do to get away.

In like manner she now thought of John Underhill. She could not sleep for thinking of John Underhill.

"In just this way I ought to think of Christ," she said to herself. She seized upon the thought of Christ. How sweet, how full of wonder He must be. And constant: once she had Him, He would never go away. And loving. Gentle and sweet and truly loving, as Jacob at his best had been. She laughed her bitter little laugh in the dark. Did she think Christ was a man, to come and ravish her? But then wasn't *ravish* just the word they liked to use, those fortunate elect who had Him already?

Oh, God, how she wanted Him. Without Christ her life would be nothing. She could clearly picture how it was going to be—groping from man to man in search of what only Christ could give her, she would end with a rope around her neck on the scaffold in the market place.

Her garret room was hot. She felt herself stifling. And she felt herself wrenched and pulled. One thing was sure, she could not bear to stay there between those closing-in walls. Without leaving her bed she drew on some clothes, then in an old way she knew well, crept barefoot out of the room and down the steep stairs, staying close to the wall in case a board should creak, out the back door, which was easier to unfasten than the front, and finally into the moist and soft-starred night.

There under the stars he would surely come.

She knew just where John Underhill would be, and how to avoid the watch. Those few low-spoken words at the meeting had let her know he would make the same arrangements he had made before. But she did not want John Underhill; she wanted something new and better than that. Not Christ exactly. Or no, she wasn't sure. It wasn't really possible He could be what Mistress Hutchinson said. Or was it? When Elizabeth Joan was in her presence, listening to her voice, there seemed no room for doubt. The woman knew.

The night was wonderful. Elizabeth Joan had always loved the night. Not nighttime, shut up in a narrow room with the walls slanting in upon her, but the real night, a night like this, a May night with the scent of bloom and grass and fresh-turned earth in the air and the stars near and sweet like the scent turned to light, a night of pale moon hardly strong enough to show the difference between substance and shadow.

Standing in the lane, with the sense of all this wonder strong upon her, she glimpsed a figure—a man with a lantern standing at the bottom of the lane. A wave of revulsion moved startlingly, sickeningly, through her, at a sudden recollection of the mingled odors of tobacco and wine and all the different leakings from his body. In that instant, she knew she wanted her night to stay pure, free of this old familiar man smell.

She began to move as swiftly and silently as she could, keeping near garden fences, turning into the high street, taking still another turn down a narrow lane that led to the sea. That man with the lantern was John Underhill, she had not the least doubt, and was equally sure he would take a different turn from hers, expecting her to be waiting in that empty barn that still stood by the burned-down house. She turned to look. No lantern blinked behind her. She stepped onto the shelly shore with a sense of being free.

The air was different here—clearer, cleaner-smelling. Less of earth it seemed, with a pungency that stirred and challenged her. She stood in the foam at the water's edge and looked out over the faintly glimmering sea to where a gray line marked its meeting with the sky. That mark of distance beckoned her, nay, more, it seemed to become a silver thread that looped her heart and pulled it, so that if she failed to follow, she would lose her heart out of her bosom.

"What is it?" she cried, and began to run along the foamy shore, as if she could that way reach the light beyond the sea. As she ran, the answer came to her, in one word that yet was not word but spirit. No sounds came to her ear but the roar of pounding waves, and yet she heard it spoken clear. Christ. He was there, He was come. Wait, the woman in the chair had said, and Elizabeth Joan had waited; but now He was almost in reach and she could wait no longer, she must go to Him. He wanted her. Come to Me, He said; she could hear His voice.

The shore curved, the sea seemed to rise in front of her; yet she could not change her course, drawn straight to Him. The water grew quickly deeper, a wave enveloped her. She lost her footing but regained it and then without conscious thought resumed her sea walk, now unknowingly moving straight toward the center from which the great waves rolled. "I am coming!" she cried. The water was cold and beautiful, like a crystal in the sun. The waves engulfed her, but the light still shone. Their force was great, a thousand times stronger than the little servant girl, and yet she knew Whose force that was and never struggled. What happened to her frail, slender body was no longer of any concern to Elizabeth Joan.

# XIV

In his sermon on the Lord's Day after the body of Elizabeth Joan had been found and swiftly buried, John Wilson spoke of her as though the whole world knew she had gone out that night unlawfully to meet a man. He spoke of the Lord's first warning to her last autumn, when He had let her live after bringing her to the edge of death (though how he knew anything of that affair Anne Hutchinson could not surmise). And he said now the ungrateful girl had gone once more a-whoring and the wrath of God had rightly struck her down. He alluded to the belief some had that she had committed suicide; if so it were a worse sin still. But Wilson declared there was a wicked man in it somewhere whom God would punish in His own good time. Meanwhile, he was thankful the lewd girl had been struck down in the midst of her sinful life and so sent straight to hell. It was a God-given lesson to other young women both within and without the church.

Mistress Hutchinson rose as he was speaking and with her chin lifted and her eyes straight ahead walked the length of the meetinghouse, to the open-standing door. To the tithing man who accosted her there she whispered something that made his face turn red, and he let her go, with a bow. Occasionally any woman might be forced to leave in the middle of a sermon. There were certain excuses, peculiar to the sex, that no man ever questioned. Who knew whether, through strange coincidence, some mysterious female complaint struck Mistress Hutchinson just as Pastor Wilson was invoking the covenant of works to send her little servant girl to hell?

At the women's meeting next day, Anne spoke with a fierceness none had ever seen in her before. It flashed and crackled like a lightning storm—in her eyes, in her voice, indeed in every gesture of her hands and movement of her body. She said she knew to a certainty the girl had found Christ. On the very night of the drowning she had waked from a dream she could never remember, but on waking had felt herself filled with a spirit of tranquillity that clearly was linked to Elizabeth Joan. She thought she would see the girl transformed the next morning. She saw her drowned, with seaweed mingled in her yellow hair: yet she was sure—more sure than ever when she went to view the lifeless body—that Christ had been at home there. No more than John Wilson could she say how Elizabeth Joan came to be in the sea; but knowing what she did, she grieved the less for her.

These things she told the women in the meeting, but she said that even had she been given no intimation that Christ had come to the girl at last, even if no one on earth had any inkling He had come, John Wilson still could have no right to speak as he had done. The girl was honest, no whore, and longing for Christ, but even if these things were not true, John Wilson was wrong to say that God condemned her for her sin. God saves through grace, said Anne, not absence of sin, and if Wilson did not know this it seemed very clear he had not learned God's truth. John Wilson had never known or cared to know this loving girl, so dear to her mistress' heart. If he had cared, he might have helped her to happiness in the Lord long before.

Anne's listeners, most of them, had not known Elizabeth Joan very well. Of those who had known her, some had found her sullen and few had offered her a hand in love. But now they all believed they had cared for her deeply, and their anger toward John Wilson grew until they half believed they had seen him strike down with a wrathful sword this bright and beautiful creature.

Goodwife Faber went home to find that Captain Underhill was waiting by her bed. As they undressed, she told him Elizabeth Joan had known Christ before she died. He said he thanked God for it. The goodwife said she understood at last the wickedness of the covenant of works. He thanked God for that, too, and prayerfully fell upon her.

2

Two or three weeks before election day (which was May 25), William Coddington and Henry Vane went on a round of visits to colony towns. Everyone had heard of Henry's success in reconciling Winthrop and Dudley, everyone seemed ready to accept him as governor, but Coddington believed it would be politically wise for Henry to see the outlying towns of the commonwealth he would govern, and make himself known to all the people who rarely or never came to Boston. The tour was a great success. Everywhere the young man went, people loved him as they did in Boston. When Coddington would tell some farmer or shopkeeper, as though in confidence, that Vane in all likelihood would soon be governor, the response was invariably smiling approval. And wives liked him quite as well as their husbands did, if not better.

That the two men came back somewhat disturbed in their minds had nothing to do with Henry Vane's reception. In their travels they had occasion to hear sermons and lectures delivered by ministers of several churches and were appalled at the discovery that every one of them, like John Wilson, preached a doctrine clearly based upon a covenant of works. Soon after their return they went to call on Mistress Hutchinson.

"I had suspected it," she said, "and it does trouble me that so many good people are building their hopes upon this weak foundation."

"Sister," said Henry Vane, "we believe you should speak openly about this false preaching that prevails throughout the colony."

"We know," said Coddington, "that you are modest and forbearing, as becomes a Christian of your sex, and have not wished to speak against any minister. And yet if you do not, who will?"

"Who else can speak so well and clear, who else can move hearts hardened by the cold unbending covenant of works?" said Henry Vane.

"I think you must know the answer to that as well as any man," Anne said, "for you dwell in his house."

Henry shook his head. "I know not," he said. "John Cotton

does not wish to believe there is so much difference between himself and the other ministers. I have tried to talk to him, but he always says it is not so much—a matter of emphasis, he thinks it may be. 'But there is a difference, sir,' I've said to him, and he will answer always with these words, 'A narrow scantling, Henry—a very narrow scantling.'"

"Through the goodness of his heart, he may be partly blinded," Coddington said, "and of course he does not wish to offend his brethren."

"You are the one," said Henry Vane, "the only one. Christianity in the Massachusetts Bay depends on you."

"Can you tell me what they said?" asked Anne then. "Exactly what you heard them say?"

Prepared for that question, they brought out notebooks from their pockets and read to Anne the false incriminating words. And from that time, in her main meetings as in any gathering of her friends and followers, she spoke to the full extent of her belief and understanding.

3

About the time Coddington and Vane paid their visit, or not so long afterward that the new strain in Anne's teaching had become very widely known and talked of, she one day received a message from John Cotton, delivered to her by his servant, who said he must wait for an answer.

"Deare Sister Hutchinson," it said. "I have for some time now been somewhat unclear about your spirituall estate, and fear I have been remiss in failing to deal with you about it. If you can come to my house and talk freely with me about some things that make mee doubtfull, I believe we shall both find ourselves the better for it. The reason I ask you to come to mee is because I know your house is often filled with family and friends, and I would deal privily with you. If you can come to mee between two and three of the clock tomorrow, please send word by the servant that brings this." It was signed "Your teacher and brother in Christ, J.C."

Frenziedly, Anne found pen and ink and wrote three lines assenting to Cotton's request. Only after the messenger was gone did she feel the storm subsiding in her brain. She sat to her spinning wheel (where the messenger had interrupted her on his arrival) and waited for the steady hum and rhythm to slow her pounding heart and quiet the thunder in her ears.

She had been in the New World nearly two years now and rarely failed to hear John Cotton's preaching twice a week or more. As she had foreseen so long ago in England, she never tired of it. She might drink in his words forever and remain thirsty still. If she had experienced any disappointment where Cotton was concerned, she never let herself know it, but there might have been a secret hope unrealized. Though she saw him not seldom in the private houses of Boston—including her own, where he came when invited—very infrequent were the times she had sat down and talked with him at length about the doctrine they two shared. And never had she been summoned to his house since that early time when she had to go and defend herself against the accusations of Zachariah Symmes. (Who now, she knew from reports brought by Coddington and Vane, preached the most flagrant covenant of works.)

In terrible distress of mind, she tried to think what she might stand accused of now. Although she never to her knowledge spoke a word at variance with what the teacher taught, she knew there were those who from spite or jealousy might go to him bearing lies. Mistress Hibbens, whose brother Bellingham became increasingly powerful, had ever looked sourly upon her, since the first and only time she had called upon Anne. And Goody Hawkins would bring a tale from time to time of someone who came to a meeting and then went out to speak disparagingly about women who neglected their proper calling.

Anne did not mention the summons to anyone else in the household, but talked to William when they lay in bed that night.

"To speak truth, I think I really be a-feared," she confessed to him.

"Thou hast naught to fear," he said.

"No," she said, "for I have examined my conscience since the time that message came. I know I have naught, but I know not what our teacher may mistakenly believe. And more than anything else in this world, I want John Cotton to think well of me."

William was silent awhile before he answered her. He knew she would never intentionally say a word to suggest his love meant less to her than another man's good opinion. He knew her needs went far beyond what he could ever give, but he also knew she was a faithful wife, who loved him. Not as he loved her, he had always understood that. Even before her father took her away to London (and she but fifteen), he knew no earthly duty or hope of heavenly reward could keep him from Anne Marbury's side if once she said she loved him. Before he spoke he kissed her.

"He may have heard some lie," he said then. "There may be some misunderstanding. But when you talk together face to face, he will see he has no slightest cause for doubt."

She sighed. "Dear William," she said, "I do thank thee."

Other men might arouse her to a fuller sense of her spiritual duties, or tune her heart strings to such a pitch she could scarcely dare ponder the glory of God for fear they would break with the tension of one such added joy. But there was no other man who loved her with this comforting, caring, earthly love. There was no other man in the world who by speaking a few gentle words and holding her close with her head on his bosom, could still her doubts and fears till she lay at his side as serenely sure of herself as of his love.

Nor was there anyone else of either sex in all the world into whose deepest soul she would refuse to search for signs of Christ.

It was a warm gray day. The sun did not quite shine. Anne walked the familiar way to the house by the Trimontaine scarcely aware of the spring growth in dooryards and back gardens, scarcely nodding to the people that she met along the street. Her thoughts were disordered, unclear. More than once she had tried to withdraw into a state of meditation, but household sounds that normally never intruded upon her thoughts became annoying and kept out all awareness of anything from God.

John Cotton's house had changed. This was the first time she had seen the addition Henry Vane had built for himself—a separate little house it was, actually, joined by a covered passageway to the main house. Somehow that gave her heart. It made Henry seem as permanent as houses, a friend in Christ who would always be near her to understand and share the messages that came to her from God. He had come, under leave of King Charles, to stay three years; but there was really no way the King could draw him back to England, if Henry thought God wanted him to stay.

Thinking of Henry Vane led her into a far more hopeful mood, so that when Cotton himself opened the door to her she was able to smile and speak with her accustomed buoyancy.

Cotton's greeting was rather more grave than hers, and he wasted little time with it but took her at once to his study where they sat, as once before, with the door standing open.

He sat at his table, where he had a page of notes that he looked at, more than he looked into her face.

"Sister," he said, "I hear very much talk of your meetings here of late. They grow larger week by week, so people say."

Surely he could not be saying her meetings crossed any rule of Scripture. Even from John Cotton, Anne could not accept that opinion. "Yes, sir," she said, "I bless God they do."

"I hope that before you began to teach others you felt full satisfaction about your own estate."

"At one time," she said, "as I have told you before, I felt lost and full of doubt. But since I have been in Boston I have walked always in certainty of grace."

"But may I ask you, sister, whence this certainty arises?"

"Why as you know, I am sealed with the spirit. I have made my confession of faith before the church."

"And do you find your faith strengthened in any way by the teaching of public ministers?"

"By some I do."

"But more strength comes to you, I believe, from private meditations."

"At one time that was surely true. When I can find the time, I still do like to meditate, but I do not absent myself from any service of the church if I can help myself."

"No, sister, you do not, and I know it is through your effort and example that your entire family is at meeting every Lord's Day. Still I wonder whether duties and ordinances mean as much to you as they should do. For let us say you are sealed with the spirit, as I do truly believe, and sure of your justification, do you ever likewise seek for signs of sanctification?"

"Not so far as to go aside to a covenant of works."

That was an answer he could not quarrel with. "But you do believe that such a thing there be?"

"Oh yes, by plain Scripture."

He nodded. That seemed clear enough. "The third thing I wish to mention," he said, still looking mostly at his notes, "is that you are more censorious of other men's spiritual estates and hearts than the servants of God are wont to be, who are more taken up with judging themselves before the Lord, than of others."

"Nay, sir, I hope not." She actually did not know what he meant. If he had heard what she said about Pastor Wilson, he would have said so, she thought. He might have charged her with a lack of respect for ministers, if indeed such a plain statement of truth could be construed as disrespect. "I do not think you can mean the times I have helped some woman discover how hopelessly she has been going on in a covenant of works. And yes, I do confess it, sometimes her husband has come to me too."

He looked up, pushing his fair hair from his forehead, and almost imperceptibly sighed. "I have been very glad to believe," he said, "that in these ways you do support the public ministry."

She valued Cotton's approval above all men's, as she had confided to William. He seemed ready to dismiss her, yet she felt she must know whether she had satisfied him about whatever had moved him to call her for this conference.

"May I ask," she said, "whether you have heard anything to suggest there are ways in which I do not support it?"

He looked at her with an expression of sadness or perhaps resignation. "There have been suggestions," he said, "but no true witnesses."

She wanted more than that from him. "I long to do the Lord's work, that is all," she said. "Do you believe that a woman may have such a calling?"

Gravely he shook his head. "I know not how far a woman may by Scripture be allowed to go," he said. "It is something that has never concerned me before. But as long as you help people to discern their true estates and do no harm by bringing forth dissension, I believe your work will be fruitful for the Lord."

The last part of his answer was to her like the fulfillment of a promise; she forgot the rest. So joyous was she in her heart that she was not surprised when the sun broke through the clouds to shine upon her walking homeward down the lane, and light up a spot of color such as she had not seen before in Boston. It was an apple blossom. The trees planted by the first settlers were just beginning to bear fruit. No doubt there had been a few blossoms before this spring, but here lifted above the fence of Penn the beadle was the first one Anne had seen; and that delicate pink so clear in the sudden sunshine seemed like a candle unexpectedly lit in a dim room. Anne took it as a sign.

# XV

When Henry Vane was elected governor, the ships in the harbor fired off volleys of great shot and all Boston cheered. Or so it seemed, from the crowd that gathered in the market place to celebrate election day. Actually there were a few not wholly pleased with the outcome of the election. John Winthrop, returned now to the office of deputy governor, managed a smile of congratulations as he silently prayed that he would be able to exercise some control over this pink-cheeked boy who looked incapable of governing even himself. John Wilson was bitterly opposed to this choice which seemed so widely popular, but he kept his disapproval to himself. He had not learned enough yet about the opinions of those who gathered at Anne Hutchinson's or how far John Cotton was involved with them. Neither magistrate nor minister would do himself any good by opposing John Cotton. Yet as for what John Cotton thought, he might not even know himself. He had been struck from the first by Henry's qualities of mind and spirit, but he well knew how young twenty-three could be.

Among the Hutchinsons there was nothing but elation. There was any number of reasons why they were all so delighted. One of the lesser ones had to do with William's brother Edward. Vane (so sure of election he was) had already made arrangements for halberdiers to accompany him on all official business, wherever he might go, and one of these fine-looking men in helmets and mirror-bright breastplates was Edward. Every Hutchinson was proud of him. Anne was secretly proud of Henry himself, as if he had been her own son. The whole family might feel a little puffed up whenever anyone said, "Oh yes, the governor goes to Mistress Hutchinson's meetings."

To Anne it seemed that a new day was dawning. William felt the same way but for different reasons: like his fellow merchants, he believed that trade with England as well as relations with the Crown would improve. Anne believed the election signified the time was at hand when the truth of God would reign supreme in Boston.

Her conviction was strengthened when on the day immediately following Vane's election the *Griffin* came into harbor bringing John Wheelwright with his wife, children, and mother-in-law, who was Susannah Hutchinson, mother of William and Edward. They had been expected for some time, with growing impatience on Anne's part, for she felt the colony had dire need of this minister, who was the only man besides John Cotton she had ever heard preach a true covenant of grace. She had been writing, urging him to come, until at last he had grown tired enough of being without a pulpit or any safe means of preaching truth that he gathered his family about him and made the fateful journey over the sea. He did not know what awaited him in New England, but Anne had assured him he would soon find a place as minister in the colony, where his talents and understanding of God's word were so badly needed.

On the evening of the day the Wheelwrights arrived, there was a family gathering at the house of Anne and William. The old grandmother Susannah sat in a place of honor (not Anne's wainscot chair, as William tactfully let his sister Mary Wheelwright know when she would have moved it to the table). She smiled toothlessly upon the reunion: her oldest child and her two youngest, with their spouses and children, the husbands of William's two married girls, and the two nieces, daughters of her husband's sister. Anne was quite willing to give the occasion over to family and sat quietly listening to talk about the brothers and sisters left behind in Old England.

But she meant to have a talk with John Wheelwright next morning, and was up early disposing of the duties of the day. Mary Wheelwright and all the little children were to go and spend the day with Sarah Hutchinson and her brood. Edward, as the family were all happily aware, would be escorting the governor to a fine dinner he was giving at Samuel Cole's inn for the masters of the fifteen ships in the harbor. This was a very wise move, William said; it would help settle problems about the selling of goods from the ships and the behavior of sailors on shore. He said anyone who feared Henry Vane was too young for the job could rest assured now.

In Anne Hutchinson's kitchen corner, the cousins were at work and old Susannah sat comfortably with Zuriel on her lap. She had taken to this youngest grandchild at once, but then she had always loved all the babies. She knew what his name meant: God is my rock. "That's right," she said, "and let him never forget it. If they would all remember that in England now, instead of quarreling about a hundred things that make no difference, how much better off that land would be. What is it to God if they bow or kneel or light a waxen candle at the altar? Or if they don't? He is still the same."

Susannah was complacent about everything, including God and the church. Zealous she never was, though she would worship every Lord's Day in whatever house of God stood nearest. Anne had learned long ago not to speak of doctrine to her mother-in-law. The two women had little in common beyond the family tie; both recognized this unchangeable condition, and so they never quarreled.

When William and the older boys had gone to work, Anne asked John Wheelwright to come and sit with her a little while. She sat in the wainscot chair, where it stood at the end of the room as if ready for a meeting, and it was significant that she held no needle in her hand. He pulled a low stool close to her and sat with his long muscular legs stretched before him and crossed at the ankles. He was nothing like the Hutchinson men; though he was evidently relaxed, his physical and spiritual forces were so strong that he seemed always on the point of a struggle with some powerful adversary. There were people who remembered well his prowess on the football fields of Cambridge twenty years before; they said he had shown the same aggressiveness in the pulpits of the Church of England. In recruiting a new lieutenant for the war against the covenant of works, Anne could hardly hope to do better. Whether this was a man to let himself be led by a woman remained to be seen; but Anne had never really thought in those terms about what she would be asking of John Wheelwright. She simply assumed that he would join the fight.

"I have written you somewhat," she said, "about the difference between the two ministers of the Boston church. Now in the last few weeks I have been hearing more about the preaching in other churches—and John, I very much fear that Master Cotton is the only man in the Bay Colony who preaches a true covenant of grace."

"Surely not the only one, Anne," he said.

"About Thomas Shepard of Newtown I still maintain some doubt," she said. "And of course I must concede I have not heard them all. I hoped you and I might go together to some churches in towns not too far away and hear for ourselves."

"I would be very much interested in hearing all the ministers," he said. "But say we learn what you believe is true. What is it you would have us do about it?"

"Only preach," she said. "Only spread the word. I do what I can at my meetings. Francis is very helpful, too; you will find him an excellent speaker."

"Does he preach, then?"

"You might say so." She decided to confide in him something she had not mentioned even to William, and leaning close to him, speaking low and almost passionately, said, "John, I feel sure he is called."

John thought about the slender, big-eyed boy, with whom he had talked in some seriousness already. He could not doubt his sister-in-law was right. "But how can you prepare him?" he asked. "Even if you could afford to send him to a university, he would sure not ever agree to take the oath."

"No," she said, "I have thought of that. And it is a sad thing, for I have always hoped above all else among worldly things that one of my sons at least might be educated at Cambridge, as my own father was."

She sighed. He looked at her keenly. If this ambition for a son came somehow out of a hopeless need of her own, she probably did not understand the source herself.

"Does he read?" he asked. "Does he know Latin?"

"He has hardly any chance," she said. "But yes, to both. A little."

"I might work with him," John said. "I may have very little else to do for a while."

"That would be generous of you, John," Anne said. "But I trust God you may have more than that to do. I believe He will provide you a pulpit somewhere. For as I say, all we can hope to do is spread the word."

"I must preach where I may," he said.

While they still sat talking, John Cotton and one of the elders of the church (Thomas Leverett from old Boston, who had come on the ship with Cotton) arrived to greet their old friend and invite him to speak as a private brother in the meeting the next Lord's Day.

"See!" Anne cried to him gleefully when they were gone. "The Lord doth not delay. You shall begin at once to do His work in Boston."

## 2

Some of the hardest preaching ever done in the colony took place that summer. Anne thought it started with John Wheelwright's sermon in the Boston church, but the concern of the ministers was already great. Undoubtedly, though, the response to Wheelwright's sermon seemed to them cause for alarm. A sigh of approbation and delight came as with one breath from the congregation when this brother-in-law of their well-loved Sister Hutchinson climbed to the pulpit and told them, with more vigor and less equivocation than ever they had from John Cotton, just what they wanted to hear: Salvation comes from grace not works and brings with it a personal union with the Holy Spirit.

Free and joyous these words rang to the ears of Anne Hutchinson's followers. Bitter anathema they were to some two or three. After sunset, when the Lord's Day had ended, John Wilson and John Winthrop came together and unleashed their fears and fury.

They sat together in Pastor Wilson's study. Winthrop smoked

a pipe of tobacco, but finding at last that he was like to bite the stem in two, laid it aside.

"They say Mistress Hutchinson carries both these errors to even more dangerous lengths than appeared in Wheelwright's speaking," John Winthrop said.

"So I have heard," said Wilson.

"Which is worse, think you?"

"To say a man is joined with the Holy Spirit is to make him no longer a mere creature. To say a man can be one with God is the blackest blasphemy."

"Yet to tell men they need observe neither the sacraments nor the law is to tempt them straight to hell. Surely the devil incarnate stood in our pulpit this day."

"Brother Cotton would say that although we are saved by grace alone, our works may be a comfort to us after our experience of grace."

"Aye, he doth equivocate."

"Not necessarily. But I admit it's hard to tell sometimes how close he comes to antinomianism."

That fearful word had not precisely occurred to John Winthrop before. It brought before his mind's eye scenes of debauchery and destruction such as had occurred in Germany a hundred years before, when a sect with antinomian tendencies had seized the city of Münster, and killed and raped and plundered churches before they could be brought under control. There is no telling what people will do when they deem themselves so close to being God that they are raised above the law. Winthrop found it difficult to believe the people of his church would bring to literal ruin the colony of Massachusetts Bay. He did not quite envision rivers of blood and blazing churches, but he thought of drunkenness and adultery uncontrolled, of extortionate prices and starvation and thievery, of deep destructive dissension within the congregations. And he thought with desperate longing of a city upon a hill, where every resident walked ever in the way of Christ.

"Something will have to be done," John Winthrop said, and Pastor John Wilson agreed.

It turned out that in the next few days Master Symmes and Master Shepard, ministers from Charlestown and Newtown, came to see John Wilson about Mistress Hutchinson and her disciples. These men had heard from a reliable source that there were persons among them who claimed to have revelations straight from God, and others whom the spirit moved to speak in unknown tongues. These things and worse would stem from antinomianism, the preachers all agreed. It was difficult to believe that men like Cotton and Wheelwright, ordained ministers, their brothers, would condone such things. Wheelwright was new and might not know what went on at his sister-in-law's meetings. Cotton, on the other hand, was extolled by the opinionists as the fountain of all that they practiced and believed.

They went to see Cotton, who seemed to have heard nothing at all of the heresies they came to report.

"You may remember I warned you of that woman almost two years ago," said Zachariah Symmes.

"I do remember," Cotton said, "but I think you agreed at the time that her opinions were sound."

"She might dissemble," Wilson said.

"I have been assured she does no more than repeat my own sermons and lectures."

Thomas Shepard sighed. "Aye, brother," he said. "So have we, so have we."

Only then did Cotton fully understand what they had come to accuse him of. He decided not to tell them he had already called in Mistress Hutchinson for a conference; and although the rumors they brought were more alarming than any he had heard before, he did not promise any specific investigation. They were too easily misled, was what he privately believed.

"I shall make inquiries, brothers," he said. "Meanwhile, I see nothing better for us to do than redouble our efforts in preaching the truth."

3

"You see, John? You see?" Anne would say again and again as the two of them visited such churches as lay in easy walking or boating distance of Boston. Francis usually accompanied them, and often other members of the family as well—the two young married couples, likely, for it made a pleasant excursion. And always little Zuriel in Anne's arms, for he depended upon her breasts for sustenance.

Their notebooks were filling with incriminating words spoken by these ministers who, Anne came more and more firmly to believe, were not themselves sealed with the spirit.

"Suppose that all miseries and sorrows that ever befell all the wicked in earth and hell should meet together in one soul, as all waters gathered together in one sea; suppose thou heardest the devil's roaring, and sawest hell gaping, and flames of everlasting burnings flashing before thine eyes? It's certain it were better for thee to be cast into those inconceivable torments than to commit the least sin against the Lord. Thou dost not think so now, but thou wilt find it so one day."

From such sermons, there would be some departing pale with terror. Anne longed to hold them tight against her bosom and comfort them with words about the grace of God. At the same time fire leaped in her great dark eyes. Soft pity and fierce anger warred for full possession of her heart.

She ever thanked God for John Cotton's sermons. New England through pride was losing its hope of grace, Cotton preached—pride in what it mistakenly assumed to be its godly behavior. We may walk in the ways of God, till all the world lift its hands in amazement at our virtue, but this is no assurance God has made an everlasting covenant with us. We had best concern ourselves more with our own hearts and less with the eyes of men upon our good behavior.

How Anne loved to repeat such words at her meetings. And how John Winthrop, hearing the minister preach them, did inwardly writhe on the magistrates' bench.

## 4

Once more summoned to John Cotton's house, Anne wearily trod the crooked, dusty lane. Her heart was heavy. One thing had she clearly learned by now: her teacher did not summon her to praise her.

Cotton was not alone. Henry Vane was there, and William and Mary Coddington. Cotton invited them all into his boxlike little study at the head of the stairs, where he had extra stools placed so that all could be seated. It was crowded there, close and hot with only the one narrow window open to the humid summer air. He had shut the door; the occasion called for privacy.

He politely apologized for bringing them there from their callings. In fact, he regretted the occasion quite as much as he told them he did. He had judged it best to bring together the leading men known to frequent the Hutchinson meetings. None ranked higher than Henry Vane and William Coddington. They were able, trustworthy men, so he believed. Mary Coddington could testify about the women's meetings, should anyone deem Anne Hutchinson herself an unsuitable witness.

"Do not think," he said to them, "that I have brought you here to accuse you."

No one answered that. They would wait to see how far that remark would prove true.

"Questions have been raised," he went on, "as to certain opinions brought forth at meetings in the house of Mistress Hutchinson. Strange opinions they be, some of them, and far from my beliefs, yet I am told you say nothing is held forth there except what I deliver in my lectures and sermons." He looked at Anne.

She scarcely knew how to answer. For the first time she suspected some secret enemy working against her, deliberately misleading Master Cotton. "That is true, sir," she finally answered. "It is what I always say, and it is true. But I know of no strange opinions; nor, I think, do my sister and my brothers here."

Mary Coddington looked troubled. William's face was bland and unreadable. Henry had drawn himself up with an air of injured innocence. They all looked at Cotton and gravely shook their heads.

"With your permission," Cotton went on, "I will give you some account of these doubtful teachings."

They sat quietly while he spoke of revelations through spirit without any reference to the scriptural word, of salvation accompanied by neither faith nor works, of God speaking through a believer in tongues unknown to anyone on earth, of abuse heaped on the ministers on account of their great learning.

Anne felt such anger rising in her as when she heard preachers frightening innocent people with their raging hellfire sermons based upon the covenant of works. It would be some of them, she guessed, who were spreading such tales, having heard she compared them unfavorably with John Cotton. She stood up, her eyes flashing.

"I know not who hath told you these things," she said, with difficulty keeping her voice low and steady, "but I have heard none of them spoken in my house. It would not occur to me to say that you yourself had ever preached such opinions."

Vane was standing too now. "Sir," he said to Cotton, "I find it incredible that you have brought us here to urge these suspicions against us." His eyes were large and luminous; there was a perceptible tremor in his voice.

"I have no suspicions, my dear Governor," Cotton said placatingly. "I merely have hoped for your help."

Vane sat down. Anne still stood. Mary Coddington sat staring, as though she had not yet comprehended what the minister had said to them.

"Do you speak, Mary," William said to her, "and say whether you have heard these opinions vented."

"Never!" she said, as in horror.

William reached out and placed a soothing hand on her arm. "I think," he said then, with no sign of emotion such as the others had shown, "that we need not feel so personally affronted. It appears to me that our teacher wishes, for our own good as well as the sake of the church, to clear the air of any heretical opinions that may be anonymously circulating." He turned to Cotton. "Have we not given you satisfaction, sir, by our simple denials?"

Cotton admitted that they had. He said he would assure his informants of his satisfaction, and he hoped and believed there would be an end to such talk as this that so much disturbed them all.

He accompanied them down the stairs, and then stood at his front door watching as the four of them went off together down the lane. He wondered why Henry Vane was making one of the party. After all, the boy lived here, more or less under the minister's own roof. He shook his head. There was much he did not understand about all this, but God knew he spoke truth to them when he said he hoped their denials would put an end to this strange unrest that was moving in the colony. But he did not know. He felt like a fish somehow caught in two nets by two fishermen at the same time.

5

Half Boston must have seen them as they came down Prison Lane and passed through the market place, on the way to Mistress Hutchinson's. They walked close together, talking earnestly: the two women in everyday sad-colored clothes with their black French hoods neatly rolled and tied under their chins; William Coddington, portly and tall, wearing a plain broad-brimmed hat and a suit of russet kersey. Only Henry Vane, with the notion that some degree of majesty belonged to the governor's office even in ordinary times, wore gayer things—green velvet and a feather-trimmed hat with a narrow brim that one might suppose the latest fashion in England. Slender and graceful, he moved along lightly beside his plodding elders.

"Where are they going?" it was whispered in the market place. "Where have they been?" There were those who knew that they had been to Master Cotton's, and others who guessed their destination. Old Goody Hawkins, questioned by a cluster of matrons gathered to watch a drunkard in the stocks, looked bright-eyed and knowing, as if she could tell a great deal more if she would.

"I cannot say," she told them, "but Boston will never be the same again."

She had no idea why she said that. A revelation it might be, such as those Mistress Hutchinson had. Of course Mistress Hutchinson never openly admitted to revelations, but it was common knowledge that she had them. Anyway, it was clear something was happening. Those closest to Mistress Hutchinson would be gathering together, she reckoned, and that meant news to be gleaned tonight and an extra big supper, at which a place could be found for Goodwife Hawkins.

Jane was right. At home, Anne sent Samuel with a message to the Cogshalls and Aspinwalls, and one of the little girls to the shop after William with word that John Wheelwright should come if he happened to be there. John was not there though. The Wheelwrights and Susannah were staying with the Hutchinsons until some permanent work could be found for John. Meanwhile, he might be in the market place or at the harbor or any place he could find a job to do, for he was strong and active, and detested idleness.

When the meeting was finally gathered, Anne sat in her tall armchair with the others clustered around her. All who received her request had come, and in addition, Francis, who had begged Anne's permission to be present.

"Let us take up the accusations one by one, in the order that he made them," said Anne in the confident high voice that she spoke in at her meetings.

They considered the questions fully and honestly. However it may have been later, no one then had any wish to dissemble or delude. They considered revelations. Calvin, they were told, taught that the Bible was the total of God's revelations to man.

"But what is it Master Cotton teaches when he talks of the direct witness of the spirit?" asked Mary Cogshall. "Is this not revelation?"

"I conceive not," said Anne. "That we may be sure of our election is a comfort of God and not to be thought of as a revelation. I do confess, though, I have sometimes believed He spoke to me." She paused, remembering. "I know He did, but it came out of my study of the Scripture."

"Aye," said Francis, "and so it was with me when I knew I must teach the mixed meetings."

"Then it was clearly not the spirit without the word," said Coddington, "and I do not believe such a thing as that has been spoken of by any of us here."

They all agreed it had not. Nor would any admit to doubting that faith was necessary to salvation, though it came only after God's initial gift of grace (as Cotton often had told them).

"But what about unknown tongues?" asked Elizabeth. "How could there be any gossip about that?"

They were puzzled until Mary Cogshall remembered a story she had heard about Jane Hawkins. "They say that one night at a birthing she suddenly began to babble till they thought she was crazed. Someone said they recognized some Latin words, but when it was over Jane said she did not know what she had said, but sure she was she'd never studied Latin."

They laughed at the thought of poor old Goody Hawkins as a

Latin scholar. But it was kindly laughter—they all felt kindly toward her, and ever welcomed her to the meetings.

"I shall find out about this speaking in tongues," said Anne.

"Now as to abusing the learning of the ministers," said Henry Vane, "I have a notion about that." He told them what the barber said about the blackcoats that had been at the Ninniversity.

Then Francis spoke in some heat of passion and said, "Now I know my mother never gave anyone cause to say such a word as that, for if any have respect for learning it is she."

Vane, looking with admiration at Anne, spoke tenderly to Francis. "Nay," he said, "but your mother has the gift to make God's promise clear to the meanest understanding."

"If so, I thank Him," said Anne. "But my son speaks true. My father was an educated man, and therefore, I have always believed, understood and could preach the word of God better than most ministers I have heard in my lifetime. Would that my son could follow in his footsteps."

It was not the first any of them had heard of that. They knew what Mistress Hutchinson extolled in her father and hoped for in her son.

"No, it is clear," said John Cogshall. "These false reports are being circulated by someone who wishes to discredit Mistress Hutchinson and those who love to listen to her teaching."

But his wife, reminding him of Goody Hawkins, said, "No, John, I think this is not necessarily so. Although I agree with Governor Vane that our sister has a special gift for making all things plain, still there are those among us who might misunderstand. I confess it is sometimes hard for me to see exactly what it means to be united to the Holy Spirit."

In the end, agreeing that at least for the time being, they could know neither the identity nor the nature of the enemy, they determined that the best thing to do was to speak plainly and simply, whenever the opportunity arose, about the meaning of free grace.

At the supper table they all still talked freely of the strange accusations and their plans to combat them. John Wheelwright, who had come in from working at the docks, listened intently.

"There are no religious truths so simple and clear that they are not subject to exaggeration and distortion," he said. "And minds of new converts are most fruitful of such strange shapes." He paused, watching Goody Hawkins gobble her porridge, then addressed her so suddenly and sternly that she choked and he had to wait for her to get over a fit of coughing before he could continue speaking to her.

"Goodwife," he said, "where did you ever hear of folk speaking in tongues?"

"Why, 'tis in the Bible," said Jane innocently.

"And can you read the Bible?" he asked. "And if as I think you cannot, then I repeat: where did you hear of this?"

She looked at him unblinking. "On the Isle of Ely," she said.

"Aha," he said.

"Yet all may not be error there, John," Anne interposed.

"Error spreads like weeds and deprives the truth of sustenance," he said. "I think we should take this we have learned as a warning to be careful."

"Well, I am sure I have never mentioned speaking in tongues —have I, Jane?"

"Oh no, mistress," said the old woman. "But I did hear you talk of them of old times, that acted when the spirit moved them."

"And did the spirit move you so to speak?" asked Wheelwright.

"Well, I thought of it and I did do it," she said.

"So I surmised," he said. "And where did you learn the Latin words?"

"I didn't know they was Latin," she said, "but I learned them on the Isle of Ely."

After supper, he talked at length with Anne about the danger of encouraging Jane Hawkins. "I do not believe she is the main source of this talk that has been brought to Brother Cotton, but she is a little foolish and may easily do and say things that an ill-wisher could use against us."

"Of course," said Anne. "I will talk with her."

"And we ourselves should be very careful not to add anything to what the preachers preach, in our reports of them—whether it be John Cotton, or brethren who emphasize a covenant of works."

Anne looked at him searchingly. "Do you think I also be a little foolish, Brother John?" she asked.

"Foolish—no," he said. "But enthusiastic, my dear Anne. Uncommonly enthusiastic."

6

In those days of doubt and confusion, many came to Anne Hutchinson for spiritual aid and comfort—more, it was said, than resorted to all the ministers put together.

Most came seeking desperately for some way to assure themselves of their election. For what if one minister told them to search their hearts for sin, of which even the smallest sign portended eternal damnation, and another in the same church said wait for Christ, only wait for Christ, and He will wash your sins away?

But also there were those who, having Christ clearly within them, still wrestled with matters of conscience. (Whatever Anne's enemies might say, calling her familist and antinomian, she did not teach or believe that the experience of free grace canceled out a person's conscience.)

Even the most pious and highly placed men in the colony thus might come to Anne, and several did, young Governor Vane most frequently of all. His matters of conscience now often concerned affairs of state, as when he came to Anne worried by the threat of an Indian war. The old trouble with the Pequods seemed certain to emerge again. The tribe had violated the treaty more than once. Several of the magistrates thought the colony had dawdled too long, and it was time to teach the Indians a lesson. Henry thought such lessons too costly in human life.

"I know there are many," he said to Anne one day as he sat in the place he always preferred, a low stool by her tall armchair, "who still do not believe the Indians are children of God, and some even insist they are devils that in the service of God we ought to destroy."

"No," said Anne, "this is not true. An Indian may be saved as well as any man, for I have talked with some myself and clearly seen signs of Christ. One thing I have learned surely: we are all one people in the sight of God."

"So I believe," said Henry. "Yet Indians do keep killing helpless Englishmen, and most of the magistrates insist we must protect the settlement in Connecticut." He sat dejected, his head bowed low; she reached out and touched his soft hair.

"Hold fast," she told him. "God does not want His people murdering each other." And Henry went on working for a new and more useful treaty of peace.

But on another day he came to her in great torment of mind, hatless, his hair disheveled, and dropped to the stool at her feet. "It is all over," he moaned, and covering his face in his hands commenced weeping.

Shortly he gained control of himself and told the story. Two Indians, Narragansets, had come to him with the news. There was a man named John Oldham, from Watertown, not a godly man but an Englishman even so, who while out in his trading ship with two English boys and two Narragansets had been brutally murdered. Another trader, coming upon his pinnace adrift and full of looting Indians, succeeded in frightening off most of the Indians and going aboard. When he searched the ship he found Oldham's body, not yet cold, concealed under an old seine. His hands and legs were hacked nearly off, his head split open so deep the brains had spilled out.

"Oh, dear God, dear God," cried Henry Vane. The magistrates, he said, would hardly hear to postponing war now, and perhaps they were right. They said if this act went unpunished there would be no end to murder and torture of innocent Englishmen, and women and children as well. Such deviltry had happened before in New England, and clearly would happen again and again, if no steps were taken to prevent it.

"It may be," Anne said, "that as governor you have bound yourself to put the protection of your people above what you in your heart would choose to do."

She did not deem it a good answer, but it was the only one she had for Henry Vane. Within a few days a company of ninety men under John Endicott sailed for Block Island to avenge the death of the ungodly John Oldham.

"I am afraid God will not bless us for this," said Henry Vane.

## 7

Other matters besides war concerned the General Court that summer. One was the establishment of a school that would serve the colony in the stead of a university. At last they voted to give four hundred pounds for the purpose. Francis had not said much when the subject was discussed at home, but after the court decided to support the plan he came to his mother one day and sat at her feet, as Governor Vane was wont to do.

"Mother," Francis said, "have you heard that there is to be a school?"

"Yes, son, it will be a good thing for the colony."

"It will be a good thing for me, Mother, for I know now I can stay in Massachusetts and still become a minister of God."

"Will it be such a school?"

"They say it will. Uncle Wheelwright says he believes it will soon be teaching everything he learned at Cambridge, and that if I continue to study with him I shall be ready for it by the time it opens."

"It would please me very much to see you ordained a minister someday," Anne said. Such a boundless joy as it really would be she hardly wished the boy to know, for she would not have him confuse his love for her with a true calling from God.

"You will see it, Mother," Francis said solemnly. "For I know I am called, and I know what I will become."

"You are confident, Francis."

"The Lord has spoken," he said, "and revealed His plan to me."

She did not inquire of him the nature of this revelation. He may have meant simply the call to preach that every man must know ere he become a minister, but the way he answered her suggested more than that. She was herself beginning at this time to believe revelations from God to be a corollary of what Master Cotton preached about the direct witness of Christ. But no matter what rumors might be circulating, she had not spoken publicly of her growing conviction. Nor did she speak of it now.

"So be it," she said, and clasped her son's hand, and they silently prayed together.

She thanked God for coming into his heart and showing him the way to go. In truth she had feared to lose this boy. Though his work at the meetings had seemed so satisfactory, it had undeniably made him restless. She had half expected him to come at any moment and say he was sailing to England—or more likely to the Lowlands or Germany, where he might think to find more freedom than in the mother country, as well as a university where he could matriculate. Now with this revelation from God and the action of the General Court, she could hope to keep this beloved son by her side. It pleased her to believe that Henry Vane was most responsible for establishing the school.

8

Gradually that summer, Anne became aware that she had changed. Or the pattern of her days had changed. Once again she had women enough in the household to do all the work, and this time she did not even try to take all the responsibility herself. Though her own hands were seldom idle, she had so much confidence in Mary Wheelwright that she felt free to turn the management of the household over to her. In fact, she saw that she must do this or give up her other work, the work God called her to: the large meetings, the private interviews, the impromptu strategy planning sessions when men as well as women would stop in and talk. The old days when Goody Hawkins and the three Marys came in for a pleasant chat seemed over and done with. They were often about, but Mary Wheelwright had in a sense taken Anne's place as hostess as well as housewife, because Anne was so often involved in a conference or else making notes for her meetings. To provide some semblance of privacy for those who came seeking her aid, she kept her chair by the window at the opposite end of the room from the kitchen, where the women gathered for most of their work, and set up a screen of green baize.

One day Mary Dyer sought her there. The old friends came somewhat apologetically now, for Anne Hutchinson seemed not quite one of them any more. Anne knew this and tried to put them at their ease; yet her mind stayed almost constantly on matters not often dwelled upon by her sex, so that she sometimes felt she was speaking to them across a newly opened chasm, and would almost unconsciously raise her voice as if they had turned somewhat deaf. The women thought this was because she had become so used to speaking at the large meetings, and she thought well, after all, perhaps it was.

"I have come," Mary Dyer said that day, "as so many others come to you now, and not as a friend."

Anne thought she knew what Mary meant, but felt rather

chilled, almost rejected, by those words. "Yet surely, Mary, we are always friends," she said.

"Oh yes, dear Anne," said Mary, and kissed her. "And yet I have come to you asking more than mere friendship can give."

There was a new little chair that Anne kept by her now, from the shop of John Crabtree the joiner (who came to the meetings and had seen a thing he could do to help Mistress Anne). She motioned for Mary to take a seat there; only two or three of all who came to her did she care to have sitting on the stool at her feet.

"Two things I would ask of you," Mary said. "I shall speak first of what I must think is the lesser one, even though it is breaking my heart."

"Dear Mary, what is it?" Anne cried.

"I want a child, so terribly. I hunger for a child," Mary said.

"You do not think it will come in God's time?"

"Oh, I know not. We have lost one, as you know, and now it has been so long. Can there be aught I have done, to be punished thus by the Lord?"

"Is this what you have come to ask?" Anne did not think it was. Mary knew very well she did not believe God dealt in such a way with His children.

Mary shook her head. "No," she said. "But there is something else I badly need to ask you." She looked down. "I don't know, it may be wicked. I can't tell."

"You will not tell me you are contemplating anything wicked," Anne said.

Mary waited a little while to speak, and Anne did not urge her. At last she said, "Jane Hawkins has herbs that can make me conceive."

"Do you think so, Mary?"

"She assures me that she does."

"Mandrake, I doubt not."

"Does it work as she says?"

"Aye, it may. Not every time, but it may."

"I have heard"—Mary almost whispered this—"I have heard it be the devil's root."

"No, Mary. God made everything for man's use. But we have to learn its properties. It is doubtful to me that we have learned all God would have us know about the mandrake."

"Have you never used it then?"

"Never."

"What do you think—it might be dangerous?"

"I think it might be—either to you or the child. But I do not know."

"Goody Hawkins says it is safe and that more often than not it has worked for her."

"Then, Mary, I have told you all I can."

"You do not think knowledge like this is something God would reveal?"

"I do not think so, for it is something we can find out through common sense, and we can let the plant alone unless we know what it will do."

"Then what?" asked Mary. "What is it God reveals?"

"What course to take in living out our lives in His service. As Francis when he heard his call to preach."

"And you when you came to New England."

"Aye." But then Anne frowned and slightly shook her head. "And yet not quite the same."

"No," said Mary, "I thought it was not."

Anne looked up keenly at this young woman whose dreamy eyes ever seemed to be searching her own soul instead of looking outward upon the world. It was impossible that she had come to accuse Anne of believing in direct revelations. She saw something she might well have guessed long before.

"God spoke directly to my son when He called him to preach," she said. "And I think that you yourself have heard the voice of God in some such way."

"Yes, He has spoken to me," Mary said. "He sent me to you."

Anne had no doubt at all that Mary meant what she was saying, or any doubt that it was wholly true.

"The spirit without the word," she said.

Mary nodded. "Without Scripture, without a sign, and without even a dream to be interpreted."

Anne said then, "It will happen to me if I let it."

"I thought it would," Mary said. "Is it not part of our union with the Holy Spirit?"

"I have long believed so," Anne confessed.

"Others want to believe so, too," said Mary. "We want to be

free to speak the truth of what we know by our experience, but we are waiting for you to unlock the ministers' iron bonds."

Anne gazed into her inward, dreaming eyes. "Let us wait here a little while longer, and He may speak to us."

They had no idea how long it was they sat there, hand in hand. But after that time alone with Mary Dyer, Anne knew she must no longer keep back this truth of God from the people who trusted her.

# XVI

In the late summer and early autumn of 1636, every man and woman in the colony—and every prating child as well—seemed consumed with the raging controversy over how God saves men's souls. As John Winthrop would write later, it began to be as common to distinguish between men as being under a covenant of works or a covenant of grace, as in other countries between Protestants and papists.

One cold night in October, the Winthrop family were sitting by the fire. John's little grandchild Thomas, visiting with his mother from Ipswich, was playing with a servant's child on the floor, making a governor's mansion out of scraps of wood saved from building a new barn on Winthrop's Mystic River farm. Suddenly Thomas, annoyed by the other child's manner of stacking blocks, stood up and kicked the whole structure to pieces. "You don't know nothing," he shouted. "You're under a covenant of works!" "Grace!" shouted the other child, trying to push Thomas down. "Works!" cried Thomas, kicking and hitting.

John Winthrop leaped from his chair, grabbed a child under each arm, and carried them both to the woodshed, where he whipped them thoroughly. "Never let me hear you say those words again," he ordered them.

"Are they wicked words, Grandfather?" sobbed little Thomas.

"They are wicked in the mouths of fools and children," he said. "Now go back and play peacefully together, and let me not hear you raise your voices to each other any more tonight."

He was unable to settle down again in the family circle by the fire. Anger at that fierce ungodly woman across the high street mingled with cold, creeping doubt about her brother-in-law, the minister, and the reverend Master Cotton, who had once seemed God's greatest gift to His people in New England. He could not force his mind back to the talk of his daughter's ever-recurring problem of finding a maidservant who would follow instructions and keep a respectful tongue in her mouth. Mary said if the war continued she hoped her father would find a way to get her an Indian girl or two. Everybody was saying that English servants were getting more difficult to manage all the time. It was too easy for them to have their own house and land here in New England. Soon there would be no servant class at all.

Winthrop told her he would keep her need in mind. Ever gentle and thoughtful with his womenfolk, he apologized for removing himself. He said there were papers that needed his attention, as indeed there always were, but when he sat down in the study at his desk, the turmoil of the colony possessed his mind. The Indian trouble—Mary's request brought that to mind—seemed at least temporarily under control. He had to admit that young Vane, with the help of Roger Williams, had done well in arranging a treaty with the Narragansets. It was to be signed the very next day. On the other hand, John Endicott's tactics had probably done more harm than good, stirring up the Pequods to greater hostility without really settling anything. Certainly William Bradford at Plymouth thought so. He complained that the Bay Colony had sent forces against the Pequods without even notifying Plymouth, and then left them and the Connecticut settlers at the mercy of the angered tribe.

But these difficulties could be overcome. The young governor had some experience in matters of state and seemed willing to learn about colony affairs from the magistrates who had been involved in them from the beginning. If only that emotional and impressionable boy had stayed away from Anne Hutchinson!

Internal conflict was the thing John Winthrop feared most. Unified, this colony could still become a model for Christian communities throughout the world. But the opinionists were capable of turning it into a ragged collection of little settlements all struggling against each other, at the mercy of the Indians, the Dutch, the French, and the devil. Already in England, nonconformist brethren were predicting the experiment would fail because of the congregational form of church government that was evolving in New England. The experiment had to work: before the eyes of Englishmen at home, there must be a demonstration of its value. And the form of government that left each congregation independent would work as long as they all accepted scriptural truth as the basis of all doctrine. Such lawlessness as Anne Hutchinson preached was not compatible with any form of government at all, and in a colony where matters of church and state moved always hand in hand it could only result in total devastation.

Up to this time, John Winthrop had not written anything about Anne Hutchinson in the journal he was keeping as a basis for the history of this colony. He had always considered his writing an integral part of his work. In years to come—even centuries to come, so he believed—when people still marveled at this model community of God's elect, they would want to read the account of how it came to be. He scrupulously entered every event of any significance. Once his son left over a thousand books in storage, among them one in which the New Testament, Psalms, and the Common Prayer were bound together. When he came to take up this book, he discovered that mice had eaten up the Common Prayer entirely; but not another page of this volume, or any other of his many books, was even touched. Signs from God as well as events that affected the condition of the colony, he always recorded. Until recently he had hoped Anne Hutchinson would somehow vanish without making any mark that would have to be remembered.

Perhaps, indeed, he had hoped so until this very night. But when the truth of God had been held up publicly to scorn, so that these two infants of his own well-taught family used doctrinal terms in their childish name calling, the antinomian threat could no longer be ignored. Here was a segment of the history of Massachusetts Bay. He dipped his quill into his ink and began to write the story whose end was still veiled in the dark future. He trusted in God, but that night he could not guess what the end would be or how far ahead of them it lay.

"One Mrs. Hutchinson," he wrote, "a member of the church of Boston, a woman of a ready wit and a bold spirit, brought over with her two dangerous errors: 1. That the person of the Holy Ghost dwells in a justified person. 2. That no sanctification can help to evidence to us our justification." He thought, as he had often done before, about the implications of these two errors. Man is no more man but God-man and so above God's law. When fear of eternal punishment is taken away, as surely it must be when man no longer must look to his good works as evidence of his salvation, then conscience must vanish as well, and sin will flourish like rampant weeds. He wrote a few more lines. Then he thought of John Wheelwright. Not the instigator of the dangerous opinions, still he had by his evident approval deepened the division in the colony. "There joined with her in these opinions," he added, "a brother of hers, one Mr. Wheelwright, a silenced minister sometimes in England."

He felt a little better. He had faced the problem, given it the recognition it had come to demand. He did not know then what he could do about it, but from that time he knew he would give his full powers to achieving a solution.

He was about to have the opportunity to take his first public step against the opinionists, but of course he could not know that in this very same moment they were hatching a plan to make their own first public and strategic move.

2

In the meetinghouse, on the morning of the Lord's Day, one might have sensed something uncommon about to take place. Anne Hutchinson walked in straighter and stiffer than usual, her chin slightly lifted, her eyes straight ahead. Most of her followers lacked her control and could not help giving quick little meaningful glances at each other. In the back of the house, Goody Hawkins whispered shamelessly, until the tithing man touched her with the fox tail on his pole. Those in hearing had learned at least that something was going to happen that would put old thundering Wilson in his place.

In later years it was said that only four persons in the Boston church refrained from joining Anne Hutchinson's party. Anne herself neither knew nor cared how many there were. Probably it was more than four. But as for the number who actively opposed her, that may have been fewer still. Among the laymen only one—Winthrop—clearly made himself known. He sat through the sermon wondering what the opinionists might be about to do, and was not surprised when, after it ended, Atherton Hough rose and asked permission to make a proposal to the congregation.

In view of the fact that God had sent to Boston an able minister of the Church of Christ, silenced in England for his true beliefs, he wished to propose that this man, this brother John Wheelwright, be called as a second teacher to their church.

From his place on the foreseat, Winthrop could see the sly little smiles on faces throughout the meetinghouse. He might have predicted this move, he thought, might have made plans to forestall it. Even now, though, there was something he could do, and he was on his feet before any other member had a chance to speak, reminding the congregation that by church rule a week must elapse before a vote on this kind of measure was taken. Hough expressed himself as being quite willing to wait, but there were signs of frustration and annoyance among the Hutchinsonians.

John Winthrop thanked God that He so arranged things that in the week following the move to call John Wheelwright, there occurred in Boston both a conference of ministers and a meeting of the General Court. Winthrop had little doubt that the opinionists were plotting to remove John Wilson from the pastorate, put John Cotton in his place, and leave Wheelwright as the only teacher. These two public events, he thought, could help to thwart their devious purpose by bringing all opinions clearly into the open. The ministers, so Winthrop had been told by Pastor Wilson, would attempt to discover once and for all exactly where each of them stood in regard to the errors emanating from the Boston church.

To make sure the results of the conference would become widely known, Winthrop determined to have the ministers appear before the court. Henry Vane enthusiastically agreed. Like Winthrop, he believed God had decided it was time His children brought the truth out in full view, that it might prevail through all the churches in the colony.

On Tuesday morning at nine o'clock, the court convened in the meetinghouse. Deputies from every town in the Bay filled the seats of the congregation. Henry Vane sat at the head of the long table, with Deputy Governor Winthrop and the other magistrates ranged around him. The ministers were seated to one side, in the places of honor always kept for them should they wish to attend the court. Every extra seat and every corner were crowded with spectators. All Boston knew what was happening today. The same two questions that everyone had been discussing in private were to be publicly resolved by the ministers at last. Yet as the session proceeded, it appeared that they had reached no consensus in their own conference, so that few could find much satisfaction in their answers before the court. Did they believe sanctification could help to evidence justification? Oh yes, they all believed that. But Cotton added his usual difficult disclaimer: No amount of good works can be true evidence without the witness of the spirit that we are justified. Was not this dangerously slanted against scriptural law? Winthrop thought so, but Cotton's brother ministers indicated without enthusiasm that this was their belief as well.

It was harder to be certain of just what each one held about the union of the elect with the Holy Ghost. Did they believe, as Mistress Hutchinson purportedly taught, that this was a personal union? Cotton thought not. A union, yes—at least to the extent of the indwelling of the Holy Ghost—but not if one meant any communication of personal properties.

The governor then, unasked, stood up and said that he believed, with Mistress Hutchinson, in a personal union; and if any wanted witness of that he would gladly testify. No one did. It was the opinion of the ministers that was wanted, Winthrop reminded Vane. But it seemed that on this point the ministers could nowise agree. Wheelwright thought as Cotton did, he said, and several spoke for that view. Pastor Wilson saw no reason to suspect that there ever was any divine spirit dwelling within any man. To his mind, such a concept went clearly against Scripture.

John Winthrop felt perplexed when the meeting was over. He had thanked God for this opportunity to see how each minister stood in regard to true doctrine. But as he walked wearily homeward, across the market place, he had to admit to God that he wasn't much clearer about most of the brethren than he had been before.

## 3

It was not entirely true, as Winthrop suspected, that the opinionists were plotting to get rid of John Wilson. They wanted another teacher who knew how to preach the covenant of grace, and they admitted to each other some hope that with two such men in the pulpit, the pastor would see how out of place he was and accept a call elsewhere. Many had wanted John Cotton as pastor from the day they heard he was coming to New England. Now they envisioned Cotton as pastor and Wheelwright as teacher in a church where nothing would ever be preached again but God's pure grace. But Wilson might stay. That would be well enough, provided they could have John Wheelwright, and since the court session with the ministers they could see no reason why any member of the church would vote against him. Although several of the preachers and some few of the court had seemed uncertain about both Cotton and Wheelwright at first, when that session was over most of the ministers professed to hold no greatly different opinions.

So now on a cool, bright autumn morning, the last Lord's Day in October, the Boston congregation made their separate ways to the meetinghouse in a triumphant and anticipatory mood. The Hutchinson household, all dressed in their best, looked properly well-to-do and sedate; but inwardly they were not so very calm. Anne did not consider herself embattled, but she understood for the first time in her life the way God's angels must have felt when they toppled Satan out of heaven.

When the time came, Atherton Hough rose and made a motion that the church call John Wheelwright as an additional teacher. But before it could be seconded, John Winthrop sprang up from his place on the magistrates' seat and with a cold dignity that belied his blazing eyes declared he never could consent to call this man to preach.

Stunned, Anne heard him go on to explain that the church had able ministers enough, and certainly would be better off without one of such dangerous opinions as Brother Wheelwright had recently expressed. She knew what this meant: she understood that one dissenting member could end all hope of moving the Boston church into the true covenant.

But as Winthrop took his seat, the governor rose to speak. He had not Winthrop's remarkable control. He spoke passionately. He would remind his brother that Master Cotton himself at the General Court had said he was in agreement with Brother Wheelwright's opinions; so he failed to see how Brother Winthrop could call them dangerous. He spoke well, Anne thought, for surely Master Cotton's approval must serve to persuade Winthrop. But then Cotton arose from his seat beneath the pulpit, and in gentle tones explained that he believed in a general way his brother's doctrines, yet must admit he was not altogether clear about his meaning when he talked about union with the Holy Ghost, and also did find that Brother Wheelwright was apt to raise doubtful disputations.

So incredible were the teacher's words that Anne felt tempted to rise and challenge them, but then Wheelwright stood and spoke a few words about the nature of the union he believed in, to which Cotton nodded as if in assent. Even then, John Winthrop did not change his mind. Brother Wheelwright was a godly man and an able minister, he said, but much too likely (as Master Cotton perceived) to bring about doubtful disputations.

Wheelwright's friends, having faced the strong possibility of Winthrop's unyielding opposition, had another plan, which they immediately presented. Several of them, including William Hutchinson, had been granted land at Mt. Wollaston, and they were in need of a church there. They would like to have John Wheelwright as their pastor. No one spoke against this compromise; and so there was a kind of victory.

But after sundown, a group of angry men and women gathered at Anne Hutchinson's. They could not be content without taking some action, and decided at last to demand that the deputy governor apologize to John Wheelwright. They would have him at the meetinghouse for that purpose on the following afternoon.

## 4

It was cold and misty the next morning. John Winthrop stood at his upstairs window and looked across the high street at the house that stood there ever taunting him. It had a phantom quality in this weather. He wished it were a phantom house indeed, if such a thing were possible, and would vanish with the mists that wreathed it.

At least he wished away its inhabitants. The woman had been bad enough, luring good Christian people into that accursed house and infecting them with her devilish notions. But now this man—this ordained minister of God—must move into the house and take up with her and preach her false doctrines in the meetinghouse under the sanction of the church. It might have been better if he had opposed the organization of a church at Mt. Wollaston, but on the spur of the moment, caught unprepared, he had judged it best to oppose that faction no longer. (For though it pleased him to call it a faction, was it not close to comprising the whole church of Boston?)

And now they had sent him word that he must stand before them and apologize to John Wheelwright. Oh, God, he prayed for patience and strength. As he stood praying, and growing somewhat more calm, he determined to go and pay a visit to this man, that they might peacefully reason together and if God willed avert the catastrophe that he seemed to see about to strike this city upon the hill.

Having reached his decision, he walked rather heavily down the stairs. Margaret came into the front entry as he was taking his cloak from a peg, and he told her only that he must be out for a while upon some business of the church.

Scarlet-clad and imperious, he strode across the street and came for the first time to the door of that abhorred house. A child stood on the top step.

At least he thought at first glance it was a child. It was a slight figure enveloped in a gray hooded cloak, and if he had been inclined to pursue that passing and uncharacteristic fantasy of the phantom house he might have taken her for a ghost child. She was in the act of knocking timidly (as it seemed almost silently) at the door, when she heard him and turned around. It was no child, but a woman grown and, to judge by her sad eyes and pinched face, accustomed to no very happy manner of life. Alarm widened and darkened her eyes when she saw Winthrop. He knew she was some young woman from the church, though he could not call her name, and guessed immediately that she had come to ask some kind of help from Mistress Hutchinson. He had seen them here before—brainless, godless creatures: if they needed spiritual help, Boston had ministers; if they were sick, there was Master Oliver, a surgeon by profession.

Stupid woman! She ducked her head and quickly turned away, so that he seized her arm as though she had been a thief trying to escape the law.

"What are you doing here, young woman?" he demanded in a voice charged with the anger he felt for all who would lead such as she into the devil's snare.

As she turned her face to his, tears ran out of her wide, scared eyes. "I came to see Mistress Hutchinson," she said. "They say she can help when all else fails."

"Then they are wrong," he lashed out at her with barely contained fury. "You had better go home and pray God to forgive you for coming to such a house as this with such a thought in mind."

"I only want to ask about the grace of God," she said wildly.

"This is no place to seek anything pertaining to God," he snapped. "Now get on away from here and never let me see you at this door again."

She gave him one more fearful glance, then hastily turned and ran. A voice from the doorway called, "Sister, come back!"

But the childlike figure bobbed off into the mist, and never looked around.

And Winthrop turned to see Anne Hutchinson staring at him from behind the partly open door.

"May I ask what it is you do, sir," she said in a high, brittle voice, "driving my guest from my door?"

"I do not think she can have been an invited guest," he said.

"I never yet have driven anyone from my door, invited or not," said Anne. "And yet I know not what your business here may be." Though she did not admit to herself any fear of this man, she felt him to be her mortal enemy, and when she looked into his face he held her with his piercing eyes, so that she quite forgot the girl whom she had heard cry for help and let her run away without even seeing what direction she took.

"I have come to see John Wheelwright, if you please," said Winthrop then, never calling her by name or showing by any respectful word or gesture that he knew she was the mistress of the house.

"Well," she said, and stood aside to let him pass within.

John Wheelwright was sitting by the fire, and she simply gestured in his direction and walked away toward the other end of the room. She did not know when she had been so near to shameful tears.

The two men were left in seeming privacy, but the whole household could hear their talk. After considerable discussion of doctrine, the real question in Winthrop's mind came to the surface, and he asked directly for clarification of Wheelwright's views on union.

Wheelwright gladly gave them. "Do you recognize the physical union that exists between a man and wife," he asked, "as both the symbol and the reality of their love? Do you see that they are become in actual fact each a part of the other?"

Winthrop grunted.

"Just such a union exists between God and every person who loves Him."

Winthrop said little more, but went home soon after that, taking a barely polite leave of his brother in Christ. That afternoon he appeared before the Boston congregation as requested and offered no apology. He said that after further talk with Brother Wheelwright he remained of the same opinion about the man's dangerous doctrines. He offered to impart his own belief to any brother who desired enlightenment. But to that offer, as he wrote later in his journal, "no man spake."

John Winthrop, quite singlehandedly, had won a small skirmish in the antinomian war. But it was far from a decisive battle. He knew that, and so (as they all went out declaring to each other) did the friends of Anne Hutchinson and John Wheelwright.

## 5

Anne, like Winthrop, had recognized the young woman at her door as a sister in the church and yet knew neither her name nor her dwelling place. That night, when the turmoil in her bosom had died down, she found her thoughts strangely drawn to that girl. She told William about her.

"I ought to have run after her," she said. "I ought to have gone and fetched her home with me. I saw her eyes—she needed me—and yet my hatred for John Winthrop held me back. Our hatred for each other held us as if it had been the link of love."

"Anne," said William, "thou hast never hated any man or woman in thy life."

She believed that had been true. "Until now," she said. "Until, I verily believe, this very day."

"It is anger, not hatred," he said. "It will pass."

"I pray it will," she said. "But, William, why cannot they see and understand God's truth? They profess to be Christians—they believe themselves to be Christians—yet their eyes burn like hellfire at the thought of being possessed by God's love. Oh, I have seen hell in their eyes—John Winthrop's and John Wilson's."

"Perhaps through prayer and patience," William said, "that too will pass."

"Oh, I pray for patience, William," said Anne. "And yet I cannot think God wants me not to speak, and those two men will never rest until they silence me."

"What of the girl who ran away?" said William, to take her mind from what distressed her so.

"I shall look for her in meeting on the Lord's Day," Anne said. "But I do fear, oh I do so sadly fear, that it will be too late."

The mist had cleared next morning; the day was sunny and though not very warm not freezing cold either. The young Hutchinson and Wheelwright children ran out to play and so, through meeting their friends in the street, were the first of their household to come home with the news.

A woman had thrown her baby down a well. Then she went into the house and told her husbnad that all her worries were over. It seemed she had been much troubled as to whether she could believe she was truly saved, until at last, finding no way, she had drowned the child that she might know for certain she was damned.

Anne knew at once who it was. "Where is she?" she cried. "I must go to her."

The children did not know where she was.

"Then I shall find her," Anne said, and leaving her wheel (at which act her mother-in-law but silently shook her head), she drew her cloak around her and set off down the high street and through the market place toward Prison Lane. Along the way she heard what she expected to hear. The young woman had been taken to jail and would of course be hanged as soon as the magistrates could act upon the matter. "And none too soon," said everyone. All Boston was aroused and incredulous at such unheard-of wickedness. In the market place, Anne met Mistress Hibbens, who declared malevolently that she would never rest until she saw this wicked and unnatural slut hanging from yonder gibbet.

"Hush," said Anne. "You may hang there yourself one day."

The woman walked off loosing a spate of vituperative language.

"But do you not agree," asked Mary Dyer, coming from her husband's market stall, "that the poor girl must be hanged?"

"Aye, they will hang her," said Anne bitterly.

A little cluster of women and a few men soon gathered around Anne, as nearly always happened when she showed herself in the public parts of town. They were angry and disturbed; Anne felt some part of their hostility directed at herself, an experience she had scarcely known before.

"Would you not have a law against murder, mistress?" asked one goodwife who had frequented her meetings. In truth, they all had—all in this group gathered around her—and were accustomed to hang onto her every word. But they were capable of turning against her. Anne saw that now in their set unsmiling faces and their unspeaking eyes. Only Mary Dyer came and put her arm through Anne's. "I know what you mean," she said softly.

Anne faced the little cluster of her followers. Persons whom she did not know, as well as some who she suspected might oppose her, came and stood at the edge of the group as she began to speak. As if out of nowhere, a little brown hunched creature appeared, working her way through the huddle towards Anne. "Tell us, mistress," she importuned, "tell us why you do not wish to see her hanged."

"Do you not remember," Anne said, "what I have told you many times? That the convenant of works is the devil's snare? Do you know what drove this pitiable woman to do the unthinkable deed she has done?"

There were murmurs from the group. They shook their heads.

"I might have said *who* drove her to it, for I can name the very men."

"Name them, mistress," called out Goody Hawkins, and "Name them!" echoed the crowd. Their eyes were bright and hungry now.

Anne thought of the pinched face of the girl who had come to her door. She wanted to be with her and comfort her, but here and now truth cried out to be told.

"You must hear, then, and quickly," she said, "for I needs must go to her." She paused a moment, though, tossed back the hood of her cloak, and stood bareheaded with the sun finding out silver strands in her glossy dark hair. "Yes, you must hear," she said—indeed, with passion, cried. "You may know," she began, "the report of what she spake unto her husband. That she could have peace of mind at last, since she knew she should be damned. But let me tell you this: no one could reason so, not even a madwoman could reason so, unless she had been led by false preachers into a covenant of works. More than one minister in the Bay preaches thus, as all of you well know, but we know too the one man who preaches this false doctrine in the church of Boston." She stopped, her eyes on the meetinghouse roof, and her listeners hissed, "Pastor Wilson!"

"Aye," she said. "He who tells us every Lord's Day that the least trace of sin in our hearts is the sign of eternal damnation. He who tells us it is what we do and are tempted to do that can save our souls or damn them. He who balances a measure of good works against our bad deeds and thoughts and forgets how the grace of God outweighs them all."

"And who else, mistress?" urged Goody Hawkins, who had made her way through the crowd to Anne's side. "Tell us about the other man who led the poor girl to do the deed."

"Yes, tell," cried the crowd, and Anne, remembering John Winthrop's lashing voice as it whipped the slight creature from her door like a dog, told in detail what she had seen and heard there. "John Winthrop is more to blame than John Wilson," she said, "for it was he that drove her away from the one place she might have found help."

"You could have saved her, mistress," piped Goody Hawkins.

"Aye," said Anne, her voice thick with the hatred that rose in her breast, "and yet may. But that man will prevent me if he can."

And no one thought to remind either woman that only Jesus Christ can save.

Before Anne resumed her course along Prison Lane, someone slipped away from the listening group and hurried off in the other direction, toward John Winthrop's house. Then a running boy with a swiftly scrawled message in his hand set off across back lots, and cutting behind the meetinghouse, was able to pass the paper to Jailer Brackett before Anne Hutchinson reached the heavy iron-bound door.

Patches of dead weeds uncut all summer long drooped soddenly among the faded grasses on the plot in front of the jail, which was a plain wooden structure, narrow and gray as a grave. A rosebush bare of bloom and leaf thrust out thorns that caught at Anne's cloak as she stood lifting the heavy knocker.

Even before it had sounded, Master Brackett appeared there.

"No visitors allowed," he said gruffly.

"I only want a word or two with the prisoner they brought in this morning," Anne said. "I need not even be in the same room if you deem that unwise."

But Master Brackett was already closing the door. "My orders are she must see no one," he said, and Anne stood facing the bands of iron across the oak door.

She knew where those orders must have come from, and she knew the only man in the colony who could rescind them. So she plodded on up the lane to the two-part house at the foot of the Trimontaine, where she knocked at the door of Henry Vane's lodging, only to be told by his servant that the governor was gone for the day, on business in Charlestown and Newtown.

Sadly, she went back home. She would try again, of course. But so expeditiously did the trial court go about its work that by the time Henry Vane was able to effect admittance for Anne the girl was already condemned to die. She lay on the jailhouse cot and turned her face to the wall when Anne tried to talk to her.

A few days later, Anne, along with nearly all the rest of Boston's population, stood and watched the girl die on the gallows. Anne prayed some word of hers had touched that troubled heart, though it had evoked no visible response, but as she watched the death jerk she felt a profound conviction, heavy as a stone in her bosom. What she had witnessed was the sign of victory for John Winthrop and the devil.

At her next meeting, Anne's concern with this affair was still so great that she talked of nothing else. She made not the slightest pretense of reviewing John Cotton's sermon, and many said afterward that on this day Mistress Hutchinson became a preacher in her own right.

# XVII

Now after a little more than two years in the Massachusetts Bay Colony, William Hutchinson could have been well content. He owned six hundred acres of land at Mt. Wollaston, where his brother-in-law John Wheelwright had recently removed. He had an interest in the new town dock and possession of an island in the harbor. As he gained property, he gained prestige; now in addition to being a deputy in the General Court, he was a selectman of the town, and, most gratifying of all, would soon be ordained a deacon in the Boston church.

And like his property, the mercer's trade, which had always been his chief source of income, continued to increase. He had excellent help from his two eldest sons, or would in a few months when Edward returned from England with his bride. Francis, he now perceived, would never be a man of business; but it pleased him to think of having a son in the ministry. He saw no reason why the boy should not attend the school at New-town when it opened in a year or two. People said it would be the New England Cambridge, a certain means of entering this loftiest of professions.

William was proud of all his children. The two grown girls had married uncommonly well, and he could foresee no trouble from any of the boys or girls coming on. They were healthy and biddable and, he modestly thought, well-appearing. He was somewhat sorry to think Zuriel might be the last of them, but the time had to come someday. Anne was forty-five years old now and had told him she was experiencing some little incon-veniences and discomfort that might mean her change of life was approaching. Her supply of milk for Zuriel was already drying up.

He was thinking of all these things one gray November day, riding home from the farm at Wollaston. The thought of Anne disturbed him. He was afraid for her. When she came home from the hanging (which he was one of the few in Boston to avoid), and began to speak of it, her face flushed wine red and a dark fire flared in her eyes. Pacing the floor, she preached so angrily to the whole household (which then still included the Wheelwrights and the ancient Susannah) that the little children ran away frightened and he himself muttered something about business in the shop and left the house.

Now he regretted that act. It was a cowardly thing to do: he had been frightened, like the children, and ignorant like them of any reason why. Later, though, going over the incident in his mind, he knew there was a reason for his fear. At Anne's time of life, such passions could be dangerous. He feared for her health and even, though secretly almost from himself, her sanity. In addition, he dared not predict the outcome of her open condemnation of John Wilson and John Winthrop. A strange thing, which he had mentioned to no one, had happened on a day when, most uncommonly, he went to the spring for a pail of water. As he turned back toward the house he met Winthrop, and so convenient was this meeting for the deputy governor that William could only believe he had been watching and waiting for some such chance. "Sir," he said to William without preamble, "if you do not begin to control your wife, you may have the dissolution of the colony to answer for."

And William, standing with the pail in his hand, respectfully answered, "I thank you, sir."

He recognized the warning, but he had no intention of trying to control Anne's religious life. He had not doubted her when she told him God would have them move to New England, and he did not doubt her now. Without dwelling much on matters of doctrine, he could readily see how the preaching of Wheelwright and Cotton differed from that of Pastor Wilson. But he wondered if she had ever questioned whether God meant her to use up all her strength and call down upon herself the wrath of ministers and magistrates. For was this God's only truth, this truth she preached? (Oh yes, she preached; there was no use denying it now, she preached, and he could not help a deep instinctive sense of a woman preacher as out of keeping with the natural order of the universe.)

Riding along the Neck, nearing home, he made up his mind to have a private talk with his wife. Most husbands would have demanded such a talk long before (or exercised their rights without talking at all), but he was not thinking even now of husbandly rights. His thoughts had never run that way. Anne had the right to do whatever God required of her, William granted her that; nor was there any way he would have denied it. Still, he wanted to have a talk.

It was nearly suppertime when he came home. Goody Hawkins was there, helping in the kitchen. He thought with a small smile of what his brother Wheelwright said of Goody Hawkins, that she followed Christ for loaves. He begrudged her not a whit the food she ate at his table, but he wondered sometimes why Anne indulged her. Perhaps only because it would have been hard to turn away this ingratiating little creature who seemed to find in her Mistress Anne the whole meaning of her life.

Henry Vane was there, too, but he was leaving, due at a supper meeting with some friends from out of town. When the governor entertained, he chose Samuel Cole's hostelry, which stood just north of the Hutchinsons' house, and unless it were an official occasion that called for his escort of halberdiers, he would stop by for a little while before the hour appointed for the feast.

He was taking his leave as William entered, and after an exchange of greetings between the two men Anne saw him to the door, speaking a few soft words to him and giving him her hand. From where he stood in front of the fire, William watched the two. He had observed before how on parting Henry leaned to Anne, reluctant to say farewell, rosy with youth and the fervor of youth. Pious and pure as Henry undoubtedly was, William felt convinced that earthly love figured in the young man's attachment to his wife. At the same time, he was satisfied that Henry himself did not fully recognize the nature of his feeling. He could hardly avoid awareness of carnal urgings, but he could easily ascribe them to the devil's jealousy of a pure and spiritual love. What Anne felt for Henry, William did not ask himself.

He did not know whether Henry Vane was one of the matters he would speak of, but he made up his mind then that this very night he would talk to his wife. After supper and prayers, which Goody Hawkins stayed for, the family all went up to bed and Anne placed the sleeping Zuriel in his cradle. As she was about to put out the candle that stood on a stand by the bed, William came and put his arm around her.

"Stay," he said. "Let us drink a cup of wine together."

He poured out a little of the best Madeira and the two sat side by side on the settle in the corner by the fire.

She sighed and leaned against him. "I am tired, William," she said.

"Thou art not angry with me, Anne?" he asked.

"With thee, William?" she said, genuinely surprised. "How could I ever be?"

"Yet there may be some lack of sympathy in me?"

"In thee, William?"

"Compared, it may be, with young Governor Vane." He wished immediately he had not said that. It revealed to him and thus perhaps to her, some small degree of resentment he had truly not known that he felt.

"William, he is a boy," Anne said.

"Aye," said William.

"And yet a boy with such experience of the Holy Spirit as no one else that I have ever known."

"Such sympathy is what I mean," he said. "Only that."

"I do know that. But it's such sympathy as detracts not the least in the world from the love between husband and wife."

William kissed her. "I never really thought it could," he said, "but yet I am a weak man, with such jealousies sometimes as weakness may allow."

"Such a man, with such a weakness, is a truly loving man," she said. "I never doubt thy love, nor must thou ever mine."

"I never did," said William. "It was not that boy I meant to speak of anyway."

"Of what, then?"

As they sipped their wine, he told her; and as they talked, her weariness abated.

"Oh yes, William," she cried, in answer to his question as to whether she believed God wanted her to work so vigorously against those ministers who preached a covenant of works. "Oh yes, for He hath told me so." Her eyes glowed in the candlelight with a softness far different from the baleful fire that gleamed there when she talked about the hanging of that pitiable murderess.

"And must there be dissension and strife?"

"Aye, William, for the sword is with us always."

"Then the thought of making enemies of powerful men is not a stranger to thee?"

"Nay, William, I have thought. Never fear, for God will save us, in this world as in the next."

He recognized the way she spoke, somewhat suggestive of a minister reading Scripture from the pulpit. There was no way of reasoning with that tone of voice, that utter certainty.

"Let's to bed," he said.

And for the first time in many weeks they knew each other as husband and wife, and she was full of carnal love and energy.

2

On a bleak day toward the end of November, a delegation from the Boston church went to Newtown to discuss certain propositions concerning sanctification and justification with members of the congregation there. Anne Hutchinson went, and her son Francis, along with a number of her closest friends, both men and women; but William, though a deacon now, pled pressing business and stayed away. The truth was that he ever shunned dissension of any kind and could not believe in it as a Christian way, no matter what certain troubling passages of Scripture suggested to the contrary.

Yet it was also true that he did have business to attend to. He had an appointment with William Coddington, who like himself vastly preferred peace to a sword. A few words exchanged after Anne's last meeting had revealed to them their common concern, and they had agreed to meet and talk about it at Coddington's house on this morning of the Newtown conference.

Coddington's study was a large, well-furnished room that might have been brought in toto from England, with heavy carved oak chairs and tables and handsomely wainscoted walls. A good fire burned in the fireplace that opened into the room from the great central chimney, as the two men sat within its warmth and smoked their pipes.

"You travel outside Boston more than I do," said Hutchinson to Coddington. "Has the whole colony taken sides in this dispute?"

Coddington shook his head in doubt. "To some extent," he said, "but the farther away from Boston you get, the less the ordinary person knows about it. The ministers, though, feel themselves threatened. Every one of them is preaching against what they consider the false opinions being spread in Boston."

"Thus Newtown—"

"Oh yes, Master Shepard has incited his congregation to demand this conference. I've heard he has been engaged in a very disputatious correspondence with Master Cotton."

"Aye. Nor are they by any means the only letter writers. It seems to me the store of paper in the Bay must shortly vanish, at the rate these letters and proclamations multiply."

"Well, it is better to keep it on paper. I mistrust this conference. I mistrust all these various disputations, no matter how they come disguised as reasoning together in brotherly peace and love."

"What can happen, think you?"

Coddington frowned. "I know not," he said. "The plain truth is there are two parties formed, and one of them must win a victory."

"Is there no hope for a compromise?"

"Very little. Although Master Cotton will keep on saying there is not so much difference between him and the other ministers."

"I know," said Hutchinson. "A narrow scantling."

"And yet," said Coddington, lifting a hand with thumb and forefinger nearly touching at the tips, "just so much could cause a house to fall."

"This, I believe, is what John Winthrop fears," said Hutchinson.

"He has talked to you?"

"Aye," said Hutchinson, his lips pressed in a wry smile. "He desires that I should control my wife, he says."

Coddington laughed. "I wonder what you answered."

"I answered not much. But I might have told him where God is concerned I could not interfere."

"And you are right in that," said Coddington.

"It has occurred to me that he might bring the General Court to take some action," Hutchinson said, "though I confess I cannot see how, with Henry Vane in the governor's seat."

"The governor's opinions are making him suspect outside of Boston. Are you not aware of that?"

"How would I be?"

"He went rather far at the court in October, you know. Neither Master Cotton nor your brother Wheelwright will go so far as to say there is a personal union of man and God."

"I don't see the difference between that and what they do say."

Coddington smiled. "A narrow scantling," he said. "But Winthrop and Pastor Wilson have made of it a board to partition a church withal."

"Among the magistrates, I judge it's Winthrop has the power."

"'Tis true. Richard Dummer and I are the only ones prepared to oppose him, and therefore you may understand the governor can do very little if they unite against him."

"And what do you think of the court as a whole?"

"The deputies are less predictable," said Coddington, "as you yourself must know, and may or may not do Winthrop's bidding."

"And what will he bid them do?"

"I doubt he knows that himself yet. But I can tell you this: he will brook no division in the churches that threatens to weaken the colony. He will find a way to silence dissent, and although we dominate the membership of Boston church, he considers us the dissenters."

"And yet," said Hutchinson, "in the settlements around Rhode Island, where my wife's sister has removed, it seems no man imposes any belief upon anyone else."

"That is Roger Williams' doing," said Coddington with a smile. "He finally became so strict in his beliefs he could find no man to worship with him—and even his own wife failed the test. And so it finally occurred to him that since absolute purity was impossible, the alternative was absolute toleration."

"And why not?"

"Indeed, why not? And yet this colony was established as a place for Christians with common doctrines and a common church. This core of religion is the foundation of the colony, and it is not surprising that Winthrop fears any weakening of it."

"And you agree?"

"No, for you see, to my mind the worship of God is a personal matter. And I must say I did not fully understand at first the nature of this settlement."

"No more did I—if in fact I do now."

"It is what might be called a Bible commonwealth. And if it is to be ruled by the Bible, then it follows that those who rule and those who consent to be ruled must not only believe the Bible but believe it in the same way."

"Few here think otherwise, I judge."

"'Tis certain at least that Winthrop and Dudley conceive of governing in this way: that in a young colony, where the pattern of life and politics is still forming, there is precisely no room for dissent. I did once think Winthrop might entertain some notion of leniency, though whether in religious belief I know not. But he does not so now, I can tell you that."

"And so it comes back to what you said in the beginning: one party must win."

"Aye."

"Will Coddington, I have no stomach and no talent for this kind of fight. I would take up my sword if necessary to defend my family and friends, but if service in the court becomes a battle, it may be my best part is to retreat."

Coddington studied his friend for a long silent moment. "Would you be glad if the church would ask to have you excused from the court? No one would question your motives then."

"Who would take my place?"

"There would be an election called, of course, but I think I can assure you it would be William Colburn."

"He would know how to build strength for our side—and would not be closely tied to one of the chief causes of dissension."

Coddington nodded, smiling slightly. "That is true," he said. "As things stand now, anyone might say that you could not without prejudice look to what is best for the colony, and that would be a difficult charge to refute."

William Hutchinson, then, would resign from the General Court. Only that one small point was decided that day, but it prepared the way for happenings that William Hutchinson dreaded without being able very clearly to foresee.

When he reached home, Anne and Francis had already returned, frustrated and angry. The Newtown delegation had walked out of the conference, threatening to charge the Boston church with fifteen heinous heresies.

## 3

On another day, Governor Vane, finding himself free from any pressing duties of his office, went to call upon Mistress Hutchinson. It was a cold day, with a light snow falling. Indoors, the family worked and played near the fire, but Anne received her guest sitting in her wainscot chair, at the end of the room where she kept it for her meetings. She was wrapped in her length of blue wool, and he kept on his hat and cloak as he sat on the stool at her feet. With them it was always as though no one else stirred or spoke there, the communion they experienced was so complete.

Yet Anne realized from the beginning of the visit that they were not to enjoy the peaceful, gentle intercourse of thought and spirit that at other times had made them both content. The young man's eyes were liquid dark, with faint lines of pain drawing his brows together and shadowed circles underneath them that suggested sleepless nights.

"My dear brother," Anne said to him, "can it be some sickness has come upon you?"

He sat with his elbow on his knee, his chin resting in his hand, and looked up at her with those hurt eyes that seemed to pour her own heart full of tears.

"I am in no pain," he said, "but sore troubled. These dreadful letters come to me without end."

"Do you mean the correspondence with John Winthrop?" she asked.

"Not that so much, for indeed I suppose it is ended, with the compromise I told you of before."

"When I was at Westminster School," he began, and she knew what would come, she had heard it before. She could picture him there, a forlorn and lonely child, in that grim place in the shadow of the ancient abbey. She could see him beginning to grow up, beset by temptations invented in his own imagination because few others made their way through those thick ancient walls. How he hated himself and cried in vain for help out of this situation made worse by prayers they forced him to say—prayers composed by mortal men who never knew Henry Vane or, more than likely, God. Then something happened. Through no strength in himself, through nothing but his passive suffering, God's rich grace came down. The wells of His spirit flowed (so Henry himself described the marvelous phenomenon), and as if in outward manifestation of his spiritual condition, uncontrollable tears flowed from his eyes. A master caught him crying like a baby, and he was flogged for his weakness.

Those tears flowed now. And Anne's own tears flowed afresh. And the two rose and embraced each other, it might be in farewell, while their tears mingled as did their very souls.

When William came in, some hour or so after Henry had taken his leave, Anne rushed to him crying that Henry Vane was going back to England and something had to be done.

"Very well," said William, "I will go to William Coddington."

# XVIII

Governor Vane called a special session of the General Court for December 7, 1636. Only a few knew what the purpose was. Winthrop and Dudley knew; for Vane had showed them his letters from England, and they readily agreed that the state of his affairs demanded his presence there. Coddington was pretty sure, after hearing from William Hutchinson, and he thought he was prepared for what he expected to happen.

Anne Hutchinson carried the knowledge heavy in her breast all through the morning of that fateful day. Of course she did not know how fateful it was to prove—what a chain of events Henry Vane would start that day. No intimations came to her then of the way her enemies were about to move against her, or how long and how relentlessly they would persevere. *Henry* was all her thought and all her passion, that day; it would have been hard for a revelation to get in.

No matter what Henry had told her, she did not believe he really wanted to leave Boston. He might be kept where he belonged if his friends on the court could somehow prevent his resignation from being accepted. But his ruthless enemies could move so swiftly—she feared there was no room for hope.

When William came in at noon, he still had no word from the court, which had not recessed for dinner yet.

"But couldn't you go to the meetinghouse?" asked Anne, and added, "I believe I had been thinking you were there yourself, and would know everything when you came." (This was the first session of the court to meet since William had resigned as deputy.)

"Will Coddington said he would come to us," William said, "when there is anything to tell."

While they were eating, Coddington did come, and at Anne's invitation joined them at table, where he gave an account of the morning's events.

The governor opened the session with an explanation of his need to leave the colony. Winthrop testified that although the reasons were private, he himself knew they were urgent. No one could tell what to do, so a recess was proposed in which the governor's request could be fully considered. At that moment Coddington jumped up and spoke of what a great blow to the colony it would be to lose such an excellent governor in times of such great danger from the Indians and the French. This expression of loyalty proved too much for Vane, who burst into tears and confessed he would stay at the risk of losing his whole estate, rather than desert his people, only that he feared the judgment of God upon them for their differences and dissensions. Scandalous imputations had been brought upon him, as though he were the cause of all the trouble, and therefore he thought best to remove himself. All this was spoken with great difficulty, through his sobs.

Anne as she listened began to cry quietly. She felt her heart break when Coddington told how the court through stony silence had given their consent to his departure. The only protest offered was that the troubles in the colony should not be considered grounds for Vane's release, for such an affair would appear disgraceful in the eyes of Englishmen at home and draw unwelcome attention from the King's court, where Henry Vane still had connections. Vane then gained control of himself, and apologizing for his outburst, said the troubles with his estate were indeed sufficient grounds and he still wished to be released. After a certain amount of debate, the court agreed to hold elections the next week. And so things stood when they recessed for dinner.

Anne leaped to her feet, her tear-stained face now blazing. "This cannot be," she cried. "They cannot treat him this way. Something must be done to keep him here!"

Gently, Coddington spoke and soothed her. "Please, sister," he said, "be calm and patient, for this affair is not ended. Losing the governor would be too great a blow to all of us who have espoused the cause of truth. We will not let him go."

Anne, quietened, looked at him with hopeful eyes. "What can you do?" she asked.

Coddington had in mind a deputation to protest Vane's departure in the name of the church.

"Oh yes," cried Anne. "William will go." She thought to add, "Won't you, William?"

William declared that if needed he would certainly go, and the two men set out immediately to call upon the elders and the other deacons. Anne sat and spun and silently prayed until at last William returned, to say that all was well. The deputation had informed the court that they did not apprehend the necessity of the governor's departure upon the reasons alleged. In response the governor said that as an obedient child of his church he dared not go away, even though he had the permission of the court. The court, accepting this change, then rescheduled the election for the following May, the regular election time.

"Thank God!" breathed Anne.

She was not then aware of the matters her husband and William Coddington had been speaking of: how even such a weakling as Henry Vane would furnish symbolic support in the fight they saw ahead.

2

The court was to meet again before the session adjourned. Meanwhile the colony ministers, hearing the news, converged upon Boston. One more time, they would try to draw out of their brother Cotton an unambiguous statement of his own opinions. If they clearly differed from those of the erronists, that would be a great blessing for these preachers of the Gospel truth. If not, it was time they knew who the enemies of truth really were.

But Cotton, as usual, gave them no satisfaction. He said the same old things he always said. They accused him of encouraging Mistress Hutchinson. They said if he couldn't or wouldn't control her, it might be time the magistrates stepped in. Cotton said he thought it not according to God to bring in the magistrates and suggested that they talk to her themselves. Thus it was that Anne was summoned one more time to the house by the Trimontaine.

It was Monday afternoon. The messenger came at the very moment she had begun to speak at her meeting. Calling Faith to replace her, she took her cloak from its peg by the door and leaving a roomful of speechless, astonished women behind her, answered the peremptory command.

"The ministers are now awaiting your presence at Master Cotton's house, to answer certain questions that are troubling them," was all the message said.

She never once thought of refusing to go. Without even knowing which ministers were calling her, she would unhesitatingly go. As a member of the church, she owed such obedience, and besides, it was the habit of a lifetime. What questions they would ask her, what disposition wish to make of her, she had no idea. If they interrogated her about her teaching, she would simply have to tell the truth, as she had always done, and always would. And yet these men with their university degrees, trained in logic and argument—what might they not do against her if they chose? What might they trick her into saying if she ever lost her head? Then she remembered her father saying, "Make no statement for which the grounds are in any way uncertain in your mind." The image of him in the great chair in his study in London, serene yet ever charged with the excitement of some fresh idea, steadied her so that as she knocked at the heavy door she felt quite calm.

Then she saw them waiting to attack her—a roomful of black-clad, gloomy-browed men. She had seen them all before, and heard many of them preach; but they were like strangers now, she could scarcely have called them by name. They were like an anonymous army marching against her. She gained some strength from Master Cotton's gentle smile, and noted thankfully the presence of John Wheelwright and two elders of the Boston church, John Cogshall and Thomas Leverett. Master Cotton invited her to take a seat near the fire; he may have seen how she shivered upon entering, but that had not been from the cold.

For some little time no one spoke. Then a broad-faced, heavy-shouldered man stood up from a chair in the middle of the room. His name came easily back to her: Hugh Peter. She knew him well by sight, though she had never been able to get to Salem to hear him preach. One thing she did know: he had betrayed Henry Vane. Henry had showed her a letter denouncing his views—when once they had been such close friends.

Hugh Peter roared at her, as if he might be standing in the pulpit. He said he and his brothers had been told it was her table talk that their ministry was no true ministry of the Gospel and that they taught a covenant of works. All they wanted, he said, was that she would speak plainly and clear herself if she could. He paused. Her brain seemed blank. He towered above her, glowering, yet something quizzical played about his tiny mouth that contrasted almost comically with his large, fleshy nose. He was said to be quite a joker in the pulpit sometimes, and it crossed her mind that Henry Vane had told her of a rumor that before his conversion Peter played the fool in William Shakespeare's company of actors. Henry had never dared ask the preacher about that, and she could see why.

"Mistress," he suddenly thundered, "can you not answer a simple question?"

She had almost forgotten where she was. She tried to bring her thoughts together.

Then another spoke. It was Thomas Weld, a fierce preacher too. She had heard him at Roxbury, and knew how deceptive was his mild sheeplike face with his gray hair curling around his ears like unshorn wool. He spoke, though, more softly than he was wont, and that manner, she suspected, was deceptive too.

"Now, Mistress Hutchinson," he said, almost wheedling, "why is it you cast such aspersions on the ministers of our country? For though we be only poor, sinful men, and care not for ourselves, still the doctrine we hold forth is precious and we cannot but grieve to hear it so blasphemed."

She was no blasphemer. Give her a moment, and she thought she could answer that. She tried to say some few defensive words.

But the ministers were not willing to give her a moment. Suddenly, their patience was used up and they were all talking at once. "Speak to the question, mistress," someone shouted.

Desperation seized her. Oh, God, she inwardly cried, and He

put a passage of Scripture into her mind, Twenty-ninth Proverbs, verse Twenty-five. And she spoke it out to them as loud and clear and certain as they spoke themselves, for God was with her. "'The fear of man bringeth a snare, but whoso putteth his trust in the Lord shall be safe.'" From that moment she knew she would be safe, and she was not afraid.

She rose and faced them. "I will speak to you freely and plain," she said.

Pastor Wilson, seated at a small table by the window, took up his pen and began to write. Weld moved near a window, too, and took out a small notebook.

Then they began to fire questions at her, and she answered them with all the confidence she now wholeheartedly felt in her beliefs and her abilities. They asked her what difference she found between their brother, Master Cotton, and themselves, and she said a wide and broad difference, for they did not hold forth a covenant of grace as clearly as he. She said (for she had often thought of this) that they were no able ministers of the New Testament because they knew no more than the Apostles did before the Resurrection of Christ.

"But how doth Master Cotton do better?" she was asked.

"Because," she answered, and she was utterly clear in her mind about this, "you preach of the seal of the spirit upon a work and he upon free grace without a work or without respect to a work."

Master Cotton interrupted then, with a pained expression, saying he was sorry she put comparisons between his ministry and the others'.

"I find the difference," Anne said simply.

Then they began to ask her what she thought about certain brothers, and because they asked she told them, exactly as they appeared to her. The truth was, she could not see that any of them were sealed with the seal of the spirit.

"What do you mean by that?" Master Shepard of Newtown finally asked her. She said she had heard him preach a sermon in which he gave love as an evidence by which a Christian might reach assurance. This use of love as an evidence was to her mind a result of dependence upon a covenant of works, and so she could not think him sealed.

"What do you think of me?" put in Zachariah Symmes. And she looked at her old acquaintance and said, "Alas, you knew my mind long ago."

Then George Phillips from Watertown asked what she thought of his ministry. That might have been a trick, for she had never heard him preach; but she had detailed notes at home taken by her daughter Faith when she went to hear him. No, she said, he was not sealed either, any more than the rest.

At last they began to press her to say just what she meant by seals, and then the whole company fell into a discussion of the meaning of the term.

Master Cotton said he understood her to mean the full assurance of God's favor by the Holy Ghost. Anne said that expressed it very well, but by that time no one was paying her any mind and someone suggested that they distinguish between a broad seal and a little seal.

"If you will have it so, be it so," said Nathaniel Ward of Ipswich, in apparent exasperation. He had said not much at this conference, and Anne was thankful for that, because he was known for a slashing wit with which he liked to cut down women.

The conference lost its focus completely at this time, as the ministers began to be more interested in each other's hairsplitting arguments than in Anne's alleged erroneous opinions. She talked to Master Ward a little while about that place in Second Corinthians that says able ministers of the New Testament are ministers of the spirit and not the letter, "for the letter killeth, but the spirit giveth life."

"That's the letter of the law," said he.

"No," said she, "it is the letter of the Gospel."

She was surprised that he neither ridiculed nor attacked what she said, but listened seriously.

After this, she had a long discussion with Master Weld about exactly what constituted an able New Testament minister, and she thought she might talk thus with some of the others, except that many now were putting on their cloaks to go. She heard one or two say that in the future they would not so easily believe everything they heard, and she thought this a hopeful sign.

John Wheelwright, who was to stay the night with the Hutchinsons, walked home with her, and he assured her she had comported herself very well. It was true that the ruling elders had been adjured to watch more closely over her, but as they already agreed with her teachings, this did not seem likely to inhibit her work very much.

Anne chatted happily with her brother-in-law as they hurried over the purple-shadowed snow toward supper and home.

3

Next day the court reconvened and went about its usual business of governing the colony. There was so much sad news everywhere, at home and abroad, that a fast day was named, to be observed on January 19. The Indian menace was one of the reasons for the fast, others being the sad state of the Protestant churches of Europe and the advance of papistry in England; but the reason of most concern to the Bay was the dissension in their own churches.

John Cotton of all men was aware of this dissension, for on this very day, the eve of another conference of ministers and the court, he received a list of sixteen questions, to which the other ministers demanded short, plain, and, most of all, speedy answers. They must have gone to work drafting them almost as soon as the meeting at Cotton's was over. And yet they had seemed to him well satisfied at the time they took their leave of one another. It was really beyond his understanding that they kept on searching for heresy in his preaching, but with his usual patience he carefully wrote out the answers they asked for. They had to do with the meaning of the seals, the signs of assurance, the uses of sanctification and of faith—with all those questions that had been proliferating now for many months.

Most of the matters could be dealt with easily, but for Question Thirteen he had no short and simple answer. It lay at the heart of the dissension, and he labored to avoid all suspicion of ambiguity and obscurity. In seven separate propositions he told them all over again what he had so often said before: to depend upon sanctification, or good works, as evidence of justification, or the experience of grace, is to go on in a covenant of works. Or a believer may be justified, and not altogether under a covenant of works, yet sometimes go aside to a covenant of works. This is what Abraham did when, though believing the free promise, yet for speedy satisfaction of his faith and hope, turned aside to go into Hagar for the hastening of the promised seed. So some Christians, too anxious to feel Christ within them, seek Him in their own works of sanctification. Such works can never bring assurance, and sad doubts will still beset them until reliance upon such works be burned up with the Fire of Temptation, and the clearer daylight of God's word and spirit. And then, though their own building be burned, yet their souls will be saved in the day of the Lord Jesus.

He wearily brushed back his hair and laid down his pen. Surely, surely, that was clear—if not as clear as God's own daylight, then at least as clear as the steady flame of the candle on the table where he worked. He took up his pen again. He must finish as soon as possible, for he had a sermon to prepare. He was scheduled to preach in the meetinghouse next morning, before the conference began. He prayed he could find words that would serve to reconcile and heal.

And the sermon was well received, but then as soon as the meeting of the court was begun, it was evident that nothing had changed. Vane opened the meeting, announcing that the purpose was to unify the churches in point of opinion. Thomas Dudley said he hoped men would be free and open with each other. Everyone seemed quite eager to be free and open, so that Vane himself spoke out what he had been feeling, that perhaps this discussion with the court was unnecessary since he understood the ministers were already about it in a church way and had sent Master Cotton a list of questions to be answered.

Henry saw at once that it had been a mistake thus to show his private feelings about having been left out, for Hugh Peter was on his feet as soon as Henry finished, declaring that it saddened their spirits that he should be jealous of their meetings or seem to restrain their liberty. Henry apologized, but Peter showed him no mercy. He went on to say that before Vane came, the churches had been at peace.

That was unfair. "The light of the Gospel brings a sword," Henry angrily replied.

Then Peter (whom till then Henry had still thought of as his friend, in spite of an unpleasant letter) lectured him on his youth and short experience in the things of God. "Beware of peremptory conclusions," he warned, "which I perceive you are very apt unto."

Peter went on preaching a little longer, and then John Wilson took up the fight. To John Cotton's astonishment, he heard himself accused by his fellow minister of corrupting the whole Boston church with his erroneous opinions. The next day, in such anger as he seldom allowed himself, he agreed to go with a delegation that called on the pastor to admonish him.

On Saturday, December 31, the membership called Wilson to the meetinghouse to defend himself, and all the church joined Vane in bitter condemnation. Cotton, calmer now, kept them from proceeding to formal censure, but even so he spoke more sternly to John Wilson than he had ever done before.

The next day Wilson preached a conciliatory sermon, and Cotton thanked God that one more time the church had been saved from an irrevocable split.

4

In spite of the temporary air of peace in the Boston church, and the loving letters exchanged by some of the leaders of both church and state, no one's temper really cooled, unless it were John Cotton's.

When Anne Hutchinson thought of all the events that had transpired since the sad day Henry Vane tried to resign the governorship, she would come near to choke with frustration and rage. "They do not even want to see the truth," she would cry. "They cover their eyes."

For the preaching went on as before, with the covenant of works ministers preaching harder than ever about the difficult labor of achieving salvation and the followers of Anne confusing people with talk about the "fair and easy" way of getting to heaven by waiting for the spirit. If only it had been that easy! But doubt was rampant everywhere.

One morning Mary Cogshall came by on her way home from market. "Have you heard about the Weymouth man?" she asked, and no one had. This man, known to have been much troubled about his spiritual state, jumped out of bed in the middle of the night shouting, "Art thou come, Lord Jesus?" And before anyone could stop him, he had gone out a window and off into the bitter cold dark. He ran seven miles through the snow, stopping often to kneel and pray, until at last he froze to death. They had tracked him to his last stopping place the next morning.

Faith was there, and Sarah Hutchinson; the cousins and the little girls were sewing by the fire. All the women mournfully shook their heads and talked about the ways of God. There was no way any one of them could have been reminded of the drowning of Elizabeth Joan, not Anne any more than the rest, for there had been no tracks in the sea. Yet Anne said, "We must hope that the poor man did know Christ at last."

She spoke calmly, but could not conceal a familiar fire in her eyes, and Faith said, "Do you really think so, Mother?"

"No one on earth may know," said Anne. "But failing revealed knowledge, I believe as strongly as can be that the ministers of works sent him out in the snow, a-feared unto death on account of his sins."

The women looked up startled.

"The men in the court prate on and on about dissension," Anne continued, "as if that is the problem to be solved. But the terrible price is paid in lost souls of men and women, and the deaths of babes."

They saw what she meant now, reminded of the mother who murdered her child, and they looked at each other and nodded. "What should be done?" asked several.

Anne did not know what could be done, but for the first time saw a need for strategy, and after some little thought (while the others respected her silence and awaited, perhaps, a revelation), she decided to call a meeting of the women who had from the outset been closest to her in friendship and the sympathy of God's love.

Mary and Faith and Sarah carried the word around, and that afternoon they gathered together. Daughter Bridget came, and Mary Dyer, Mary Coddington, and Elizabeth Aspinwall. And old Goody Hawkins, too, though no one had sent for her.

"Oh dear," said Anne to herself when she saw her come in, "I forgot Jane again."

But she welcomed the uninvited guest with true affection, and if Jane knew she had been slighted she gave no sign.

This was a different kind of meeting from any they had known before. In earlier times, they used to come together, excited at the prospect of the joyous messages they knew Mistress Hutchinson would reveal. Now they came anxious, angry, and full of frustrations they needed to vent.

"It is clear now," Anne said to them, "that the ministers of works, with their friends in high places, have determined to fight till they have silenced us. Our duty to God is to find out some way to fight back."

"But what can we do?" Several, hopelessly, asked that.

Form committees, and go and talk with these men? But Anne had experience of such talk already, and although the men had listened to her with evident respect and even written down what she said, they proceeded exactly as before and paid no heed to her well-reasoned arguments. Invite the members of other churches to discussion groups? But no one could take that suggestion seriously, after the way the Newtown delegation had behaved.

Mary Coddington, who never could avoid a placid expression, folded her hands and lightly sighed. "Mayhap we needs must leave it to the men," she said.

"And really, Mother, what can women do?" said Bridget. "I mean to change anything in the government or church."

"If they would only listen to reason," said Mary Cogshall.

"Yet there must be some way we can make them notice us," said Mary Dyer. "John Winthrop and John Wilson and their kind."

No one spoke for a little while, until Goody Hawkins began to giggle. "I know what we can do," she chirped.

"Yes, Jane," said Anne, with mild encouragement.

Faith and Bridget looked at each other with raised eyebrows, nor did the others appear much more hopeful, though it was doubtful that Jane noticed.

"Do you remember, mistress," she asked, "the time you walked out of the meetinghouse when old Thunderer preached of Elizabeth Joan?"

"Aye," said Anne somewhat heedlessly.

"I mind me of the look upon his face," said Jane.

"He was angry, to be sure," said Mary Cogshall.

"What was it you said to the tithing man that day?" asked Jane.

"Oh, I know not," said Anne, flushing a little. "Something about a woman's ailment come upon me. It was no lie, but still I might have managed to stay if I had so desired."

"But he dared not question you," said Jane.

"I knew he would not," Anne said. "I simply could not stay and hear such false words spoken."

Jane looked up with her little one-sided nod, and peered around knowingly. "Why should we ever stay and hear false preaching?" she asked.

"Oh, Mother, I see what she means," cried Faith excitedly.

"They would notice us then," said Mary Dyer, her eyes shining.

Suddenly they all saw, and they began to plan how they would walk out of meetings when the covenant of works was preached and what they would say to the tithing man if excuses were demanded.

"All the women of the church will join us," Mary Dyer said, seeing more imaginatively than any of them how it all would be, "and then John Wilson may see what it means to his ministry to persist in old false ways."

Anne herself clearly saw the possible effectiveness of such a show of disdain. She could visualize the reactions of Wilson and Winthrop. Yet she wanted as well something more articulate and explicit. She saw that only within the meetinghouse could the women make a public statement of any strength at all, and she knew that many women whom she had taught were fully capable of rational and cogent argument. Thus out of Goody Hawkins' gleeful notion came another plan. Church members had always been encouraged to raise questions and enter into discussions after the sermons of lecture day and the Lord's Day; but women had never taken much advantage of this opportunity, though there was no rule that they must remain silent after lectures. Now, they determined, they would speak up when they could.

So it came about that often a sizable body of women would rise and, quietly and modestly, walk out of the meetinghouse when Pastor Wilson preached or prayed. And not only in Boston, but in many neighboring towns, Hutchinsonians of both sexes (for the men soon followed the women in this) would contradict the preachers and argue the points of their sermons to a degree called scandalous and shameless by their adversaries.

"Now," John Winthrop wrote, "the faithful ministers of Christ must have dung cast on their faces, and be no better than legal preachers, Baal's priests, Popish factors, scribes, Pharisees, and opposers of Christ himself."

This had its effect, but it was not what the women had hoped for.

5

Nothing ever seemed to have the effect that was hoped for. The much talked of and long awaited fast day, for instance, left both parties hungry but unhumbled.

John Wheelwright, invited to speak as a lay brother in Boston, was the Hutchinsonians' hero that day.

"If we mean to keep the Lord Jesus Christ," he preached, "we must be willing to suffer. We must not love our lives, but be willing to die like sheep." He called for a fight, for a war, and whether he meant only a war of words who could be entirely sure? The enemy were those "wondrous holy people" who lived under a covenant of works, and though he urged his own side to watch their behavior so as not to be taken for libertines or antinomians, no one of either party much noticed that.

What his audience remembered was his exhortation to beat down the enemy, and his concession that he knew "combustion in the church and commonwealth" might follow if they took his advice. What lingered was the power with which he shouted words like these: "Brethren, we know that the whore must be burnt. It is not shaving of her head and paring her nails and changing her raiment that will serve the turn, but this whore must be burnt." Antichrist must be destroyed, and few would need wonder who it was John Wheelwright was alluding to.

In the Hutchinson house that evening, Anne embraced her brother-in-law and shed tears of joy. Never mind what his enemies were saying in private rooms in Boston and neighboring towns. It would be known soon enough.

Meanwhile, John Cotton may have been the only man left in the colony who thought the differences in the churches could be resolved. On the third of February, a ship sailed for England, and so concerned were the leaders about the reports that might be carried back there, that they asked Master Cotton and Master Wilson to go and speak to the passengers on board. Cotton urged them to say in England that the strife among them was about magnifying the grace of God, with one party seeking to advance the grace of God within Christians and the other to advance the grace of God towards them. And so, he concluded, with a pathetic attempt at lightness, they should tell any in England that were striving for grace to come at once to Massachusetts.

But Pastor Wilson was having none of that. He said that as far as he knew, every minister in the colony labored to advance the free grace of God in justification, so far as the word of God required. And he went on to make his usual points about the uses and necessity of sanctification.

So it ever went. Whenever John Cotton spoke of compromise, there was somebody on one side or the other seeking to destroy the balance.

William Hutchinson said something like that to William Coddington one day as they sat talking in Hutchinson's shop.

"One day, though," said Coddington, "he will have to give up trying to walk the edge of his narrow scantling."

"Something will push him over, you think?" asked Hutchinson.

"A very powerful something, so I fear," Coddington said. "And if he goes over the wrong way we have lost—"

"What have we lost?"

"Something big—I know not—a rallying point."

"What can we do?"

"Look ever to the May elections," Coddington said.

"Think you Master Cotton's position is political?"

"Everything depends on the election," Coddington said, "as long as nothing happens to destroy the balance before May."

# XIX

Anne kept in her heart the assurance that God's true way would soon prevail in Boston. She never explained why she felt so sure. Some might believe she had experienced a revelation, but if so it was not by God's direct voice. It might be, though, that the sense she had of being carried by swift winds over smooth seas to some far shining place of perfect love was indeed a message from God.

When she rose and led her women out of the meetinghouse at some offensive word of Pastor Wilson, it was as though she were lifted above the rough boards of the floor. When at a lecture in some nearby town she questioned the preacher—"Sir, do you mean to say that it must be either sin or the absence of sin that determines our salvation?"—and then when he sputtered and turned red, she felt the spirit rejoice within her. When she spoke at her own meetings, she never used notes any more or took thought of what words she would say or what Scripture appropriately cite. She spoke as the spirit moved her, not by the cold, mechanical syllogisms so favored by the Pharisaical ministers of works.

At home, every day seemed a feast day. The house was full of people from morning till night. After Lord's Day and lecture day, there would be groups reporting on their experiences in the different towns they visited. There would be conferences on the best way to attack certain common doctrines that the ministers (except Cotton and Wheelwright) all preached. Upstairs, little Anne would have the younger children together, lined up near the warm chimney wall, going through their primers or their catechism. In the kitchen, the cousins would be at work turning meat on the spit or making pumpkin sauce or pease porridge, or some other way preparing for the meals that often had at the last minute to serve an unexpectedly large number.

Thus it was with the household on a blustery day in March, near the end of the year 1636. Anne sat with some mending, drawn up near the fire, while the wind whistled eerily outside. On a stool near her sat an anxious thin-faced woman not well known to her, though an occasional spectator at her meetings. Anne, searching her memory, could recall only a blank white face, staring from the edge of the gathering.

The face was blank now, but the eyes were strained and bright with threatening tears. "Help, oh, please do help," was all she had yet been able to say.

"Now tell me just what it is that is wrong," Anne demanded briskly. Too much sympathy, she felt, would unleash the flood and then she might never learn what the poor creature had come for.

"They've got my husband," the woman said.

"Who, dear?" said Anne, keeping her patience. "Who has your husband?"

"The court. The beadle came this morning, banging like he'd tear the door down."

"But what has he done?"

"Nothing. My Stephen never done nothing wrong in his life."

"Stephen? Do I know Stephen?"

"Well, you ought. He comes to your meetings all the time, when I keep telling him I don't see why, as he won't go to church."

"Tell me his whole name, then, and perhaps I'll remember."

"Stephen Greensmith. He's a merchant and as good as any man in Boston, and what they took him away from me for I don't know, unless it's got something to do with you."

Anne remembered Stephen Greensmith. He had come to one of the small training meetings for persons who expected to visit other towns and might wish to enter discussions after lectures or sermons. And in fact, she now recalled his saying that he seldom went to church but might be willing to if he could set some of the Lord's brethren down a peg or two.

"But what has this to do with me, Mistress Greensmith?" Anne demanded.

"The beadle said your name, I don't know."

At this point a knock sounded at the door, and Frances went to answer it.

"Cousin John!" she exclaimed, and Anne unthinkingly jumped up and went to meet her brother Wheelwright.

He was not expected; something extraordinary must have happened, or he would not be in Boston at the end of the week and in this bitter weather.

Recalling her visitor, she turned back briefly to say, "Forgive me, I must greet my brother."

"What is it, John?" she asked somewhat breathlessly.

Frances stood with a wooden spoon in her hand, waiting to hear.

He came near the fire and stood as always with broad shoulders thrown back and legs a little apart. He had ridden from Wollaston, and in his worn leather breeches and doublet didn't look much like a parson.

"I'm called before the court!" he said heartily, almost as if he took this astonishing predicament as a joke.

Mistress Greensmith jumped up from her stool. "Called to court!" she exclaimed.

He looked down at the mousy little thing, and then to Anne with a questioning expression.

"This is Mistress Greensmith, John," Anne said. "The court has called her husband, too."

"Aye," he said. "Stephen Greensmith. I saw him there."

"Oh, what have they done to him?" the woman cried.

"Nothing you need have great fear of, mistress," said Wheelwright. "They fined him forty pounds, and sentenced him to acknowledge error before every congregation in the colony." He paused and frowned, then went on, "I regret to say they are keeping him in jail, but I think I can assure you it will be no longer than one night."

The woman burst into tears. "But he did nothing wrong!"

"What did they have against him, John?" asked Anne.

"Why only that he was fool enough to speak the truth of his convictions," Wheelwright said. "He said all the ministers preach a covenant of works, except for Brother Cotton and me, and he thought Master Hooker."

Anne laughed bitterly. "He must never have heard Master Hooker," she said.

Mistress Greensmith had sat back down on her stool and with her head in her hands was now weeping almost silently. Anne, impatient to hear John's account of himself, forced herself to kneel at the woman's side and try to speak comfortingly. "They cannot keep him," she said, "nor is the punishment so very harsh."

"We don't have forty pounds," the woman sobbed.

"Then they can't take it, can they?" Wheelwright said. "Now don't worry, mistress. I doubt that they will force your husband to travel all over the colony recanting, either. They were simply testing themselves, to see how far they can go."

Anne resumed her chair, and motioned to her brother-in-law to sit on the settle. "But, John, how could the court punish this man for something that concerns the church?"

"Ah," he said, doffing his cloak and taking the seat that she offered, "that's the trick, isn't it? They called in some of my brother ministers, and they agreed with the magistrates that heresy threatens the safety of the commonwealth, and so the court need not tarry for the church."

"But what has this to do with you?" Anne insisted.

"Everything," said Wheelwright. "Or to be absolutely truthful, I don't really know. I came as soon as they sent for me, but by then they had discovered they would not have time to deal with me until the first of next week."

"I cannot believe this," Anne said.

"Now you know how I feel," said Mistress Greensmith. She lifted her head and looked at Anne, who now at last recognized pure hostility and partly understood the reason for it.

"Dear Mistress Greensmith," Anne said, suddenly sinking to her knees before the woman. "Nothing very bad can happen to us who live by God's love for us and our love for Him and each other. Now tell me—have you children at home?"

Dumbly, the woman shook her head no.

"Then you shall stay with us until you have your husband back again."

The woman looked up doubtfully, but her eyes were somewhat softer now. "Well," she said.

Anne took her to the kitchen corner then, and found a damp

rag so she could wipe her eyes, then left her in the care of Cousin Anne Freestone.

When she returned to John he was sprawled on the settle, staring gloomily at the fire.

"What is it, John?" she said. "What is it really?"

"They think they've found a way to silence us," he said. "Sedition." He hissed the word.

William Coddington and John Cogshall came by from the court, wanting a few words with Wheelwright, and were persuaded to stay for supper. William had already told his Mary not to expect him home, and Anne sent little Katherine next door to tell Mary Cogshall and ask her to come if she could.

"Now do tell us, Will Coddington," said Anne when everyone was seated and supper had begun. "What madness has seized the General Court?"

Coddington smiled faintly. "Where shall I begin?" he asked.

"Why with poor Master Greensmith, I think," said Anne. "I can partly guess why they have called in Brother John, but how can they proceed against Master Greensmith without putting all the rest of Boston in jail too?"

"It was easy," Coddington said. "Old Thomas Dudley and his son-in-law Bradstreet heard him themselves, the day he went to the lecture at Ipswich. They say he traduced the ministers, and with such witnesses it was hard to find any defense."

"I still think it a church matter," said Anne.

"So it would seem to be," said Coddington. Then he went on to explain what John Wheelwright had already told her, that offenses against the church might be construed as dangerous to the state as well.

Mistress Greensmith stared at him in fascination, scarcely remembering to dip her spoon in her bowl, but appeared too shy to speak up in such a company.

"Now do not be distressed, mistress," Coddington said to her. "If your husband has not forty pounds to hand, we will take care of that matter in the morning. They cannot keep a man in jail for distinguishing between ministers."

At that Mistress Greensmith began to cry so hard she had to leave the table, and Anne Freestone went after her.

Then William Hutchinson asked a question. "Is this to be the crime they charge my brother with? Traducing the ministers?"

"Aye," said Coddington.

"Aye, but there may be more," said Cogshall.

"It will be my fast day sermon they're attacking, I suppose," said Wheelwright.

"I should take a copy to court if I were you," said Coddington.

"But will they proceed against him merely on the ground of his distinguishing between the covenant of grace and the covenant of works?" asked Anne.

It seemed there might be more. If interpreted in a certain way, certain parts of the sermon might be construed as inciting the colony to strife and contention. Those words about drawing swords, and binding in chains, and setting fires—they could be considered dangerous, could they not?

"But they must know I meant spiritual combat."

"What they may know in their hearts and what they can make your sermon seem to say are two different things," said Coddington.

"We had better see exactly what it does say then," said Anne, "and predict how they might twist it and tamper with its meaning."

Wheelwright drew out of a pocket his own original copy of the sermon and laid it on the table. "Cut it to pieces then," he said.

"Let us clear the table," Anne said, "and put the family to bed. Then we shall see what must be done."

The cousins cleared the table and scraped the bowls and trenchers. The children made their nightly trips outside, the boys to one side of the house and the girls to the other. Then Anne led a long, passionate prayer, that the eyes of the ministers and magistrates might be opened to the truth, not forgetting that her own family might sometime be deluded and asking God's protection from that snare.

At last the small children, the cousins, and Mistress Greensmith all went up to bed, while the rest of the company gathered at the table, around John Wheelwright's sermon. For some hours they analyzed it, in terms of the action Coddington thought they might expect from the court and the best attitude for Wheelwright to adopt in answering their questions. Dudley and Winthrop, Coddington knew, had been working on ways to move against the Wollaston pastor ever since the January fast day. Most of the magistrates were against him, and were making what he suspected was an attempt to use the techniques of Archbishop Laud against the nonconforming ministers in England—to turn the affair into a Court of High Commission, convicting Wheelwright behind closed doors, without a chance for a true defense or appeal.

"Sir," then spoke up Francis Hutchinson, "would it not be possible for the court to vote against such a thing? Could not Governor Vane call such a vote, before Master Winthrop has a chance to start the proceedings?"

Coddington gave Francis his neat little smile. "A good suggestion," he said, "but I very much fear there is a scheme already set in action, with the secret approval of most of the court already secured."

"The people, then—the people of Boston—have they no rights in the matter?" Francis asked.

"We could try a petition, Will," John Cogshall said.

They would try a petition. They framed it that night. All freemen of Boston and the colony, it said, had a right to be present when the court sat in matters of judicature. Also it questioned whether the court had a right to act in matters of conscience.

"Every man in our congregation will sign this," Coddington said.

Not much happened on Monday, when Wheelwright was called to the meetinghouse. He was asked whether he would own certain passages in his sermon, and by answer laid his own copy before them. Very well, then they would need time to study that; he could go, until they sent for him again. The next day Coddington brought in the petition: Winthrop was already prepared for it. Vane tried to get it accepted before Winthrop could speak against it, but the governor seemed helpless against the plan already so well set in motion. In no time at all the court had agreed with Winthrop, that the petition had no just grounds, since the court used privacy only in preliminary hearings; and as to any matter of conscience that might come before them, the court itself would advise what to do.

Therefore when Wheelwright was called up again, he was examined behind closed doors. And yet the court came to no conclusion, but decided to ask the opinion of the ministers, who had all gathered in Boston for the occasion. These men too wished to consider the case in private, and so it was the following morning before they brought in their verdict against their brother. With the exception of Master Cotton, who had not been invited to the meeting, they all agreed that what they taught was exactly what Wheelwright had preached against so inflamingly. After that it did not take very long for him to be judged guilty of contempt. Immediately his friends presented a protestation on behalf of Wheelwright as a faithful minister of the Gospel; and perhaps because of this (perhaps not, it was hard to say), the court decided to defer his sentence until the next regular session.

"If they attempt nothing further," said Coddington to Vane that day, as they took their dinner together at Sam Cole's inn, "we shall be lucky indeed."

"What do you expect," said Vane, "and what do you think I can do?"

"Try not to let any motion they make be put to vote," Coddington said. "I do not know what to expect."

Vane valiantly tried, but at the end of the session, taking advantage of the fact that most of the deputies came from outside Boston, Winthrop had made two extremely significant gains. For the first time in the history of the colony, votes by proxy would be allowed at the May election. And the election would be held not in Boston but in Newtown.

It might have been this last action, moving the court of elections to Newtown, that changed the Boston men from a state of frustration and dull anger to one of raging fury. They rushed out of the meetinghouse together, all talking at once, and then suddenly, just outside the door, stopped and as if in one voice cried out, "Another petition!" John Underhill said later that the idea came into their heads all at once, as though it had been a revelation.

This protestation, written by William Aspinwall and signed by seventy-four men of the Hutchinson party, went dangerously far in its attack upon the court. It pointed out that there was a notable lack of evidence that Wheelwright's sermon was seditious, and suggested it must have been Satan himself who stirred up the court against free grace, so irrational did the action seem. And at the last it warned the magistrates against meddling with the prophets of God.

Like the other papers in favor of Wheelwright, this protestation was rejected by the court. But Winthrop quietly laid it away where he could get his hands on it. Here was evidence against the Hutchinsonians that might be put to good use someday.

2

After the March court, Anne held small meetings almost daily, not only for the purpose of coaching men and women in doctrinal debate (as she had been accustomed to do for some time), but also to increase their awareness of the coming election at Newtown. "They have not dared take such action against us as they first intended," she told everyone. "The men put a halt to that with their petitions; else Brother Wheelwright would be in prison now." But greater challenge lay ahead, how great no man could know, and keeping Henry Vane in the governor's chair was the only hope for the party of God's truth in New England.

Those things she spoke often, and if anyone ever recalled how ineffectual Vane had been when Winthrop and Dudley began to move against his party, no one reminded Mistress Hutchinson. It might be no one dared, or perhaps, while she stood before them with her enraptured face and golden tongue, no one really remembered. It is certain, though, that more than one man whispered in his neighbor's ear: "'Tis too bad we cannot have her for governor." And sometimes the answer might be, "Mayhap we do."

On a showery afternoon in April, Henry Vane went to see Anne Hutchinson. All Boston presently knew where he was, and some were saying, "See there. He needs must go and ask her what to do."

Few, perhaps, fully believed this, and yet in some sense it was true. The governor had always found that certain matters of state were managed better if his decision was compatible with his spiritual nature. When he was troubled about some seeming incompatibility, it often helped to talk with Sister Anne.

He had grown thin. Those faint lines slanting out from his eyes had grown deeper. A little ache caught at Anne's heart as she met him at her open door.

Her chair was in its place by the western window, and he begged her to sit there. The sun would bathe her in warm golden light; he loved to see her so. He sat at her knee and looked up into her expectant face.

"There is trouble," she said.

"Aye," he said. "Indians."

"I have heard the Pequods are raiding again."

"Endicott did us no good last summer, that's sure. If he had followed our instructions then, they might have been peaceful now."

"But is it so bad now? Must there be war again?"

"It is bad. This last thing—I don't know whether I should even tell you."

"Yes, go on. I've heard bad things before."

He told her. Two men hunting fowl near Saybrook were ambushed by Indians, who killed one but captured the other, a man named John Tilley, and cut off his hands. He lived on for three days. They cut off his feet, they tied him to a stake, they put coals of fire under his skin. It was reported that he never cried out, and the Pequods greatly admired his courage.

"Dear God," Anne breathed, "are they not Thy children?"

"Be sure they are, sister," Henry said. "But they have been much provoked. Nor have they heard of Christ, the most of them."

"If only there were time—" Anne had a fleeting vision of herself going into the wilderness to tell the Indians of Christ.

"The day will come," Henry said. "Meanwhile, it is my duty to protect the people who elected me to govern them."

"Aye," said Anne.

"You think I must proclaim a state of war again?"

"You think so, do you not?"

"Or else resign. I may not be governor much longer anyway."

"Oh, my dear Henry, you must be elected, and you must not resign. Every man and woman in the Boston church, except for those four or five you know of, is talking of the need for you. Wherever they go in the colony, they talk of this need. They are making special trips to the far towns, in order to persuade the men who have not known you well. But you know these things."

"I know also what Winthrop and Dudley are doing." He smiled wryly. "I knew not what a partnership I was creating when I worked with Hugh Peter to reconcile those two."

"Well, you must not desert us," said Anne. "You must persevere and pray to God. And if you see no way but war, then war I suppose it must be. God's people fought wars through all the time recorded in the Scriptures."

Henry sighed. "But surely, someday, the end to that must come, and I could wish I might be part of it."

"I pray you will," said Anne.

"Pray with me now," said Henry, "that I may see my duty clear."

The way those two prayed was in silence, with hands clasped together, communing with each other and with God. At the end of their time together, Henry said he knew what he must do. Anne knew, too, and she tried to give him courage. The prayer had not reconciled her to the thought of men killing men, but she could not give up Henry Vane.

Within a few days, Henry called a special session of the court, and preparations for war began. Captain Underhill would take twenty men and go on to Saybrook. Meanwhile, another hundred and sixty men would be armed and trained, to join him immediately after the election.

That day Anne had a visitor who had never come to her for counseling before. He had been to meetings at her house since the first ones for men had been held; she knew him but not very well, and could never feel quite sure that he was in a state of grace. Although it was true she said once in a moment of exuberance that she could tell whether a person was saved or not by talking to him for half an hour, she had since regretted that statement. She had believed it when she spoke, but since then she had begun to suspect she might sometimes be deluded. And Captain Underhill, who came to her now in his high-plumed helmet, with his sword at his side and his breastplate gleaming, was one who ever made her doubt.

He asked if they could talk privately. She indicated her chair by the window, but there were women working in the kitchen part of the room, and it bothered him to have them there.

"There is a bench in your back garden," he said, "and it's a fine day, though cool from yesterday's showers."

So they went and sat on the crude bench that William had built and placed beside a little apple sapling that he planned would one day make a shade to sit in. Sammy was digging in a fence corner, but Anne bade him run away and ask his father for tasks to do in the shop.

"Are you satisfied?" Anne asked John Underhill.

He said he was. It was true they might be seen by anyone looking out the window of the house, but no one could hear what they said.

"Well, then?" Anne said. He seemed strangely reluctant to speak, having made such demands and such preparations.

"I hope you will excuse my dress," he said. "I have been at the training field."

Anne nodded.

"I am about to go and fight the Indians," he said.

"Well, 'tis your profession," she said, "and surely not at this date become a matter of conscience for you."

He was quick to set her straight about that. "Oh no," he said, "I am a soldier and a good one. I work in my true calling. Nor am I afraid to fight and die."

"Then what is it?"

"And yet, you see, I *may* die. When a soldier goes to war, that is a possibility."

"Death is always a possibility," said Anne.

"But at a time like this, it seems closer . . . and you think about your sins."

"Why should you think about your sins, Captain?"

He took off his helmet and laid it on the bench between them. He ran a hand through his thick black hair. He did not answer the question but said, "I have heard you say that thinking about your sins means you go under a covenant of works."

"I do not think I can have said that."

"So you would not say I am under a covenant of works?"

"I suppose not, Captain, but I fail to understand just what you want of me."

"To tell me what I must fear for my sins."

"Why nothing, I have told you before, if you have Christ within you."

"But can I sin and go on sinning, and still have Christ?"

"Of course you can. We are all sinners, and ever shall be. Though we try to be perfect as Christ, we know we never can."

"But if I sin, and know I sin, and knowingly go on sinning?"

*Yes, even so, you are saved.* Anne might have said that, but something about his look, anxious and—no matter what he said—frightened, stayed her tongue. After a moment she said, "Perhaps you had better tell me what you mean."

"Do you know Joseph Faber, the cooper, and his wife?"

"I think I may by sight. But they are not church members, are they? Nor do they come to our meetings."

"Goodwife Faber has been here once or twice. She is most anxious to know Christ and be saved. I have talked with her about this many times."

"Sure that could be no sin."

"Shall I tell you what I said to her?" He gave no time for an answer, but went on. "I told her no sin could send her to hell, not even breaking the Commandments."

"So I myself have said and do believe," Anne said. "God's grace will allow of no other condition."

"But listen to why I told her that. It was to further my own scheme, not for her good, because I wanted her to commit adultery."

Anne was startled. "With you, Captain?" she burst out.

"Alas, yes," he answered her, and forthwith began to sob.

There he sat, the stalwart soldier, with his breast heaving sadly inside its bright armor.

"Now, sir, this gets you nowhere," Anne said. "You must control yourself, and if it please you tell me more." She would have liked to send him away from her; her patience was growing very thin.

He became able to go on. "For six months and more I struggled," he said, "and truly amazed I was, for it had never taken me so long before."

"To seduce a woman, you mean? You had done it before?"

"Oh yes, many times," he said. "I need the love of women, sister."

"You have a wife."

"She is but one."

"And you want me to tell you—what? What kind of comfort is it you have come for?"

"Before I can ask you that," he said, "I have to tell you more."

"What more? Do you mean you are still living in adultery with this woman?"

"Oh yes. But it's not that I mean."

Thus it was that Captain Underhill came at last to talk about his love for Elizabeth Joan, and to reveal the secret that the girl herself refused to tell—the paternity of her child that was never born. "I did love her, sister," he protested, "she was such a sweet and tender wee thing." And again he broke down weeping, and the tears ran down into his beard.

Anne felt herself confounded, unable to speak, suffocated by a wave of deep emotion. She was not sure what its source was, her great grief for Elizabeth Joan or the terrible temptation to hate this man who had caused the girl such misery. Not only the sickness that ensued from aborting the child—there were others as much to blame there, even perhaps Anne herself, for sure it was she saw and might have spoken. But the deep depression and deadness of spirit Elizabeth Joan had experienced all that winter before her drowning in the spring: was not that because this man would not leave her alone?

"And at her death," she said, "you still pursued her?"

His tears gushed afresh, and he cried to her, "Oh, Sister Hutchinson, I do fear I drove her to it."

His words well-nigh turned her to stone. She sat a moment still and unbelieving; then, "What can you mean?" she said.

He found some way to control himself, and stopped the tears. "I begged her to meet me that night," he said. "She came out, but then turned not the way I expected. There was a little slice of moon. I could see her like a shadow moving from me, toward the sea. I started after her. She ran, and I lost her. Next morning I knew she had drowned herself, but I swear to you, sister, by the Book of God, I never had a thought to hurt that girl. I loved her."

Anne did not scold him for swearing; in fact, she hardly noticed what he said. She tried to envision what had happened, but she could not understand why Elizabeth Joan had gone into the sea.

"She could have returned to me," she said.

"What I fear," said the captain, "is that she thought if she lived she could no way resist me."

Anne stared in astonishment at the man—his red eyes, his tousled hair, his teeth tobacco-stained and rotting. She could only suppose he believed what he said, but it was impossible to think a comely young woman like Elizabeth Joan could have found him irresistible. While she stared, he discovered that he had more tears to shed.

"Why do you weep?" she asked him.

"For my sins," he answered.

"And why do your sins make you weep?"

"Because—" he sobbed. "Because I am afraid of hell."

"Then surely," she said coldly, "you will sin no more."

"I cannot tell," he said. "The Lord hath made me weak."

For a long moment she dared not speak, for fear of what she might say to him. He said he wept for his sins, when what he wept for was himself, his selfish fear of punishment. It was not the fate of Elizabeth Joan that moved him so, and certainly it was no thought of Christ wounded by his wickedness—and then to blame God with it all!

"Go," she said to him bitterly at last. "For I have no comfort to give you."

He went, and she kept sitting on the bench in the weakening sunshine. She thought of Elizabeth Joan, her frail fair face and her sad, uncertain seeking, and she wept thinking of her as sometimes she would still do remembering her own dead daughters. She had been so sure the girl had known Christ, but this incredible interview had left her shaken, unsure. Yet there had been the expression on the face, and her own clear sense of the presence. She chose to keep hope for Elizabeth Joan.

But John Underhill—what of him, the confessed and practiced sinner? Her throat veritably closed up with disgust at the thought. God's grace could *not* have touched him.

The sun sank so low at last that its rays seemed no longer to touch her. She grew cold within and without, and yet sat on, until at last came daughter Mary, sent to tell her it was supper-time.

In bed some hours later, William spoke to her anxiously. "Art thou ill, sweetheart?" he asked her. She answered him nay, but spoke no further. For a little while she thought she might tell him about John Underhill, but she knew the captain expected her to keep his confidence. The midnight cocks were crowing before she fell asleep.

When she awoke, with the cocks of dawn, exhausted and still troubled in her spirit, she made up her mind to go to the man who had brought her first clear understanding of grace and sin. She would not have to tell him Underhill's name, but she could present to the minister her own predicament. As she walked along the lane (muddy from showers that now came almost daily), she wondered if she exercised her best judgment in going to John Cotton. He doubted her now, that was clear, and whatever support he lent to Brother Wheelwright seemed divided and unsure. Well, she could but ask, and he might turn her away if he would.

She asked John Cotton the question: "If a man should come to you, professing to know Christ, and at the same time giving evidence that he has sinned and still sins, what comfort could you give him?"

"That would depend," said Cotton gravely, as they sat in his little room at the head of the stairs. "Is he of the Boston church?" he asked.

"Aye," said Anne.

"Then he should come to one of the ministers instead of to you," he said sternly.

Anne flushed. This was the first time she had admitted to her teacher that she might be performing a duty rightly belonging to him or the pastor.

"I shall tell him so," she said, "should he return."

"Well, then."

"But for my own sake, that I may feel less troubled. What would you say to such a one? Could you give him assurance?"

"No man can ever give assurance."

"But if he believe he knoweth Christ, and yet has sinned and goes on sinning."

"And is he sorry for his sins?"

"He weeps and says it is for fear of hell."

"Not for sadness at the wounds he inflicts on our Saviour."

"So he did not say."

"I would, I think, cast doubt upon his certainty."

"What worries me," Anne confided then, "is whether I am judging on the basis of a covenant of works when I say that because he sins he cannot be saved."

"No, sister, for I think your reason is really what you feel to be in the man's heart."

"And I am right—I am saying no more than you preach yourself—when I say that the presence or absence of sin is evidence of neither damnation nor salvation?"

"That is true."

"But some accuse me of going beyond your teaching and creating my own doctrine, as you have told me yourself."

"In this case, I would say you do not so."

"But in others?"

"Sister, I know not what you may teach in your meetings."

"Only what you have ever taught to me," Anne said.

"I hear strange things repeated," the preacher said. "Such as that no one need obey the Commandments, and that a man may do good works and know Jesus Christ, yet still be damned.

Anne felt a familiar rage rising. Her eyes flashed. "If any say I said so, they are my enemies," she said fiercely.

"So I have believed, sister," said Cotton, "yet you must take care not to be misunderstood in these parlous times. Do not take on more than your position allows."

Her position? Did he mean that because she was a woman, with duties to her family and the burden of a house to keep, she was ever to keep silent? And if not, where was the line beyond which she must not step? She did not ask these questions, only bowed her head so that he should not read her eyes. But presently, when she was walking home, she realized that she had a new attitude toward John Cotton. In the past he had often inspired her, and sometimes had chastised her, leaving her with a bruised heart. Now, dragging her iron pattens through the mud, she thought of him and thanked God for all he had done for her, and prayed they might continue to be friends. But she knew she would never again believe he knew any more than she did about God and the way of salvation. What she felt in her heart she would teach, and what she believed in she would do. But never again would she make the mistake of seeing Cotton as a surrogate of God. He was a man.

And as for John Underhill—her view of him was just what it had been when he left her in the garden. No matter what kind of soldier he might be, he was a sniveling coward who had never known the presence of Christ in his heart and was sorry for his sins only because of his selfish fear of hell. He might come to her meetings—she never would turn anyone away—but she would nowhere confess him as a follower or fellow Christian.

When she got home, Mary Dyer was waiting for her. For a brief instant, something inside her rebelled at what she assumed would prove an added burden. Mary had been so unhappy lately that God sent her no more children, and Anne supposed she had come again about that worry. But when Mary turned and came to her with glowing, smiling face, she knew she was wrong and reproved herself.

"Anne, I am with child," Mary cried.

They hugged and kissed and then sat down together to offer prayers of thanksgiving, silently, with linked hands. It was such a happy, uncomplicated time, of sharing this ordinary womanly joy with a friend, such a relief after the turbulent thoughts that had accompanied her home from John Cotton's, that it never occurred to her to ask if Goody Hawkins' remedies had played any part in producing that delightful condition.

# XX

The opposition to Vane lay outside Boston. No one knew how much support he would have in the mainland towns, but his friends in Boston accepted the fact that the March court had made it easier for freemen from these places to make their opinions count. For the first time, vote by proxy would be allowed, so that if a farmer needed to be planting corn, someone else could go and cast his vote. Moving the election to Newtown would make it a little easier for these mainland men to come to the court, a little less likely that every man in Boston would be present or take enough interest to send a proxy.

Vane's friends had not been able to think of any strategy to combat these two clever moves, but they had one thing in mind to do. They would present still another petition on behalf of John Wheelwright, and this time it would go before the entire court instead of the handful of magistrates who had convicted the minister in the first place. The saving of John Wheelwright would be a victory, should the election happen to go the wrong way.

Wednesday, May 17, election day, dawned clear. For a while after sunrise, there was a faint haze of moisture in the air, but it soon burned away. The weather would not keep anyone from voting.

Henry Vane was already in Newtown. He had gone the day before, taking with him the sergeants that formed his honor guard. It seemed fitting to him that he should not be seen on the day of election until the time to came to open the court. Then, dressed in his finest and flanked by his halberdiers, he would make his appearance.

Otherwise, the leading Hutchinsonians sailed to Newtown in William Coddington's shallop, leaving early in the morning from the landing near the meetinghouse. Besides Coddington, there were sailing together John Cogshall, Atherton Hough, William Aspinwall, William Colburn, and William Hutchinson with his sons Edward, Richard, and Francis. His brother Edward was of course already in Newtown, as halberdier to the governor. Other boats were sailing to Newtown at the same time, and many men were going on foot by way of the Charlestown ferry. Election day in Massachusetts was traditionally a time of merrymaking, the best holiday of the year, but these men going to Newtown were not much inclined to shouting and laughter.

In Coddington's shallop there were solemn faces and quiet talk. "Who has the petition?" Coddington asked.

Aspinwall had it, the man who had written the first draft of the paper from which this one sprang.

"Do you wish to be the one to present it?" Coddington asked.

"Why not?" said Aspinwall, concealing his eagerness.

When would it be presented though? That was a crucial point to consider, thought Atherton Hough, whose experience in politics reached back to Boston in Old England.

"We want the full attention of the assembly," said John Cogshall. "If the freemen hear it read as well as the court, so much the better."

"Before the election then, you think?" said Coddington.

"Aye!" cried all the rest.

Certainly before the election, while the attention of every man could still be counted on. Getting the truth before the electorate in time might well determine the outcome. They decided to send a message to Vane at his inn, as soon as they reached Newtown. As governor and presiding officer, he could accept the petition and have it read before John Winthrop could prepare to move against it.

The election was held in a public field outside the palisades enclosing Newtown. A big crowd had already gathered when Coddington and his party got there.

"Not good for our side," muttered Coddington to Cogshall.

Men were already asking when the governor would come, but no one knew. As noon came near, little knots of men grumbled to each other, and some began to take bread and cheese out of wallets and pockets. A goodly number of them sat under a big oak tree on the north side of the field.

"How long did he mean to hold off?" said Hutchinson to Coddington.

"I don't know," said Coddington. "He wanted to wait until everyone had gathered, but he could go too far with this idea of a royal entrance."

"Where is that sweet-faced governor boy?" a rough voice shouted.

Several voices were raised in support of that sentiment. One said, "We've got to get home before dark."

Winthrop stood up and looked over the crowd. "Hey, Governor," someone cried, "let's get started."

"We'd better send for him," Cogshall said to Coddington.

Then, "Here they come!" someone shouted.

Everyone looked across the common to see the governor and his guard, just emerged from the town gate. In silence they awaited the leader, who came to his place with majestic mien and if the truth be known, a hint of a pout about his handsome, full-lipped red mouth.

He went through the ritual of formally opening the meeting, and as soon as he had finished Aspinwall stepped forward, petition in his hand. "May it please the governor," he cried, "here is a petition from the Boston church which we beg the court to receive."

"What's this?" "How now?" "Is this the election court or not?" Such mumblings came from the crowd, but Winthrop's sharp voice cut a swath through them.

"Out of order!" he shouted. "The first business of this court is the election of magistrates."

"Aye!" cried many voices. "Listen to the good old governor!" someone called out.

Vane under the oak tree was trying to shout them all down, insisting that no election would take place until the petition was read to the court.

"Look here," cried a sturdy freeman from the country. "I come here to vote, not listen to a lot of barnyard yap about some preacher."

Aspinwall, who happened to be standing near the man, told him to keep his silence; the reply was a fist in his face, which Aspinwall looked ready to return. Coddington pulled Aspinwall back, and the citizen subsided. But here and there, an exchange of blows was completed.

Somewhere among the Bostonians someone cried, "Watch out for the covenant-of-works boys!"

And just then a strange sight was seen: John Wilson up the oak tree. The stout black-clad pastor pulled himself up to one of the large spreading branches and perched like some great bird of prey. "Brethren!" he roared in his huge pulpit voice, and they looked at him in amazement. "Look to your charter," he demanded, "and consider the work of the day."

What the charter had to do with the order of procedure few could know, but the reminder was enough to quiet the crowd. Any threatened loss of that document worked like magic among the men of Massachusetts Bay.

"Election, election!" the chant began, running through the crowd, and Winthrop, taking advantage of the relative calm, shouted to the voters to indicate their preference by dividing. "You who want election over here"—he gestured to the right—"and you who want the petition read, over here"—he gestured to the left.

After a moment or two in which men turned and looked questioningly at their neighbors, the crowd divided in two. There was no question of where the majority lay. But the little cluster of Bostonians still held apart, and Vane still refused to go on, until Winthrop threatened to proceed without them. And Vane realized then that he had lost the election. The outcome was already as clear as though the votes had been counted.

## 2

At home, the women waited. Family and friends had come to the Hutchinson house: Sarah and Katherine, wives of the two Edwards; the faithful three Marys, Elizabeth Hough and Elizabeth Aspinwall. And yes, Goody Hawkins was there, too, although her husband was not a freeman and so had not gone to the court.

They knew not when the business at Newtown would be ended, or how long the men would take getting home. By mid-afternoon they were beginning to look out for them, asking each other why the election should go on much past noon. About this time Anne sent Sammy, with some other boys of his age, to wait at the long wharf till they saw the shallop coming. Meanwhile, the women watched over the smaller children, who were playing in the front garden, and kept themselves busy with various kinds of handwork they had brought.

Mary Dyer, embroidering a design of flowerets on a baby cap of fine linen, was the center of attention, on account of the exceptionally delicate work that she did, so that someone would frequently be getting up to see whether she had finished another of the tiny white silk rosebuds. Yet somehow no one had noticed her for a little while when Mary Cogshall, about to go and admire the latest flower, saw that her head had fallen down onto her knees crushing the cap under her forehead.

"She has fainted," Mary cried, jumping up from her stool, and several women rushed to her. She was only asleep, though deeply asleep, and they managed to wake her. She said she fell asleep thus every day. "I get so tired," she said, "that I truly cannot go about my housework."

Most of the other women said they had experienced great weariness, too, when they were with child. But Jane Hawkins, looking into Mary's eyes while she held her limp wrist in her hand, said it seemed to her more than ordinary tiredness.

"Have you borrage, mistress?" she asked Anne.

Anne did, and Jane made a potion of it for Mary Dyer to drink. "I will bring you something better, another day," the old woman said vaguely.

"I should be careful about using too many kinds of medicine for something that may be altogether natural," Anne said.

"Oh yes, mistress, I am always careful," Jane said earnestly.

Mary had brightened enough to smile and say, "Jane has many medicines at home that few even know the names of."

It occurred to Anne that she would like to know more about

the nature of these medicines and where Jane learned of them; but at that time Sammy came flying in at the open door, shouting, "They're coming, they're coming!"

Then all the women except Mary Dyer, who felt too tired, and Goody Hawkins, who thought she had better stay to look after Mary, hurried off to the wharf, with all sizes of children running pell-mell around and behind and in front of them.

They stood on the wharf watching and wondering, not talking much among themselves, while the little sailboat drew slowly near the shore. When they could see the men's faces clear, they looked at each other anxiously: their expressions did not suggest victory.

Then Sarah noticed her husband was among them, and exclaimed, "There's Edward," just as one of the children cried, "There's Father—but he hasn't brought his halberd."

"Nor the governor either," said another child.

By this time the men were wagging their heads, and all that remained was to hear the full story of defeat as the little company made its plodding way up the high street and along past the market place and the meetinghouse to the Hutchinsons', at the corner of Sentry Lane. Every once in a while along the way, someone would call to them, "Who's governor now?" and the answer—"Winthrop!"—would crack in the air like a whip. No one cheered.

It was a disappointment to Anne that Henry Vane had not returned with the men in the boat. She could imagine his hurt eyes and trembling lips, and thought how she would like to enfold him in her arms like a child come home weeping from his play. Henry, though, had felt it suitable to stay in his room at the inn another night and be present if the court should convene very early the next morning. (If some of the men thought he was sulking, they did not say so to Mistress Hutchinson.)

It was not Vane alone who had lost his office. William Coddington and Richard Dummer of Newbury, the only two magistrates among Anne's supporters, were defeated as well. The old team was back in power—Winthrop as governor, Dudley as deputy governor, and the entire court of assistants on their side.

When the official word had come—when Vane stepped out of his place beneath the tree and Winthrop came forward—Edward Hutchinson and the other sergeants of the guard had laid down their halberds on the ground and walked away. At that news, the plodding little band did cheer a little.

In the Hutchinson house, their first thought was to pray. Although they had no kind of ritual for prayers, and might pray either sitting or standing (so long as they did not bow), several of them had come to feel that in clasping each other's hands they could feel the spirit stronger and commune with God more freely. Anne found herself with Coddington's hand in hers: he is the one, she thought; God may send us strength through him.

After prayers they were able to smile hopefully at each other and speak of plans for the future. Anne decided to serve early supper, for she knew the men still had work to do. They had devised a scheme even before the election in case the worst happened. Most towns elected deputies before the meeting of the court, but they had decided to wait, and now must quickly arrange an election for early the next morning, so that their own people could have some part in the actions of the court. After the meal, the men scattered, to give notice of the election, and the women remained, again waiting.

Light lingered a long time this warm May evening, but inside the narrow-windowed house dusk came early. The women did not take up their handwork again, but talked, in murmuring voices, about their own closest concerns. Mary Dyer was feeling well now. Katherine Hutchinson, young Edward's wife, who was expecting a child a little before the time Mary's was due, had not felt ill at all, not even having to vomit in the mornings. She wanted to borrow the pattern of the cap Mary was making.

All the time Anne sat apart from the rest in her wainscot chair. Her mind was not on women's things, but on the things of God, and whether they might ever be brought to prevail in the colony of Massachusetts Bay.

## 3

John Winthrop ruled again in Massachusetts. The court was a Winthrop court. Boston elected its deputies—Vane, Coddington, and Hough—but their votes would count for nothing when Winthrop opposed them. The governor knew his own town was displeased with him, but he prayed God to guide him aright in preserving the colony, and kept faith that, when he had succeeded, Boston as before would gladly follow where he led.

On one matter at least the colony seemed in agreement: the war against the Pequods. Much had happened in Connecticut since John Underhill took his twenty men there. On April 23, two hundred Pequods had attacked some settlers working in a field, killed nine of them, and carried off two girls. Connecticut decided not to wait for Massachusetts to send additional men and went ahead, with their allies the Mohicans, to win a decisive victory. Now in order to have some credit in the affair, Massachusetts had already prepared to send an army to hunt down the remnants of the tribe still hiding in the swamps and forests. All the court had to do was provide them a chaplain. Lots were cast, and John Wilson won the post. (How could Winthrop have guessed that even this simple act would become a target of the hated antinomians?)

Business clearly related to the antinomian affair was expeditiously completed. The Hutchinsonians scarcely bothered trying to make their voices heard.

John Wheelwright was brought before the court again, and again his sentence was deferred, so that he might be given time to retract his error. Wheelwright rejoined that if he were really guilty of sedition they should go on and put him to death, for he had no retraction to make. But Winthrop had his reasons for waiting about this.

Finally, with such haste that few had heard of the proposal before they were voting on it, a law was passed prohibiting any newcomer from staying more than three weeks in the colony without the approval of two magistrates or one member of the Council for Life. Winthrop did not know whether it was generally known among the legislators that friends and relatives of the Hutchinsons and Wheelwrights were already on their way to Boston. He assumed they would have given him what he wanted whether they knew or not.

When the session of court was over, Winthrop went home guarded by two of his own servants carrying halberds. People along the way turned their backs on him. Doors were closed all up and down the high street, and no one came out to greet him.

He had experienced nothing like this in his political career, and his heart was heavy. All the same, he knew he would pay any price to keep the colony united and secure. He had taken the first necessary steps and was prepared to take more.

Meanwhile, bewildered and frustrated, tasting defeat, the Hutchinson party kept on doing things that could hardly have any other effect than to annoy John Winthrop. On the Lord's Day, Vane and Coddington, no longer eligible to sit on the magistrates' bench, went to sit with the deacons; and although Winthrop graciously invited them to sit with him, the invitation was declined.

Then the men of Boston congregation refused, as a matter of conscience, to go to war with John Wilson as chaplain. They could not bring themselves to put their immortal souls in the care of a minister who preached a covenant of works. Fortunately, the war was nearly over, but the principle was the same as if they had put their homes and families in jeopardy. So Winthrop said to himself, grinding his teeth, as he wrote in his journal that Boston had been willing to send only those men they did not mind being rid of, and a few others "of the most refuse sort."

To promote harmony in the colony, and to give himself a much needed change of scene, Winthrop went in late June on a journey of state to Saugus, Salem, and Ipswich. His reception in these towns raised his spirits greatly, for he was met everywhere by enthusiastic supporters and provided with an honor guard that escorted him from town to town.

Yet he could not go lightheartedly home to Boston. There were many burdens bearing down on him, not least of them the heat. During this time, a number of people newly come from England had died of heatstrokes while looking for homesites; and Winthrop himself found it necessary to travel by night on his way home, to avoid the searing sun.

Was this heat wave God's sign of a wearisome, difficult summer ahead? Winthrop thought it might be. But he thought he was well prepared for whatever God might send to test him.

4

About this time there arrived in Boston the friends and relatives whom the Hutchinsons and Wheelwrights had long awaited. Some of them went to stay at Mt. Wollaston; others went to various Boston families, believers in the covenant of grace. Samuel Hutchinson, with his wife and children, stayed a few days with his cousin William.

The New World appeared a strange world indeed to these people who had come hoping to find good homes and a congenial church way. At the dock they were met with news of the alien law and a summons to be questioned by Governor Winthrop. As a member of the Council for Life, Winthrop was able to question and dispose of them without consulting any other magistrate or any minister. And this he did, without delay.

On the morning of the hearing, the women waited. Anne, though she tried to cheer her kinswoman, thought how weary she was of waiting for Winthrop, who seemed ever to be discovering new actions he could take against her and her friends. She could not say how many times, since last December's court, she had found herself sitting at home while the men fought through decisions that always came out the wrong way. If women could go to court—if she herself could argue these cases that so closely concerned her and the doctrine she believed in—might the outcome not sometimes be different? She still thought she had comported herself very well when the ministers questioned her during the time of that December court.

None of this was what she was talking about with Margaret Hutchinson. To her Anne spoke of house lots that were available, of the good supply of produce coming in from the farms, of the heat which was—yes, Margaret was certainly right about that—almost beyond the belief of any Englishman.

They sat in the open doorway shelling garden peas (a little shriveled they were from the burning sun) and watched for the men to come from the direction of John Winthrop's. They were almost unbearably hot but, having no way of dressing for such heat, called it the will of God and endured it.

The men came in, roasting in their breeches and wool doublets, with streams of sweat pouring down their faces under their heavy, broad-brimmed hats. "The news is not good," they said. But Anne would have them come inside and take a cup of the drink she made from bruised mint and honey before they began to give their disappointing account of the meeting.

"This does seem cooling," said Samuel, fanning himself with his hat.

"Now tell," said Margaret, "for I can wait no more."

The four of them sat on benches just inside the front door, where the air moved slightly and breathing seemed easier.

"Winthrop has been generous," said William bitterly.

"Aye," said Samuel. "Since we had no way of knowing about the law before we came, he has decided we can stay in the colony four months."

"But what has he against us?" Margaret cried.

Samuel shrugged.

"The governor let me stay for the questioning," William said, "and I can tell you there was nothing."

"He asked for their beliefs about the covenant of grace, I suppose," said Anne.

"Aye," said William, "and the indwelling of the Holy Spirit. But I can assure you no one said anything more than Master Cotton says all the time in the pulpit. I had already warned them not to use the word *person* in their answers."

"So really," said Anne, "there was nothing more against them than the error of being our relatives."

Samuel, feeling better from his drink and his fanning, laughed lightly. "I did say," he admitted, "that I had never experienced such heat as this in England and I fear the governor took offense at that."

"So he will send us back, because we can't stand the heat," said Margaret.

"Oh, I don't think we shall go back," said Samuel. "There are other places to settle. John Wheelwright talks of going to New Hampshire, and it might be that William and Anne will be moving, too. The climate of Boston does seem to leave something to be desired."

Anne shook her head, and William answered, "No, I think we shall stay. My business is well established here, and the two oldest girls have married Boston men."

"But since you are not established, you may be just as well off not to stay in Boston," Anne said, then added thoughtfully, "although we need you sorely here."

"There are those who think we don't have to put up with such a law," William said. "Much may happen in four months."

In the miserable heat, Anne felt a shiver go through her body, a presentiment, she half believed, of something that would be happening four months from that day, which was the sixth of July. But she shrugged it off, and standing with a bowl of peas in her hand said, "Let me ask Cousin Frances what she wants to do about cooking these peas, and then we shall take you out to see the town. It cannot be much hotter in the streets than in the house."

As she went back to the kitchen corner, where the cousins were at work, William said wryly, "That's a good idea. You may discover you'll be happy not to stay in Boston."

The newcomers had not yet been able to go about the town much. The way between the harbor and the Hutchinsons', and the high street between them and John Winthrop's, was all even Samuel had seen.

The two couples walked along the high street, past the meetinghouse and on into the market place. Men, women, and children of all classes were gathered there, for a reason both William and Anne had quite forgotten in the excitement of welcoming their guests and learning what their fate would be.

"Oh, you will see something indeed," William said. "Something that will tell you even more about the men who govern us."

He led them through the crowd as near as they could come to the scaffold that stood in the open square. Along the edge of the platform were nailed severed hands and even a few withered heads. At the center, and higher than the rest, hung a scalp with a long hank of coarse black hair.

"Oh, William," cried Anne, "I had not seen this."

"The heads and hands have been here some days now," said William. "The Narragansets have been bringing them in, so as to collect the bounty offered by the colony. The scalp belonged to Sassacus, the last of the Pequod chiefs. Our own men brought it, along with the captive women that they marched in yesterday."

"'Tis not a pleasant spectacle," said Anne, and the others

agreed, though it was true they had seen sights not dissimilar in London.

"There's more to see than this," said William, "for as I now recall, this is the day the Boston matrons choose their slaves, and I believe the Indians will be arriving any time now from the pen the governor had built for them on the common."

"Slaves?" Margaret exclaimed.

"Oh indeed, slaves," said William. "Let's walk toward the common, and we may meet them as they come to market." They moved back along the high street, in the direction whence they had come.

"Bond servants now," said Samuel, "I would have said might be as near a thing to slaves as you would have here in the colony."

"It's hard to get enough English servants," William said.

"And I don't think Indians make very good servants either," said Anne. "They are always running away, back to the wilderness."

"So there really is a servant problem," William said. "Emanuel Downing—Winthrop's brother-in-law—has a solution for it. He wants to trade Indians for Negroes. He came down here from Ipswich to tell us his views one time while I was still on the court. He wants us to capture all the Indians, as many as we can, for he says it would in any case be sinful if we left them to their devil's powwows in the forest. Then they can be traded for blackamoors, who make better servants. And of course, as he said, even if you can get English servants, you can maintain twenty blacks cheaper than one Englishman."

Soon thereafter they had to make way for a herd of squaws, roped together and moved along to the market place by some soldiers home from the war. The men hollered at the captives from time to time and cracked whips at them to keep them in line. None of the Hutchinsons had seen anything like this before —these savage, staring women, scarred and painted, some of them dressed only in skirts made of animal skins, driven along the high street like so many wild cows.

While the Hutchinson party was standing aside for the herd to pass, Henry Vane came up to them with a young man—no more than a boy, years younger even than Henry—whom he introduced to them as Lord Ley, a visitor from home, son of the Earl of Marlborough. The young lord stood in openmouthed amazement as the women passed by.

Anne and Henry stood back a little from the rest. "Do you realize that this is what remains of the entire tribe of Pequod Indians?" Henry said to her. "And I with my proclamation of war set in motion what has ended with this." He gestured sadly toward the passing band.

"We must pray for them," Anne said. "Some of them, strange as it seems, may be among God's elect."

"Aye," said Henry, "we must pray."

"Look a-yonder," said Samuel Hutchinson suddenly. "Across the street there, ogling the women. I think I know that man."

"'Tis Hugh Peter," Henry said, "a preacher you might have seen in England. I've heard he wrote to have a squaw saved for him. No doubt he's come to pick her out."

The Hutchinsons, not having come to watch the parceling out of the slaves, were about to continue on home, when they noticed everyone along the street standing back, as they had done for the Indians, and not with much more of an air of respect. Looking on down the street, they saw that John Winthrop was coming. Dressed in his finest, and accompanied by two servants as halberdiers, he was going to the market place to make a state occasion of the disposal of the slaves.

And now he was stopping, apparently on purpose, to speak to someone in the Hutchinson group. He said a cold good morning to them all, but then directed his speech to Henry Vane and Lord Ley. It would afford him the greatest pleasure, he said, if the two young men would dine with him on the morrow. He only regretted that his absence on affairs of state had kept him from extending an invitation sooner, as he had not even known of Lord Ley's arrival; but now he wished to give a suitable dinner in the noble visitor's honor.

To this long speech, for which a not inconsiderable audience had gathered, Henry responded with regret that his conscience withheld him from consent; and that, in any case, such an affair would undoubtedly continue far into the afternoon, at which time it would be necessary for him to attend a meeting in the home of Mistress Hutchinson.

Lord Ley replied politely that he too must refuse, as he had agreed to go with Master Vane.

Winthrop looked coldly into Anne's face and then without another word turned and continued on his way to the market place.

"Three cheers for Henry Vane!" shouted someone in the crowd. "Hurray for his lordship," another cried. And among cheers for his enemies, Winthrop marched on with his halberdiers.

## 5

As news of Winthrop's manner of invoking the new exclusion act spread through Boston, feeling against the government reached the greatest intensity ever. After the mixed meeting at the Hutchinsons', at which the new arrivals including Lord Ley expressed much gratification, a small number of the leading persons stayed on to discuss what could be done about the tyrannical new law.

"It's worse than England," Samuel said, "for there you may believe anything as long as you keep quiet about it; but here they will root out your most secret thoughts and expel you before you ever have a chance to express them."

"And the worst of all," said Vane, "is this: that it is tyranny not only against men, but against Christ, when men and women known to be good Christians are refused for cause of their true belief."

"Yet what can be done now?" asked Coddington. "For court will not convene again till August, and since that session will be called for special purposes, it is doubtful that Winthrop would agree to hear our protests then."

Then Anne, who rarely spoke out at meetings of a political nature, said something she had been thinking of since she realized to what an extent the law could be taken. "Since it concerns the suppression of true belief, why should we not make our protest in the meetinghouse on lecture day? Then the ministers might see it as an act of Antichrist and demand that some action be taken."

This suggestion was deemed a good one, and the discussion turned to the formulation of the most cogent arguments against the act. It would be as well, all agreed, if their intentions remained secret until the set day. But of course the secret was not quite kept. Goody Hawkins was there, in her corner in the kitchen.

John Cotton, though not taken into the confidence of the Hutchinsonians, heard some talk and began to articulate his own objections to the act. John Winthrop guessed something was in the wind, and began to make notes. There was no one in Boston who had not at least heard vague rumors that something was going to happen on lecture day.

The meetinghouse was filled with people not nearly so attentive to Cotton's lecture as ordinarily they were. When it was over, Atherton Hough, who as one of the most moderate speaking of Anne Hutchinson's supporters had been chosen to raise the question, stood up to speak. He said very little: only that there was a doubt in his mind whether any man was so well able to judge another's religious principles that he might in the fear of God refuse to allow a professed Christian to take up residence within a Christian commonwealth.

John Wilson seemed about to arise in some sort of protest—perhaps to say that this was not the proper time and place for such discussion—but John Cotton was on his feet and speaking before Pastor Wilson had decided what to say. It seemed to Cotton that this new law would work against the balance of power necessary to a Christian commonwealth, for the ministers might question a man and perceive him to be a good Christian, and then the magistrates for reasons of their own might turn the man away.

"Yet," said John Winthrop, stepping out from the magistrates' bench, "this law would do nothing less than preserve the commonwealth. And without the commonwealth, what good can our ministers do?"

At that speech Henry Vane jumped to his feet. "This is nothing but a covenant of works!" he cried, his dark eyes bright and his nostrils flaring.

A murmuring wave of approval went through the congregation, but Winthrop, ignoring it, said coldly, "I wish you may explain your reasoning, brother."

"I wish you would first say clearly, brother," said Vane, moving out from where he stood beside the deacons' bench to face Winthrop more directly, "whether in your interpretation of this law a true Christian might be turned away."

"Yes," said Winthrop, "I conceive he might be, for the saving of the commonwealth."

"Why then, 'tis clear," said Vane, "that you are more interested in presenting an appearance of Christianity than in witnessing for the true Christ."

"I am interested in preventing seditious opinions—and actions that may tear the state apart."

"But remember, Christ may sometimes bring not peace but a sword. And if you reject the sword you reject the truth of the Gospel and Christ himself."

"You argue somewhat emotionally, brother," said Winthrop, and it was true: tears stood in Vane's eyes. "Surely if you would allow the scriptural exhortation that we should reason together, you would see that unless we have a time of peace we have no commonwealth. And since it follows that we must keep out troublemakers who would destroy the very foundations of our commonwealth, then surely it were an unhappier thing to let a man come into us and then to cast him out than simply to let him know in the first instance that he does not fit in."

Now Vane was burning in fury, and he cried, "I see, sir, that you now intend to banish from the colony all who disagree with your own opinions."

Winthrop, standing face to face with Henry Vane, fixed his eyes hard upon him. "I could wish that such a thing need never be," he said, "and yet if it must be, then the Lord's will be done."

Henry spoke swiftly and tonelessly then, struggling against his threatening tears. "Since I know that by this you mean your own will," he said, "I understand that I am no longer wanted here, and should have left this colony long ago."

He meant to say more, recalling to them the time he offered to resign the governorship, but realizing he could no longer speak with any assurance of control, he turned and walked out of the meetinghouse. Anne Hutchinson rose and followed him, and no man tried to stop them.

The partisans found more to say in the meetinghouse, and yet to no avail, until finally John Wilson put an end to the discussion, saying it had reached a level inappropriate to the occasion.

## 6

Outside in the high street, Henry turned toward the mouth of Prison Lane, on the way to his house by Cotton Hill. He trudged along through the dust like a man bearing a heavy burden, for he was indeed weighted down, both by the oppressive heat and the sense of his terrible failure here in the New World. He took a silk handkerchief out of his pocket, and wiped tears and sweat from his face.

"Brother! Dear brother!" called someone behind him. He knew that voice. It was strong, somewhat high-pitched—a female voice, yet with little of the sweetness or softness with which another woman might have spoken. No matter for that: it was the most beloved voice in all the world to him. He turned and saw Anne Hutchinson coming toward him, and felt his heart burst with joy and sorrow at the sight. Tears flowed; he no longer tried to control them.

Forgetting to lift her skirts from the dust, Anne hurried towards him dragging a path behind her. She reached out her hands and he took them; with an effort that made her arms and bosom ache, she kept from clasping him against her. She thought she could not bear his great hurt, nor let him try to bear it, as long as they must hold themselves separate, one from the other.

They stood a moment, her hands in his; some bit of comfort flowed between them.

"Where are you going?" she asked.

"To my house," he said. "Come with me."

"Come to my house," she said. "We must talk."

"Come with me," he said again, pleading. "My servant is gone. We can be alone there—God would have us speak alone, one time before I leave New England."

She let him lead her there, not wondering if there was anyone to watch, for she believed, with him, that God would have it so.

When they sat side by side on the settle in the corner of

Henry's little hall, they did not, after all, soon start to speak. Both wept a little while, pressing each other's hands.

"When will you leave us?" Anne finally asked. She knew there was no use protesting any more.

He would sail on the ship with Lord Ley, he said, within the next few days. He bemoaned his failure in Boston.

"No, it has not been a failure," Anne said. "You have helped make plain the truth of God. If our enemies suppress it, God will not blame you.

"Thou knowest," she said, "I have nothing to blame thee for, but much to thank God for, because He sent thee here to me, e'en for a little while."

"And thou knowest," he said, "that I never could consent to go away, or even leave thy side, if—"

He did not finish, but turned to her and embraced her, and she took him to her bosom. Then for the first time they kissed, mouth to mouth, and each knew surely what might have been surmise until that moment.

"God wished it thus," she said at last. "If He had sent us into the world at different times, so that we had been young together, who knows whether we should ever have found the work that was ours to do?" (For though she loved William, and would put no other man before him as long as they both should live, she could not tell whether a different kind of love might not have kept her bound so close to the bed and the hearth of a man that she never would have turned away to teach the waiting multitudes about the love of God.)

Henry sighed. "Nevertheless," he said, "I shall thank God all my life that He did bring us together, that we might share His work on earth for as long as He was pleased to have it so."

"And so shall I," said Anne. "Yet we must put the work before the sharing."

"And must go," said Henry, "where our work leads us, as mine to England now."

"The Lord knows there is work to be done there," said Anne, "and if when the prophecy of England's destruction be fulfilled, thou art caught in the midst of it, remember I have loved thee."

"I shall remember," Henry said, "though I stand on a scaffold with a rope around my neck."

Anne's brow clouded; but if his words started a revelation, she thrust it away from her. Let the future remain dark, she prayed to God.

Presently they said a last good-by, for although they might meet again in public, they knew that never more on earth could their hearts speak thus to one another.

Anne walked alone out of the little house, and a few steps down the lane met John Cotton and his wife returning home.

"Good day," she said to them, looking straight into their faces.

They answered her as though not certain she was anyone they knew, and she went on, smiling faintly to herself though tears still stood in her eyes. This one thing God had given her, these moments all alone with Henry Vane. She could never regret them no matter what her life might hold.

When the two young men sailed for England, there was such a crowd come to say farewell to Henry Vane that one might wonder whether anyone stayed to keep a shop or tend the sick. Those left on shore fired volleys of shot in his honor, while others went out on the barge that took the two passengers to the ship in the harbor. Then as the ship passed Castle Island, they at the fort fired five pieces of ordnance.

Anne sat at home alone, proud and anguished. New England would never forget Henry Vane, and she thanked God for that.

# XXI

And now there would be a great synod, comprising all the churches in the Bay. Now heresy would be clearly identified, so that the churches could deal with it whenever it arose. Now the ministers would understand each other, for doubtful doctrines would be explicated so thoroughly that there could no longer be any question of what any brother believed and taught. The colony would be in full truth a Christian commonwealth, with all men united in their acceptance of God's way, from which in turn would stem all civil law and family rule.

Winthrop saw now, as he recalled the history of the colony, that it had been overweening of him to suppose he could govern according to the will of God, lovingly and firmly, without error and without opposition. It was not so easy to serve God, even for an individual; how much more difficult then, for an entire state. Yet with the right leadership, in the ministry and in the magistracy, he well believed that such a thing could be: his long cherished dream of the city on the hill, engaged in right dealings with all the world, serving as an example to every nation, helping the needy at home and abroad. From such a pinnacle as he envisioned, what outward foe need any nation fear?

His hope for all this now rose again. After this long time of tribulations accompanied by agonizing prayer and soul searching, he thought God would let them go on. Men of faith and good will now formed the government, and once the ministers had come to terms with each other and defined heresy, the magistrates would know surely how to rule. There must be a line beyond which none dared go. Once that line is established, a nation need never fear the foe that lurks within.

Although Winthrop had the support of John Wilson from his first intimation of a desire for church unity, not all the ministers had been quick to agree. Most were doubtful about John Cotton and whether it ever would be possible to nail him down on either side of his narrow scantling. But at last the brethren all agreed that for the sake of peace it was imperative that they agree among themselves.

Cotton recognized the necessity for a synod, if for no other reason than to clear himself of charges of familism. Over and over, he had preached sermons clearly showing the great gap between his views and the doctrines of the Family of Love. Yet invariably there would be someone coming to him after a sermon, reporting what the Hutchinsonians declared: "No matter what you hear him say in public, we know what he says to us in private." He still could not believe Anne Hutchinson would tell such a falsehood as that, or pretend to know his secret mind. He never had thought she was teaching anything different from what he himself always preached; but he had finally accepted the possibility that the way she expressed herself might lead to misunderstanding among persons not well versed in theological dispute. And so he thought that, far from causing trouble for Anne Hutchinson in the church, the clear definition of heresy might prove a blessing to her.

The congregation of Boston church, including Anne Hutchinson, were by no means so hopeful. They saw the synod as a battle between the covenanters of works and the covenanters of grace, and they knew the world well enough to understand that power wasn't always on the side of truth.

For three weeks before the public meetings began, the ministers held conferences in Boston preparing for the arduous labor of weeding error out of Massachusetts. In particular, they were striving to pick out all the errors from Master Cotton's sermons; the difficulty in that task was being sure what Cotton meant. Anne Hutchinson thought she was sure, but Cotton's brother ministers often found his words too slippery to take hold of.

Among the preliminary work was a meeting of the ministers in which Cotton was required to answer five questions about faith, justification, and the covenant of works. He said all the same things he had always said, if possible in more equivocating terms. They spent many hours on the question "Whether the Spirit of God in Evidencing our Justification doth bear witness in an absolute promise of Free Grace, without qualification or condition?" To which at last Cotton gave answer, plainly and roundly, "the Spirit doth Evidence our Justification both wayes, sometime in an absolute Promise, sometime in a conditionall."

So they went on with the synod.

## 2

At first Anne thought she would not go. The Boston church had selected its delegates—"messengers," the ministers would have them called—and they of course were all men. No woman would be allowed to speak in a public conference on matters of such grave import.

"What good would I do going?" she said to William.

"It might set your mind more at ease," William said, "to understand exactly what it is they are about."

"I shall go the first day," she decided.

So she went, she and William and at least half of Boston. She found a seat, packed in with other spectators at the back of the little meetinghouse in Newtown, where the synod proper was to be held.

Master Shepard prayed the opening prayer, in which he told the Lord about the unscriptural enthusiasms that troubled the colony.

"Hypocrisy!" Anne would have liked to spit out that word, but it stayed unformed among a profusion of mental reactions. If he had a true communion with God, he need not bore Him with a recitation of what He would already know if there were any truth in it.

At last, Master Wilson rose at his seat. "You that are against these things, and that are for the spirit and the word together, hold up your hands!"

Hands flew up all over the meetinghouse, except among the

Bostonians at the back. "Dear God protect us," Anne inwardly prayed. Most knew not what they were voting for, but followed their ministers like sheep, and in any case who ever heard of voting on a prayer? It was clear Master Shepard had only made a pretense of talking to God.

Then it was time to let the people know more fully just what sorts of things they had held up their hands against. One of the elders climbed to the pulpit and read the list so laboriously compiled.

Eighty-two errors! Plus nine "erroneous expressions." Anne listened in utter astonishment. Where had they ever heard such things? Some of the expressions were close to her belief, and she might even have spoken a few of them in her meetings. But she had never in her life heard anyone say that "to take delight in the holy service of God, is to go a-whoring from God." If anyone had so expressed her condemnation of the covenant of works, she could only suppose the devil himself in the guise of an earnest Bostonian had been attending her meetings.

After the people had a little recovered themselves from the horrors of this "litter of fourscore and eleven brats hung up against the sun" (as Winthrop liked to call them), two of the ministers explained the procedure that would be followed in the synod. No names would be named; the concern was merely with the errors, and anyone who wished to enter into debate upon any point could do so freely without suspicion falling upon him personally.

"Hah!" said the Bostonians audibly to each other.

"Silence!" cried the ministers.

At home that night Anne said, "I see how it will be. I shall not go back."

She was right. Nothing could have changed the course the ministers were set upon. When some of the Boston church seemed about to speak in favor of one of the opinions, Master Cotton took them aside and scolded them. "Brethren," he said, "if you be of that judgment which you plead for, all these bastardly opinions will be fathered upon Boston."

He told them if they were in doubt about the erroneousness and danger of the opinions, they should have dealt with their doubts in the church at home when they were chosen messengers. (But it would have been hard to find any in the Boston church who would not have expressed the same views about justification before faith; they thought they were saying just what Cotton himself had been preaching all the time.)

At his uncommonly harsh speaking, some of the Boston messengers withdrew from the synod. And Cotton was left doubting for the first time whether there might in fact be a real and broad difference between himself and those brethren who leaned to Mistress Hutchinson.

Each day the reports brought home to Anne confirmed more fully what she had suspected all along. More of the Boston delegation walked out one day after Winthrop threatened to have them arrested for disturbing the peace. The magistrates had no authority at a church meeting, Aspinwall rejoined. Winthrop dared him to make trial of it.

At the end of the week every one of the opinions was labeled heresy. Symmes of Charlestown asked (as apparently no one had thought to do before), "What is to be done with them?" And Pastor Wilson had the answer. "Let them go to the devil of hell from whence they came," he roared.

On hearing this last report, Anne only said that she was not surprised. "Nothing has changed," she affirmed, "except that now the ministers who oppose us have made their opposition open and clear."

William and their friends thought she was more worried than she would confess about the blanket condemnation of opinions, but in truth it was no fear of being called a heretic that held her thoughts and made her seem withdrawn and absent-minded. Although some of the errors came near being what she believed, the whole collection of them appeared to her so absurd that she could not imagine anyone being seriously charged with holding such views.

What concerned her most was the business taken up next by the ministers, who deemed it essential that all of them must believe exactly the same way. About John Wheelwright she entertained no doubt. She knew exactly what he believed and how long he would hold to it. He would come to them sometimes at night, and tell them of the long, hard (and to him useless) arguments. That a man was saved by God's grace and could take no active part in his own salvation was as clear to him as it had been to John Calvin. But he was not as sure as he once was that John Cotton was in perfect agreement with him.

Anne now knew that she had not been sure either, not for many months. She had learned that she could bear her teacher's doubts of her, but she did not know how to deal with her own doubts of him. For if he no longer held the full meaning of the covenant of grace as once he taught it when he awakened her soul to true experience of the spirit, then why had God led her to New England?

On another day, they heard in Boston how the ministers had wept and begged and wrestled with the teacher's soul. For Cotton had still clung to his belief that only through justification could man acquire faith. "He will not change," said Anne, but inwardly she quavered. The truth was clear, so shining clear and beautiful to her, it was like a great thin crystal sphere that enclosed her in God's glory. It was John Cotton who had first revealed to her that glorious shimmering happiness that was resting in the certainty of God's grace and power. One who had ever known so great a truth—that salvation flows like light from the flame of God without regard to man's puny efforts to strike a spark—one whose heart had soared as hers had done at the gift of this heavenly marvel—oh, could such a man ever turn away from such a glory? And if one could lose sight—if Cotton did—She could find no way to finish such a proposition.

Yet Cotton did lose sight. (Or at least, perhaps, not entirely.) And yet they pulled him back. (Oh yes, that was sure, they pulled him back, and turned his head away.) For the sake of harmony and better understanding, he allowed his views on the place of faith in the order of conversion to be phrased in such a way as to give some comfort to those who said man's faith comes first, before God's act of justification. There were three points at last that Cotton accepted to bring to an end the terrible ministerial ordeal. William Coddington copied them and brought them home to read to Anne:

1. That the new creature is not the person of a believer, but a body of saving graces in such a one; and that Christ, as a head, doth enliven or quicken, but Christ Himself is no part of this new creature.

2. That though, in effectual calling (in which the answer of

the soul is by active faith, wrought at the same instant by the spirit), justification and sanctification be all together in them; yet God doth not justify a man, before he be effectually called, and so a believer.

3. That Christ and His benefits may be offered and exhibited to a man under a covenant of works, but not in or by a covenant of works.

These things Cotton put his name to, and the crystal sphere was clouded as if with God's own tears.

The synod ended on September 22. A few more resolutions were passed. No member of a church henceforth would be allowed to withdraw from it because he disagreed with the theology. There would be no more discussion periods after sermons. And whereas neighborhood prayer meetings might still be encouraged, "yet a set assembly where sixty or more did meet every week and one woman (in a prophetical way, by resolving questions of doctrine and expounding Scripture) took upon her the whole exercise, was agreed to be disorderly and without rule."

At this last news, Anne faintly smiled. To Coddington, who had brought it, she said that she would be the judge as to whether her meetings were disorderly.

# XXII

After the synod, Samuel Hutchinson's family went to stay with John Wheelwright at Wollaston, because there was work to do there on the farm and also because the two men were studying together the prospects of settlement in New Hampshire. Once more Anne's household consisted of her own immediate family and the Freestone cousins, so that there was more silence and space in the house as well as more time for the work of the Lord.

But that, too, had changed. Fewer persons attended the meetings now, and the task was less one of proselytizing than it had been before. Nor was Anne displeased with this change. She had always known there were some who came out of curiosity or simply because her house was a place to go for refreshment in a grim and monotonous life. She had never turned a soul away and never would, believing that for whatever reasons anyone came, there was always a chance she might help him discern the meaning of his election. And then in union with Christ such a person would realize a life new formed and wholly satisfying.

But it seemed likely to her now that she had reached everyone in Boston whom God had marked out for salvation. Now those who came to her were so sure of their spiritual state that they could not be frightened away by her enemies. They were loyal to Anne Hutchinson as they were loyal to Christ. Each meeting was so completely a communion of love that Anne thought she could understand why John Winthrop and John Wilson liked to call her and her friends familists. When they came together they were so much like a large and loving family that she sometimes wondered if that old Family of Love founded by Hendrik Nicholas had not been falsely maligned. Men unable to understand such love as this would be bound to see it as a source of wickedness.

From her meetings she missed no one whose absence troubled her. If she now experienced defeat, it was only in the hope she once cherished of taking to all the churches in the Bay an understanding of the covenant of grace. But there is a time for everything under the sun, and the time for that gift was not yet.

There was one whose continued presence surprised her: that was John Underhill. He had been coming to the mixed meetings ever since his return from the war, and on the Lord's Day often went to Mt. Wollaston to hear John Wheelwright preach. She was tempted to break an old promise to herself and turn the man away, but if Brother John felt he was fit to worship in his congregation, she could not afford to judge him otherwise. Then, too, there was his wife, that poor little Dutch woman who could scarcely speak an intelligible word. She came more often to the meetings now, bringing with her a younger, comelier woman who seemed to be her close friend. God's design might be to draw them in.

Anne worried about neither the ones who came nor the ones who stayed away. She was exceedingly troubled about John Cotton. She could not find out whether he had actually gone over to the enemy or had been in some way misrepresented. His sermons sounded very much the same as always, save that he emphasized the need for harmony in the church more than he had ever done. John Wilson was the one whose wrath came down on erronists. And now no person was allowed to question him—a rule that failed to keep Anne and a good number of other women from walking out whenever they were displeased.

Sometimes Anne thought she would make one more visit to her teacher, and beg him to tell her the whole truth of his beliefs. More than once she had tied a hood over her head in preparation for going to him, and then something stopped her. She had wondered if it might be the little connecting house left empty by Henry Vane. Sometimes when she had to walk that way, along the road by the Trimontaine, to attend a woman in childbirth or carry food or medicine to someone in need, she could not keep back the tears for thinking of that loss.

Yet something else kept her away from her teacher. She knew that. It was the way he had spoken to her at their last private meeting, coupled with his evident desertion of those who had loved most the doctrine he had taught. If she had gone, he might have thought she came to seek forgiveness, when to her mind she was the one who had most to forgive. Could she possibly be waiting for him to come to her? She refused to admit to herself she had a thought of such a question.

But then, as days went by, this burden on her heart grew somewhat lighter. She had so little time to think of him. Edward's wife would soon come to term and had frequent need of her. Bridget had taken to bed with a stomach complaint that many suffered from that summer and fall; she was ever one to think herself sicker than she was. And strange though it might seem, as attendance at Anne's meetings diminished, and fewer came to her for spiritual counsel, there were more calls than ever upon her skills of midwifery and nursing. Never mind. Her time as ever was at the disposal of God.

Tuesday, October 17, was washday. This was no regularly appointed day at the Hutchinsons', but once a month or so, when the weather was good enough, Anne would decide that it was time to do the washing. She would have all the soiled clothes brought together the night before, the worst to be soaked in chamber lye, and next morning by the time the horn blew, the great kettles would be hung over the fire. It would be a long, hard day's work for all the women and children of the household.

About midmorning Anne went into the back garden to spread a tub of linen things to dry. The weather was so uncommonly good—for the season had been cold and wet—that she let herself stand a minute or two enjoying the perfect balance: warmth enough for comfort without heavy clothing, wind just strong enough to blow the remnants of cloud away and dry the linens soft. It seemed to her a long time since she had taken time to thank God for sun and air.

She stood staring out toward the sea—she could see the masts of the ships in the harbor, and gave a glancing thought to England, whence they came. It struck her that when she thought of England she no longer suffered any twinge of homesickness; when she watched the ships, she never had to stifle a deep desire to get aboard one and go home. Home was here. In spite of all her troubles, she had come to like Boston: her dear friends, and her house, plain and gaunt but comfortably furnished, and her garden—

"Mistress Hutchinson!" The urgent screech came from the back gate and drove out of her mind all pleasant musing. She turned and went to meet Jane Hawkins, with her basket of childbed needs on her arm.

"I'm on my way to Mary," said Jane breathlessly, "and I thought you'd want to come."

"Mary?" said Anne.

"Aye, Mary Dyer."

"But her time—" Anne broke off. "Yes, go on, Jane," she said firmly. "I'll be there as soon as I can get my things together."

Mary had gone seven months, Anne knew that. No use to demand explanations that would keep Jane standing there. The midwife hurried on along the back lane, and Anne flew into the house, thinking through a list of all that would be needed. Mary would have ready all the linens normally used in childbirth, but she would not have done the brewing and baking necessitated by the women who would come crowding in, offering to help but not really expecting to, with an appetite for groaning bread and groaning beer.

In the house Anne quickly gave instructions. The cousins would oversee the rest of the washing; they would have to send one of the little girls to watch the linen, that a bird did not light upon it and that it did not blow off in the dirt.

"What bread have we in the house?" Anne asked Frances.

"Plenty of rye, but no wheaten."

"Well, put what we have in a basket, with some cheese or cold meat if you think fit, and send Mary and William with that and a gallon of beer, whatever you can spare. I shall not wait for them."

Anne caught up a basket kept ready with her medicines and

instruments, in case a need might arise for something Goody Hawkins was not supplied with, and set off alone at a fast pace. She heard Anne Freestone calling after her, "Pray God all will be well," but she thought not much about a special need for prayer. A seven-months child was not uncommon, and Mary had seemed quite well since early summer.

As she expected, the house was filled when she got there. Children were standing around in everybody's way, till she shooed them out to play in the yard. Several of the older girls refused to go, but kept trying to crowd in close to Mary's bed, which stood, half curtained, in a corner of the tiny downstairs room.

Everyone moved back for Anne, though, both women and children, as she made her way to the bed and stood looking down at the swollen, sweating woman. Mary tried to smile and lifted a hand for Anne to take.

Jane Hawkins was standing by her. "She's been having bad pains," she said.

"How long?" asked Anne.

"A good while. She did not send for me at first, thinking her sickness was brought on by something she ate, because of course her time had not come."

"You have given her basil?"

"Aye, as soon as I came."

Anne picked up a damp rag from a stool and wiped Mary's forehead. "Where is William?" she asked.

"Outside," said Mary. "He said he would chop wood." Her last word was lost in a sudden sharp scream.

"It will soon be over, dear," said Jane.

Anne squeezed Mary's hand once more and turned to the door, where her children were coming in with the baskets from home. She put some of the big girls to work setting out victuals and drink, which in their turn gave the women something to do besides get in the way. She sent someone to take a drink to William.

There was really nothing to do now but wait with Mary, keep cool rags to bathe her face, and hold her when the worst pain came. But suddenly there came something different and strange: a shriek that scarcely seemed human, and a terrible convulsive movement that shook the very bed where the poor woman lay. Some claimed later that there was also a "noisome savor," but Anne never remembered smelling anything beyond such odors as always accompanied a birth.

The gossiping women grew abruptly quiet; some turned pale. "Something is dreadfully wrong," Anne whispered to Jane. "These women are not helping, and we do not need spectators."

"I can fix that," the midwife mumbled, and to all appearances went to get herself a cup of beer.

It was not very long afterward that two of the women rushed to the door and could be heard retching. Then others ran out, crying that some pestilence must have come upon them. Two of the children defecated where they stood in the middle of the floor and then began to vomit into the liquid stinking mess. All, whether presently ill or not, began to talk loudly about going home.

"It would be best you do," Anne said to them, "for although I am sure Mistress Dyer is glad of your presence, you certainly are not able to help her now. And it may be if you leave at once you will not be stricken."

Everyone agreed and went home, except for one old grandam who had drunk no beer since it was first brought in because she was fast asleep. She had failed to wake through all the excitement and showed no sign of waking now.

"Well, let her stay," said Anne. "What was it you gave them?"

"Groundsel and gentian," said Jane, "but not too much."

"I should not have done it," said Anne, "but perhaps in this case—" She hurriedly cleaned up the mess in the floor and then went to join Jane at Mary's bedside.

"I want to see about something," Jane said, and pulled back the sheets to examine Mary's poor distended abdomen; then with skillful hands she felt inside the womb. "Just as I thought," she said. "It's coming hiplings."

Then Anne with an effort almost beyond her strength held Mary in her arms while the midwife turned the child. Yet things went no better.

"I've got powdered ants' eggs in my basket," Jane said. "We could surely find a virgin half Mary's age, and get a lock of hair."

Anne shook her head. "That old charm," she said. "I really cannot let you use a charm. You must see if she can swallow basil water one more time."

"If you say so, mistress, but it has worked for me," said Jane.

"I do say so," said Anne, and Jane argued no more. She brought basil water, then bent again to feel Mary's belly. She rose and looked at Anne, then slightly shook her head. Anne felt with her own hands, then turned to Jane with a look of confirmation. She would be very much surprised if there were life left in that little body inside the suffering body of her friend.

The two walked a little distance away from the bed, although it seemed doubtful that Mary would notice anything they said.

"What now?" said Jane. "In bringing away dead children, I've had some luck with dittany."

"I have some," said Anne.

"We'll use it," said Jane, and Anne took a twist of paper from her basket.

"If you will prepare it," said Anne, "I think I had better go and fetch William."

She brought him in, a pale and frightened young man who could not stay seated but walked about the room, sometimes coming to stand by Mary briefly and lay his hand on her head, then walking to every corner of the room and back again.

Anne went and held his hands. "Pray," she said, and they stood a little while together.

Not long after came one last terrible scream.

"She has fainted," said Jane, and brought out the child that Mary and William had so long desired and prayed for.

The women looked and stood as though turned to stone by the sight. William cried out hoarsely, "For the love of God," and staggered away, and out through the back door.

The ancient grandam sat up and opened her eyes. "What is it?" she said sleepily.

No one could say what it was. It seemed, as Jane Hawkins stood with the red slimy mass in her hands, to have no head, yet somehow a face, a face with horns. (Nightmarishly, Anne seemed to see herself seeking some place to set a fine linen cap, with white rosebuds.) As for the body, no one could well say whether it most resembled a child or some prickly creature from the sea.

It was, as they had thought, dead. They could thank God for that, that and the fact that Mary was alive.

Only seconds did they stand helpless. Almost at once Jane wrapped the creature in a swaddling cloth and laid it on a bench in a dark corner, then turned to the care of the still unconscious Mary. Anne had already decided what she must do.

"Can you manage?" she asked Jane.

Jane nodded.

"Then tell William I have gone to Master Cotton," she said. "This birth must not be known, and I can think of no other way to get help."

She went to the old grandam, who seemed about to go back to sleep. "Come with me," she said. "It's all over now, and time to go home."

The old crone followed like an obedient child or dog.

Outdoors, the sun was low and the little crooked lane lay in shadow. Anne turned to her. "Where do you live?" she asked.

"Close by," the woman said.

"I'll walk with you," said Anne.

Anxious though she was to reach John Cotton, she must try to make sure the old woman did not go back to get another look at the baby before Jane had hidden it well from sight. She did not think the woman could have had a very clear view of it.

"Was it deformed?" the dreaded question came.

"Aye," said Anne dismissingly, "but it was dead. We need say nothing of it."

"Less said the better," the old woman agreed.

Anne had no idea whether she could trust her not to talk, but dared not insist too much. After all, the old thing had been half asleep. Dim as the light in the house had grown, she could not have seen much, and she might begin to think she had dreamed what she saw.

Anne left her inside her front door and hurried westward then, toward the three-humped hill reared up against the yellow sky.

## 2

John Cotton did not share the triumphant exhilaration of Winthrop and the other ministers, but he believed the synod had done the best and indeed only possible thing in defining heresy and bringing the churches together. He himself could conceive of no other way to have uncovered the extent of error among those aligned with Anne Hutchinson. Yet it troubled him that this woman who had so warmly embraced his doctrines and seemed to serve the church and God so well should be snared in the synodical net with never an opportunity to speak in her own defense. Some said that when she went on holding meetings in defiance of the synod's resolution, she was admitting and even flaunting her guilt. But Cotton was not yet ready to give up on Sister Hutchinson.

When Sarah came to his study on that evening in October and told him Mistress Hutchinson was downstairs, he thanked God and prayed a hasty prayer for guidance in dealing with his old pupil. Surely it was a hopeful sign that she had come to him voluntarily.

Sarah was in no prayerful disposition. "The nerve of the hussy, coming here now," she said. "I started to tell her to go away at once, but then I thought you might have something to say to her."

"I do," said Cotton. "Send her up."

At the door Sarah turned back and added, "She looks strange. I think there's something wrong with her."

Cotton's first thought when he saw her was, Can she have committed some crime?

Her face was flushed, her eyes glittered, and when she threw off her hooded cloak he could see that her hair was in disarray and her dress sweat-soaked. Some dark stains on her sleeves and bodice looked like blood.

He prepared himself for something other than the peaceful, fruitful conference he had prayed for.

"Sit down, sister," he said.

She sat on the edge of a chair facing him across his big pine table. "I need help," she said.

"Are you in trouble?"

She shook her head as if uncertain. "There is trouble," she said. "Bad trouble."

He said nothing but turned on her a placid, expectant gaze.

"I have come from a childbed," she said. "From Mary Dyer."

She paused. She had thought all the way here about the best way to tell her story and present her case and had decided the only thing to do was tell the worst at the beginning. But now, when she tried to say what it was, the sight came so clearly back to her that she was (as at her first look) too stunned to speak.

"Is Sister Dyer well?" Cotton prodded her.

"Aye," said Anne. "Or so I think. The child is dead."

"It was a hard birth?"

"Oh—hard." Anne struggled with herself; she must do what she came for. "It was a monster birth," she said.

"Bad?"

"Oh, sir, so very bad. I pray that Mary need not ever know how bad it really is."

"You desire that I should go to the young parents?"

"More than that—" She saw then that she could and must describe the monster child. She did it calmly, almost coldly, by making herself think of it as a figure in a nightmare. Then she ended as calmly: "I know that by law the birth must be chronicled. But, sir, it scarcely seems a human child. I dare not do this alone, but if you help we could conceal this birth. If the body could be buried tonight, people need know nothing except that the child was born dead."

"But surely there were women present. Did no one see?"

"They had gone, all but one. Some fell ill." She paused, remembering Goody Hawkins and the beer. No need to speak of that. "There was one ancient dame, asleep most of the time. She saw very little, and I think she will not talk of what she saw. Goodwife Hawkins knows, of course. She is there now. But certainly she will never tell. She loves Mary Dyer so, she would do anything to protect her."

Cotton did not like this. Such a creature would not be born without some reason. "I know not but that we might sin if we should go against some design of God by keeping this thing dark," he said, then thoughtfully added, "And yet, 'tis passing strange that nearly everyone had gone. It may be God meant it as instruction for only those few who remained."

"Oh, I do think it," said Anne. "What it can mean I know not as yet, but I pray that I will come to understand."

Cotton sat staring out at the pearly sky for a few minutes longer. "Do you know that Mistress Cotton goes once more with child?" he surprisingly asked.

"Yes, I had heard," murmured Anne.

"I think of her—what such a thing would do to her, especially if it became the subject of extravagant talk and speculation."

"As of course it would."

"I fear so." He looked out the window again, then abruptly arose from his chair. "I will go with you and talk to Brother Dyer. If he wishes, I think he should go on and bury the child."

Downstairs he said a few words to Sarah, who did not speak to Anne; then the minister and his pupil walked out together.

The minister set a pace somewhat slow. He had in mind to speak to Mistress Hutchinson about those doings of hers that had been bothering him. "You are tired, I think," he said to her.

She sighed. "It has been a hard day," she said, "to have begun with such promise."

"Sometimes we do not read the signs aright," he said, "and may mistake a warning for a promise."

"It may be so," she said, "and yet the time has been when I have known so surely."

In her voice there was a sadness, a regret, that made him wonder. "What is it you have known thus, sister?" he asked.

"I knew who spoke the truth that nourished my soul," she said. "I knew I should perish without it."

They walked on down the darkening lane. He did not answer.

"So certainly did I know these things," she finally went on, "that I caused my whole family to uproot themselves and come with me to New England."

"And now you doubt the wisdom of that move?"

"No," said Anne slowly, studying what was implied in his question, knowing she would do it all again. "No," she said again more firmly, as in her heart an old passion renewed. "No!" she cried. "I dare not doubt—you *cannot* have changed."

The minister's steps slowed almost to a stop. He peered into Anne's face; the light had dimmed too much to read it by. "I—changed?" he said, truly puzzled.

"At the synod," she said. "I heard reports of statements I could scarce believe you made."

He shook his head, moved on a little faster. "There was so little difference," he finally said. "Such a very narrow scantling."

"But did you change?" she insisted. Disrespectful to a minister this might be, but still she had to know.

"In what way, sister?" he quietly asked.

"In such a way as to suggest that by taking thought a man can bring unto himself the grace of God."

"No," he said, "I never suggested that."

"But did you say that man's consent by faith is necessary before God's act of justification upon the soul?"

"They would have it expressed so," Cotton said.

"But you would not?"

"I agreed, for the sake of peace," said Cotton, "yet they knew the distinction I have always made. It is true that faith is present before complete union, but it is as a vessel waiting to be filled with oil, it can take no action that will cause the pouring in. This is union, this is justification. Afterwards, faith may be more active in receiving help to grow in grace, as a child receives milk out of his mother's breast by sucking."

"And this you still believe?"

"And this I still believe, and think the manner of expression cannot alter the meaning of it. We be not active in laying hold on Christ before He hath given us His spirit."

"Then I thank God I have been misinformed," said Anne.

Cotton in his earnest attempt to explain his part in the synod had completely forgotten the questions he had meant to ask. They approached the Dyer cottage now, and he had some need of further elucidation of the situation there. Only the next day, at home in his study, did he remember he had intended finding out about Mistress Hutchinson's meetings.

3

For many days after Mary Dyer's child was born, Anne felt weak and strange, almost as though she herself had given birth. Or more, perhaps, as though she had long lain ill and knew herself about to die. In fact, she knew she was not ill, or no more than was common for a woman of her age who had borne fifteen children. That night when she came in from the Dyers', after going with William to bury the child at the edge of the burying ground, she had fainted. She had soon revived, to the scent of lavender water that little Anne brought to bathe her face.

It was nothing, she told everyone, except that she had been so busy with the hard, sad work of the day that she had forgotten to eat. (They had all heard already that Mary's baby was born dead.) Cousin Frances brought her bean porridge with good bits of meat, and she ate it dutifully but without appetite. Then she sent the children back to bed and let the cousins help her cleanse herself and put on her nightdress. To them she explained that she had been flooding much of the day—the blood on her clothes came from that as well as the birthing—and they brought her strips of linen cloth to use through the night. By then she felt able and made herself an infusion of goldenrod, which ought to slow the blood.

It was a relief to tell William (in the privacy of their bed, with no one nearby but baby Zuriel) the whole story of that day. He comforted her and told her she had done the best for everyone concerned. Even so, she did not sleep well, but awoke from time to time feeling unsettled by dark, confused dreams, none of which she could clearly remember.

The next day she kept mostly to her chair by the fire, wrapped in her length of blue wool. (She would never use it any more without heart-wrenching memories of Henry Vane, and yet for memory's sake would cling to it forever.) Sometimes she stared into the flames, as though hoping they would sear from her eyes the image of that frightful creature she had helped to bring into the light. And "Oh, dear God," she prayed, "what, oh what, can the meaning in this be?"

On the day after that, she went to see Mary Dyer. She was still slow and weak but had ceased to lose so much blood. William insisted that she take a child or two with her, in case she had need of help along the way. She let Katherine and little William go, and left them playing in the lane when she went in to Mary.

Goody Hawkins was there, she had never gone home. Mary seemed asleep.

"Does she know?" Anne whispered.

"Not all," said Jane. She said Mary was recovering, or would be if her mind were set at ease. "Otherwise, I know not if she ever can be well."

Jane had a pot of clothes boiling over the fire. She said she would go on and finish the washing if Anne would sit with Mary for a while. She took the clothes up in a large tub and Anne helped her carry them outside, where she would rinse them and spread them to dry.

Then Anne went in to Mary, and as soon as she sat down—on a stool pulled up next to the bed—Mary opened her eyes.

"I'm glad to see you, Anne," she said, smiling. Her smile did not light up her face.

"I thought you were asleep."

"No. I heard what Jane said."

"Well, is it true? Are you grieving too much to get better?"

"Is it grief?" Mary's eyes sought Anne's, begging an answer to something more than this question.

"Is it not?"

"I would grieve if a baby had died. But what was this?"

"A poor misshapen creature. God was good and never gave it life."

"Anne, I have to know what it was like. Jane and William won't tell me. Why can't they see it's like to drive me mad with wondering?"

"But if you know?"

"It cannot be worse."

Then Anne told her, not everything, but at least as much as appeared to her when Jane first held the creature in her hands.

Mary did not weep or moan but lay silent a long time. At last she said, "What did God mean?"

"Aye, what?" said Anne. "This question haunts me too."

"Master Cotton came and talked to us—William and me. He said 'twas meant for our instruction, but he could not say what we must learn."

"Nor do I know," said Anne. "I feel it might be meant for me as well, yet I cannot interpret the sign."

"It is not for you, only for me," said Mary. "And I lied, for I know what it is. It is punishment for me because I would not wait for God's time."

"What do you mean?"

"I took the mandrake root Jane Hawkins gave me, to make me conceive," she said. "And other things," she added vaguely.

"What other things?"

"I know not, she would not say. And then more: after I had

conceived, and when I felt tired or distrait, I took more. There too I fear I went against God's will, for a woman with child must feel ill sometimes."

Anne pondered, frowning. This was not against her belief. God does not punish his sealed children everlastingly but may sometimes chastise them for their own good here on earth. Yet what a terrible chastisement. Still, as she pondered, it came to her that this loss might in time seem easier than to have, still-born, a perfectly formed child such as all of hers had been. She mentioned this to Mary, and she told of the death of her first little William, whom she had kept just long enough to feel she knew what God would make of him. "There are worse things," she said. "If a punishment it be, then we must somehow learn to thank God for it."

"Pray with me," Mary said, and they sat silent, hand in hand, a long time.

When Anne finally went home, both she and Mary felt better and believed that they could with loving thankfulness accept the will of God. The mood did not last—not with Anne, and she feared not with Mary. She herself could not get over a sense of dread foreboding, but she no longer experienced such anguish of mind as she had known at first.

Jane Hawkins brought news that Mary was much better. She had come to bring a strengthening medicine for Anne, but Anne felt somewhat reluctant to take it and questioned her about what it was. Anne was not surprised to hear it contained powdered frog livers and salts made from a dead man's skull, for she knew of the use of both. She never used such ingredients, always herself preferring herbs in every sort of illness because they seemed to her to come directly from God's hand.

"Are you sure about the effect of these?" she asked Jane.

"Yes, mistress, very sure," Jane said eagerly, holding out the small vial in her hand.

"I am better, though, and will not try it," Anne said. "I but wish to be completely clear—are you always sure of medicine you give?"

Jane looked hurt. "Oh yes," she said. "I learned these from a woman of St. Ives, who learned them from a man who learned from Paracelsus."

Anne sighed. She had meant to question Jane closely about what she had given Mary, but suddenly saw there was no use. Jane would not give any medicine that could do harm if she knew it, and surely nothing anyone might swallow could produce such a monster as Mary Dyer bore. No, it was God's will, and no doing of poor Jane.

Anne thanked Jane for her kindness and sent her to Mary with a basket of cakes that Frances had that hour taken from the oven. "And take some for yourself and Goodman Hawkins," she urged her.

"I had better make another batch," said Frances, resignedly. It was not the first time Cousin Anne had given away food she had labored over.

It was true what Anne told Jane, she felt better. But still the strangeness continued; she kept thinking that her state was like that of one about to leave this world. Everything about the house appeared to her with such clarity, such intensity and sharpness of detail, that it seemed she was seeing things she never saw before: the breastplates that William and Richard wore on training days, though tarnished, reflected the fire and a copper pot hanging on a trammel over it, in a way she had never noticed. She saw how smoky the joists overhead were getting, and how heavily the cobwebs hung. It must have been a long time since she had really looked at her house, so busy she had been with things of God.

She longed to keep close to her children. She sent for Faith and Bridget to come, and they talked a long while together. Faith told her something she and Thomas had been thinking of: that these meetings and this effort for the Lord might be too much for Anne, at her age.

"Do you not think my work needs to be done—and who would do it, would you?" Anne said somewhat sharply.

Faith hesitantly said that perhaps since the synod, it need not be done.

"Oh no, even more!" Bridget cried.

Anne thought she saw her daughters going different ways. Since her marriage, though visibly faithful, Faith had ever spoken less frequently of her experience of Christ. Yet they were both good girls, and in Anne's judgment sealed with the spirit.

Nothing about her children disturbed her very much. She loved them, it might be, as God loved His elect.

On another day, when a thick, swirling snowstorm was hurled upon them in a driving northeast wind, all who dwelled in the Hutchinson house kept at home. William closed the shop and came to sit by the fire while he worked at his accounts, for he said no customers would come on such a day. The children, though they would run excitedly to the window sometimes to see how high the snow was drifting, were kept pretty much to their tasks. The littlest ones sat just inside the great chimney, with their pumpkin shell full of toys.

Richard decided this was the day to polish his armor, and Sammy was allowed to help. They would do William's, too. Francis, who had never found much time to study with his uncle Wheelwright since the move to Wollaston, elected to spend the day with his books, and to please his mother recited some verses from the *Aeneid*.

"What good will that do him?" said Sammy, who kept away from books all he could.

Then Francis got up and went to lecture him, standing over him where he sat on the floor with a helmet between his knees and a rag in his hand. William could not help smiling. Francis looked so much like his mother when she spoke to her meeting about some matter that deeply concerned her—or, as to that, like himself at the mixed meetings—or like his grandfather Marbury. He had not the Hutchinsons' rather phlegmatic way of responding to life and religion.

Francis had to be prepared, he explained to his brother, to study at the new college when it opened. Uncle Wheelwright believed that at the rate he was now going he could finish in two years. He might even be an ordained minister at twenty, if he worked hard.

"They've been talking about that college a long time," said Richard.

"Aye, but it's almost a reality now," Francis cried. "And do you know what I heard, they are going to change the name of Newtown to Cambridge, and so I may go to Cambridge after all."

"Would it might be so," said Anne softly.

"I have it on very good authority," Francis said, "that the

court convening tomorrow will vote on it. Why the college may be open by next spring."

"Pray God it will," said Anne, "but I could wish you had not spoken of this court."

"Then I am sorry, Mother," Francis said, "but 'tis not impossible they might do some good."

"So they may," said Anne. She would have preferred not to think about the General Court. For some reason, Winthrop had decided the colony should have the opportunity to choose new deputies, and without precedent had called a special election. The reason, whatever it was, had something to do with the outcome of the synod—perhaps with the final decision about Brother Wheelwright. The new court had few friends of Anne and Wheelwright on it, that was sure—perhaps only Coddington, Cogshall, and Aspinwall.

But she brushed thoughts of the court away. It was no business of hers, and she knew John Wheelwright was preparing to leave the colony anyway. He wanted justice, but he was sick of Boston.

She preferred not to think at all, but to sit wrapped in her blue wool and listen to the chatter of the children and the crackle and roar of the fire. If she were somehow nearing the end of her life, she mused, she would have very little to regret. For the love of God, she had rejoiced in spreading understanding of His way; and through earthly love, too, much happiness had come to her. Though she had lost dear ones through death and separation, she knew she would meet them all again someday. The family left to her now all lived close around her—every one would be able to stand by her deathbed. She would like to see Katherine's child, her first grandchild, into the world (oh, Lord, please let it be all right), and then she would willingly take leave of friends and family for a while. She would be sorry to think she was leaving any of God's work unfinished, but she knew He would not call her until He was satisfied with what she had done.

For the next few days, in a world muffled in sweet silence by the snow, she still lived in a state of detached contentment. Katherine gave birth to a baby daughter that they christened Elishua; it was an easy, natural birth, of a beautiful, well-formed child. "My cup runneth over," Anne said.

And perhaps it was part of the strangeness that she should say such a thing, for of course she knew better. On November 2, the day after the snowstorm, the court had already begun to act, and there was no way she could keep from hearing full reports of all the actions they were taking.

# XXIII

Winthrop had moved the court back to Newtown. Boston did not sympathize with him; Newtown did not sympathize with erronists. In time, he would again make Boston his capital, but this temporary displacement was preferable by far to the permanent uprooting of the institutions that formed the foundation of the colony.

On the first day of court, his side exulted over what they read as signs that God was with them. Two of Boston's deputies (strong supporters of Mistress Hutchinson's) were immediately discredited. As the roll was called, Dudley rose to question whether Master Aspinwall was fit to be received as a member of the court, having signed the petition in favor of John Wheelwright. Asked whether he was still of a mind to join in such sedition, Aspinwall assured them that he had not changed; and consequently, he was dismissed with no further discussion.

Cogshall jumped up then, out of order, and boldly spoke to this effect: that seeing they had put out Master Aspinwall for that matter, they were best to make one work of it. His hand was not to the petition, he said, but he approved of it and had signed the protestation.

The court was entirely pleased to oblige Master Cogshall. Coddington, who kept his head, was instructed to ask Boston to elect two more deputies.

Then Coddington moved, in accordance with the wishes of Boston freemen, that the censure of Master Wheelwright be reversed, and the alien law be repealed. The results of this motion were that Wheelwright was sent for to be questioned again, and Winthrop promised to bring forth on the morrow the whole proceedings about the law.

Thus the first day ended, and when the news was received in Boston, Anne merely said, "They can pass laws against us and refuse our deputies, but what can courts of men do against the truth of God?" She asked the question without any expectation of an answer. News of the court then was like an annoying cluster of gnats; she brushed it aside.

On the second day, Winthrop read in full the lengthy correspondence with Henry Vane about the alien law, in which he himself was easily able to have the last word. Most, perforce, declared themselves satisfied.

On the third day, which was Monday, November 6, John Wheelwright came to the court; and in the Hutchinson house that night, sitting at the table where the cousins served the unexpected guest a late supper, the family heard the news from him.

"There's no room to be had in Newtown," he said. "And I thought, besides, it would be well if you knew what happened in court today. You have not heard?"

"Not yet," said William, "though we expect Will Coddington to let us know."

"He found a place to stay," Wheelwright said, "and did invite me to share his bed. But I told him I believed I should come to you, and he thought it well."

"We knew you had been called," Anne said.

"Winthrop offered me a chance to recant," Wheelwright said. "I told him I never preached anything but the truth of Christ, and so had nothing to recant. They told me that before I came, there was no dissension in the churches or the state."

"What a lie!" interposed Francis.

"Everything is turned upside down because of me," Wheelwright went on. "Members of congregations are set against each other, and even husbands and wives divided. It was my fault Boston would not go to war against the Pequods. And, maybe the worst of all, the blame was mine when the governor had no halberdiers to attend him. My sedition had affected the granting of town lots, the setting of tax rates, and the peace of neighborhood meetings. Like Cain, and like Hagar and Ishmael, I am a troublemaker and must be expelled."

In the midst of that speech there came a heavy knocking at the door. All looked at each other in astonishment at such a pounding on the door at such a time of night, and as they still sat dumbfounded (trying to listen to John Wheelwright, who seemed deliberately to keep talking against the sound), it began again and did not stop until William went and pulled open the heavy shutter.

A tall heavy man in breastplate and helmet, bearing a carbine in a military manner, stepped into the room. They knew him: James Penn, the beadle of the town.

"Mistress Hutchinson!" he bellowed.

"You may tell me what you want," said William quietly.

Anne, at the sound of her name, seemed to feel a weight descend upon her, as though it would press out both sight and hearing. She could still see her family and the fire-lit walls around her, and the beadle just inside the open door; yet as to understanding what any of it meant, she might—for the moment—have been deaf and blind. The man spoke more words, which she did not comprehend, as he came across the room toward where she sat. Instinctively, she rose and went to meet him.

He extended a paper that he had in his hand, and she took it in hers. He said something about it, she did not know what. William came and took her arm.

"I must have your answer, mistress," the beadle said. "Do you hear, I must take your answer to the court that you will come, or else I must take you to jail."

"Jail." That word rang like a bell in her head, an alarum bell that cleared her mind, restored her sight and hearing.

"It is a summons you have?" she asked then.

"Aye," he said with apparent relief. "Will ye come? Will ye be at the court in the morning?"

"Of course I will come," Anne said coolly. "I am subject to the authority of the court."

"She will come," said William, escorting Penn to the door.

"I am sorry," Wheelwright said, as William and Anne resumed their seats at the table. "I should have already told you this might happen."

"You knew?" Anne asked.

"I guessed," he said. "I saw what they were about—to rid themselves of any they call troublemakers."

"Which means," said Francis, "any who get in the way of their own designs."

"Are you banished, then?" asked Anne.

"Not yet. They put off sentencing until tomorrow, but I expect it."

"You have long expected it," Anne said.

"Oh yes. I shall fight them to the end—but I am ready to go. I have already made inquiries about New Hampshire. Samuel plans to take his family too."

"It must be bitter cold there," William said.

"Aye, but free," said Wheelwright. "Why do you not get your affairs in order and come with me?"

Anne shook her head. "No, we must stay in Boston."

"They might banish you, Mother," Francis said.

Anne knew it had been in all their thoughts. It had crossed her mind, but she did not believe Winthrop could find grounds for banishment in her case.

"They might try," she said. "But unlike your uncle I have preached no public sermon that could lead to anything they might call sedition."

"If you have ever laid the ministers and magistrates under a covenant of works," said Wheelwright, "they are capable of calling that sedition."

"I never have," said Anne. "Not absolutely, or in any public way. I see not any matter they can prove against me."

Wheelwright shook his head. "You may be right," he said. "And in any case I doubt your banishment is what they have in mind. If it were William instead of you, it might be—but a woman— No, I expect they will seek some other way to silence you."

Anne rose. "It is time we had prayers," she said, "and then bed."

But she had no expectation of sleep. After the rest had gone to their beds, she sat with William and John at the table, going over all John thought the court might find to use against her. Then when the men went to bed, she still stayed at the table making notes.

2

What sleep Anne got refreshed her. She awoke early and perfectly clear in her mind about what the day would bring forth. She arose in the dark and went out to squat behind a bayberry bush, thus saving one of the girls from the hated task of cleaning the chamber pot. Snow still covered the ground, but now no clouds threatened. The sky was sprinkled with sharply glittering stars, while out over the sea, gray dawn was rising. She stood cold and conscious of the sky, where God seemed in some sense to show Himself. Her soul's eye saw Him and her soul's ear heard Him. He loved her and filled her with the certainty that all things would be well.

Remember, He said, the fear of man is a snare.

As she went back into the house, she felt uplifted and exhilarated. Bodily weakness was gone. Her spirit was quick with renewed life. Her mind held the promise of sharp wit and clear expression. She was eager to depart for Newtown, and said so to John Wheelwright, who was coming down the stairs.

"No hurry," he said. "They set no time for you to come, and as for me, they may not be best pleased if I miss their appointed time, but they cannot do much more than they've already made up their minds to."

There was not much delay though. The cousins were already busy in the kitchen, and the children were up. They had prayers and breakfast, and then Anne took leave of the children. She had not talked to them much about the possibilities of the day; but they understood, those who were old enough, and were brave. Only Susannah cried, but that was because she still wanted to go everywhere her mother went.

Bundled thickly against the cold, Anne, William, and John made their way to the Charlestown ferry, where Thomas Marshall, the ferryman, spat out Winthrop's name like a curse. "I heard he sent for you, mistress," he said.

"Pray," said Anne.

The forest path to Newtown, dark and cold in the shadow of great, rimy trees, seemed long today. There was still unpacked snow to plough through, which wet the bottoms of their cloaks and Anne's heavy skirt. They grew cold to the bone before they reached Newtown; nor was there any heat in the meetinghouse there.

Winthrop was impatient and angry at Wheelwright's tardiness. The court had quickly dealt with Boston's new deputies: they accepted Colburn but rejected young Sergeant Oliver, who had signed the petition and did not repent of it. That done, they were ready for Wheelwright, who ought to have been there long before. Winthrop paced the floor. When the door opened and the three latecomers entered, he called up the minister at once. Meanwhile Anne and William found places in the crowded hall. A man from Boston got up and gave Anne his seat; William stood near her, leaning against the wall.

Wheelwright went to stand in the proper place for one called before the court—he knew it well already, the space in front of a long table, where the governor and assistants were seated. Behind them, to one side, were ranged the thirty-two deputies of the towns, seated on the backless benches with which the hall was furnished. Their faces were cold and gray, like the rime on the trees in the forest.

Anne examined the scene carefully. Not much longer, and she would stand where Wheelwright stood.

They disposed of him rather quickly. He was asked to show reason why sentence should not be passed against him. He said he had not been proved guilty of sedition or contempt. He said though he was charged with setting forth ministers and magistrates as enemies of Christ, yet he had named no names. The court had ample precedent to show names need not be named, from Scripture and from recent history. The court had answers for everything and soon passed the sentence they had evidently already resolved upon: that he be disfranchised and banished, and kept in safe custody, unless he would give security to depart by the end of March.

Wheelwright said he would appeal to the King's Majesty, whereupon they assured him that by the terms of the charter no appeal could be made. "If an appeal should lie in one case," said the governor, "it might be challenged in all, and then there would be no use of government among us."

Accepting this pronouncement with a shrug of his broad shoulders, Wheelwright answered the next question by assuring the court that he had no intention of providing security for his quiet departure.

So they sent him off to jail to think about these things a little longer and proceeded to deal with John Cogshall. Anne caught her breath in surprise as he was called. Could they mean to banish every man who called himself her friend? She thought of Mary and the children at home in Boston. They would have no idea of this.

Cogshall evidently was dumbfounded at the charges against him: of disturbing the peace, of threatening the court. He had meant no threat, he protested. When a motion was made to banish him, he said he had never heard of an example in Scripture where a man was banished for his judgment. "If you had kept your judgment to yourself," snapped Winthrop, "we should have left you to yourself. We do not challenge power over men's consciences, but when seditious speeches and practices discover such a corrupt conscience, it is our duty to use authority to reform both."

In the end they did not banish him but disfranchised him, with an admonition to be careful about disturbing the peace in the future. Anne sighed, and thanked God.

Then Aspinwall. He said his heart was to the petition as well as his hand. He said it was not unlawful to petition; but Winthrop said this was no petition but a seditious libel—"the misnaming of a thing doth not alter the nature of it." When sentence was about to be passed, Aspinwall demanded that the court show a rule in Scripture for banishment, and Winthrop again cited Hagar and Ishmael.

Anne wanted to weep but controlled herself. The court was furious with William Aspinwall, because he had not adopted Cogshall's conciliatory manner. She could see what was about to happen to him: banishment at the very least. They banished and disfranchised him. They said he could stay in the colony until March if he tendered security. Aspinwall agreed to that.

It was well past noon, and Winthrop at last recessed the court. William Coddington came at once to Anne, to take her and William to his room at the tavern. Anne was grateful for the warmth there, and the food and wine that Coddington brought her. In the press of human bodies in the meetinghouse, she had lost the bitterest chill, but now felt really warm for the first time since she left her house in Boston. Aspinwall and Cogshall, with several other friends, came to the room after they had dined, and their presence comforted her. No one found very much to say though. They all seemed stunned.

At the meetinghouse she and William found a place to sit together on a back bench. "Keep calm and respectful," he whispered to her, "but fear not to tell the truth."

That was just before John Winthrop called her name, in a voice that rang with triumph through the hall.

3

She stood now before a court in which judge, jury, and prosecutor were all the same. There was such a court in England—the Star Chamber. Men had crossed a wide ocean to free themselves from such justice as it meted out—some of the same men she faced here in this cold house, in this wilderness they had chosen for their refuge. And where was her refuge?

She knew the answer to that question. She lifted her head, looked Winthrop in the eye, and waited. She heard God say He would not fail her now.

Winthrop spoke. "Mistress Hutchinson, you are called here as one of those that have troubled the peace of the commonwealth and the churches here; you are known to be a woman that hath had a great share in the promoting and divulging of those opinions that are causes of this trouble, and to be nearly joined not only in affinity and affection with some of those the court has taken notice of and passed censure upon, but you have spoken divers things as we have been informed very prejudicial to the honor of the churches and ministers thereof, and you have maintained a meeting and an assembly as a thing not tolerable nor comely in the sight of God nor fitting for your sex, and notwithstanding that was cried down you have continued the same. Therefore we have thought good to send for you to understand how things are, that if you be in an erroneous way we may reduce you that so you may become a profitable member here among us. Otherwise if you be obstinate in your course that then the court may take such course that you may trouble us no further. Therefore I would entreat you to express whether you do not hold and assent in practice to those opinions and factions that have been handled in court already, that is to say, whether you do not justify Master Wheelwright's sermon and the petition."

She had listened raptly, she had heard all he said. There was no clear charge there. She answered: "I am called here to answer before you but I hear no things laid to my charge."

"I have told you some already and more I can tell you."

"Name one, sir."

"Have I not named some already?"

"What have I said or done?"

"Why for your doings, this: you did harbor and countenance those that are parties in this faction that you have heard of."

"That's matter of conscience, sir."

For the first time, the governor lost a little of his lofty magisterial air. He snapped at her. "Your conscience you must keep or it must be kept for you. And if in this cause you shall countenance and encourage those that thus transgress the law, you must be called in question for it, and that is not conscience, but your practice."

He meant her friends, she supposed. He meant Cogshall and Aspinwall and Wheelwright. "What law have they transgressed? The law of God?"

"Yes, the Fifth Commandment, which commands us to honor father and mother, which includes all in authority. Their seditious practices have cast reproach and dishonor upon the fathers of the commonwealth."

He seemed to be trying to use the petition, for which Aspinwall and Cogshall had been punished, to create some sort of charge against her. "Suppose I had set my hand to the petition—what then?" she asked.

"You saw that case tried before," he answered.

"But I had not my hand to the petition."

"You have counseled them."

"Wherein?"

"Why in entertaining them." He seemed to have brought them full circle, and to what end she could not tell.

"What breach of law is that, sir?"

"Why," he said in some exasperation, "in dishonoring of parents."

"But put the case, sir, that I do fear the Lord and my parents, may not I entertain them that fear the Lord because my parents will not give me leave?"

"If they be the fathers of the commonwealth, and they of another religion, if you entertain them then you dishonor your parents and are justly punishable."

"I may put honor upon them as the children of God and as they do honor the Lord."

Winthrop cleared his throat. "We do not," he said, "mean to discourse with those of your sex but only this: you do adhere to them and do endeavor to set forward this faction and so you do dishonor us."

"I do not acknowledge," she said, valiantly keeping resentment out of her voice, "that I ever put any dishonor upon you."

But the governor had ended that subject. "Why do you keep such a meeting at your house as you do every week upon a set day?"

This she could certainly answer, plainly and with no chance of offending the governor. "I will show you how I took it up. There were such meetings in use before I came, and because I went to none of them, this was the special reason of my taking up this course. We began it with five or six, and though it grew to more in future time, yet being tolerated at the first, I knew not why it might not continue."

"There were private meetings indeed, and are still in many places, of some few neighbors. But yours are of another nature. If they had been such as yours, they had been evil, and therefore no good warrant to justify yours. But answer by what rule you uphold them."

"By Titus Two, where the elder women are to teach the younger."

"So we allow you to do as the Apostle there means, privately and upon occasion. But you take upon you to teach many that are elder than yourself; neither do you teach what the Apostle commands—to keep at home."

He wanted women kept in their place, of course, as he saw their place. She had long known that was one reason for his enmity. "Will you please to give me a rule against it, and I will yield?"

"You have a plain rule against it: First Timothy, 'I permit not a woman to teach.'"

"But that concerns authority over men."

"If a man in distress of conscience should come and ask your counsel in private might you not teach him?"

"Yes."

"Then it is clear that it is not meant of teaching men, but of teaching in public."

What logic! But she decided not to call him to account. "I teach not in a public congregation. We do no more but read the notes of our teacher's sermons, and then reason of them by searching the Scriptures."

"You are gone from the nature of your meeting, to the kind of exercise. But you do not confine yourself to searching for points of confirmation. You declare his meaning and correct wherein you think he hath failed, and so abase the honor of the public ministry and advance your own gifts, as if he could not deliver his matter so clearly to the hearers as yourself."

That was unfair, to accuse her of putting herself above her teacher. And how could she defend herself against accusations that she was proud? For the first time, she came near losing her temper. "Prove that," she said, "that anybody doth that!" In her attempt to control her passion, she had used up too much of her strength. She felt weakness pour through her—she reached for the back of a chair for support.

"Sit down then," Winthrop said shortly. "I would not have you faint before we have finished."

William Coddington stepped forward and pulled out an empty chair from the table. She met his eyes, which seemed to tell her she was comporting herself well. When she sat down, she felt strengthened and encouraged.

Winthrop's next question concerned the authority by which she taught, and she gave him the case of Aquila and Priscilla, who taught Apollo.

But he did not care for that, and said sarcastically, "See how your argument stands: Priscilla, with her husband, took Apollo home to instruct him privately; therefore Mistress Hutchinson without her husband may teach sixty or eighty."

"I call them not, but if they come to me, I may instruct them."

"Yet you show us not a rule."

"I have given you two places of Scripture."

"But neither of them will suit your practice."

She felt her face flame at that; she lost patience. "Must I show my name written therein?"

With a show of magnanimity, the governor refrained from answering this, but began to deliver her a gentle lecture on the troubles that she caused, seducing many honest persons with her strange opinions, and besides causing women to neglect their families.

"Sir," she said, "I do not believe this to be so."

But still he ignored her. "Well, we see how it is," he said. "We must therefore put it away from you, or restrain you from maintaining this course."

This then would be the punishment—to deprive her of her meetings. She would not so easily accept it, though. "If you have a rule for it from God's word you may."

Winthrop did not like that. "We are your judges, and not you ours and we must compel you to it."

He could, of course. "If it please you by authority to put it down I will freely let you, for I am subject to your authority."

There did not seem to be much more to say on that score. She would be grateful if the governor had used up his store of accusations, if the end of her ordeal were nigh. She was so tired, she almost believed she might give up her meetings, if such were the sign of submission the court would demand.

But then old Thomas Dudley cleared his throat, pushed back his chair. It wasn't anywhere near over, he seemed to be saying. "Here hath been much spoken concerning Mistress Hutchinson's meetings," he said, "and among other answers she saith that men come not there. I would ask you this one question then, whether never any man was at your meeting?"

Winthrop interposed. "There are two meetings kept at their house."

That seemed to surprise the deputy governor. "How?" he said. "Is there two meetings?"

"Aye, sir," said Anne, "I shall not equivocate. There is a meeting of men and women, and there is a meeting only for women."

John Endicott then spoke up with a tricky question about

that. "Who teaches in the men's meetings? None but men? Do not women sometimes?"

"Never as I heard, not a one," Anne said. Thanks to Francis, she could say that with a clear conscience; for if she answered questions at the end of his presentation, that was no more than any other woman might have done. They were not going to prove any breach of law, either God's or man's, about her teaching.

But suddenly it seemed her teaching was not the point. Dudley reared back in his chair, and settled his jowls. "I would go a little higher with Mistress Hutchinson," he said insinuatingly. "About three years ago we were all in peace. Mistress Hutchinson from that time she came hath made a disturbance, and some that came over with her in the ship did inform me what she was as soon as she was landed."

Then he told that old tale of Master Symmes's accusation against her, and her delayed acceptance as a member of the Boston church. He was satisfied for a while, he said, but then she began to vent her opinions, which it appeared at first that both Cotton and Vane agreed with. Cotton had said he did not, but still the fact remained that Mistress Hutchinson had endangered the very foundations of the colony by saying that Master Cotton was the only minister who preached a covenant of grace, while all the rest preached a covenant of works.

Anne had been careful about that; she thought she had made no public accusations. "I pray, sir," she said, feeling almost sprightly again, "prove it that I said they preached nothing but a covenant of works."

"Nothing but a covenant of works!" Dudley exclaimed, his face reddening. "Why a Jesuit may preach truth sometimes."

She kept denying she had made the accusation; he kept repeating that she had. At last he said, "I will make it plain that you did say that the ministers did preach a covenant of works, and that you said they were not able ministers of the New Testament, but Master Cotton only."

"If I ever spake that," she said confidently, "I proved it by God's word."

"Very well, very well," said Winthrop, intending a stop to that.

But this charge was something Anne had not expected. She wanted to know the source of it. "If one shall come unto me in private, and desire me seriously to tell them what I thought of such an one, I must either speak false or true in my answer."

Dudley ignored this. He had more to say and was determined to say it. "Likewise I will prove this—that you said the Gospel in the letter and words holds forth nothing but a covenant of works and that all that do not hold as you do are in a covenant of works."

She said something like this once, mostly to find out what a well-esteemed minister thought of the idea. It was not what she believed—not expressed this way—and she hotly denied it.

Then Winthrop said, "It is well discerned that Mistress Hutchinson can tell when to speak and when to hold her tongue."

Unfair, Anne wanted to scream. But she continued to restrain herself. "It is one thing for me to come before a public magistracy and there to speak what they would have me speak, and another when a man comes to me in a way of friendship privately. There is difference in that."

"What if the matter be all one?" said Winthrop, and then she knew what would happen. The ministers to whom she had spoken freely, sometimes only by way of testing her own beliefs, were there to use against her everything she had said in that meeting last December. They had professed themselves satisfied then, but it was very clear to her now that they were only waiting there in their corner seats to drag out every word she had spoken.

First it was Hugh Peter. He brought out all she had said about the differences between Master Cotton and the rest of them, that none but Cotton was a truly able minister of the Gospel.

In truth, Anne did not remember the exact words she had spoken, but she felt this was going beyond what she had intended. "If our pastor would show his writings," she said, "you should see what I said, and that many things are not so as reported."

Master Wilson said he had no writings with him, and besides he did not set everything down.

Dudley said he wanted to hear from the other ministers, and they all spoke and accused her. Master Phillips came near to calling her a liar when he told how she had characterized his ministry even though she had not heard him preach. Then finally Dudley summed up the case. "I called these witnesses and you deny them. You see they have proved this and you deny this, but it is clear. You said they preached a covenant of works and that they were not able ministers of the New Testament. Now there are two other things you did affirm which were that the Scriptures in the letter of them held forth nothing but a covenant of works and likewise that those that were under a covenant of works cannot be saved."

"Prove that I said so," Anne challenged.

"Did you say so?" Winthrop asked.

"No, sir, it is your conclusion."

Dudley in frustration seemed about ready to give up the case. Hoarse and red-faced, he demanded, "What do I do charging you if you deny what is fully proved?"

It was growing dark now, and very, very cold. Anne in her spurt of anger had seemed to gain strength, but now she felt herself losing some of the clarity of mind she had counted on. She could feel her body drooping.

Fortunately, Simon Bradstreet, the court secretary, who had sat beside the governor taking notes, said in a low voice to Winthrop that it had grown too dark for him to tell what he was writing on his paper. Dudley was not quite ready to give up, wanting to talk about something Anne said to Nathaniel Ward about the letter and the spirit of the Scripture. But hardly anyone seemed to be listening any more, and the governor finally adjourned the day's session.

"We shall give you a little more time to consider," he instructed Anne, "and desire that you attend the court again in the morning."

As soon as the crowd thinned out enough, Coddington came and supported her to the door of the meetinghouse.

"I do not believe Sister Anne is able to go home to Boston this night," he said to William. "I want you two to stay the night in my room at the tavern."

"Anne?" said William.

"Oh, I am able," she said. "I must be able, for there are some notes I took out of what Master Wilson wrote down at the conference. I believe they would prove things not to be as they say."

"I will go get them," said Coddington.

She wavered. She was tired.

"Anne, stay here," said William.

"William, I will," she said, glad of his strength. "Francis can find the notes," she said to Coddington.

"I will bring them in the morning," he said, "early enough for you to peruse them before you go to court. And I will say a word or two to some who may speak in your defense if the court will allow them."

"Thank God for friends," said Anne.

## 4

Anne read for an hour or so in her Testament after supper, while William went to visit Wheelwright in the jail. On his return he reported that his brother John was about ready to give the required security; he could hardly afford to take his family north at this season.

They slept well. The bed was straw, but clean. As early as he had promised next morning, Coddington was there with the notes Anne had asked for. She had made them from a copy Henry Vane had lent her of Wilson's account of the December conference. It angered her now to remember that time, how they had all implored her to speak freely, because it was a private meeting. And as before, anger seemed to bring her strength. She assured the men she felt well this morning and would be entirely able to answer to any charges the court would bring against her.

"If there be any doubt about the ministers' testimony," Coddington said, "they should be required to testify under oath."

The idea shocked Anne. "They would not like that," she said. "They would say it amounted to an accusation of lying."

"Nevertheless," said Coddington, "out of fairness to you it ought to be done."

"I shall think upon it," Anne said.

In the court, Coddington took his place among the deputies. Anne waited with William at the back of the house until Winthrop came in, flanked by halberdiers from the Newtown militia. He too seemed to have renewed his strength in the night. He wore a fresh band and cuffs and the expression of an avenging angel.

Before giving his attention to Mistress Hutchinson, he had the marshal bring in John Wheelwright, who now said he would provide the assurance the court asked for. Winthrop said very well, but he would also have to agree not to preach any more before he left the colony. This Wheelwright would by no means agree to, and so he was told he would have to leave within two weeks or go back to jail. Having agreed with those terms, he stalked out of the meetinghouse.

Then Winthrop called up Mistress Hutchinson. She stood erect before him, her chin slightly lifted, while he summed up the case as it now stood against her: the regular meetings, the speeches in derogation of the ministers, and the weakening of the hands and hearts of the people towards them. The evidence they had given of her speeches at the conference was cited. "And this was not spoken as was pretended, out of private conference, but out of conscience and warrant from Scripture, she alleged the fear of man is a snare and seeing God had given her a calling to it she would freely speak." Then he gave her a chance to speak further.

Though she felt herself able to stand there as long as they could require her, she was grateful when Coddington came and (without a word to Winthrop) pulled out a chair for her to sit in. She sat, and began to offer her defense.

"The ministers come in their own cause," she said. "Now the Lord hath said that an oath is the end of all controversy; though there be a sufficient number of witnesses, yet they are not according to the word. Therefore I desire they may speak upon oath."

The faces of the ministers darkened, and Winthrop spoke rebukingly. "It is not in this case as in case of a jury," he informed her. "If the court be satisfied, there is no need for an oath."

"I have since last night looked at some notes out of what Master Wilson did then write, and I find things not to be as hath been alleged."

"Where are the writings?"

"I have them not, it may be Master Wilson hath."

Winthrop turned to Wilson then, who rose bunching his black gown around him. He did not seem very sure of what he spoke. "I do say that Master Vane desired me to write the discourse out and whether it be in his own hands or somebody's else, I know not. For my own copy it is somewhat imperfect, but I could make it perfect with a little pains."

No doubt he could, Anne thought. The governor evidently did not wish to pursue the matter, anyway, but turned back and addressed himself to Anne. Wilson sat down.

"It is not true what you allege against the elders," Winthrop said, "for they are not prosecutors in this cause but are called to witness."

"They are witnesses in their own cause," Anne repeated.

"It is not their cause," Winthrop said, "but the cause of the whole country, and they were unwilling that it should come forth, but that it was the glory and honor of God."

"If I be accused, I desire it may be upon oath," Anne said patiently.

There followed a long discussion, mostly among the seven magistrates who sat in judgment. Endicott spoke for them all when he said the ministers were so well known to them that no oath was needed.

Anne turned slightly and lifted her hand in a gesture against him. "Ah," she said, "but there are some that will take their oaths to the contrary."

Then the governor said, "Let those speak that are not satisfied without the taking of an oath."

Many voices rose: "We are not satisfied!"

Then Winthrop said that if the elders would agree to an oath it should be given; but Dudley said, "Let us join the things together that Mistress Hutchinson may see what they have their oaths for."

Once more, the governor repeated the charges: "that she hath traduced the magistrates and ministers of this jurisdiction, that she hath said the ministers preached a covenant of works and Master Cotton a covenant of grace, and that they were not able ministers of the Gospel. Now the ministers sent for her seeing she made these things her table talk, and she said the fear of man was a snare and therefore she would not be a-feared of them."

And Anne said, "This that yourself hath spoken, I desire that they may take their oaths upon."

Then the ministers seemed reluctant to agree, for it had been almost a year since the conference, and without a certain record of what they said, many of them felt they dare not trust their memories upon an oath before God.

One magistrate suggested, "Put any passage to them and see what they say."

The thing that came into Anne's mind was the thing they had spoken of so much, as evidence of her disrespect: that she said the fear of man is a snare. She mentioned it.

"This is not an essential thing," said the magistrate.

No, it was not, Anne realized. She wished she had thought of something else, she was on the wrong track. Yet even so their testimony was wrong. "Aye," she said, "that was the thing that I do deny, for they were my words, but they were not spoken at the first as they do allege."

Hugh Peter then jeeringly said, "We cannot tell what was first or last."

And Dudley said, "Mark what a flourish Mistress Hutchinson puts upon the business that she had witnesses to disprove that was said, and here is no man to bear witness."

For once she was glad of Thomas Dudley; this new subject suited her better. "If you will not call them," she said with a shrug, "it is nothing to me."

In truth, she did not know whom she would name, if they gave her the opportunity to call witnesses. John Cotton? He was the one she longed to rely on, but she did not know if she dared.

But for a time they did not ask her for names. There must still be more discussion about the oath, until at last John Cogshall (though under disfavor) stood and asked for recognition. "I desire to speak a word," he said. "It is desired that the elders would confer with Master Cotton before they swear."

"Shall we not," Winthrop answered him, "believe so many godly elders in a cause wherein we know the mind of the party without their testimony?"

Hardly waiting for Winthrop to finish, Dudley turned toward Cogshall and spoke with cold fury. "I will tell you what I say. I think that this carriage of yours tends to further casting of dirt upon the face of the judges."

Ah, it was certain the magistrates did not want to hear from John Cotton. Anne asked to have her witnesses called, yet still she did not name names. Wait and see, she told herself.

Then William Colburn spoke from the deputies' bench. "We desire that our teacher may be called to hear what is said." As Winthrop indicated assent, Cotton came from his place among the ministers and sat down at the table by Anne.

Endicott was not satisfied with this move. "This would cast some blame upon the ministers," he said, then shrugged. "Well, but whatever he will or can say, we will believe the ministers."

Then there was further talk about the oath, but finally the deputy governor said, "Let her witnesses be called."

"Who be they?" asked Winthrop.

Anne made up her mind to take the risk. "Master Leverett and our teacher and Master Cogshall," she said.

"Master Cogshall was not present," Winthrop said.

"Yes but I was," said Cogshall, "only I desired to be silent till I should be called."

Winthrop asked, "Will you say that she did not say so?"

And Cogshall answered, "Yes, I daresay that she did not say all that which they lay against her."

Then Hugh Peter rose with a flourish. "How dare you look into the court to say such a word?"

There seemed no satisfactory answer to that question. It meant, Anne supposed, that her witnesses would be disallowed. Unless John Cotton—

Thomas Leverett was asked to speak next, and his recollection was that what Anne had said was that other ministers did not preach a covenant of grace as clearly as Master Cotton did.

"Don't you remember," asked Winthrop, "that she said they were not able ministers of the New Testament?"

He shook his head, and Anne spoke to that. "Master Weld and I had an hour's discourse at the window, and then I spake that, if I spake it."

But Weld did not remember that.

Then Winthrop called for Cotton's testimony, and what John Cotton would remember who could tell?

He spoke in his mild and conciliatory manner, so familiar to them all. He said Mistress Hutchinson had made some difference between him and the others, but only that he preached a covenant of grace more clearly than they. "And I must say that I did not find her saying they were under a covenant of works, nor that she said they did preach a covenant of works."

Thank God, her teacher was not lost to her, was all Anne's thought then.

The ministers fell into a cacophony of talk amongst themselves, in which they somehow found it necessary to wrangle about the broad and little seals, as on the day of the fateful conference. Finally Dudley interrupted and said (it was not clear to whom), "You should have brought the book with you." And someone else said that Mistress Hutchinson's witnesses failed to answer requirements.

Winthrop chose to ignore that. He was not ready to make such a statement about John Cotton, yet he did say to the teacher, "I wonder why the elders should have asked our congregation to deal with her if they saw not some cause."

At that Cotton smiled gravely and would have spoken, but that Dudley, determined to bring them back to the essential point, repeated, "They affirm that Mistress Hutchinson did say they were not able ministers of the New Testament."

So this at last was the thing that must be answered. It had been answered before, but to no one's satisfaction. Cotton must speak to it, or Anne Hutchinson was lost. And yet perhaps he would only say that he could not remember clearly enough to answer under oath.

A murmur began to arise in the court; then Cotton stood, and all were silent. He cast his mild gaze upon the gathering, as though he might be preaching from the pulpit. At last he spoke. "I do not remember it," he said.

The only answer to that was to call John Cotton a liar. No one rose to do so. It seemed no one could doubt that Mistress Hutchinson was exonerated, and yet John Winthrop spoke no word. Everyone else, including the spectators, seemed to be speaking at once; their voices came like a roaring river risen in the hall.

They must have wondered why he did not call them to order. He sat as if stunned.

Anne herself wondered. Was it over? Was this really all? It seemed the court might dismiss her now, without taking action against her. But she had no sense of finality: something was missing. There was more she should have said. The court would disperse now with no understanding, with nothing different from before. She wanted them to know the truth, to see how it was that she had come to know it, and why she had come to Boston and begun to witness in its cause. Even now, she might bring many to this truth of Christ. She thought God called her this moment to give her testimony in full, to hold nothing back. The call came not as unmistakable as others she had felt, yet she knew no doubt. Her mind and spirit had been sorely tested this day, and might be somewhat clouded; still, as ever, the truth was crystal clear.

She rose from her chair. She stood turned somewhat sidewise, facing the court, but in a position to address the spectators as well.

Voices at once lowered. There were hisses for silence. The magistrates stared in astonishment. Before them stood this woman they had brought here to accuse, and nothing had been proved against her; and still she would speak, unsolicited. Many in that house knew well this stance—this lifted chin, these glowing, slightly bulging eyes, this listening air, those full moist lips barely parted.

When the noise had almost subsided, Anne spoke. This was no soft, respecting, clucking woman's voice; these words pierced the doubt-filled air of the meetinghouse as a cock's crow comes through the darkness before dawn.

"I beg leave to speak," she said.

There was full silence now; all heads turned toward her. Winthrop lifted his eyebrows in a high arch that deepened the lines arched above them. "Well?" he seemed to be saying.

"If you please to give me leave," Anne said, "I shall give you the ground of what I know to be true."

Still no one spoke. She went on. "Being much troubled to see the falseness of the constitution of the Church of England—"

At that Winthrop interrupted her. "This is not to the point," he said brusquely.

What point? She ignored him, and went on. Seeing what she was about, he made no further move to stop her.

"I had like to have turned separatist," she continued. "Whereupon I kept a day of solemn humiliation and pondering of the thing. This Scripture was brought unto me—he that denies Jesus Christ to be come in the flesh is Antichrist. This I considered of, and I found that the papists did not deny Him to be come in the flesh, nor we did not deny Him. Who then was Antichrist? Was the Turk Antichrist only? The Lord knows that I could not open Scripture; but then he brought before me this Scripture out of the Hebrews: 'He that denies the testament denies the testator.' And thereby did I see that those who did not teach the New Covenant had the spirit of Antichrist, and ever since, I bless the Lord, He hath let me see which was the clear ministry and which the wrong. Since that time I confess I have been more choice and He hath led me to distinguish between the voice of my beloved and the voice of Moses, the voice of John Baptist and the voice of Antichrist, for all those voices are spoken of in Scripture. Now if you do condemn me for speaking what in my conscience I know to be the truth, I must commit myself unto the Lord."

She paused. There was a long silence. The magistrates might have been asking themselves whether she was not imploring them to condemn her.

It was Dudley who spoke at last. "How do you know that was the spirit?"

Without hesitation she answered him. "How did Abraham know that it was God that bid him offer his son, being a breach of the Sixth Commandment?"

Now Dudley leaned forward eagerly—he was onto something he had been waiting for. "By an immediate voice," came his answer.

And Anne looked him in the eye and said to him: "So to me, by an immediate revelation."

"How!" Dudley exploded. "An immediate revelation!"

"By the voice of His own spirit to my soul."

Now again was there much murmuring and exclaiming; yet no one spoke to Anne, to restrain her, and she went on, for there was more she must tell them.

"When our teacher came to New England it was a great trouble unto me, my brother Wheelwright being put by also. I was then much troubled concerning the ministry under which I lived, and then that place in the Thirtieth of Isaiah was brought to my mind. 'Though the Lord give thee bread of adversity and water of affliction, yet shall not thy teachers be removed into corners any more, but thine eyes shall see thy teachers.' The Lord giving me this promise and they being gone, there was none then left that I was able to hear, and I could not be at rest but I must come hither. And then this place in Daniel was brought unto me and did show me that though I should meet with affliction, yet 'I am the same God that delivered Daniel out of the lion's den, I will also deliver thee.'"

She stopped. It crossed her mind that she might well stop here, yet her spirit still was full and overflowing. Up to now, she had simply told what had happened to her in the past. Yet more was happening now, this instant, and she went on. "Therefore I desire you look to it, for you see this Scripture fulfilled this day and therefore I desire you that as you tender the Lord and the church and commonwealth, to consider and look what you do. You have power over my body but the Lord Jesus hath power over my body and soul, and assure yourselves this much, you do as much as in you lies to put the Lord Jesus Christ from you, and if you go on in this course you begin you will bring a curse upon you and your posterity, and the mouth of the Lord hath spoken it." She leaned upon the chair.

There came a long moment of shocked silence, followed by cries of astonishment throughout the house. Winthrop waited warily until the exclamations died down. Then he spoke to Mistress Hutchinson:

"Daniel was delivered by a miracle. Do you think to be delivered so too?"

She was not careful; she was buoyed up by the Lord. "I do here speak it before the court," Anne said. "I look that the Lord should deliver me by His providence."

Zachariah Symmes then rose in the ministers' corner and said, "I would remind my brother Cotton of what she said on board the ship, that England would be destroyed."

"As I recall," Cotton said, "she explained that this was a revelation of Master Hooker's."

"So she said," Symmes replied. "But I would add that it hath been reported to me since, by a man that met her in London before we sailed, that in speaking of Master Hooker's prophecy she said it was very acceptable to her because she herself had never had any great thing done about her but it was revealed beforehand."

"I say the same thing again," said Anne firmly.

John Eliot of Roxbury stood up among the ministers then, to say it was his belief that this revelation they spoke of came from Mistress Hutchinson herself, for it was against his brother Hooker's mind and spirit to make any such prediction as she laid to him. (And all the ministers agreed; and since Master Hooker was not there that day, he could not tell them that he had indeed made such a prophecy as he took his leave of Old England, so that their concept of his mind and spirit was the evidence accepted by the court.)

Then Endicott spoke, saying he had heard rumors before this of Mistress Hutchinson's revelations, and it seemed to him this discourse of hers proved it. But since her reverend teacher was there with her, he might speak freely whether he approved of such speeches and revelations.

All eyes were upon Cotton. He had saved her with his testimony once, but few believed he could save her now.

"May it please you, sir," said Cotton. "There are two sorts of revelations. Some come through the word of God, and these are lawful for Christians to receive. Those which come direct, without the word, I look upon as satanical."

"You give me satisfaction in the thing," said Endicott, "and therefore I desire you do give your judgment of Mistress Hutchinson."

"I would demand," said Cotton, "whether by a miracle she doth mean a work above nature or by some wonderful providence that is called a miracle often in the Psalms."

He wanted to help her. Anne believed he was trying to help her—and perhaps, anyway, she had gone too far, beyond what God intended. "I desire to speak to our teacher," she said. "You know, sir, the different ways of God's deliverance. I believe that by the kind of miracle you speak of He shall deliver me, yet I would not have the court so to understand that He will deliver me now even at this present time."

Dudley was no way willing to let this go. "I desire Master Cotton to tell us whether you do approve Mistress Hutchinson's revelations as she hath laid them down."

Cotton clearly was not sure. "I know not whether I do understand her, but this I say, if she doth expect a deliverance in a way of providence, then I cannot deny it."

"No, sir," said Dudley harshly, "we did not speak of that."

"If it be by way of miracle," Cotton admitted, "then I would suspect it."

Dudley persisted. "Do you believe that her revelations are true?"

And Cotton answered, "That she may have some special providence of God to help her is a thing that I cannot bear witness against."

Dudley was to have no equivocating. "Good sir, I do ask whether this revelation be of God or no?"

But Cotton obviously could not answer that. "I should desire to know whether the sentence of the court will bring her to any calamity, and then I would know of her whether she expects to be delivered from that calamity by a miracle or a providence of God."

Anne now had returned to her cautious, respectful, soft-spoken manner, and she said simply, "By a providence of God I say I expect to be delivered from some calamity that shall come to me."

Then Winthrop, as though to say "Enough now!" declared that the case had been altered. It seemed to him that through the providence of God this woman had confessed that she was guided by revelations that bore no relation to God's word. "And this hath been the ground of all these tumults and troubles, and I would that those were all cut off from us that trouble us, for *this is the thing* that hath been the root of all the mischief."

And all the court—the seven magistrates—exclaimed, "We all consent with you!"

Well, it was God's will. Anne awaited their disposal of her, but meantime there were those, apparently, who would also like to dispose of John Cotton. He had stood perilously close to her this day.

She listened unbelieving as Endicott and then Dudley conducted the attack. Endicott asked for clarification about Cotton's view of his pupil's revelations, and he answered that if she looked for deliverance by God's providence then he could not deny it.

"You give me satisfaction," Endicott said.

"No, no," said Dudley, "he gives me none at all."

"But," Cotton tried to explain, "if it be in a way of miracle or a revelation without the word, then I do not assent to it, but look at it as a delusion, and I think so doth she too as I understand her."

And Dudley said, "Sir, you weary me and do not satisfy me, for I am fully persuaded that Mistress Hutchinson is deluded by the devil."

Winthrop agreed with that. "I am persuaded that the revelation she brings forth is delusion."

"We all believe it, we all believe it!" the magistrates and ministers cried.

Then one of the deputies wanted more from John Cotton, but Winthrop put a stop to that course. "Master Cotton is not called to answer to anything, but we are to deal with the party here standing before us."

Anne lifted her head. What they were about to do, she knew not, nor when she could expect deliverance. It lay all with God.

Yet her friends had not yet done all, for Coddington rose and came forward a step or two from the deputies' place. "I do think that you are going to censure; therefore I desire to speak a word."

"I pray you speak," the governor said.

Coddington said, "There is one thing objected against the meetings. What if she designed to edify her own family in her own meetings—may none else be present?"

Winthrop spoke impatiently. "If you have nothing else to say but that, Master Coddington, it is a pity you should interrupt our proceedings.'

"I would say more, sir," Coddington went on. "Another thing you lay to her charge is her speech to the elders. Now I do not see any clear witness against her, and you know it is a rule of the court that no man may be a judge and an accuser too. And for the other thing which hath fallen from her occasionally by the spirit of God, you know the spirit of God witnesses in our spirits, and there is no truth in Scripture but God bears witness to it by His spirit. Therefore I would entreat you to consider whether those things you have alleged against her deserve such censure as you are about to pass, be it banishment or imprisonment."

Banishment or imprisonment! The words struck at Anne's spirit, yet scarcely could she tell what they meant. She had expected no such thing, and why should Master Coddington speak such words?

"Her own speeches have been ground enough for us to proceed upon," said the governor.

"Go on!" cried several. The whole court and the spectators were becoming impatient, and hungry too, for it was long past the hour of noon. Yet some would go on talking, and redefining the charges against Anne Hutchinson.

"We shall all be sick with fasting!" grunted Dudley.

Even so, her friends would not give her up so easily. "I dissent from a sentence of banishment," Master Colburn said.

"And I desire," said Master Stoughton, who though no follower of Anne's did follow justice, "that no offense be taken if I do not formally condemn her because she hath not been formally convicted as others are by witnesses upon oath."

"That is a scruple to me also," said Coddington, "because Solomon said, every man is partial in his own cause, and here is none that accuses her but the elders, and she spake nothing to them but in private."

But it was Stoughton whose opinion counted—he was a magistrate, and an impartial one, at that. Winthrop at last agreed that there should be an oath required, but after some distress appeared among the ministers, he ruled that any two of them would serve.

The duty devolved upon John Eliot and Thomas Weld, who repeated all that had been said before of Anne's words at the conference.

And Coddington spoke again. "What wrong was that to say you were not able ministers of the Gospel because you were like the Apostles—methinks the comparison is very good."

"Well," said the governor, frowning, "you remember she said but now that she should be delivered from calamity."

And Cotton still speaking in her defense, said, "I remember she said she should be delivered by God's providence, whether now or at another time she knew not."

But Israel Stoughton was satisfied now. "I am fully convinced," he said, "that her words were pernicious, and the frame of her spirit doth hold forth the same."

And so Winthrop at last could proceed. "The court hath already declared themselves satisfied concerning the things you hear, and concerning the troublesomeness of her spirit and the danger of her course among us, which is not to be suffered. Therefore if it be the mind of the court that Mistress Hutchinson for these things that appear before us is unfit for our society, and if it be the mind of the court that she shall be banished out of our liberties and imprisoned till she be sent away, let them hold up their hands."

And all the court but three did lift their right hands.

"Those that are contrary-minded hold up yours." He paused, to count. "Master Coddington and Master Colburn only."

Then the one who had not voted either way, a deputy named Jennison, from Watertown, spoke up and said, "I cannot hold up my hand one way or the other, and I shall give my reason if the court require it."

But Winthrop did not care to know. He turned to the woman accused, who still stood erect before him, and said, "Mistress Hutchinson, the sentence of the court you hear is that you are banished from out of our jurisdiction as being a woman not fit for our society, and are to be imprisoned till the court shall send you away."

And she lifted her chin, and spoke out high and clear. "I desire to know wherefore I am banished."

And Winthrop answered: "Say no more. The court knows wherefore and is satisfied."

# XXIV

In Boston they had learned Anne Hutchinson was on trial, and on the second day her friends came to Newtown, drawn by their own need as much as hers. Most were kept outside the meetinghouse for lack of room within and stood about in the softening snow, determined to stay for the end. Then at last the door opened, and those who had seen the trial burst forth with the news. There was a long silence, followed by weeping and cries of protest.

Then all crowded as close as they could to the door, for everyone (friend, foe, and curiosity seeker) wished to see what Mistress Hutchinson looked like when she came out of the meetinghouse.

She came down the aisle at the side of the marshal in whose custody she had been placed. William walked a step or two behind. She would be parting from him shortly, for they had told her she would be taken to Roxbury and kept prisoner there in the house of Joseph Weld until next March when she must leave the colony.

All this the governor had spoken to her while she still stood before him at the table, but the meaning of his words had yet to reach her. As earlier, during the examination, she felt lifted up in God's hands. When she came out of the house, she was blinded by the dazzle of snow under cloudless sky and thought at first it might be the presence of God. The marshal, pondering the best way to get through the crowd with his prisoner, paused on the doorstep. Anne waited beside him and, blinking and shading her eyes with her hand, began to see and understand her surroundings.

As they stood thus, a slender, cloaked woman wearing a steeple-crowned hat pushed her way to Anne; and before the marshal could interfere, Mary Dyer had flung her arms around her friend and, weeping, called her name. At that touch the reality of her situation came clear to Anne, and she too wept.

"What can I do for you at home?" asked Mary quickly, knowing they must soon be parted.

At home, she thought, and full understanding possessed her. "My children!" she cried. And there in Mary's arms, in front of enemies and friends, she broke at last. "Mary," she moaned aloud, "they won't let me go home to my children."

She broke into loud wailing and sobbing, and the image in her heart was of tiny Susannah, reaching after her with tears in her wide brown eyes.

"Who is that?" asked some woman then, who stood near them.

"Oh," said an ancient grandam at her side, "that's the woman that had the monster."

Just inside the door, John Winthrop heard, and his eyebrows lifted with the lines on his forehead.

The marshal pushed Mary away and roughly taking Anne's arm strode through the crowd, which parted before them like a biblical sea.

Anne was taken to the tavern then, where they let her eat a meal and have a short private talk with William. She did not cry any more.

"Tell the children that when they pray, by morning and night, I shall be praying with them, and all will be linked together in God's spirit."

As she spoke these words, the husband and wife were standing together, ready to take separate paths. They kissed each other gravely, and then she was led away. She did not look back, but walked erect and tall beside the black-clad marshal armed as though for war. Others from Roxbury came following them, but she seemed not to know.

William stood and watched her out of sight. He prayed she had the strength to walk proudly all the way to her prison.

## 2

The court recessed for a week, during which time Winthrop drew up in careful detail a design to break the opinionists forever. He was now about the work of saving the holy commonwealth of Massachusetts Bay from utter ruin, and he saw nothing to stop him if he acted swiftly and with just so much mercy as God's enemies deserved.

In session again in Newtown, the court began to call those enemies before them. Uppermost in Winthrop's mind were those two sergeants who had laid down their halberds to dishonor him at the May election. They were charged with having their hands to the Wheelwright petition and they readily admitted that they did and would again. Both men were disfranchised and heavily fined. William Baulston said if that petition had been made anywhere else in the world there would have been no fault found with it. Edward Hutchinson—turning himself in a scornful manner, as Winthrop later wrote—said if they took away his estate they would have to take care of his wife and children. For this impertinence he spent the night in jail.

Then came four more men who had done a deal of talking to spread Anne Hutchinson's satanic teachings: Marshall, the ferryman; Dyer, the milliner; Dinely, the barber (who as soon as one sat down in his chair would be cutting of his hair and the truth together); and Gridley, the brickmaker, an honest poor man, but very apt to meddle in public affairs beyond his skill. (Pondering that characteristic, Winthrop later realized and set down the fact that this was the trouble with many others in the country: if such men would attend to their own business and let the governors govern, a model commonwealth might readily be achieved.) These four men, though justifying themselves in signing the petition, spoke with sufficient modesty that they were disfranchised but not fined or banished.

Another day, they called John Underhill. He had known he would be called and thought of some defense, so that when they asked him how he could justify signing the petition in defiance of the sentence of the court, he cited the example of Joab's rough speech to David on the occasion of Absalom's death. The court knew many reasons why Underhill was nothing like Joab and the situation altogether different. They said Underhill was but a private man and had no calling to meddle in court affairs. Then Underhill insisted that all countries allow more liberty to military men than to private citizens, recalling that when he fought in the Low Countries he used to talk quite freely to the Count of Nassau.

"We are not here to look at what some do tolerate," Winthrop told him sternly, "but what is lawful. And there may be a reason for disorder at some season, which may not with honor and safety be permitted at another."

And still Underhill refused to retract anything he had said, or repent of signing the petition, and so he was disfranchised and discharged from his position.

When they were through with Underhill, ten men from Charlestown came begging to have their names stricken from the petition. Winthrop smiled with grim satisfaction; his plan was working.

On the morrow, though, he speedily showed Boston how far he was from being satisfied. He had devised still another way of bringing opinionists to their knees. Perhaps he really believed, as the court record stated, that there was "just cause of suspicion that they, as others in Germany in former times, may, upon some revelation, make some sudden irruption upon those that differ from them in judgment." When people act through revelation rather than reason, there is no way of knowing what they may do.

Consequently, all powder and shot were ordered taken out of Boston and kept at Newtown and Charlestown. Next, with no warning, a court order was presented at the doors of fifty-eight Boston men, plus five each from Roxbury and Salem, three from Newbury, and two each from Ipswich and Charlestown. By the end of the month every one of these men was required to deliver to the house of Robert Keayne "all such guns, pistols, swords, powder, shot, and match as they shall be owners of." Only by acknowledging his sin in subscribing to the seditious libel could any of these men keep arms.

3

With resentment boiling beneath his bright breastplate, John Underhill marched down the high street on his way home from the ferry that brought him across the river from Newtown. He and Thomas Marshall had looked at each other accusingly, as though each thought the other had betrayed too much, and been punished too little. Underhill himself wondered why the court had not stripped him of his armor when they relieved him of his office, but he thought that he would wear it, when it pleased him, till they did. He caressed the sword hanging at his side—he would like to have drawn it against Winthrop. He remembered the fine talk when the governor enticed him to join the company and emigrate to New England—to serve as a military officer of high rank, with all the usual rights and privileges. Why, Winthrop knew nothing whatsoever about the relationship between a true prince and a captain. Baulston was right: nowhere else in the world could such things be as these now happening in the court of Massachusetts Bay.

What he would do now he had no clear notion. He had some land, of course, granted by the colony. But he was no farmer—God forbid. Helena might make a farmer's wife, he supposed. That was about what she was good for—what she might have been, in Holland. Would he had left her there.

Thinking of getting home to Helena made the news seem worse than ever. Where could he go every day, he wondered—he could certainly not sit at home with her; there was nothing he wanted there. Then he remembered something he did want very much—something to challenge any soldier of Underhill's spirit, with a chance of getting it this very day, if he had read the signs aright. He could forget the god-damned court for a while.

Just when he realized he was growing a little tired of Goodwife Faber, Helena had made a new friend for herself, a young married woman whose blue eyes sparkled promisingly. The captain had made two private visits to her house already, and she had dallied with him just enough. Dalliance would not be the goal another time.

As usual, he thought himself too clever to be suspected, but there was one looking out from her back door across the empty lot behind Henry Webb's house. "I know what you're about," said Goody Judkins to herself, "and I know who'd like to hear about it, too." At least she had strong suspicions, and if they turned out to be true, Winthrop might find work for Job, her husband, and Pastor Wilson might look on them both with more favor when they asked admittance to the church again.

While she watched, Underhill knocked three times at Dosabell's back door. They had not arranged any signal, but she would know who was there. Quickly, she let him in.

"I had not expected you," she said, locking the door behind him. She had on a ragged short petticoat and a bodice without either kerchief or band, a style of dress that made him think she lied. He wondered if she were not cold, but then she led him to the hearth, where she had spread a rug. She had been lying there on her stomach staring into the fire, he realized—that was why she looked so rosy, and also why she had a pattern of rough woven wool pressed into her bosom. She sat on the rug, and he drew up a stool and sat near her.

"I like it when you wear your sword and armor," she said.

Thereupon he decided not to tell her he was put out of office. Sympathy would have been nice, but he knew of something else much better.

"I heard they put her in jail," she said.

"Who? Mistress Hutchinson? Yes, sadly, that is true. But they cannot change the truth of Christ by silencing His messengers."

"You still believe all this you have been telling me?"

"Of course. Truth does not change. God never frowns on Christian love. And you and I are Christians, and in love."

"Well—but *Christian* love. That's different."

"Why should it be? Can you say love is not love? What kind of logic is that?"

She stuck out her lower lip, pouting. "What do I know of logic?"

"What do you know of love?"

"I am married, if you have not forgotten."

"Ha!" he snorted. "And have you forgotten that I have the honor of being acquainted with your husband?"

"Why should I think you know more than he?"

"Mayhap I could show you."

"Mayhap you could, if 'twere not that I want to be a Christian."

"No one can stop you, I have told you that. And you have been to Mistress Hutchinson's meetings. You know that there is nothing wrong with love—but if it be not true love, even if it be what men call sin—"

"I know. Christ does not turn away. But you see I do care what people think as well as what Christ thinks. I want to be somebody. I want to be in the church. And if they've banished Mistress Hutchinson—then maybe she is wrong. And if I said I think like she does they might never let me in."

"As long as John Cotton is teacher, the church cannot reject the covenant of grace."

She lay back on the rug. "Grace," she said. "I like the sound of that."

He took off his helmet. "Help me off with my armor," he said.

She lay lazily looking up at him. "I've never done that," she said.

"You might like to learn. As you say you like to see a man with armor, you might like to help him with it off and on."

"But I do not wish to help you undress."

"I'm not undressing. I just want to be comfortable."

But when she leaped to her feet and began to fumble with the buckles of his breastplate, he knew she would let things go farther today. By God, she'd better.

He reached out and touched the fading pattern of the rug upon her breast.

Someone knocked at the door.

"Oh, Christ!" she said, and turned and ran. She snatched up a mantle to cover her breast and left him with a strap hanging down. He tucked it up out of sight.

The knock came again. Dosabell turned the key, and the door swung in. "I am sent in search of Captain Underhill," said a well-known voice. John stepped forward. "There is no captain here," he said gruffly. "They've stripped me of that."

"Well, sir, I'm sorry to hear that," said the beadle—for he it was, with his staff in his hand and his peaked hat on his head.

"What is it you want?" said Underhill.

"Well, sir, seeing that the ministers and magistrates was all gone, Goody Judkins she come to me."

"The old sow!" said Underhill.

"She thought there might be something wrong here, she said."

"Nothing is wrong," said Underhill.

"But I think I will have to report to the authorities that you and Goodwife Webb was here behind the locked door."

"Now look here," said Underhill. "There's nothing going on here. I've come to pray with Goodwife Webb, and comfort her. That's all."

"Behind a locked door, sir?"

Underhill drew himself up high enough that he could almost look the beadle in the eye. "We did not wish to be interrupted," he said.

"Yes, sir," said the beadle. "I will report it as you say."

When he was gone, Dosabell burst into tears. "Now I never will get into a church," she cried.

"Here, fasten this strap," said Underhill.

She obeyed with pouting lip, and he took up his helmet and started home. To wait for a warrant, he supposed, thanks to Goodwife Judkins, that filthy old bawd.

He was not likely, though, he realized upon consideration, to hear anything till the next week, with the court still in session in Newtown. In fact, he need not think about the court at all. He turned back up the high street, in the direction of Samuel Cole's tavern.

4

The meetinghouse in Boston seemed strangely quiet on the Lord's Day. Everyone knew what had happened in the court, and looked for consequences of some sort in the church. There never was, of course, any tittering or chatter. This quiet was more a matter of light breathing and still feet.

As the service progressed, many members of the congregation began to realize that the thing they waited for was about to happen. Pastor Wilson had an air of hurrying to be done, although he turned the glass and preached out the sand.

When he had prayed the last prayer, he announced that there was a young woman present, not a member of the church, who had come to them for help. "Goodwife Dosabell Webb," he called, with a purr of satisfaction lurking beneath the sternness of his voice, "please come forward."

"My God," said Underhill inwardly, but moved not so much as an eyelid.

Then Dosabell, as requested, came forward, dressed all in

black with plain sleeves and a clean white band. With some few becoming tears, she told how she had put her trust in Captain Underhill, who had promised to come and pray with her about her great longing to be a Christian and a church member, but then had locked the door and solicited her chastity under pretense of Christian love.

Then Underhill, called forward, confessed there was an appearance of evil, when they were found together behind a locked door, but in truth they were engaged in private prayers. Goodwife Webb had been mistaken about his intent, he said, perhaps because she had never had a close acquaintance with any Christian men.

Now Underhill was a member of the church—if not altogether in good standing, yet an accepted Christian—and Dosabell had asked for admittance already and been turned down. Wilson was thus in duty bound to pay proper attention to his words, and so he turned to Master Cotton and inquired of him, "Brother, does it seem to you that this is correct behavior for a man and woman, even when engaged in private prayer?" And Cotton, gravely surveying the scene below the pulpit, mildly said that he himself would not have done the like and doubted that his brother Wilson would.

And Wilson agreed that he would not. No, it would not have been of good report, even for the elders, they agreed, and in such a case they would have called some brother or sister to be with them, and not have locked the door.

That settled, Wilson turned once more to Goodwife Webb and inquired of her whether she considered Brother Underhill's account of their meeting to be true. And she admitted that he did from time to time pray and talk of Christian love. With such an air of childishness that her audience might well forget she was married and presumably no virgin, she said, "He told me he often had his will of the cooper's wife, and all out of strength of love."

"What cooper's wife?" blasted a voice from the back, where the unregenerate sat.

"Sit down, sir," shouted Wilson, "and wait your turn."

On the magistrate's seat Winthrop lifted his brow and said to himself what good advice that was. There were devils a-plenty to out now, he had no doubt. He knew of some himself, but they must wait their turn.

Presently, though, the cooper was allowed to come forward, and his wife, too, neither of them being church members, and in the end Underhill had to confess that he had committed adultery with Goodwife Faber, for which he was sorry before God and man. So miserable was he that he commenced weeping and saying how sorry he was to grieve his Lord, for though he did go under a covenant of grace and knew himself saved, still it was a heavy burden to him to fall into sin. Then he sank upon his knees before Joseph Faber, entreating his forgiveness. The cooper, who had never seen any man behave so in his life, was so amazed that he forgave Underhill on the spot.

Then the church, seeing how contrite and brokenhearted Brother Underhill was, moved to censure but not to excommunicate. The pastor gave an additional sermon on the evident perils of antinomianism, warning Underhill that he had better not feel so confident of being saved, and a chastened congregation went thoughtfully home. Winthrop privately congratulated Wilson upon his handling of the Underhill matter. Ordinarily, he said, he would deem it a matter for the court (in addition to the church, he hastened to say), but the court had so much business on hand already that he could scarcely see an end to it. Having all this deviltry brought to light in the meetinghouse would do much good both to those involved and to the public at large.

John Underhill was of the same mind. He was pretty sure he had escaped another summons to court, and so he supposed he must be grateful to Dosabell. He was also grateful for the fact that in time of great trouble his tears had always flowed easily, and that Helena never had seemed to mind in the least about his other women.

## 5

Joseph Weld, marshal of Roxbury and brother of the pastor, Thomas Weld, was said by some people to be the wealthiest merchant in the colony. He had a fine house, in which Anne was given a small, sparsely furnished, upstairs room. She was locked into it, except when she was brought downstairs to prayers and the evening meal; but it had its own fireplace, opening from the massive central chimney, and she was not uncomfortable there.

She was taken to worship service on the Lord's Day, and ministers of the colony were to visit her as often as they pleased. Otherwise she would see no one except members of her immediate family, who were to come for two hours once a week, and no more than two at a time. William brought her clothing and a Bible on Thursday, the day after her imprisonment began, but Weld said he must not see her. Later she was able to believe this deprivation was for the best, because on Thursday she could only have wept when she saw him. By the next Wednesday she had reached a kind of acceptance. God had a purpose in her imprisonment, and as she realized how she would be kept—shut up alone, with only her Bible and an occasional minister for company, she saw what it must be. There was more she must understand about God's plan for His people. She must search the Scriptures diligently, and pray and listen to the ministers when they came.

Until now she had not been able to dedicate herself wholly to an understanding of God. She had never wished to, or thought such dedication suitable for a Christian woman with a husband and children. But now, since God willed it, she would do her best to submit. She protested at first, in her heart, and wept much, that God would separate her from her husband and children; and she grieved for the sake of her many friends in Boston who often depended upon her for their own spiritual comfort. But at last she found herself able to forget them for whole hours at a time, and turn herself to God, as a lone traveler, lost in a cold dark wilderness, knowing not the direction of home and discerning no landmark to guide him, turns himself at last toward the light and warmth of the sun and hopes for nothing more.

When William came, she greeted him calmly, with a loving smile and no tears.

"Thank God you seem better," he said.

"I believe you find me reconciled," she said.

He had found her sitting by the window wrapped in her mantle of blue wool. When the ministers came, she was taken downstairs to them; but the rule was, she could see her family in the privacy of her chamber. There was a young servant maid who kept the key and came to fetch her for visitors or meals, or as now to let someone come in to her.

"I am to leave the door unlocked while you are here, sir," she said to William, "but you must lock it behind you when you leave."

When she was gone they embraced and kissed. Then Anne resumed her chair by the window, and he sat on a stool by her side.

"I had not thought they would go so far as to lock you in," said William.

"Aye, they put a lock on the door especially for me," said Anne. "I told Master Weld I would not even think of trying to escape, but he had orders from the court; and now I am somewhat glad of it, because no one can come in upon me until I have first heard the key turn in the lock."

William squeezed her hand. "My dearest Anne," he said.

"The children," she said to him first. "Tell me of the children."

"They are well." He reached under his loose coat and pulled out a packet of letters. "I thought it best not to bring any one of them until I saw for myself what your condition is here, but they have all written to you. Even Zuriel, I believe, has made his mark."

She clasped them to her breast. "I shall read them when you're gone," she said. "Now tell me, what further news? I have heard hints of something happening in Boston, but no one talks to me."

"I could wish you need not know," said William.

She sat with her hands folded in her lap and waited. At last he spoke, and told her of the actions of the court against all who had signed the petition, of the fines and disfranchisement of some, and the disarming of almost every man the Hutchinsons might think of as their friend, both in Boston and outlying towns.

"But, William," Anne said, "what can they do without their guns? Many families depend on game for food, and in some places they still need protection from the Indians."

"They can have them back," said William grimly, "if they recant and take their names off the paper."

"But of course they cannot do that," cried Anne.

"Some few have," said William shortly. "But let me tell you about Captain Underhill."

"I suppose they took away his armor, along with his sword and his gun. Poor man, he must feel naked."

"So he must. But that is not the story I would tell you."

"Can there be more bad news?"

"There can be, indeed." He told her then of the charges of adultery in the church and Underhill's pitiful confession.

"And he was not excommunicated," said Anne.

"Only censured."

"He deserves the worst," she said. "I cannot trust that man, no matter what he may profess about the love of Christ."

"Nor should you—for I still have not told all."

"I cannot conceive of more."

"Then what think you of this? Though he professed repentance, he claimed the covenant of grace protected him from punishment. And then Pastor Wilson preached a second sermon, using Brother Underhill as an example to show how this doctrine of grace has been warped by the devil to fit his own evil purposes."

"And spoke of me, I guess, as the devil's disciple."

"He did not call your name."

"But whether he did or no, they know the truth in Boston. They know who I am, and they know whose spirit lives in me."

William did not respond to that. "And more news," he said. "Brother Wheelwright is gone to New Hampshire, and Cousin Samuel with him. They will prepare a place and come back for the rest of the family in March."

"Well—they may be better off there," Anne said.

"Where would you like for us to go, Anne?" William asked then.

She shook her head. "I still cannot believe we must go," she said. "Could not the sentence somehow be rescinded?"

"I fear not. And we too may be better off somewhere else. We could go to our kindred to the north."

"Katherine likes Rhode Island."

"But she likes Roger Williams."

"And so might we, if we knew him better."

"Well, there is time enough to decide," William said, "and, thank God, some choice remaining to be made."

Anne realized she had not thought overmuch about what they would do in March. In trying to accept her imprisonment, she had even made an effort not to look to the end of it. Now she pondered on how it would be.

"William," she said, "they will all go with us, won't they? Son Edward, and Bridget and Faith?"

"Most will stay with us, of course. Richard talks of going to London."

She was silent a moment, accepting that. "Well, Brother Richard has wanted him to come. And he would like the business. But the others, I suppose, will go with us. The girls—"

"Anne," William interrupted then, "I don't know. I had better tell you about Thomas."

"Thomas? And Faith, too, perhaps? She could not begin to guess what had happened to them. Some terrible accident?"

"Thomas," said William tonelessly, "asked to have his name marked off the petition, and so will have his arms again."

Anne felt stricken. "What does it mean?" she asked.

"I know not. I have talked with him, and I know he is unhappy about it. They said he wept when he appeared before the court. He tells me he has not changed his religious views, only he sees now the paper was in contempt of court."

"And yet—"

"Some thirty other men have done the same. And most do take it as a sign that they recant."

"So many turned against me?"

"I think not, Anne; 'tis that they fear the law."

"Aye," she said bitterly. "Winthrop's law. And they set it above God."

"It may be."

"And Faith, my Faith?"

"She says not much, only that what her husband does is right, and so it should be."

Anne's head sank, and she sighed. "Aye," she said.

William got up and stood close to her. He took her head gently in his hands, and stooped and kissed her. "My dear sweetheart," he said, "let us not speak of these things any more, but trust God in His own time to guide us right."

She lifted a hand, to find one of his and hold it. "I thank God for thee constantly, William," she said.

He sat on the stool again, and leaned against her knee. "Does it make thee sad," he asked after a little while, "to remember the days when we were children together in Alford?"

They spent a long time remembering those days, and the days when their children were young there in that Lincolnshire village.

"How green and sweet it was," Anne said.

"We could go back," said William, and was startled at the fierceness that rose then in Anne's eyes.

"Never!" she said.

Not long after that, the little serving maid Lucy tapped gently at the door.

When William was gone, Anne wondered herself at the fierceness with which she answered him about going back to England, and she felt sorry for it. Yet she knew she never could go back. That would be as much as to say that in bringing her to New England God had been mistaken. Or that she had been?

That question did not linger in her mind—or perhaps had never been there. Whispered by the devil, it might have been.

She turned then to her letters from the children, and wept over the little ones' precious attempts to put their love for her on paper. Then she came to the letter from Francis.

"My dear Mother," he wrote. "Your absence from us leaves a great sadness, especially for the young children and for Cousins Frances and Anne, who do not understand God's plan for you much better than Zuriel does.

"I could weep as he does and call out Mother, Mother, were I not sure that out of your imprisonment, as out of Paul's at Rome, great good will come. Somewhere, some time, we will be together once more, living and preaching for God's greater glory.

"I know not whether you will have remembered anything about the college. The court did pass a law about it, and they said it will be open in the spring, I suppose it may be about the same time we leave the colony. I would not mention this, only I fear you may have thought of it and be sorry if I do not go. Please do not be. I know now God calls me on to higher things."

After reading this letter, Anne wept a long time. She did not know whether she wept for the education lost to her son, for herself that she caused his loss, or for her heart pierced by his love and constancy. Some of her children might separate from her and go their ways. Francis would be with her forever, in the Lord.

## 6

It was ordered by the court that Anne should be taken to worship services on the Lord's Day. There the two ministers, Thomas Weld and John Eliot, preached assiduously against the heresies condemned by the synod. These had never been publicly ascribed to Anne Hutchinson, but everyone (except her own friends) was convinced they all came from her teaching. Consequently, the Roxbury meetinghouse was filled and overflowing at each Sabbath service. People would wait outside to see the tall pale woman in black cloak and hood come attended by the marshal through the snow, and then in the house would crane their necks to see her face when the minister told how the devil made use of his disciples in spreading error through the land.

She was thankful to be denied the privilege of going to the lectures. To have deprived her of Lord's Day worship would have been a sin on the part of the court, but the fifth-day lecture was a luxury, inappropriate for such a one as Mistress Hutchinson to enjoy.

Hence, on lecture days, she was left alone in the house except for the little maid Lucy. One Thursday afternoon about mid-December, a day of low gray clouds that threatened snow, she was surprised to hear the key turn in the lock on her door. It was not a day for visitors; neither did Lucy ordinarily come at this hour to do any of the tasks assigned her. When the door was thrust open, a little hunched figure came in sidewise and stood peering uncertainly about her, as the door closed and the key turned again in the lock.

Unexpected and forbidden, the visitor startled Anne so much that at first she hardly recognized Jane Hawkins as she stood in the gloomy corner by the door.

"Mistress?" cried Jane uncertainly.

Anne was sitting by the window with her Bible on her lap. "Come to me, dear Jane," she said, and laying her book aside rose to embrace her friend.

"I can't stay long," said Jane. "I was a-feared to come, but I knew not what else I could do."

Anne sat down in her chair and gestured Jane to the stool beside her.

"But how did you know you could get in?" she asked. "And how persuade the servant to open my door?"

"'Twas lecture day," said Jane. "I heared how they left you alone on these days, and I heared about Lucy from a friend of mine."

"What about Lucy?"

"She's in love with a boy in Boston. My friend said she wants him so bad she would do anything to have him. So I offered her a love potion."

"Oh, Jane, surely love cannot come from a potion."

Jane smiled her knowing little smile. "You might not call it love," she said, "and I might not. But for such a girl as Lucy, 'twill be as good a thing."

"I don't know, Jane," said Anne. "That troubles me."

"No, please, mistress, do not be troubled. 'Tis but a passing, pleasant thing."

Anne shook her head. Sometimes Jane's reasoning seemed dark and strange to her, yet she put her doubts aside; for it was clear Jane was in sore need of her now, to have come on such a day, at such a risk.

"Then tell me why you're here," she said.

"Winthrop," said Jane. "That's why."

Winthrop. The sound of the name, like that of some diabolical engine designed to squeeze the spirit out of the word of God, tightened her throat till her voice (when she spoke) came forth thin and dry.

"What has he done?" she asked.

"'Tis Mary," Jane said, "or that's the start of it." At Newtown, at the meetinghouse door, Winthrop heard a woman say that Mary Dyer had given birth to a monster. He had been too busy for a while to investigate that birth, but he did not forget. "He found out I was the midwife, and he come to me. I told him Master Cotton knew of it, and said it need not be writ down.

And then he got Master Cotton and Master Bellingham together, and they called me to Winthrop's house. They wanted me to tell it all, what part you played, and what the child looked like."

"But surely," said Anne, "Master Cotton might have told the governor all that he could wish to know."

"Master Cotton did not see the child, he said."

"No, he did not," Anne said, "but I told him something."

"And so did I tell something. Yet 'twould not do, but I must tell all, or they would dig it up. So I tried to tell them everything, all I could any way remember." She paused, screwing up her face as if to frown or cry. "They dug it up after all, then," she said.

"So cruel could he be?" cried Anne.

"More cruel than you know, mistress."

"How? What do you mean?"

"He made her watch. Her and him."

"Her and him?" Anne scarcely understood her.

"Mary and William. They had to stand there in the snow, and half Boston besides, for they said it was meant for public eddy—eddy *what*, mistress?"

"Edification," said Anne grimly.

"And he got the gravediggers there, to scrape off the snow, and dig down, and the ground was froze hard as a rock. But at last they dug down to it, and brought it up, and the governor examined it and called out every last thing that was wrong with it, loud and clear so everyone could hear, and had it set down on paper. The claws and the horns and the holes in the back—mouths, he called them—everything about it, and more than you'd believe."

"My poor dear Mary. What did Mary do?"

"She stood there and got whiter and whiter, till you couldn't 'a' told her face from the snow, and then William told Winthrop he was going to take her home. Whether the governor liked it or not, was what he meant, though he did not say it. And he took her away from there."

"How is she?"

"I went and stayed with her that day and night, and Mary Cogshall stayed too. She prayed. *We* prayed, I guess. She seemed better next day. But she hasn't heard all folks are saying."

"What do they say?"

"Many things. They say it sprang from devil's seed."

"Oh my dear Mary."

Goody Hawkins gave a wild little laugh, or a cry. "You had better say your dear Jane," she said.

"Yes, I know it was hard for you too, but—"

"No, you don't know. You don't know yet what Winthrop's done to me."

"What could he do to you?"

"He says I consort with the devil. I reckon the truth be he thinks that I planted the seed."

"Why, Jane, what can you mean?"

"Oh, he meant in some potion, I guess, that he thinks the devil give me. He's called me to come before him tomorrow—him and Master Cotton and Master Bellingham. He means to get proof that I'm a witch and then feed me to the court, like them Christians in Rome you used to tell about that got fed to the lions."

"No, no, he cannot do that."

"Maybe he can. He put you here."

"This is different, for the Lord will deliver me, but if John Winthrop should have you convicted of witchcraft—"

"I know. They would hang me or burn me. And, mistress, I be bad a-sceered, either way."

"Be not afraid, Jane." Anne saw that she must be the teacher now, be all that she had ever been to Jane and more. She remembered her own doubts about Jane's medicines, but looking at her now, her round eyes bright with tears and trust, she knew whatever the little midwife had done was born out of nothing worse than a need for love. If the devil had used her, it was through her ignorance and need, but not with her consent.

"But how can I not be a-feared?" Jane asked.

Anne tried to think how Winthrop might proceed. If it were true that Cotton and Bellingham were to sit with him at the hearing, the plain truth might be of some use. "Tell the truth," she said, "and if possible, before you are questioned. Offer to take them to your house and show them all your medicines and instruments." She remembered having heard that Winthrop knew something of physic. "Explain what everything is. Show your knowledge. Tell where everything came from. Or—" She suddenly doubted her advice. "Jane, have you ever been to the forest at midnight?"

"Why yes, mistress. Everybody knows it's the only time you can dig mandrake root."

"Then don't tell that," said Anne. "Tell them everything but that."

"No, I wouldn't tell that," said Jane.

"But everything else. All the truth except that, and all so clear and full that they will be satisfied without many questions. Now is that clear?"

"Yes, mistress, very clear," said Jane somberly.

Then Anne was near to weeping, recalling how gaily Jane was wont to chirp those words in former times. And yet she did not weep, for anger welled up in her stronger than pity; and while she longed to go to Mary and wished she could be at Jane's side when her testing came, it was neither of these vain wishes that made her clench her fists and pace the floor and strain at her lot like a tethered animal. It seemed to her then for the first time she purely hated her imprisonment: with a passion fed by a terrible desire to go and stand face to face with John Winthrop, as she stood at her trial when she told him God would curse this land.

# XXV

About this time John Cotton began to feel that he had been sadly deceived, and worse than that, used, by the members of the Boston congregation. When John Winthrop called him to demand what he knew about Mary Dyer's monster, he found himself in the position of literally having to confess a crime. He had known what he was doing—out of compassion he had deliberately decided to break the law and connive at burying the dead infant without recording the birth. He would not repent of that act now, if it had not begun to appear that he had been tricked into it by a witch and a heretic.

He explained to Winthrop how his wife Sarah's condition had led him to be perhaps too tenderhearted in consenting to help protect Mary Dyer from the public curiosity. Winthrop smiled blandly but did not say he understood that point of view. He had no intention of proceeding against Cotton in any legal way, but he expected the minister's full co-operation in proceeding against others.

Thus Cotton must endure the painful disinterment scene and then hear testimony which Winthrop expected would prove that Goodwife Hawkins was a witch. As it turned out, neither Cotton nor Bellingham could see that he had a case against her. The old woman was perfectly open with them, took them to her house at her own suggestion and showed them her stillroom and all her ingredients and instruments. It was true she was somewhat confused about some of her medical knowledge, but Winthrop had to admit that as far as he could see all she did was acceptable practice.

And then, although there appeared a goodly number of persons who had heard somebody say that Goody Hawkins was a witch, it was difficult to secure any substantial testimony against her. Several women told how the old woman would say that she could help them get better if they "believed," but they could not say with certainty what kind of belief she referred to. Jane herself said that of course she meant the Christian faith. Some of these people could affirm that Goody Hawkins was the first woman to speak a word to Anne Hutchinson, except for her own kin, but Winthrop had to point out that nothing resembling witchcraft had been charged against Mistress Hutchinson.

Then Mistress Hibbens, Master Bellingham's own sister, came forward declaring she had seen Goody Hawkins in the form of a sparrow that had caused her garden peas to wither away. But as it was well known that only this kinship with one of the magistrates had prevented her being brought up as a witch herself, she was hushed and banished from the meetinghouse. Someone knew of a man who had seen the shape of Goody Hawkins in a boat on the way to Ipswich, and found out later she was really in her yard at home all the time. This man was located at Samuel Cole's tavern and led staggering into court to testify. Gloomily, Winthrop had him placed in the pillory with a wooden letter D hung round his neck, and called a halt to the testimony.

One more thing remained to be done. Two other midwives were called in to examine Jane for extra teats, but when they reported nothing extraneous, the governor reluctantly gave up hope of a conviction.

"There's smoke and must be fire somewhere," he said, "but witchcraft is hard to prove—I remember that from my days in Suffolk." He decided he could be satisfied with having her banished for her self-confessed connection with Anne Hutchinson. Meanwhile, as she showed some uncertainty about her craft, she would be forbidden to meddle in surgery, or in physic, drinks, plasters, or oils. And to question matters of religion.

Cotton was left relieved but uncertain, a familiar condition for him ever since Anne Hutchinson came to Boston. Even as recently as the trial in Newtown, when the woman convicted herself out of her own mouth, he had been unable to see that Mistress Hutchinson had adopted any views that he himself could clearly reject. That about her revelations was dangerously close to heresy; yet he believed, as he told the court, that the spirit might make revelations through the word and beyond the word.

But now, just since Anne Hutchinson had been imprisoned, a whole new brood of strange opinions had hatched out in Boston. It had earlier been reported to him how some of her disciples would say, "I have many things to tell you, but you cannot bear them now; and there is a great light to break forth, if men do not resist it." And now it began to appear that the time had come and the great secret would be bared at last. There was talk everywhere of revelations without the word, of the abrogation of the law (yea, even to the extent that the Commandments were declared a dead letter), of the uselessness (after union with the spirit) of baptism with water, and other conjectures so wild and alien to Christian doctrine that one could conceive of no source for them but the devil. Winthrop and Wilson insisted they could all be traced directly to Anne Hutchinson.

At the same time there was wild talk among another segment of the Boston population: persons who had never quite accepted Mistress Hutchinson's teaching and those who had believed but now feared they had been led astray by this woman of devilish revelations. These unbelievers now professed to have known for years that Goody Hawkins was a witch. (Never mind that the magistrates failed to condemn her; they were afraid of the devil, it might be.) And as everyone knew how close she had stuck to Mistress Hutchinson, the question that occurred to them now was which one taught the other.

Some whose loved ones had died watched over by Anne Hutchinson now must make great moan, for it was well known that a witch would wait by a deathbed in hope of stealing the dying one's soul. Likewise was it known that monster births came from the devil's seed. And so it was with delicious horror that many drew away from even the thought of listening again to Mistress Hutchinson.

When Cotton found occasion, he sternly castigated all who talked irresponsibly of witchcraft; for nothing had been proved against Goodwife Hawkins or even charged against Mistress Hutchinson. Yet in the depths of his consciousness this talk roused primordial fears, unnamed and unrecognized, that intensified his anger and resentment against his old pupil.

It would have been easy for him to say that Sister Hutchinson had made herself unworthy of his care and concern, but Cotton's conscience would allow no such washing of hands. She was perhaps not truly lost; and if not, then he of all the ministers of the Bay dared not disown her as a sister in Christ.

If John Cotton had ever believed that fairness was an element in the nature of God, he might have been bitter about his position now among the ministers and their congregations. Short of denying the very basis of his creed, he had compromised to the fullest with men who he sometimes feared did not even accept salvation by grace. Out of loving concern for his avowed disciples, he had searched every opinion they advanced, with a mind open to any saving facet of it. Yet now he was accused of betrayal on every hand; and had he not understood the experiences of Job and the theories of Calvin, had he ever once expected God to treat a man according to his evident deserts, he might almost have doubted his faith.

But Cotton never doubted, or wavered in his task. Diligently he preached against every strange opinion that came to his attention. Repeatedly he urged his hearers not to judge without cause. And as soon as he could find a free day, he went to Roxbury to deal with Sister Hutchinson. "You have a visitor, mistress," said Lucy at Anne's chamber door.

Anne did not ask who it was. It would be some minister, of course, probably Eliot or Weld. She had in any case given up asking any sort of question of Lucy, who seemed sullen and hopelessly unregenerate, with no interest in any sort of love or companionship, except that which might be purchased with potions.

Anne was astounded to see John Cotton standing by the fire. Formerly, her heart would have leaped in gladness at the sight, but she knew that she had lost her teacher's confidence if not his love. They greeted each other formally and sat in chairs that had been arranged for them before the fire.

He inquired after her welfare. She said she was treated well and could not complain, except for being so much cut off from her friends in Boston. She hoped he would respond with news of Jane Hawkins, who had been very much on her mind, and when he did not she asked about her.

"Naught could be found against her," Cotton said, "or nothing pertaining to witchcraft."

"Thank God for that," Anne said.

"You may thank God, sister," said Cotton, "but I was left wondering still if the devil were not in it somewhere."

"In Goody Hawkins, sir?" asked Anne. One could understand such a feeling, she knew that.

"In it all," he said.

She looked at him dully, for she had no idea what he meant, and as she made no response he went on to itemize the strange new beliefs flying through the Boston air. "Now I ask you plainly, sister," he concluded, "and would like a round answer. Do these things come from you?"

Anne wearily shook her head. "Sir, I can only give you the same answer I have given many times before. If they come from me, they come from you."

"Yet you seem to have had revelations that certainly did not come from me."

"At the trial I thought you understood my relevations."

"No, sister, I begin to think I have never understood you."

"If I have revelations, it is because I learned the possibility of them through your teaching about union with the spirit."

"I never taught a union that made man into God," said Cotton stiffly.

"I suppose you do not think Paul became God," said Anne, "and yet he had revelations, and without the word."

"That is all past," said Cotton.

"But, sir, how do we know it is past?" cried Anne.

Cotton suddenly rose up from his chair. "Sister," he said, "we shall never understand each other. Nor do I have time to sit here listening to your equivocations. There is only one thing now for me to believe: that you have used me as a stalking horse, to bring in your own opinions under cover of my good name."

Anne jumped up in anger, but there was a deep hurt too, a blow that left her weakened, and swaying as she stood.

"Sir," she said, "that is an unjust accusation. But let me say this—I will not in the same fashion accuse those who have come to me and listened to my words. I would deny these things you charge against me—these new notions in Boston—but since you doubt me what would be the use? And I may say that it is possible some of them came from my teaching, if any who used to come to me have misunderstood me as I seem to have misunderstood you. And one more thing I'll say—whenever new thoughts have come to me, I have never pretended they came from you or any man."

"Then you set yourself up as one who may know God without any help from a minister—or mayhap, any help from the Scriptures."

"Nay, sir, that is not so. Daily I search the Scriptures, always praying for more light, and when any minister of God doth offer to help me I thankfully let him."

If that were an invitation to Cotton, he ignored it. "Yet you expect to find more than we ministers teach," he said.

"More than these ministers who preach a covenant of works, though under your teaching I learned to believe that the covenant of grace holds forth all."

"We ministers differ not so much as you have evidently thought," said Cotton. "This was proved at the synod."

"Well, then, if that be so I confess this much: I believe there be more than any of you preach—more comfort on earth and more glory in heaven, and I will go on seeking truth in every way I can."

"Then I must leave you with a warning," said Cotton. "Those who cannot be content with what they find in the word of God have only one course to pursue—to the devil!"

2

Now another season of ice and snow came down on the colony of Massachusetts Bay. It was true that each winter away from England seemed bitterer than the last, but this one was like an enemy sent against the people. Anne Hutchinson was allowed a small fire through the day, but she must huddle over it to keep warm. At night the great central chimney still held some heat, but she shivered as she changed to her nightdress and climbed into the cold narrow bed. It was when she first lay down at night that she missed William most. She had no need of his sex and knew not if she ever should again, so drained of life she was. But she felt a great hunger for his presence, both for the warmth of it and the quiet, comforting talk they had always kept for this last waking hour.

And then because she was thinking of William, she thought of the children. They had decided it might be better if he did not bring the younger ones through the deep snow and cold to see their mother in a condition they could hardly understand. But Francis came. They had good talk together and a time of prayer that left them both certain of a bright future, even if Francis should be kept from further schooling. His uncle Wheelwright had lent him his books till he returned from the north. In his youthful innocence and passion, he assured his mother that he could learn without teachers all that man had to say, and then would wait for God.

One day Faith and Thomas came. Probably because of Thomas' recantation, they gained permission to make a visit of their own, apart from the regular family day allowed the prisoner. They did not say this was the reason, but Anne could think of no other. The young man and wife both wept, but Anne did not weep. She had shed tears a-plenty, and would more, but not for the hypocrisy of her son-in-law. That Faith was sorry she could well see. She embraced her daughter and kissed her.

In the end, no mention had been made of Thomas' part in the aftermath of the trial, but as the servant maid was already knocking on the door, he said to Anne, "Mother, we have really come to say that wherever you go, we want to go with you."

"Very well, children, very well," Anne said gently.

Then they were gone, both weeping again, and Anne sat down and thanked God that they loved her. But Thomas had further revealed himself now, and she knew he would not cling for long to his mother-in-law. For Faith's sake he might try, but in the end what mattered most to him was the good opinion of men who squeezed the spirit from the law. Thomas was part of Winthrop's victory.

At different times there came Edward and Richard with William; the young men were ill at ease and found not much to say. Bridget was ailing and never tried to come, but she sent many loving messages, which she ever signed, "Yours in the Lord."

On the days when members of her family visited her, Anne

often became somewhat disturbed in her mind. Sometimes she wondered if she would be better off not to see them at all, when they must leave her so soon. Her condition at these times was much as it had been in the days following the birth of Mary Dyer's monster. She waited for something: she thought it might be death. She remembered how she had felt in that period before the trial—the sense that soon she might no longer see her house and children, the compulsion to hold them both so close. But never an inkling came to her then of the lengths her enemy would go to. Never even when she faced him in the Newtown meetinghouse did she guess he would send her straight to prison, without even a chance to go home one more time and embrace her beloved children.

Now the sense of impending deprivation (even beyond what she had yet known) came over her again. It was no clear revelation, but whatever it was, it was real. And if she faced imminent death, then in truth she might never see her youngest children any more. Not little Susannah, who cried so hard at Anne's leaving. Not Zuriel, learning to talk now without her to guide him. Once or twice she almost said to William, "If I do not see them now, then it may be too late." But she did not want to worry him about her fears, for in clearer, lighter moments, she could not believe her death was quite so near. And whatever happened, she would see them one day in heaven, her family and all her dearest friends.

But then as she read through her Bible, death seemed to press closer and new doubts assaulted her. She came to the words of the Preacher, the son of David, and she read, "For that which befalleth the sons of men befalleth beasts . . . as the one dieth, so dieth the other. . . . All go unto one place; all are of the dust, and all turn to dust again."

Distressed by these words, she brought them to the attention of Thomas Weld when he came to her. "What if we all turn to dust, body and soul?" she asked him.

And Weld, who had said he came to help her see the light, grew wroth and would only say no child that had learned his catechism would ever ask such a question. "The spirit of man is immortal," he angrily cried, but he scorned to cite the Scripture that he said she ought to know.

Then as she went on with her reading she realized that the

Bible speaks of both the spirit and the soul. Sometimes she would search the Scriptures far into the night, until her hearth grew cold and the last candle sputtered and died, and yet she could never be sure of the difference in the meaning of those two words. Afterwards, as she lay in bed, longing for the comfort of her husband and her children, she came to ask herself, "And what if either soul or spirit rise, or both, what then of the body?" Even the certainty of heaven perhaps did not mean she would see her children again, if she died this winter in Roxbury. For in heaven they might all be invisible, unrecognizable spirits.

Remembering Paul's writing on the Resurrection in his first letter to the Corinthians, she next day read, reread, and long pondered the fifteenth chapter; and it seemed to her that if our resurrection be in Christ Jesus, then it is not our earthly body that rises. For though she was sure of her union with Christ, she did not understand how Christ could be united to our fleshly body.

At that time Thomas Shepard of Newtown came, and she confessed her perplexities to him. And though he was considered by his flock to be a mild and gentle pastor, yet did he rage at her and pace the floor and threaten her with eternal damnation. But he gave no satisfactory explanation of the passages that most concerned her.

And so it ever was. The ministers would come and talk with her and listen more or less patiently, according to their different temperaments, and still her heart was sore with confusion and uncertainty. Her only hope seemed to lie in her own reading, and so she went on and on, led from one puzzling place to another, until at times she feared she must doubt all she had ever heard a minister preach. For where is the comfort in assurance of a glorious resurrection, if the only resurrection be of the spirit which is Christ? When we die, we die, if our identity die with us. And then she would think, yet what if it be true that we are resurrected in our own bodies? Could such a creature as Mary Dyer bore have a soul and could that horrible, grotesque body be resurrected? Does a child have a soul while it is still in its mother's womb, and if so what of the bloody pulp that Jane Hawkins through misguided love brought forth from the body of

Elizabeth Joan? Would it rise to eternal life, and would it be in heaven or in hell?

Hour after hour, she hunted desperately for answers, until at night she would lie down with burning eyes and aching head and a terrible desolation in her heart. If John Cotton had come again, she might have asked him if it were possible to lose one's way even in the Scriptures, and find the devil there.

3

The worst time was a period of three weeks when no one could come from Boston because of ever-renewing storms. Often Anne would huddle by her small fire and let her inner vision wander to her family at home. When she tried to read her Bible, images of her children somehow lost and freezing in the snow rose before her eyes and blotted out the words. And then she might fear to lose sight of God Himself, for at such times either her hatred of John Winthrop or her newfound doubts about the meaning of death would take possession of her thoughts and spirit. Oh, how she would pray then for that clarity like light that once her mind seemed made of.

Those prayers were not answered. Too many earthly passions kept her from full experience of her union with Christ. Looking into her heart, as into a glass, she could see them dimly reflected, such distortions that she hardly recognized herself. Fear. Hate. She had never known hate in her life until now. She had not hated the legalistic preachers but only their mistaken teachings that she attacked in her meetings. Winthrop—she did not know. She often wished for Henry Vane and would try at such times to bring him close in spirit, as though he might again advise her, though in body gone so far away. The light of the Gospel brings a sword, he often would say. He might have seen her enmity toward Winthrop in that sense—he might have helped her keep it free of personal animosity. But God had sent Henry away from her—mayhap because it was his body as well as his spirit she had loved. Yes, carnal love. Fear. Carnal love. And hate. Ever returning, now returning—for it was Winthrop not God who sent her love away. And he had no better reason than his own selfish desires—to govern without opposition. Oh,

Lord, it was so hard not to hate. But if she had kept control of these feelings, she might not have spoken all she did that day of the trial, and so might not be here now.

Vain, foolish regrets! She had ever kept to the way of the Lord, and there should never have been any reason for her to have to calculate the effects of this way upon John Winthrop. She did not deserve this persecution he had heaped upon her.

But if the punishment really came from God— And with such thoughts as this, darkness would once more descend upon her.

When William was finally able to come to her again, he was appalled at her evident physical condition and questioned her closely as to whether she was being treated well and given enough to eat. If not, he would have something to say to Joseph Weld, for the court was making him pay for his wife's keep, and that rather dearly.

She assured him that her treatment was all she could ask. She was lonely and worried of course. She had begun to lose too much blood again, and aches that she had never known before assailed her body. But these were natural and temporary results of her age and her condition. When spring returned, bringing freedom and the presence of her loved ones, he would see her bloom again.

He tried to believe her, and thinking to cheer them both told her such happy little stories as he could think of about the children and the daily business of the household. He had thought it best not to bring any of the children in this weather; but they were all well, he said, and sent their love. Still he could not think of much to tell her, for the truth was they were not very happy and what he did remember did not always prove very cheering. She broke into a long fit of weeping when he told her it was clear Zuriel had not forgotten her because he had learned to say "Marmie gone gone."

At the end of the visit she told him not to come again when the weather was in any way threatening, or if business made his presence needful at home. Then when he was gone she cried for many hours because she had told him that.

He wondered afterward if Anne might really be better if he stayed away from her. Still, he could not be sure of that, and he knew it was better for his own peace of mind to see her as often as he could.

Each time he came she looked paler and thinner. Once he talked with Goody Hawkins about her and she sent some medicine supposed to be good for women in Anne's time of life. (She did still meddle in physic, in spite of the court, but not as openly as before.) Anne said she knew what it was, but doubted its effect upon what ailed her now. William was distressed more and more at her talk, which was all of death and the doubtful nature of the resurrection.

Then at last one day in February, he brought news that he thought must help her if anything could. William and Mary Coddington had decided to move to Rhode Island, and a whole party of Anne's friends—nineteen men in all, including William—had agreed to take their families and go with them. Coddington had not been banished, but he no longer had respect for the rulers of the colony. The Aspinwalls, Cogshalls, and Dyers would go; and even Goodman Hawkins (though not among the nineteen who had signed a formal agreement) had come to William asking to be taken along, with his wife Jane. And of their own family, there would be the two Edwards, Bridget and John, and—William smiled delightedly, at the best saved for last—Thomas and Faith.

William expected Anne to burst into prayers of thanksgiving at this news, but she had not much to say.

"Art thou not joyful, Anne?" he asked her.

"Aye," she said, "But have you not heard that I am to be called before the church?"

"No," he said, "I have not. And I am still a deacon."

"Nevertheless, it is to happen. Pastor Weld has told me and although I have not been summoned, still I know that I must go."

"But for what purpose?"

"To examine me for heresy."

"Dost thou think they look to excommunication then?"

She sighed dejectedly. "I suppose they do. And though I be no heretic, I must suppose they may accomplish it."

He changed his tone, spoke almost harshly. "This is not like you, Anne. You are certainly no heretic, and why should you suppose they can prove you one?"

"I think because I am so tired," she said. "And because there be so many errors now, since the synod. Who can know what innocent word may be construed as part of some new error?"

He moved from his stool to kneel at her side, where she sat in her chair by the fire, and he put his arms around her. "Thou must rest," he said.

She kissed him. "I will, dear," she said, and tried for his sake to believe she could meet the ordeal. He sat down at her feet then, and they talked a little about the way she might present her beliefs, to keep them free of the taint of synodical errors.

At last she seemed to take a little heart, and she said, "William, do you think there be any hope, that if I should not be excommunicated, the court might rescind my sentence?"

He shook his head. "I know not," he said.

"If my views were known to be sound, pronounced sound by the ministers, accepted by the church—would not they let us stay? Let us all stay, all our friends, and let everything be as before?"

"I do not think, Anne, that everything can ever again be as it was before."

"I could have my meetings. All my friends must miss my meetings—they would soon come back."

He saw he must tell her what she would inevitably find out when she went back to the Boston church. "I fear there could never be meetings again, Anne," he said. "For there has been a change in the congregation. Once those I told you of leave for the south, there would be very few left to come to you. If by some happenstance they should not go, they would be very nearly all."

"Doth no one believe me?"

"Many have turned away—we saw it happening soon after the synod. But since your trial—and more, I think, since Captain Underhill's strange confession and the matter of witchcraft—there has been much talk against you."

"But I could win them back," she protested, and then struck by what she had said began to shed silent tears.

"What is it, my dear love?" he asked her anxiously.

"I fear I spoke in pride, William," she said, "and that my thought was of their admiration of me and not their spiritual needs."

"No, it is wrong to speak so," he said, and told her something he truly believed as long as he lived. He had said it before and he would say it again. "Thou art a dear saint and servant of God."

She let her body droop wearily and rested a hand on William's knee. "Pray it be so," she said, "for I have found many sins and weaknesses in myself these last months."

He shook his head but she would not let him speak. "Only pray," she said.

They sat silent awhile. She did not know whether he prayed or not, and in truth neither did he.

"William," she said at last, "I could not bear to be excommunicated."

He put his hand over hers, but still did not speak.

"Even without our family and friends I can face banishment. I have often thought of that, and I regret many things. For so many reasons, it would be so much better to stay in Boston. Your work, your position in the colony and town. School for Francis—for of course I know he could not come back here. Still—for myself alone—I can accept whatever the magistrates choose to do to me. But to be cast out from the church—cut off from Christian fellowship—sometimes I think it would be the same as death to me."

"Yet I have heard you say the church is only a body of men."

"So it surely is. And yet—oh, William, there is no reason to what I say. Only—I belong to the church. You know I never wished to separate, nor do I now. My views may be different from what the ministers teach, yet I belong. It is not merely that I am a member—I belong, I am possessed by the church. I know it lies not in the power of men to cut off anyone from Christ, but if I were deprived of that communion, I think my soul would die."

"It cannot happen, Anne."

"I know not," she said. "But pray for me, and tell our friends to pray."

Soon after that he kissed her and left her alone with her fears.

# XXVI

Anne Hutchinson was called to appear before the Boston church on lecture day, March 15. William and most of the other men planning to settle in Rhode Island had gone there to locate land and prepare a place. Hence, not only her husband but all the men who strongly supported her were gone from Boston.

The elders of the church decided to allow Anne to come to Boston on the fourteenth, and spend the night before the trial in her own house. Her son Edward and Thomas Savage, the only men of her family left in town (for William had taken with him Richard, Francis, and Samuel), came to Roxbury to escort her home. (Though Joseph Weld must accompany her, too, for she was still a prisoner.) She was exhausted and ill when she got there. The walk, though easy for a well person in good weather, had been hard and piercingly cold for Anne. Snow still lay thick everywhere, and the waters on either side of the narrow Neck were jammed with ice.

At home, the children had the wainscot chair waiting for her by a blazing fire. She took a step towards it, and stopped. She was kept from that chair by something she dared not name; it might have been the hand of God. Images besieged her: Francis Marbury in that chair (and oh, dear Lord, would he know, where he was, if she should be cast out of the church?); Henry Vane at her feet as she sat there, with the blue mantle draped around her and a baby at her breast; the crowds who came thirsting for the words she used to speak.

She swayed lightly, where she stood. "No, not there," she said.

"No, she must go to bed," said Faith, and Anne let them put

her there, for it was certain she must feel her best on the morrow. She had Zuriel and Susannah in her arms, though, William and the two little girls on the bed with her, and Bridget and Faith nearby. The cousins scolded and said the children would sap her strength, but as she wept and prayed and laughed with them, she felt the force of life surging back into her.

The lecture was set for ten o'clock, two hours before the usual time, in hope that the trial could be completed that day. Anne had asked leave to wait until after the lecture to appear at the meetinghouse. ("Pretending some bodily infirmity," was what Winthrop wrote about that later.) She was slower than she expected in her walk to the meetinghouse (which she made accompanied by Penn the beadle) and so was a few minutes late in arriving. The house was packed with members of the church and visitors from all over the colony. Many stood outside. Yet Anne scarcely knew anyone was there. She was making every effort to keep her mind sharply focused on such matters as might be brought against her in the trial. She was determined to tell the simple truth, but no more than her inquisitors asked for.

When she arrived, Elder Leverett was asking the members of the congregation to draw together, so as to distinguish themselves from the visitors and make it easier for the elders to count the votes. Hearing that, Anne felt she was realizing for the first time that it was the Boston church in whose hands her fate lay—that body of Christians among whom several months ago it would have been hard to find three persons willing to make an expression against her. She glanced around her and saw faces that revealed neither friendliness nor enmity. Her best hope was that they had not yet made up their minds either way and would listen to the evidence.

She made her way to the table below the pulpit and stood as erect as she could, awaiting the pleasure of the lay elders. These two men, Thomas Oliver and Thomas Leverett, had been her followers and friends. Now there was nothing in their attitudes to show they had ever seen her before. Elder Leverett, however, in telling her she might sit down, had in his voice a suggestion of warmth that might be sympathy. Anne allowed herself to be heartened by it.

"Sister Hutchinson," said Leverett then, "here is divers opinions laid to your charge, and I must request you in the name of the church to declare whether you hold them or renounce them as they be read to you."

She had seen a copy of the list and still had not understood that all the different opinions would be charged against her, as though she unequivocally espoused them. For such was not the case.

"First," read Elder Leverett, in a toneless, nasal voice, "that the souls of all men by nature are mortal. Ecclesiastes Three, eighteen-nineteen."

Anne gasped. This was unfair—incredible and unfair—for this was no opinion, only a question that had troubled her, and she had talked to Master Shepard about it because he came professing his desire to help her.

"Second, that those that are united to Christ have two bodies. . . . Third, that our bodies shall not rise with Christ Jesus. . . ." On and on—those expressions in Corinthians that had perplexed her so much, all matters she had confided to Pastor Shepard with what she understood to be his assurance of privacy.

Other accusations, especially those that came from Master Weld and Master Eliot, were closer to her true beliefs; yet some of them were grossly exaggerated.

At last Elder Leverett desired her to "express whether this be your opinion or not."

And Anne made up her mind to protest. "I desire of the church to ask one question," she said in her high, clear public voice. (People noticed how she had to strain to make it carry through the meetinghouse.) "By what rule of the word may these elders come to me in private to desire satisfaction in some points, and do profess in sight of God that they did not come to entrap me nor ensnare me, and now without speaking to me and expressing any unsatisfaction would come to bring it publicly into the church before they dealt with me? For them to come and inquire for light, and afterwards to witness against it, I think it is a breach of church rule."

Would she accuse the ministers then? But no, she said, she would not, "for there was none with me but myself, and I may not accuse an elder under two or three witnesses."

Well, then, they would go on. Shepard spoke of his attempts to deal with her about her errors and reminded her he had told her he would bear witness against them.

But these were not her opinions. "I did not hold divers of these things," she insisted, "but did only ask a question."

Then Master Shepard spoke out to the people at large, and made clear to them what would be a basic principle of this trial. "I would have this congregation know that the vilest errors that ever was brought into the church was brought by way of questions."

"Brother, we consent with you," said Master Cotton, who now —the preliminaries done with—was conducting the examination. "Mistress Hutchinson now must answer each thing objected to," he said.

Making an effort to conceal her resentment at Shepard's proclamation, Anne tried to answer each charge by asking humbly for more light on it, and leaving herself open to persuasion if the men would find Scripture to support their own views. Master Cotton required her to speak of her alleged statement that the souls of men are mortal. She asked for an explanation of the Scripture.

"The spirit ascends upward," he said, citing Ecclesiastes Twelve, seven.

But Anne in her searching had come across confusing passages that seemed to contradict that point. "The spirit returns to God but the soul dies." This had been the hardest point, the thing that drew her on and on in those dark nights in Roxbury, until she thought her brain would twist in two.

This opinion of hers would overthrow man's redemption, if it were true, Cotton admonished her. There were black looks from the other ministers and gasps of astonishment from the congregation.

Cotton continued to labor with her on this first point, until at last she brought up the question that for her lay at the heart of it all. "Do you think we shall go into heaven with our natural life?"

Our nature but not our corrupt nature, was Master Cotton's answer.

"Then you have both a soul and spirit that shall be saved,"

Anne protested. "I desire you to answer that in First Thessalonians. Your whole spirit soul and body, and that in Psalms: he hath redeemed his soul from hell," Anne urged.

At that Master Cotton in exasperation gave up the citing of Scripture. "Sister, do not shut your eyes against the truth," he cried. "All these places prove the soul is immortal."

"The spirit is immortal," Anne agreed, "but prove the soul is. For that place in Matthew that you bring of casting the soul into hell is meant of the spirit."

"These are the principles of our Christian faith and not denied," Cotton stated. "The spirit is sometimes put for the conscience and for the gifts of the spirit that fits the soul for God's service. I know not what you conceive the soul to be."

"She thinks the soul to be nothing but a breath, and so vanisheth," John Eliot said. "I pray put that to her."

What was the soul made of? At that moment Anne could not recall whether in all her painful searching she had ever asked that question, but the answer came to her then clear and certain. "I think the soul be nothing but light," she said.

But no one paid that any mind. ("They cannot bear the truth when they hear it," Anne said to herself.)

Elder Leverett interposed to ask whether the church had heard enough on this point, and Thomas Savage then tried to speak on Anne's behalf, saying the church should have time to consider before voting. This objection was not allowed; neither did the church express itself, but the wrangling went on.

Finally Cotton put the point still another time. "I would ask our sister whether the soul, body, and spirit be not immortal. First Peter Three, nineteen."

And Anne in all honesty, and with a terrible effort at humility, answered, "It is more than I know. How do we prove that both body and soul are saved?"

"I pray God to keep your whole body—soul and body may be kept blameless to salvation," quoted Pastor Wilson.

But Anne answered, "It is said they are kept blameless to the coming of Christ, not to salvation."

"What do we mean by the coming of Christ Jesus?" demanded Wilson.

"By coming of Christ there," said Anne, "he means His coming to us in union. Romans Six, four."

Then Wilson was on his feet, shouting with thunderous wrath: "I look at this opinion to be dangerous and damnable and to be no less than Sadducism and atheism."

At this the congregation were requested to lift up their hands to show they condemned it as error, and most did. Anne felt she might have done so herself, for she was by no means sure of her expression on this point, nor did she expect the ministers to take it as her fixed opinion.

"If error be the thing you intend," she asked, "then I desire to know what is the error for which I was banished, for I am sure this is not. For then there was no such expression from me on this."

But no one answered that.

John Davenport, a minister who had come to Boston a few months ago and as yet had no pulpit, spoke at some length about this ancient heresy of questioning the soul's immortality. "The soul cannot have immortality in itself, but from God from whom it hath its being," he concluded.

This seemed more clear to Anne than anything she had heard. "I thank the Lord I have light," she said.

And yet the ministers would go on trying to define the difference between the spirit and soul as the terms appeared in Ecclesiastes and Thessalonians.

Then Master Davenport brought them back to the question about the meaning of the coming of Christ. "You do consent that it is the coming of Christ at the judgment that is meant?" he asked.

And Anne consented, saying she did not acknowledge error but an honest mistake. "For I held before as you did but could not express it so," she said.

And now for some reason it came to Peter Bulkely of Concord that this was the proper time to question Mistress Hutchinson about her familistic views. "And whether you hold that foul, gross, filthy, and abominable opinion of the community of women."

Anne had tried hard to keep humble in her heart, but at this question she could no longer maintain any semblance of humility. "I hold it not," she firmly said. "But Christ answers now, I know thou hast a devil. That was the conclusion they made against Christ when He said they that believe in Me shall not die: I do not believe that Christ Jesus is united to our bodies."

"God forbid," ejaculated Pastor Wilson.

It seemed unclear, perhaps, whether Anne was confused or simply trying to change the subject. Master Davenport was determined to keep her on the main track, and declared she could not avoid Master Bulkely's question, "for it is a right principle that if the Resurrection be past then marriage is past. Then if there be any union between man and woman it is not by marriage but in a way of community."

This was by no means clear to Anne, but she was certain no one could ever accuse her of having attacked the institution of marriage. "If any such practice or conclusion be drawn from it, then I must leave it, for I abhor that practice."

Then they were all back again to their attempt to determine what she believed about the resurrection of the body, until at last, somewhat wearily, she gave the answer: "I do not think the body that dies shall rise again."

At that John Eliot said, "We are altogether unsatisfied with her answer and we think it is very dangerous to dispute this question so long in the congregation."

And yet they would not let her go. And Anne could not by their arguments be convinced. "I am not clear," she said after long discussion. "I cannot yet see that Christ is united to these fleshly bodies. And if He be not united to our fleshly bodies, then those bodies cannot rise."

At that point Hugh Peter leaned forward, and with a threatening air that was almost like a twinkle in his eye, said slyly, "I would ask Mistress Hutchinson this question, whether you think that the very bodies of Moses, Elijah, and Enoch were taken up into the heavens, or no."

And Anne, reduced to honest simplicity, could only say, "I know not that I can believe this more easily than the other."

There, at last, was an end of discussion on that subject. So at least Master Davenport thought, for he rose and faced the congregation, now but a sea of indistinguishable faces in the thickening dusk.

"These are opinions that cannot be borne," he said. "They shake the very foundations of our faith and tend to the overthrow of all religion. They are not slight matters but of great weight and consequence."

Here was something all the ministers agreed upon, and Pastor Wilson saw no need to delay admonition any longer. "Because it is very late," he said, "and there are many things yet to go over, the church thinks it meet to refer further dealing with our sister till the next lecture day." Those who considered Mistress Hutchinson's opinions to be gross and damnable heresies were asked to hold up their hands.

Anne looked out over the congregation. It was hard to see whether hands were lifted or not. Yet one man stood up, and she saw with tears in her eyes it was Edward.

"I desire to know," Edward said, when he had been recognized, "by what rule I am to express myself in my assent or dissent when yet my mother is not convinced. For I hope she will not shut her eyes against the light."

But this objection was disallowed, on account of the natural affection which clouded his conception of the truth.

Then Master Shepard must have time to deliver a lecture to Mistress Hutchinson, who he declared was "of a most dangerous spirit and likely with her fluent tongue and forwardness in expressions to seduce and draw away many, especially simple women of her own sex."

Then once more Wilson attempted to proceed to admonition, but now Thomas Savage made an effort on his mother-in-law's behalf. Though he had recanted, and could himself see her error, still he did not see that the church should admonish her simply because she requested more light on certain opinions.

But it was dark indeed now. Someone lit a candle that flickered on the faces of the ministers but left Anne Hutchinson in darkness. And so, the elders seemed to conclude, she must remain.

Yet there was a problem. In order to proceed to admonition, the church needed full consent. And then arose young John Oliver, he who once had refused to take his name from the Wheelwright petition even though he must lose his post as deputy to the court. "Why not," he asked, "lay these two brethren under an admonition with their mother, that so the church may proceed without any further opposition?"

Wilson was jubilant at that brilliant suggestion. "I think you speak very well: it is very meet."

And so the whole church by their silence consented to the motion, and it fell to the part of the teacher to deliver the admonition.

2

Now John Cotton arrived at a certainty he had resisted even to this hour. Now at last he had proof out of this woman's own mouth that not only her misguided followers but she herself had deceived him and used his name to cloak her heresies. In the hope that all whom God had gathered here might benefit from his speech and be kept from future error, he prayed silently as he mounted the pulpit that he might be guided to choose words unsparing and true.

Someone thrust up a candle to him and it lighted his face, yet (it seemed to Anne gazing up at him) with a light that brought darkness and transformed the angelic gentle fair face that she had loved in Lincolnshire and followed to the ends of the earth. But transformed or not, he was John Cotton still, and it was in following him (by God directed) that she had come at last to this cold, dark place, this utter weariness, this deprivation. Or was it—brought down into this terrible darkness of spirit and mind she could no more be sure—could it have truly been God that so directed her?

All, all had been taken from her—all certainty, all hope. Now she felt like the empty vessel she had delighted once to hear John Cotton preach on, the one that waited passively to be filled. Yet his words filled her not, but fell against her like blows aimed to break the walls of the frail vessel.

"I do in the first place," he said, "bless the Lord, and thank these our brethren, the elders of other churches, for their care and faithfulness in watching over our churches. I confess I have not been ready to believe reports against any of our members for want of sufficient testimony, but now they have proceeded in a way of God and do bring such testimony as does make plain the truth.

"I shall address myself first to you that are her son and son-in-law. And let me tell you from the Lord, though natural affection may lead you to speak in the defense of your mother, yet in this cause of God you are neither to know father nor mother, sister nor brother, but to say of them all as Levi did, what have we to do with them? And though the credit of your mother be dear to you, and your regard to her name, yet the regard you should have of Christ's name and your care of His honor and credit should outweigh all other. So I admonish you in the name of Christ Jesus and His church to consider how ill an office you have performed to your mother this day, to be instruments of hardening her heart and nourishing her in her unsound opinions by your pleading for her and hindering the proceedings of the church against her which God hath directed us to take to heal her soul, and which God might have blessed and made more effectual had you not intercepted the course. And how instead of loving and natural children you have proved vipers to eat through the very bowels of your mother, to her ruin if God does not graciously prevent." If the two men did not labor to bring her to a sight of her sin, he said, the Lord would bring them to an account for it.

"Next," he went on, "let me say somewhat to the sisters of our own congregation, many of whom I fear have been too much seduced and led aside by her. Therefore I admonish you in the Lord to look to yourselves and to take heed that you receive nothing for truth which hath not the stamp of the word of God from it." Some of them, he was willing to admit, might have received some good from her, some help in their spiritual estates, but he feared many had drunk in poison with the good, and if so they should "make speed to vomit it up again and to repent of it."

He paused, perhaps to pray again, and then looked down directly at Anne. "And now, sister, let me address myself to you. The Lord put fit words in my mouth, and carry them home to your soul. It is true that when you first came into this country we heard some things of some opinions you held, and vented upon the seas, in the ship in which you came; yet then you did give us such satisfaction that after a little stay to your admission you were received amongst us. And since that time you have been an instrument for some good. You have been helpful to many in bringing them away from unsound principles and building their estates upon duty and the law. The Lord hath endued you with good parts and gifts fit to instruct your children and servants and to be helpful to your husband in the government of your family. He hath given you a sharp apprehension and a ready utterance, and ability to express yourself in the cause of God.

"Yet notwithstanding, we have a few things against you and in some sense not a few but such as are of great weight and consequences. Therefore, let me warn you and admonish you in the name of Jesus Christ to consider of it seriously, now the dishonor you have brought unto God by these unsound tenets of yours is far greater than all the honor you have brought to Him. And the evil of your opinions doth outweigh all the good of your doings. By this one error of yours in denying the resurrection of our very bodies, you do the uttermost to raze the very foundation of religion to the ground and to destroy our faith."

He hushed his voice, as though to emphasize his consternation. Anne took advantage of this hiatus, for she had discovered she was not drained utterly of faith and hope. The very things she had always professed and believed—that had brought her following after Cotton to New England—were the same things he himself still believed and could yet praise in her. Surely, surely, she had not been mistaken—it had been God's voice that called her. Some evil in men had driven them apart, but with God's help she could make him understand how he was mistaken in her.

She rose unsteadily. Her voice though somewhat faint still carried through the house. "I desire to speak one word before you proceed. I should forbear but by reason of my weakness I fear I shall not remember it when you have done."

"You have leave to speak," he said to her.

"All I would say is this—that I did not hold any of these things before my imprisonment."

And he answered her, but yet coldly. "I confess I did not know you held any of these things, till here of late. But I must say I have often feared the height of your spirit and being puffed up with your own parts. So therefore it is just with God thus to abase you and bring you low. So with your other errors which have been proved against you this day—they set an open door to all epicurism and libertinism. If this be so, let us eat and drink for tomorrow we die. We need not fear hell nor loss of heaven. Nay, though you should not hold these things positively, yet if you do but make a question of them and propound them as a doubt for satisfaction, yet others may hear of it and conclude them positively. And so your opinions fret like a gangrene and spread like a leprosy, and infect far and near, and will eat out the very bowels of religion, and hath so infected the churches that God knows when they will be cured. Therefore that I may draw to an end, I do admonish you and charge you in the name of Christ Jesus that you sadly consider the just hand of God against you, the great hurt you have done to the churches, the great dishonor you have brought to Jesus Christ, and the evil you have done to many a poor soul. Seek unto Him to give you repentance. Bewail your weakness in the sight of the Lord, that you may be pardoned. The Lord carry home to your soul what I have spoken to you in His name."

Someone had lit another candle now at the elders' table. Cotton extinguished the stump that was guttering on the pulpit and descended in the darkness. While he came down, Thomas Shepard rose to speak.

"Lest the crown be set upon her head in the day of her humiliation," he said, "I desire to speak one word before the assembly break up. It was a grief to my spirit to hear what Mistress Hutchinson did last speak, in interrupting you in the midst of her censure. But it was an astonishment to hear her impudently affirm so horrible a falsehood in the midst of a solemn ordinance of Jesus Christ, yes in the face of the church to say she held none of these opinions before her imprisonment, when she knows that she used this speech to me, when I was with her and dealt with her about these opinions. This makes me more to fear the unsoundness of her heart than all the rest."

And John Eliot added that it was the same trouble and grief to him to hear.

But Pastor Wilson, seeing that an end must be put to the proceedings for this day and night, only said: "Sister Hutchinson, I require you in the name of the church to present yourself here again the next lecture day, this day sevennight, to give answer to such other things as this church or the elders of other churches have to charge you withal, concerning your opinions, whether you hold them or no, or will revoke them."

3

Even Winthrop could see by the end of that day that Mistress Hutchinson was weak in body and spirit. And so, though it had been intended she should return to Roxbury, he consented to a request from John Cotton that she be kept at his house for the week intervening between her two appearances before the church. Davenport was staying there as well, in the rooms that Henry Vane had built, and Cotton assured Winthrop that there was a good chance the two ministers could reduce her and bring her to acknowledge all her errors.

With Edward and Thomas to support her, and following behind John Cotton, who held a lantern to light the way, Anne Hutchinson came one more time to the house by the Trimontaine. Sarah Cotton gave her cold porridge and led her without welcome to her chamber.

Unutterably weary, Anne lay in a high, curtained bed and could not sleep. Her back and legs ached, and the events of the day moved through her mind like an unending procession of frightening dreams. The more she tried to fix them in her mind and discover their full meaning, the more frustrated and confused she became. Now it seemed incredible to her that the spirit of God had ever spoken to her soul. It seemed possible—nay, even probable—that if she ever had a revelation it had not come from God.

She tried to remember how she had felt, in those days that seemed so long ago, when she stood or sat before a house filled with men and women eager to hear her tell them of God's wonderful covenant of grace. She could not regain the spirit she had known then, though she dimly recalled it. Her heart used to swell with joy in her bosom—and yet, was it joy? She could not distinctly remember. John Cotton had accused her of pride. "Puffed up with your own parts," he had said. Usurping a place never properly belonging to a woman, and leading other women away from their own callings. It might have been a soaring pride instead of Christian joy.

What if God meant her now to humble herself? Lay herself at the feet of the ministers and magistrates, where she had always belonged? What if He meant she should recant?

One at a time, she brought before her mind the sixteen errors as they had been read to her. They swam together in a sea of dark uncertainty; she wished she could catch them all in a net and consign them to oblivion.

Finally there came overpowering her a sleep that was worse than waking, filled with strange, monstrous swimming images. Once she awoke with gasping little terrified cries and, even after she lay with her eyes wide open, still could see glowing in the darkness a great white-bellied fish with horns and claws and a prickly, thick-skinned back. Part of its belly had been eaten away, and inside it were ranged grotesque shapes that bore heavy black numerals. She could not see them all clearly but seemed to know that all the numbers from one to sixteen were represented there.

The next morning, Cotton and Davenport sat with Anne in the little study at the top of the stairs. She had asked for this meeting, which she thought of now, as she sat beneath the gaze of the ancient Dr. Sibbes, as the end to which all her earlier interviews in that room had been inevitably building.

"Well, sister," said Cotton, with some gentleness, "can we hope you want our help in weeding out the errors from among your beliefs?"

"Aye, sir," she said, and a sigh escaped her. "I thank the Lord I see my need at last."

Thus began the painful week in which the ministers wrestled with the devil on the Lord's behalf for the soul of Mistress Hutchinson. The original list of errors charged against her had been multiplied and divided until now there were twenty-nine, and several of them required many hours of inquiry and exhortation before a satisfactory conclusion could be reached.

The first five concerned her unorthodox statements about the immortality of the soul and the nature of the Resurrection, which had been lengthily examined at her trial. She wanted to believe the ministers were right, even though they could not explain away the confusion she still found in certain passages, and so without much further discussion she submitted on those counts.

The question concerning inherent graces in the saints after union with Christ gave her far more trouble. Anne had come to believe firmly that in this saving union such graces are no longer part of man but must be ascribed to Christ Jesus. The ministers labored exhaustively with her on this point, until at last Master Davenport concluded she had not an understanding of the meaning of the word *inherent*. She admitted she might have mistaken the word, for she did believe men were born with some capacity for good. Only she thought such good as they could do had meaning only in the Lord. The ministers let that pass.

The nature of her revelations was also a difficult hurdle.

"Why did you keep them private for so long, sister?" said Cotton, referring to the fact that only in recent months had her followers talked of them openly.

As she sat in daylight, talking rationally with these men, her revelations held more of reality than they had seemed to do on that first night when she lay exhausted and aching and confused in all her thoughts. "Because I knew they would be misunderstood," she said.

"Perhaps it was you who misunderstood," said Davenport.

"In one case at least I think I might," she admitted. She said she had felt unjustly accused by the court, and thus so filled with what she believed to be righteous anger that she might have been mistaken when she predicted the ruination of the country. "Although," she felt compelled to say, "I cannot believe aught but that ruin must eventually come in a country where men persecute the seekers of the truth."

"We are not to talk of that," said Cotton hastily, "and do you not think the disrespect you showed the magistrates came from your pride, in setting yourself up as their equal?"

Anne bowed her head. "Aye," she said, "it might have done."

"And when you spoke against the ministers in your meetings, were you not thinking then about the height to which you had risen, believing you spoke better and more of truth than they, because you drew such crowds around you?"

"It seemed not so to me then," said Anne, "but mayhap it was pride."

The ministers both lectured her at length on pride, but in the end were satisfied with her answers.

On the last day before she must face the church again, Cotton said, as the morning conference began:

"In some respects, Sister Hutchinson, the most dangerous accusation against you is this, that you teach we are not bound by any law."

Anne's head jerked up. "I do deny that charge," she firmly said.

"Yet I believe you say that sanctification can be no evidence of a good estate."

"Sir," said Anne, "I mean no disrespect, but surely, this I learned from you."

"I have said something very much like it, and yet I think not with the meaning you intend."

"I intend nothing more than what the words do say," said Anne, struggling against any expression that might suggest a proud spirit. "I have never encouraged the disobedience of any law of God or man, but only said that such a legal way is not an evidence of union with Christ."

"Yet we may look to the behavior of some of your followers," Cotton said, "as a truer sign of what you do actually teach."

"Will you name me names?" Anne asked him.

"We might speak of Captain Underhill," he said.

"He is no true follower of mine," said Anne. "Nor do I think him to be saved, but rather believe he has pretended a saving union and has distorted my words as a screen for his own evil deeds."

"A feeling I know well," said Cotton, as though in spite of himself. "But we must not judge."

"No, sir, I do not judge," said Anne, "but likewise I hope the church will not judge me by his actions."

"They will not," said Cotton, "if you deny you spoke against the law."

"I will deny it," said Anne.

Then Davenport spoke, and questioned her on her knowledge of witchcraft.

"If you are thinking about Goodwife Hawkins," said Anne, "then all I can say is that I have tried to help her; and though I dare not affirm she is in a state of grace, yet I do know her to have a loving heart."

"And have you taught her what you know of physic?" Cotton asked.

"Sir," she said, "are you accusing me of having taught her witchcraft?"

Cotton quickly denied that intention. "Yet I have heard new things," he said, "that I might go with to the court, were I not assured the woman will soon leave this jurisdiction."

"I am opposed to any traffic with the devil," Anne said, "and know not what more I can say on this. I did not see witchcraft put down on the list."

"No," said Davenport, "yet revelations and lawlessness might lead that way."

"I do deny it," said Anne, "and though I know Jane Hawkins to be no witch, I hope I am not to be held responsible for what each person that ever came to me hath done."

"No, no," both ministers assured her.

And so at last they pronounced themselves satisfied she was no heretic, and the three of them together composed the recantation she would read before the church.

4

Through the snowy streets Anne trudged once more, accompanied by the beadle and the ministers. It was a sunny day, but an icy wind blew hard in from the sea, so that she had to push against it, using up her strength. When at last she stood beside the table in the meetinghouse, to read the paper of recantation in her hand, she wavered and her voice was weak and low. With great effort she finished, and then sank down, believing she had done her utmost and it would be enough.

But Master Wilson, not satisfied, spoke. "There is one thing that will be necessary for you, sister, to answer the objection that was raised at the last meeting—that you denied you held these things but since your durance."

Anne gave her answer, speaking low and fast. "As my sin hath been open, so I think it needful to acknowledge how I came first to fall into these errors. Instead of looking upon myself, I looked at men. I know my dissembling will do no good. I spoke rashly and unadvisedly. I do not allow the slighting of ministers nor of the Scriptures nor of anything set up by God. If Master Shepard doth conceive that I had any of these things in my mind, then he is deceived." (She knew at once that she should not have mentioned Master Shepard, when she saw him there waiting to catch her in error, gloating. . . .) "It was never in my heart to slight any man but only that man should be kept in his own place and not set in the room of God."

Most of the congregation had not heard what she said; Winthrop leaned over to whisper to the elders. "It is meet somebody should express what you say to the congregation," Leverett said.

Then Cotton summed up Anne's speech, adding something he perhaps had only intended she should say: "She desires all that she hath offended to pray to God for her to give her a heart to be more truly humbled."

Shepard did not seem prepared to offer such a prayer. "If this day when Mistress Hutchinson should take shame and confusion to herself for her gross and damnable errors, she shall cast shame upon others and say they are mistaken, and to turn off many of those gross errors with so slight an answer as your mistake, I fear it doth not stand with true repentance. I should be glad to see any repentance in her: that might give me satisfaction."

Neither was Eliot satisfied. He insisted Mistress Hutchinson had told him what she did Pastor Shepard: that she could have told them much more than she did, before she was imprisoned. Then Shepard wanted a more definite recantation of her old opinion that there were no graces in ourselves, but only in Christ.

"Sister," said Cotton, "was there not a time when once you did hold that there was no distinct graces inherent in us but all was in Christ Jesus?"

"I did mistake the word *inherent*, as Master Davenport can tell who did cause me first to see my mistake in that word."

Eliot and Shepard were not satisfied with this explanation. They did not like this talk about the meaning of words. They thought she was dissimulating again.

Master Symmes of Charlestown finally spoke what was in the minds of most of them. "I should be glad to see any humiliation in Mistress Hutchinson."

This was exactly what Thomas Dudley had been thinking, and

though he had little business speaking out there in the Boston congregation, he could refrain no longer. And so with the heavy sarcasm he was so well able to express, he said: "Mistress Hutchinson's repentance is only for opinions held since her imprisonment, but before her imprisonment she was in a good condition, and held no error but did a great deal of good to many." He looked around to receive the appreciative glances of his peers. "Now I know no harm that Mistress Hutchinson hath done since her confinement; therefore I think her repentance will be worse than her errors." (Tight-faced elders nodded in approval.) "And for her form of recantation, her repentance is in a paper, whether it was drawn up by herself, or whether she had any help in it I know not, and will not now inquire to, but sure her repentance is not in her countenance."

Now suddenly it seemed every man had something he had been waiting till this moment to say. There were many hard speeches, directed mainly at the meaning of her views about graces, while she struggled to speak only humble words and kept her eyes downcast for fear they should reveal some remnant of pride she did not know was in her.

But Hugh Peter had something else in mind: an evidence of guilt that perhaps no one else had heard of. "I would say this," he declared, "that when I was once speaking to her about the woman of Ely, she did exceedingly magnify her to be a woman of a thousand, hardly any like her. And yet we know that the woman of Ely is a dangerous woman and holds forth grievous things and fearful errors."

Anne answered, "I said but what I heard, for I knew her not nor ever saw her."

Peter's charge and her denial went unnoticed though, for Pastor Wilson had risen to speak, citing the sin that most deeply concerned both himself and his brethren. "I must needs say this," he insisted, "and if I did not say so much I could not satisfy my own conscience, for whereas you say that the cause or root of these your errors was your slighting and disrespect of the magistrates and your unreverent carriage to them, that is not all; for I fear there was another and a greater cause, and that is the slighting of God's faithful ministers and crying them down as nobodies. And whereas you say that one cause was the setting up of men in the room of God I do not deny it but it may be you might have an honorable esteem of some one or two men, as our teacher and the like. Yet I think it was to set up yourself in the room of God above others that you might be extolled and admired and followed after, that you might be a great prophetess."

Wilson had reached the real heart of the matter, but no one seemed ready to speak to it quite yet.

"She thinks us nothing but a company of Jews," muttered Hugh Peter, still thinking of some irrelevant point about the woman of Ely.

Master Shepard, ignoring that, must take them back to a discussion of Mistress Hutchinson's views of grace; for he believed it was useless for anyone to speak further unless she could clear herself on this score.

"Our teacher knows my judgment," said Anne, "for I know I never kept my judgment from him."

Dudley recalled that she had always professed no more than Master Cotton held. It was clear he did not think this was necessarily any defense.

Then it seemed every man in the house wished to speak about graces, and testify to what Mistress Hutchinson had said to him upon the subject.

—While Anne sat bowed and still. The stated purpose of these men around the table had been to reduce her. It was a term both ministers and magistrates had used, presumably meaning to free her of error and restore her to the true faith as they understood it. But she felt reduced indeed; it seemed to her she must appear shrunken and shriveled, as though her inquisitors had diminished the substance of her body as well as the light of her soul. Yet she struggled against herself to say what they wanted to hear.

"I confess," she told them, "I have denied the word *graces*, but never the thing itself."

Still they went on muttering about graces, without respect to anything Anne said, until at last Hugh Peter, with a weary droop and half-closed eyes, as though to say he was tired of all that, stood up with a paper in his hand and said, "I would desire Mistress Hutchinson in the name of the Lord that she would search into her heart farther to help on her repentance. For though she hath confessed some things, yet it is far short of what it should be. And therefore"—at this point he began to read his numbered conclusions—"One. I fear you are not well principled and grounded in your catechism. Two. I would commend this to your consideration, that you have stepped out of your place; you have rather been a husband than a wife and a preacher than a hearer; and a magistrate than a subject. And so you have thought to carry all things in church and commonwealth, as you would, and have not been humbled for this."

It was upon hearing these words that Anne regained herself. Vision returned to her as though a light had flared up in the dim meetinghouse. She had tried earnestly and with all the humility she was capable of to answer the objections of these ministers and church members. She had been ready, in her physical weakness and her concern for the good opinion of men, to go beyond strict honesty. She had fallen into their meaningless muddle about the distinction between the word and the thing.

But now Hugh Peter had reminded her of something she had always known quite well. She considered the ministers ranged before her along the table, looking at her with hostility unconcealed. Even John Cotton's mild eyes were hardened. She looked to the magistrates' bench, met Winthrop's dark sword-like eyes and observed the choleric countenance of Dudley. None of them was thinking nearly as much about the welfare of her soul as about his ambitions for himself and for the colony as he conceived it. Winthrop had a vision of a city upon a hill: so, doubtless, did they all. And in the shining streets of that city, there was no place for Anne Hutchinson.

Struck with horror at what she had been about to do and elated at her timely recognition of it, she sat unheeding as the hateful words of men rained down upon her. For the sake of something called a church, and forgetting that her covenant was with God instead of men, she had been about to deny herself and Christ. She thanked God silently; and the records show she never spoke another word till the Boston church was done with her.

Those who knew her best noticed at this time how her back straightened, her chin lifted, and her face began gently to glow. Some few rejoiced with her.

Meanwhile, the men went on with their work.

"Let her declare her good estate," said John Winthrop.

"Question her whether she was ever in a state of grace," said Shepard.

"We are not satisfied with her repentance," said Hugh Peter, "wherein she lays her imprisonment to be the cause of all her error, as if she were innocent before."

Thus they went on, until Pastor Wilson's harsh condemning voice reached Anne's consciousness and she realized he was bringing the proceeding near its close.

"I cannot but reverence and adore the wise hand of God in this thing," he said, "and cannot but acknowledge that the Lord is just in leaving our sister to pride and lying. And I look at her as a dangerous instrument of the devil raised up by Satan amongst us to raise up divisions and contentions, for the misgovernment of this woman's tongue hath been a great cause for disorder. She saith one thing today and another thing tomorrow, and I think it is time for a proceeding in our church, to ease ourselves of such a member. Therefore I leave it to the church to consider how safe it is to suffer so erroneous and so schismatical and so unsound a member amongst us, and one that stands guilty of so foul a falsehood.

"That you may not forget what lie she made, let me remind you that in the face of testimony from several ministers, she willfully declares she held no dangerous opinions before the time when she was kept a prisoner. And so you must now consider how we can or whether we may longer suffer her to go on still in seducing to seduce and in deceiving to deceive and in lying to lie, and in condemning authority and magistracy still to condemn."

Then Master Cotton rose, and Anne knew when she saw his gray, sagging face that he had resigned her to the will of his brethren. Unlike them, he understood the nature of her lie. It was not what they charged against her, that she held her imprisonment to be the cause of her erroneous beliefs. She had tried to lie to her own self—in that respect, her entire recantation was a lie—but her conscience in the end could not consent. He had gone as far with her as he could go, but he found a way to spare himself the last grim duty. There was a difference (a narrow scantling, maybe, but a difference) between what she would have suffered for last week and what she must suffer for today.

"The matter is now translated," Cotton said. "The last day she was dealt with in point of doctrine, now she is dealt with in point of practice. And so it belongs to the pastor's office to instruct and also to correct in righteousness when a lie is open and persisted in. God hath let her fall into a manifest lie, yea, to make a lie, and therefore as we received her in amongst us I think we are bound upon this ground to remove her from us."

Some two or three protested the suddenness of this move. Elder Leverett declared that according to Scripture excommunication should come only after a first and second admonition. Master Shepard would hear of nothing but that she had lied and lied again. And so this, she could see, was what it had come to: she would be thrown out of the church as a common liar, and all the anxious probing into her beliefs had come to naught. Perhaps they never cared what she believed.

At least she would not have to endure any more. For as Master Cotton now reminded those who would demur, "As soon as ever Ananias had told a lie the church cast him out."

Then perforce the church gave consent by its silence, and Pastor Wilson proceeded to excommunication: "Forasmuch as you, Mistress Hutchinson, have highly transgressed and offended, and forasmuch as you have so many ways troubled the church with your errors and have drawn away many a poor soul and have upheld your revelations; and forasmuch as you have made and held a lie in the face of the congregation, therefore in the name of the church I cast you out and in the name of Christ I do deliver you up to Satan that you may learn no more to blaspheme and to seduce and to lie. I command you in the name of Christ Jesus and of this church as a leper to withdraw yourself out of the congregation."

Anne knew what was expected of her now: the long walk away from Christian fellowship. But she sat a moment pondering this incredible thing that had happened here. Excommunication. Terrible, frightening word. And who was it that had done this thing to her? Men. Men who set themselves up in the room of God. They said she had deprived herself of the sacraments by moving out of her place; and yet it came to her now that they were attempting to take the only Place forbidden humankind. And who was it that determined the proper place for any man or woman in the world? She would think about these things another day—but now she was cast by men out of the Church of Christ, and the members of the congregation were waiting to watch her depart from them.

She stood briefly, looking about her; then, with stately carriage and slow steps, she started toward the door. About midway along the aisle, someone in a soft gray cloak and steeple-crowned hat joined her and took her arm. It was Mary Dyer, and the two walked side by side.

A stranger standing by the door spoke as they came to the threshold. "The Lord sanctify this unto you," he said.

"The Lord judgeth not as man judgeth," Anne answered him, in a voice that rang out over the congregation like a high-pitched, singing bell. "Better to be cast out of the church than to deny Christ."

Then the two women moved on together, out into the sunshine of that cold and cloudless day.

# EPILOGUE

On a lecture day in the autumn of 1643, the teacher of the Boston congregation climbed to the pulpit. He was heavier than he had been at an earlier time of his life, and his formerly fair angelic hair, while graying somewhat, had darkened, strangely, to a dull rusty red like that of dying coals of fire among the ashes. His voice was not as light and sweet as it once had been, yet he spoke with a conviction that some said did more properly evoke the wrath of God.

Before starting his lecture, which as ever attracted many visitors to Boston, he had a piece of news to impart to his own congregation. Their eyes brightened at that, and a rustle of skirts and sleeves told how expectantly they shifted in their seats.

"Brethren and sisters," the teacher addressed them. "Word hath come to us lately of a woman who once lived here amongst us and brought great disturbance to the peace of our churches. I mean Mistress Anne Hutchinson, and it is well that we should not forget this former sister of ours and her ways of deceitfulness—nay, her very betrayal of some of us who, not given to suspicion, accepted in full faith her lying words.

"You will remember that five years ago, some months after her banishment from this colony, word came to us that she had been delivered of a monster. At that time I read to you a full description of that strange birth, that you might know how God by this sign reassured us of the justice in our action against her. You will remember that I told you then how the monster was made up of twenty-nine lumps of man's seed, corresponding with the twenty-nine errors which were finally proved against her, and that in those lumps there was no mixture of anything belonging to a woman. By this we understood what God intended: that we should know in full certainty that there was nothing of the Christian woman to be found in Mistress Hutchinson.

"And now I bring you further news. You may have heard that after her husband died in Rhode Island, Mistress Hutchinson took most of her family and went to live under the Dutch somewhere along the shore of Long Island Sound. Many warned her of the dangers of the Indians, but in her old devilish pride she would answer them that Indians and Englishmen were all one in the sight of God. And it seems that for some time the Indians did live near them full neighborly, but then one day suddenly fell upon them, cruelly murdering the heretic mother, taking one of the daughters away with them; and another of the daughters, whom they caught as she was getting over a hedge, they drew her back again by the hair of the head to the stump of a tree, and there cut off her head with a hatchet.

"It is believed that they did burn the mother to death with fire, along with her house and cattle and the other of her children. But I am not able to affirm by what kind of death they slew her, but slain it seems she is, according to all reports. I never heard that the Indians in those parts did ever before commit the like outrage upon any one family, and therefore God's hand is the more apparently seen herein, to pick out this woeful woman, to make her and those belonging to her an unheard of heavy example of their cruelty above all others.

"The place where she lived and died was known by seamen and marked on the map by the name of Hell-Gate. Thus we see God's wondrous ways in putting an end to that most satanic life on earth."

Finished with his news, the teacher waited to let the awful import of it fill the minds of his hearers. And then a strange thing happened, something the like of which had not been known in Boston for lo, these many years. From somewhere toward the front of the meetinghouse, though not from the seats where the richer sort were placed, there arose a tall slim figure in a steeple-crowned hat and a long gray cloak. In the middle of the aisle she stopped and turned toward the man in the pulpit.

"May the Lord forgive you, John Cotton," she cried. "No woman who loved Anne Hutchinson ever will." She was out of the hall before the tithing man could reach her, without anyone seeing her go through the door.

In the dimness of the meetinghouse, no one surely recognized that gray figure, but many believed it was nothing more than the empty shape of a woman who had long since left the town. When in later years this woman returned in the flesh and was hanged for her faith on the gallows of Boston, some said it was Anne Hutchinson who drew her back to that sad and fitting end.

# AUTHOR'S NOTE

This novel is based upon an episode in American history known as the Antinomian Controversy. Because it follows true events very closely, I would like the reader to know of the most notable instances in which I have added to or departed from history and tradition.

I have in a few cases changed the chronology to suit the demands of unity. Two of these changes, I think, would be especially noticed by anyone familiar with the history. John Underhill, who was historically a famous adulterer, actually confessed his sins somewhat later than the period covered in this book; but his contemporaries linked his immoral ways with the alleged antinomianism of Anne Hutchinson, and so it seems fitting to reveal the extent of them here. The discovery of Mary Dyer's monster occurred after Anne's church trial rather than after the civil trial; but it has always been considered part of the Anne Hutchinson story, and so I thought it belonged within the confines of the novel.

Almost all the people mentioned are drawn from history, but I invented Jacob and Elizabeth Joan Hickson, because I felt sure there must have been persons of their religious and social standing involved with Anne Hutchinson yet overlooked by history.

I took the liberty of making Anne's son Francis the nominal teacher in the mixed meetings. Anne said at her trial that no woman taught at those meetings, and I do not think she lied. What I could find out about the character of Francis led me to believe he might have played that part.

Traditionally, it has been assumed that Anne was pregnant

during her long ordeal, because of the "monster" that she gave birth to in July or August of the following year. I have chosen to accept the very convincing evidence offered by Emery Battis in *Saints and Sectaries* that she did not become pregnant until after she left Boston, and that the "monster" was a menopausal baby that aborted into a hydatidiform mole.

Writers on this subject have occasionally presented Anne Hutchinson as a feminist. I do not see her that way. Although persons concerned with women's rights may appropriately find in her an inspiration, I have not seen evidence that she gave significant thought or effort to changing the established view of women. The passion of her life was bringing the truth of God as she understood it to men and women equally.

One more historical matter—a rather minor one—should perhaps be mentioned. Rhode Island was not always called Rhode Island in those days, but for the reader's convenience I have referred to it that way.

In regard to language, particularly in dialogue, I have attempted to create an illusion of the speech of the time. Language was in a period of transition (as indeed it always is), so that it is difficult to ascertain any strict rules regulating the use, for example, of "you" and "thou," "has" and "hath," and the subjunctive form of the verb. With my general reading in Elizabethan and seventeenth-century literature as a guide, I have played by ear in the matter of usage.

# REFERENCES

This is not a complete list of works consulted in writing this novel, but is intended as a guide for anyone wishing to know more about the history of the Antinomian Controversy, the social, intellectual, and theological background, or the lives of the people most prominently connected with the events.


Charles Francis Adams: *Three Episodes of Massachusetts History.*

J. H. Adamson and H. F. Folland: *Sir Harry Vane, His Life and Times.*

Emery Battis: *Saints and Sectaries.*

George Francis Dow: *Every Day Life in the Massachusetts Bay Colony.*

Alice Morse Earle: *Home Life in Colonial Days; The Sabbath in Puritan New England; Two Centuries of Costume in America.*

David D. Hall, editor: *The Antinomian Controversy, 1636–1638, A Documentary History.*

Thomas Hutchinson: *The History of the Colony and Province of Massachusetts Bay.*

Cotton Mather: *Magnalia Christi Americana.*

Perry Miller: *The New England Mind: The Seventeenth Century.*

Edmund S. Morgan: *The Puritan Dilemma.*

Samuel Eliot Morison: *Builders of the Bay Colony.*

Richard D. Pierce, editor: *The Records of the First Church in Boston, 1630–1838.*

Winifred King Rugg: *Unafraid, A Life of Anne Hutchinson.*

Darrett B. Rutman: *Winthrop's Boston.*

Nathaniel B. Shurtliff, editor: *Records of the Governor and Company of Massachusetts Bay.*
John Wheelwright: *His Writings.*
John Winthrop: *History of New England, 1630–1649.*
Larzer Ziff: *The Career of John Cotton.*